# TENNIS SHOES
## A D V E N T U R E   S E R I E S

# KINGDOMS AND
# CONQUERORS

# TENNIS SHOES
## ADVENTURE SERIES

# KINGDOMS AND
# CONQUERORS

*a novel*

## CHRIS HEIMERDINGER

Covenant Communications, Inc.

Covenant®

*For Angelina,*
*in sweetness, in perfection, in love.*

Cover illustration by Joe Flores

Cover design copyrighted 2005 by Covenant Communications, Inc.

Published by Covenant Communications, Inc.
American Fork, Utah

Printed in Canada
First Printing: August 2005

11 10 09 08 07        10 9 8 7 6 5 4 3

ISBN-13: 978-1-59156-740-0
ISBN-10: 1-59156-740-8

# CURRENT CAST OF CHARACTERS

(Listed here are the main characters who continue from previous novels. Characters introduced in this novel are not listed. Actual scriptural or historical characters are in bold.)

**Jim Hawkins Family**

Jim Hawkins—Father, original character from *Tennis Shoes Among the Nephites*

Sabrina Hawkins—Jim's wife, mother of Meagan

Melody (Hawkins) Sanchez—Oldest daughter of Jim, married to Marcos

Steffanie Hawkins—Second oldest daughter of Jim

Harry Hawkins—Oldest son of Jim, recently returned missionary

Meagan Sorenson—Daughter of Sabrina from previous marriage

Gid Hawkins—Infant son of Jim and Sabrina

Carter Sanchez—Adopted toddler son of Melody and Marcos

**Garth Plimpton Family**

Garth Plimpton—Father, original character from *Tennis Shoes Among the Nephites*

Jenny (Hawkins) Plimpton—Garth's wife, Jim's sister, original character from *Tennis Shoes Among the Nephites*

Joshua Plimpton—Son of Garth and Jenny

Rebecca Plimpton—Daughter of Garth and Jenny

**Main Ancient Characters**

Gidgiddonihah—Nephite warrior from first century BC, nephew of Gidgiddoni (from Book of Mormon)

Apollus Brutus Severillus—Roman Centurion from the first century AD

Mary Symeon—Jewish girl from first century AD, blood relative of Jesus of Nazareth

Micah—Christian convert, former Jewish Essene from the first century AD

Jesse—Jewish orphan from the first century AD

**Pagag**—Son of Mahonri Moriancumr (Brother of Jared) from (approx.) 3000 BC

**Moroni**—Son of Mormon, fourth-century Nephite prophet and captain

Tz'ikin (Zi-keen')—Fourth-century Lacandon warrioress

**Gilgal**—Fourth-century Nephite captain

Lamanai (Eagle-Sky-Jaguar)—Prince of Tikal, son of Jaguar-Paw (Lamanite)

Jacobah—Lamanite warrior, loyal bodyguard of Ryan Champion

**Fireborn**—War general of armies of Teotihuacán, conquered Tikal, killed Jaguar-Paw

## Other Main Characters

Marcos Alberto Sanchez—Nephite, husband of Melody, grew up in modern times, also lived in first century AD, son of Nephite dissenter, Jacob (of the Moon)

Ryan Champion—Teenager from modern times, former boyfriend of Meagan Sorenson

# PROLOGUE

## Jim

I once asked a Church genealogist—one who happened to live in my ward—just how many people have been born in the history of the world. He said estimates ranged from 80 to 120 billion. That's 80 to 120 *billion* human beings who have been born since the dawn of recorded history. This caused me to wonder just how many spirit children of our Heavenly Father were assigned here. What I mean is, how many souls were foreordained to go through mortality on this particular earth? If I use the lower range of that estimate—80 or 90 billion—it might mean that around 100 billion souls belong to this planet. That's a nice even number. Of course I'd also be estimating the number yet to be born before the end of the Millennium, which seems totally impossible.

Nevertheless, the topic remains rather interesting. Especially when I consider that I may actually *know* each of those 100 billion souls. Am I the only oddball who ponders such things? To me it makes sense. After all, there's no telling how long we lived as spirits before we came to earth. Time itself is apparently only measured in the mortal realm. That is, time as we *know* it, ticking away second by second on our wristwatches and alarm clocks. So it seems possible—even probable—that each person who crosses my path, all those whose faces I see on an airplane or in a crowded stadium, and all those who make the news or live lives of obscurity in faraway lands, are souls that I already know quite well.

It may be that I know every individual on earth by *name*. It seems clear from the scriptures that we all had another name before this life. Just as Michael is Adam, Noah is Gabriel, and Jehovah is Jesus Christ, we all have a name that has belonged to us since we lived as spirits with our Father in Heaven—one that we'll vividly recall after passing to the next realm. And just as I'll recall my *own* name, I might also recall the names of every other soul connected to this earth. In fact, locked in my memory may be a thousand intimate things about each person who ever lived—things that we did together on other worlds, conversations that we had, or triumphs that we shared.

How remarkable to think that a person I saw last month in a checkout line—some stranger whom I'll never see again for the rest of my mortal life—was one of my closest friends before the foundations of the world. And if the veil were drawn for just an instant, I might find myself so overwhelmed that I'd embrace this person with a breathless rush of joy. The thought is staggering. And *sobering*. It reminds us that when we speak of such things as the "brotherhood of man," or the "oneness of humanity," or the idea that "we're all in this together," we are indeed speaking of a very real fellowship—a commonality beyond anything we can presently comprehend.

I also wonder how freely we were allowed to observe events here on earth before we were born—or how freely we can observe them after our deaths. For instance, did I view the signing of the Declaration of Independence? Did I listen to the Savior's Sermon on the Mount? Do I already know who might have conspired to assassinate JFK?

Certainly we witnessed *some* events, right? Testimonials seem abundant from leaders past and present proclaiming that ancestors or descendants are watching over us. So I'm curious if I might have watched Christopher Columbus cross the ocean and declared, *"Yup, that's ol' (whatever his spiritual name was). We all knew that he was bound to do something great. Good for him!"* Or perhaps I watched someone as dark as Adolf Hitler during his rise to power and thought, *"Oh, no. I was afraid he'd do something like this. His spirit seemed twisted and troubled even during the War in Heaven. I never quite knew what side he was on. Surprised me that he was even allowed to obtain a mortal body."* Except I certainly wouldn't have been so blasé about it. Instead I was probably devastated that any spirit child of Heavenly Father could become the author of so much evil. Who *knows* what I would have thought? Perhaps some matters are more complex than I could possibly imagine.

The reason I mention such things is because at specific moments during my time-travel adventures, I've felt . . . certain feelings deep inside. Impressions which whisper to me, "You've already seen this." At such instances it has seemed as if the things I have observed while time-traveling in the ancient worlds were like watching an old movie for the second time. Events and vistas sometimes seemed shockingly familiar. Of course, shortly thereafter, such impressions would usually fade, and I would have to relive such events in the here and now. But there have been times when such impressions were incredibly poignant, and the euphoria or anguish that I experienced seemed *double* what it might have otherwise been—perhaps because the feelings were so overwhelming the first time.

But no adventure, no experience during my travels in time, was ever so replete with such impressions of déjà vu as the events I was about to report. Yet it's curious that what I remember most vividly about these events, aside from what was happening directly to me, are the myriad of faces. Not just the faces of the principal players. But the faces in the crowd. I remember the looks in their eyes. Despite their actions—or inactions—it didn't change the fact that what was happening affected them no less than it affected me.

A curious guilt settles over me as I ponder this, and as I wonder what my *own* actions would have been if I had been in their place. That is, what my actions would have been if I hadn't already known the outcome—if I hadn't had the advantage of a scriptural education. It's a terrible thing to have to admit that I don't know if I would have behaved any better than those who actually belonged to the century wherein the events took place. Like them, I doubt I'd have done much to change the outcome. And like them, I'd have been no less culpable for the crime.

But just as such a confession is devastating, it's also *liberating*. I recognize like never before that I am truly *one* with my brothers and sisters of humanity. Despite their weaknesses, faults, mistakes, and sins—whether they may like me or hate me—it's given me a keener understanding of the unconditional love of my Lord and Savior, Jesus Christ. I've felt a very real twinge of what Alma and the sons of Mosiah experienced when they wrote that they quaked and trembled at the very thought that *any* human soul might perish or suffer eternal torment. It's my sincere hope that this understanding will now become the guiding beacon of the rest of my life.

Forgive me if it seems like I'm talking in riddles. Don't worry. It will become clear soon enough. I only pray I can tell about what I witnessed in a manner worthy of the events themselves. I want desperately to help others to share the feelings, the sentiments, of what I experienced. Yet I feel so intimidated. So inadequate. Which is why I will leave some of the reporting to a person somewhat more inclined to spiritual subjects—my loving sister, Jenny.

\* \* \*

*Jenny*

*More inclined? I doubt that very much, dear brother. But thank you anyway.*

*By the way, this is a* first *for me. I suppose my own telling of one of these adventures is long overdue. I am certainly qualified. That cave in Wyoming has affected my life as much as Jim's or anyone else's. Maybe more so, considering all the stress that I've endured waiting for my husband and loved ones to come home. In a way, I always felt it was that cave that somehow caused the miracle of allowing me to have my two precious children—Joshua and Rebecca. It seemed a strange irony that this same cave could now become the very thing that would take my children away. With all my energy and strength I was determined to prevent this from happening.*

*I'm only worried that I may not be much of a storyteller. I might have to leave most of the dramatic stuff to Jim.*

Don't be silly, Jen. You underestimate your own gifts of gab and powers of persuasion.

*Really? You think so? What a nice thing for you to say. And this from the brother who tried to abandon me on the mountainside as he was about to embark on his very first adventure among the Nephites.*

You still resent that? Goodness, Sis! It was more than thirty-five years ago. You were ten years old!

*And you were thirteen—the same age as my future husband, Garth, who also accompanied us on that expedition.*

It all seems so long ago and far away.

*Not "seems." It was long ago and far away.*

*But no, big brother, I don't resent you for trying to ditch me. You were doing what you thought was best. I don't resent any of the things that have happened to us in our adventures. Except one. I admit there was one thing that broke my heart. Nearly shattered it completely. But it would be too soon to talk about that now. Still, even with that—perhaps even because of it—my conviction is no less firm that God is at the helm of all our adventures.*

*Let me start at the beginning and try to explain what brought us to this point—the point of staring into that swirling pillar of silver energy in a vast chamber several miles below the surface of the earth. What did you call that room anyway, Jim? It wasn't the Rainbow Room anymore. I knew all about the Rainbow Room. I consider myself to be the one who first discovered the secret route to reach it. I'd also heard the Galaxy Room described, though fate had denied me the honor of ever seeing it. But this room, as I understand it, was a combination of both of those areas. Am I correct?*

Correct enough. The present room, as far as I could ever determine, was created by seismic activity, or else by the power in the orb itself. The orb was that big, round . . . *spacey*-looking thing in the ceiling. It was the thing that the swirling pillar seemed to "project" down from. This, we came to conclude, was the source of power for that whole geological zone inside Cedar Mountain. I named it the Millennium Room.

*Millennium Room?*

Yes. After all, it was from that very room that a person could choose to visit any millennium in the history of the world.

*Did you say "choose" to visit? Sounds funny to hear you say that. Sure, you could choose—if you had the gift. Which you, quite obviously, did not.*

Ah, I *knew* you'd find a way to bring that up—

*Those who didn't have the* gift—*like my dear brother—were basi-cally flying by the seat of their pants. To this day I can't imagine what possessed him to think that we could leap blindly into that thing having no blinking idea where we would end up.*

A leap of *faith,* sweet sister. Faith that God knew our dilemma better than we knew it ourselves, and that He wouldn't have allowed us to end up in oblivion. At least . . . not in the *long* run—the ulti-mate scheme of things.

*It still seems very reckless—like saying if we were to jump off a cliff, the Lord would protect us from our stupidity.*

Oh, come now. You know it's not the same thing.

*I do?*
*Well . . . okay. Looking back, I suppose there's some truth to what you say. Or maybe it was merely that the Lord looked out for us in* spite *of ourselves.*

Might we get back to the story?

*Certainly. First I'll take us back to the day that I received that awful phone call in my hotel room in Austin, Texas, where I was attending an archeological convention with Garth. This was the call that informed me that my two children had been kidnapped.*
   *Their abductor was Todd Finlay—a man whom none of us had seen in twenty-five years. Mr. Finlay had apparently been plotting revenge against Jim and my husband ever since our college days at BYU—ever since Jim had taken the Sword of Coriantumr from him and destroyed it at the top of El Cerro Vigia.*
   *The moment I received that phone call my blood turned cold, and it remained that temperature for at least another two months. Virtually everyone in our two families was affected by what happened. Within days the only people left in the twenty-first century were me, Jim, Sabrina, and*

*Melody, along with their very young children. Thus began the awful vigil of waiting. The waiting had nearly driven me to a nervous breakdown. This was the state of affairs on the night when Jim received some frightening visitors to his home in Provo, Utah. They were four men, one of whom claimed to be a Jaredite king from the land of . . . What was it again?*

Morōn.

*What did you call me?*

Very funny. That was the name of the land. Just make the vowel long and put the emphasis on the second syllable. The man said he was the king of the land of Morōn. He claimed that he was searching for a sword—a sword that had been stolen from him by Mary, Becky, and Joshua. It could only have been the sword of Coriantumr. But how did Mary, Becky, and Joshua steal such a sword from this Jaredite king? What alarmed me further was that this man claimed that he had *created* the sword. I was left with only one conclusion. The Jaredite king was none other than Akish, the evil sorcerer spoken of in the book of Ether.

The confrontation ended in violence. My home was set aflame. Nearly everything that I owned in the modern world was obliterated. It was only through God's mercy that none of my family members were seriously harmed. I realized that I could no longer hold tight and wait. My loved ones were threatened in the past as well as in the present. There was no safe haven. My only choice was to take action. We had to see if there was something we could do to turn the tide of events—some way that we could save our family members who were trapped in the past.

*By "we" Jim means myself and him. My brother and I decided to go to Frost Cave and climb down to the pillar of silver energy.*

Sabrina and Melody took it especially hard. Sabrina begged me to let her come. She didn't want to be left alone with little Gid. I could hardly blame her. It seemed as if we were vulnerable no matter where we turned. Everyone that she loved in this world—aside from our newborn son—might become forever lost in another century. But because little Gid wasn't even three months old, how could I justify the risk? Still, Sabrina seemed willing to take that chance. She suggested bringing a child backpack, dressing him in warm clothes. However, I reminded her that two out of the three times I'd traveled back in time had involved water and swimming. Twice I'd nearly drowned. It just wasn't practical to take an infant. Melody was in the same boat as my wife, having recently adopted a toddler named Carter. I was convinced that it was up to Jenny and me, or it was up to no one at all. We simply couldn't go on any longer wondering when the next villain might emerge from the shadows and threaten our well being. It was apparent that complex and earthshaking events were taking place in the lives of our loved ones. If there was anything that we could do, any miracle that could be invoked . . .

Yet despite all my pleading and reasoning, there was still a significant amount of tension as we parted from Sabrina and Melody. I was afraid, despite all the dangers—despite all logic—that they would eventually do something bold and regrettable.

*So that about sums it up, I guess. Looking back, it was all so foolhardy. For all we knew, each one of us could end up in entirely different lands and centuries and never meet again. But I wouldn't accept that. It wasn't true. Despite all my fears and reservations, I was making this journey with Jim because, deep down, I felt it was* right. *I felt it was what we were supposed to do. As I said before, because of my trust in God and my faith in His ultimate control, I was willing to put myself completely in His hands.*

Although putting herself in *my* hands may have been a different matter. Frankly, I knew nothing about that silver pillar beyond what had been told me by my son, Harrison. The "gift" that my sister mentioned was apparently something Harry possessed. Harry was thoroughly convinced that he could use that pillar as a conduit to find Joshua and Becky, as well as the rest of our family members.

*And that's where our new epic begins—with me and Jim standing at the foot of the pillar.*

*To be quite honest, that silver cyclone of energy shooting hundreds of feet upwards terrified the dickens out of me. By the time we'd reached its base, I'd already felt two of its awful "power pulses." The pulses had nearly knocked me onto my keister. Then again, my fear was most certainly heightened by fatigue. The two-day climb through the caverns had left me so exhausted that I could hardly stand. Admittedly, I wasn't in the best of shape. And I'll confess right now that I had, unfortunately, put on a few pounds since those "glamour queen" days of my youth. It's not like I was obscenely obese or anything, but, well—*gimme a break! You *try worrying night and day about your husband and children and see if you don't find yourself sneaking a few extra Mint Oreos and Swedish Fish and focusing on stuff besides treadmills and carb counters—*

No one is judging you, Sis. You're just fine.

*I know I am. Anyway. Sorry. I just had to get that off my chest.*

Actually, you really are as beautiful as ever.

*Wow. Thanks, Jim.*

Besides, back then it was in vogue for women to have a little meat on their bones. Look at all those paintings from the Middle Ages with—

*Okay, thank you. Quit while you're ahead.*
*As I was saying, there we were at the base of the pillar, gazing up at that strange red, glowing orb in the ceiling. Afterwards I stared directly into the pillar itself, trying to discern some kind of pattern in the swirling bands of energy. The air around us wasn't hot or electrified, but there was a curious sort of warmth that seemed to emanate from it. So curious that I found myself reaching toward it. That is, until Jim grabbed my wrist.*
*"Don't touch it," he warned. "You don't want to touch it until we decide to leap."*
*Up until then it hadn't quite settled in my mind what our intentions really were. Jim had mentioned something about the pillar the night before, and how it was almost like a doorway—or elevator—to other*

*centuries. But for some reason, when he'd used the word "leap" just now, I felt sure I was hearing this concept for the first time.*

*With dismay I repeated, "Leap?"*

*"Yes," he said, sounding impatient. Or defensive. Maybe because upon hearing himself say it, he realized how daffy it sounded.*

*"So that's all there is to it?" I asked, alarm still present in my voice. "We just leap?"*

*Jim turned back to the pillar, suddenly unafraid to let doubt show on his face. "That's what Harry said. I'm sure that's exactly what he and the others did."*

*"And what will happen to us?"*

*Again, impatience flashed in Jim's eyes. Clearly my brother had no idea what would happen, and felt that I should have already realized this. But he fought those emotions down and allowed the better part of his personality to shine through—the confident, assuring Jim that I'd always admired. Though I have to say, that part of him could also be a tad reckless.*

*"We'll find our children," he replied, standing a little taller. "We'll put an end to all this and reunite our families."*

*The sturdy look in his eyes didn't waver. Shuddering inside, I nodded my consent. Hey, we'd come all this way. It may have been foolish to take that leap, but it seemed incrementally more foolish to turn back, so I took my brother's hand. He studied the pillar another moment, then turned to me one final time.*

*"Ready?"*

*"Ready," I answered, my voice a bit weak and cracking.*

*And so we leaped. Simple as that. One second I was staring into the swirling cloud of energy, and the next minute I was part of it. My body and soul became united with the same substance as time itself. For a moment I felt like I was enveloped in luxurious warmth, like a foaming bubble bath. I say "for a moment," but honestly, I couldn't say how much time passed before the feeling around my body began to change. First of all, there was a change in temperature. It began to cool down significantly. But more than this, my body experienced a change in . . . How can I describe it? A change in flexibility.*

*Whereas I had felt like I was floating—almost as if I could fly—I began to feel pressure against every inch of my skin. Not only that, but I began to feel disoriented. And I don't mean in the mind—like I was dizzy* or something. I mean physically *disoriented, as if gravity was working against me. I felt like I was upside down!*

*I began to feel an intense discomfort. Everything was dark. I couldn't see a thing. On top of that, I couldn't move. Yet I could still feel all my muscles. Then I began to sense something else. It was the movement of someone else. It was Jim! I felt his arm against my arm. His fingers were clasping my elbow. Yet it was obvious that he was struggling against the same sensation of being trapped that I was.*

*I opened my mouth to speak—to yell out Jim's name. At that instant my tongue tasted dirt. I realized that my face was pressed against a wall of rock and mud. A wave of fear spread over me like nothing I'd ever felt before. It was worse than the feeling of being buried alive—more like the feeling of waking up to discover that you're encased in a thousand tons of cement! Somehow Jim and I had materialized inside a mountain of dirt!*

*I couldn't breathe. I started to scream, but my mouth immediately filled with soil. I couldn't spit it out! It was turning to mud against my tongue! How could this have happened? Had anything like this ever happened before? That silver pillar had transported us directly into the earth itself. In a million years someone would find us—but the only thing left would be our fossils!*

*I heard someone yell—muffled and muted—like hearing a human voice through a thick wall. It was Jim.*

*"Hey!" he screamed, at the same time digging his fingers into my elbow. "Help us!"*

*Who was he screaming at? Who would possibly be able to hear us? We might have been miles below the surface of the ground. I began fighting against my grave of dirt with all my strength, like a mummy fighting inside its wrappings. Or better yet, like a mummy fighting against the cold, suffocating stone of its sarcophagus. Yet I was making no progress whatsoever. In fact, it felt as if I was only helping the soil to press in more tightly around me.*

*My panic was full-blown. I was firmly convinced I was about to die. Then I began to hear another sound. Or perhaps I just felt the vibrations. It was like an echo. Like scraping and scratching. Someone was scratching against the wall of dirt behind my head. It sounded vigorous and desperate.*

*Someone—or so I could only hope—was trying to dig us out of our tombs.*

# CHAPTER 1

## Rebecca

Hi, it's me. Becky Plimpton. Still ten years old. And still the youngest one to give personal reports about our adventures.

I'm also the one who gets the unglamorous job of telling about the last things that happened in our little group. I say "little" group, but it seemed like our group was getting bigger all the time. It now included me, Mary, Harry, Steffanie, Gidgiddonihah the Nephite, Jesse and Micah, who were Jews from Jerusalem, and Pagag, the son of Mahonri Moriancumr. There was even a falcon with us named Rafa!

But in case you didn't notice, one name was missing from our group. That person was my brother, Joshua. Toward the end of our last adventure, Josh had run away from the ancient city of Salem, taking with him the evil sword of Coriantumr. I followed him into the hills. He tried to hide from me in the darkness of night, but after lots of praying and help from the Lord, I found him anyway. Then we got chased into the forest by a group of horsemen from the army of King Nimrod. Mary and Pagag had also gone into the hills to find us. But while they were looking, they saw a very strange sight in the stormy sky. It was a glider—the same glider that Harry and the others had flown all the way from the Tower of Babel. After it landed, Mary and the love-of-her-life, Harrison Hawkins, were at last, after more than two long years, reunited.

They all followed Harry's falcon, Rafa, and continued searching for me and Joshua. But by the time they found us, we were already surrounded by Nimrod's horsemen. This is where the story gets hard for me. I love my brother so much. I don't know what made him do such foolish things. He used the sword's power against the horsemen. Lightning ricocheted off the blade and slew all of Nimrod's men. Their horses ran off into the woods. It wasn't as if these men weren't evil. They definitely were. It was the fact that Joshua had used the power of evil to fight evil, rather than seeking the power of God. You see, I was hit by the lightning too, and for a while it looked like I was a goner.

Harry, Gidgiddonihah, and the others had almost reached us—in fact they were running toward us—when Joshua suddenly saw Akish the sorcerer walk out of the darkness. After all these years, Akish was still trying to get back his evil sword. He took the sword from Josh and held it out as Harry, Pagag, and the others surrounded him. I wish I could have seen what happened next. They told me that Akish learned a good lesson that night—a lesson about the power of righteousness. Harry, Pagag, and Gid defeated ol' Akish quite handily. His sword was powerless against the priesthood, and against their faith in God. But just before Harry or Gid might have slain Akish for good, he grabbed my brother around the neck. Somehow he slashed the air with his sword, causing a rift in the fabric of time. Poor Josh, because he'd given in to the sword's power, didn't have the strength to resist. Akish pulled Joshua into the slash of light. In a flash, my brother and the sorcerer disappeared before everyone's eyes!

Harry and Pagag miraculously revived me with a priesthood blessing. Afterwards, Harry and I used our faith and looked into the seerstone that he'd found in Frost Cave. We learned that Josh was presently in the same century as my dad, Meagan, Marcos, Apollus, and Ryan, but they were not all together. We also learned from the stone that Uncle Jim and my mom had jumped into the pillar to look for us, but they had gone somewhere completely different from everybody else! It all seemed like a major, boffo, big-time mess, but the person I feared for most was still my brother, Josh.

\* \* \*

Steffanie

Nicely done, Rebecca. Now, if you don't mind, I'll take over for a while.

Steffanie, you have to be kidding! I do the boring part and now I have to stop?

If you don't mind.

Ohhhhh fine. But you gotta make it up to me later. For some things, I wanna be the one to tell. You probably can guess what they are.

I can. And I promise.

Okay! So the last thing I mentioned in our previous adventure was when the eight of us, including Rafa the falcon, descended into the cool lake of energy in that cave in the hills near Salem. All I remember from when I was walking down into that slowly rotating pool of mist was how *tired* I was. The scenery was beautiful—cloud-like waves swirling like fog on a winter night—except that the mist was full of tiny lights, as if the molecules themselves were illuminated—a billion tiny fireflies—purples and blues and reds. Yet it all seems like a dream now. A part of me wonders if it was a dream, because shortly after descending into the mist, I fell asleep. I guess I *was* just so exhausted, and those colors were so relaxing that I just curled up on the cave floor and faded into dreamland. But I wasn't the only one.

Several hours later (I wasn't sure how many), I was nudged awake by my brother, Harry, who was smiling. Several of the others were also just waking up. The stone walls of the chamber were smooth, as if created by running water, though at present the surface was dry. The floor and ceiling had gentle scoops, almost like ribs, as if we'd fallen asleep inside a vacuum hose at a car wash.

There was only a small amount of light. Last night Gid and Micah had made crude torches to bring us this far, but those torches had burned out. The light was coming from the tunnel up ahead—daylight, or so I hoped. As I looked behind us, the cavern was so dark I couldn't make out *anything*. Apparently, after passing through that lake of mist, I'd walked farther than I thought, obviously in a state of near unconsciousness. I realized that without torches or flashlights, there was no going back.

Harry glanced at Pagag, still asleep about five feet away. He moved away to awaken him, but I grabbed his arm.

"Don't," I said.

My brother looked at me strangely.

"Let's leave him here," I whispered. "He'll never know the difference."

Harry grimaced and chuckled, as if I was making a joke, then he ignored me and gave Pagag a nudge. Little did Harry know, I wasn't joking at all. I was trying to do my brother a *favor.*

"How're you feeling?" Harry asked Pagag.

"Good," he replied. "Like I've slept for a week."

"How long *did* we sleep?" asked Jesse, also sitting up.

"Too long," said Gidgiddonihah grumpily. He rose quickly and faced the light source.

Micah said, "It's almost as if . . . our journey into the mist *lulled* us to sleep."

"Well, we all needed it badly," said Harry.

"Except that now I'm hungry," said Becky.

None of us had brought any food. Finding nourishment would be our first order of business. That is, as soon as we figured out where we were.

Pagag moved over to Mary, who was just opening her eyes. He offered her his hand. "Need some help?"

Mary glanced at Harry. She smiled kindly at Pagag, but replied, "No, thank you. I'm fine."

*Starting already,* I thought to myself. My naïve brother *still* didn't realize this square-jawed, amber-eyed Cro-Magnon with long, blond hair was a challenger. He seemed grateful just to have Pagag along— one more able warrior to face whatever lay ahead. For me, however, the Jaredite's presence made my blood boil.

"Let's get moving," said Gidgiddonihah. "On your feet, everyone."

Harry looked around anxiously. "Where's Rafa?"

His falcon was nowhere in sight.

"Maybe he went on without us," Becky suggested.

My brother grunted. "That would be typical."

Harry helped Mary to her feet. She embraced him and tenderly brushed some hair away from his forehead. Pagag watched, his expression unreadable, though I perceived a glint of determination in his eye. What this boy required was a good tongue-lashing. The last thing Harry and Mary needed was to have this buffoon try to spoil their romantic reunion. At the first opportunity, I was determined to have a little talk with the son of Mahonri Moriancumr.

We followed Gid toward the source of light. It was about twenty yards down the chamber—emitting upward from a space about two and a half feet wide in the cave floor. Except for this hole, the tunnel more or less ended. Like it or not, we were going to have to fit inside. Gidgiddonihah sniffed the air with his large, flat nostrils. A foul odor was coming up from below.

"*Peee-eew!*" said Becky. "What *is* that?"

We all looked to Gid. I'm not sure why we expected him to know. Because he was the oldest, I think we naturally looked up to him as the expedition leader. The Nephite warrior appeared a little uneasy, but he didn't offer any theories. Everyone stood about, wondering who would be the guinea pig. Pagag moved forward, as if volunteering. I forced myself in front of him.

"Wait," said Gid as I started climbing into the hole. "Let me go first."

"How about second," I replied and disappeared inside.

There weren't many handholds, so after the first few feet, it felt like I was slipping more than climbing. The smell got worse. It reminded me of an old, musty refrigerator. A little farther and it reminded me of a visit I'd once made to the city dump on a particularly hot day. All at once the space opened up and I dropped, landing on my feet.

*Crunch!* As I hit bottom, my feet broke something. It almost felt like eggs—*big* eggs, like those of an ostrich. I stood there frozen, almost afraid to look down at my ankles.

I was inside another room of the cavern. It was very dusty, almost like a cloud of smoke. There was sunlight coming from behind me. My long shadow was cast far into a back chamber of the cave. The shafts of dusty light were cutting all around my torso and arms. My focus fell initially on the cave walls. Many of the walls were smoothed and painted. There were black and red designs—mostly red. *Blood* red. I felt a brisk gust of wind. No doubt this is what was stirring up the dust. At last I turned my eyes downward to see what my feet had crunched.

At first it wasn't clear. The dust was so thick and the shadows were so pronounced. But whatever I had broken, it appeared that there were dozens of these things all about my feet. *Hundreds* of them, extending back into the cave and behind me toward the source of light. If I'd been under water I might have thought I'd just stepped into a bed of some kind of fragile coral—except that all of it was oval shaped, like a nest with hundreds of ostrich eggs.

No, not ostriches. They were smaller than that. A dark, queasy feeling settled over me, like I'd just disturbed somebody's sacred ground. Or just the opposite. Somebody's evil chamber. I reached down and felt one of the objects at my feet. Then I lifted it until I could see it clearly in a shaft of light.

I sucked in a deep, choking gasp. I wanted to scream. I *tried* to scream. But the sound came out very weird and strained, more like I was trying to vomit. And maybe that *was* what I was trying to do.

The object was a skull—a very small human skull with a hole in the crown. The hole indicated death by violence. Immediately, I let it fall from my hand.

Gidgiddonihah dropped down from the opening overhead. He almost mashed me to the floor, but instead he latched onto my shoulders to keep us both from falling. We stumbled around a bit. Each time we planted our feet, I heard and felt that awful, hollow, stomach-turning crunch of skull bones. The entire cave floor was *carpeted* with tiny skulls.

The skulls of children.

The sound of retching came out of my throat. Gidgiddonihah's eyes made a fast scan of the area and quickly determined the cause of my speechlessness. He hugged me to his chest.

"It's all right," he said. "You're all right. Come."

He turned me around and led me across the carpet of skulls toward the source of sunlight. I shuffled, keeping my steps low, preferring to push through the skulls, or kick them out of the way, rather than hear that awful crunch. Gid, however, wasn't as careful, so I heard the crackling just the same. We seemed to walk forever, although it was only a dozen steps or so until we had crossed that abominable graveyard and my feet were again standing on flat, stony ground. He left me immediately to go help the others as they dropped into the room, and also to prepare them for the shock.

"There are bones on the floor," I heard him say as Pagag slipped down from above. "Don't be alarmed." His voice was loud enough that all those who were still climbing down must have heard.

I pulled myself together. I was no use to anyone acting like a squeamish female. Whatever the purpose of this terrible room, I had no doubt that the remains of these victims had been collecting here for many years. Some of the skulls were very old and brittle while others . . .

I put it out of my mind and focused on the other realities of our situation. Gid had left me in a spot only a few feet in front of the cave's apparent entrance. Shafts of sunlight projected into the chamber through vines and other foliage that dangled down from above. From the other side I doubted if anyone would have recognized that there was a cave here. Gusts of wind would occasionally flutter the vines, causing the spears of light to transform and shift in the dust cloud.

I began to hear expressions of revulsion from the others as they entered the chamber.

"What *is* this place?" Micah exclaimed.

"A catacomb," Jesse declared.

"It's a sacrificial chamber," said Gidgiddonihah calmly.

To my left sat a fire pit with soot-blackened edges and charcoal remains. I also noticed nooks along the walls where candles and incense had burned, probably for generations, blackening the surrounding stone. The candle mounds almost looked like stalagmites. Rivulets of wax ran all the way to the floor. In other nooks along the walls I perceived something else that was disturbing—snake heads, dried and withered, jaws pried open wide and fangs displayed. There might have been fifty of these shriveled heads arranged throughout the entrance area, as if guarding the place from intruders, or warning them to leave.

I was all for that. I stepped up to the entrance and pushed aside an armful of vines. I stopped abruptly. My feelings of revulsion and shock were replaced with vertigo. A dizzying vista appeared before my eyes. We were hundreds of feet in the air! This cave was situated high up the wall of a cliff. Instinctively, I grabbed onto the vines for support.

Jesse joined me and peered outside. "Micah, look at this!"

Micah arrived and leaned out. Four hundred feet below, a small river cut its way through a gnarled canyon. The water looked shallow, strewn with hundreds of rocks and boulders. The opposite canyon face looked like it was only about two hundred feet away.

Jesse added, "It reminds me of that water tunnel inside the Tower of Babel."

"Except that our elevation is considerably higher," said Micah. "And there's no pool below into which we might leap."

Pagag and Gid finished helping Mary and Becky into the room, with Harry entering last. Mary broke down in tears as soon as she recognized what was all around her; Rebecca began shaking in terror. I put my arm around my young cousin.

Again I turned to Gid. "Who would create such a chamber hundreds of feet up the side of a cliff? Who would bring all these skulls to such a place? Children and . . . *infants?*" I shuddered and again felt my stomach turning.

"Gadiantons," said Gid.

The word by itself evoked awful images. The sound of it echoed in the cavern depths. I stared back into those depths apprehensively. It was easy to imagine others nearby, listening, breathing, waiting for us to turn our backs.

Something on the floor at the edge of the carpet of skulls caught Pagag's attention. He knelt and began brushing away what appeared to be a mosaic design composed of jade and others stones, black and red. The mosaic was a representation of another skull, this time the skull of some kind of monster. A panther or jaguar. It wore an elaborate feathered headdress, again composed of jade and chips of red stone.

Gid seemed to recognize the design. "We used to find caves like this in the wilderness of Hermounts during the Gadianton war—always high up in the cliffs. When they weren't performing their bloody rituals, Gadiantons would use them as places of resort. Sometimes the Reds would hide up here for months while we searched. Even after we spotted them, it was easier to starve them out rather than attack. At the end they usually killed each other. We'd find their bodies with the flesh all . . ." Gid stopped.

"All what?" asked Pagag.

"Never mind," I snapped. I saw no need for further details. Becky was upset enough as it was.

"So these Gadiantons are worshippers of the Evil One?" asked Pagag. "Like the children of Cain?"

"Profound deduction," I declared.

Harry indicated the fire pit. "This hasn't been cold very long. A day at the most. How often do they . . . 'visit' caves like this?"

Gid shook his head. "Unknown."

"This place is dark and wicked," said Mary. "We must leave here now."

Jesse leaned over the edge. "It shouldn't be too difficult. We can climb down the vines."

The vines and brush descended down a rocky shaft. The shaft stretched all the way to the bottom of the canyon. The cliff face wasn't sheer. There were many ledges and outcroppings that would provide adequate foot and handholds. As I studied it, I could easily perceive the route that visitors to the cave probably used. Still, one sloppy placement of the foot and climbers would be airborne, bouncing from one ledge to the next, like a soccer ball, until they landed in the riverbed.

Harry stood aside to allow Gid a wide view of the landscape and asked him, "So where are we?"

The Nephite warrior studied the opposite cliff wall and the green mountains beyond, partially hidden by swirls of gray clouds. "Not quite sure. But the general character . . . it does appear to be Zarahemla. Those might be the misty mountains of Gideon."

"Who lives in Zarahemla?" Pagag asked.

"Nephites," Gidgiddonihah replied. "My people."

"Let's start climbing," said Micah. The former Essene yanked the vines, testing their sturdiness.

As we gathered at the cave's mouth, Becky, still wiping tears, asked Harry, "Do you still think Joshua is here? Do you really think he's all right?"

Harry touched her shoulder. "I do. On *both* counts."

"Why would the seerstone send us here?" she asked. "Why bring us to this horrible room?"

Harry shook his head, unable to reply. Suddenly something else drew his attention.

Pagag approached Mary and said, "I think it would be safer if you locked your arms around my neck. I will make certain that you reach the bottom unharmed."

Harry's eyes blinked. This may have been the first time that my brother *finally* got some kind of clue that Pagag had set his crosshairs on his Jewish princess. And yet Harry, *still* wanting to give Pagag every benefit of the doubt, said to him politely, "I wonder if that might be more awkward and dangerous than just letting her climb. She's more capable than you might think."

Pagag was looking into Mary's eyes. "Of that there is no doubt. I have, after all, seen her in action."

"Action?" asked Harry.

"With a sword," said Pagag.

My brother gave Mary a surprised look. He hadn't yet heard the story of how Mary had used the sword of Akish to defend the children.

"Nevertheless," Pagag continued, "I may have to insist. I couldn't feel comfortable knowing that any woman might be in danger."

At last Harry puffed out his chest and stood his ground. "I think I can look out for her well enough, Pagag."

Pagag looked Harry over from top to bottom. The Jaredite was taller, wider in the torso and shoulders. Frankly, the man had arm and leg muscles like a Titan. Still, I had no doubts that Harry could look after Mary's safety. However, Pagag replied, "Are you sure about that?"

The two men gaped at one another. Harry opened his mouth, ready to say something bold. But Mary spared him and announced, "*I'm* sure of it." She took Harry's hand. "But thank you, Pagag. I deeply appreciate your concern."

Harry gave her *another* queer look. I don't think he liked the phrase "deeply appreciate."

The Jaredite wasn't quite ready to back down. I feared the doofus was gonna challenge Harry to a wrestling match right there on the cave floor. Before he could say anything else, I intervened.

"Becky!" I said, putting my hand on her arm. "Pagag has volunteered to help you climb down the cliff. After all, he just couldn't feel comfortable knowing that any woman might be in danger."

I sent Pagag a tight-lipped smirk.

Becky's face brightened considerably. I realized ten-year-old Rebecca might have had a slight crush on the son of Mahonri Moriancumr. "That would be wonderful."

Pagag sent me what could only have been interpreted as a scowl, but then he smiled warmly at Rebecca. "It would be my honor. Come. Wrap your arms around my neck."

Gid was chuckling quietly.

Just then we heard something behind us. Quickly, I turned and gazed past the sea of skulls into the dark chamber beyond with all its chasms and tunnels. Everyone else had also turned. The sound was still echoing, like a fallen rock. I noticed that Gid's hand had gone instinctively to the axe on his hip. We stood there a moment, listening, but the sound did not repeat.

"Perhaps a bat," Jesse suggested.

"Or a falling stone," said Harry, "set loose by our vibrations."

Noises in a cave, I thought to myself. Why does there always have to be noises?

We waited another moment. Finally Gid said, "Let's get moving."

Jesse and Micah led the way down the cliff, following the narrow trail of footholds and ledges worn smooth by the steps of Gadianton sorcerers. We gripped vines and foliage for support, reaching the bottom in about an hour. There was only one rather close call. That was when Mary slipped, though she was quickly caught by Harry's arm. Harry and Pagag exchanged looks. The Jaredite shook his head, clearly inferring that Mary still would have been safer with him. Upon reaching the riverbed, no one appeared the worse for wear—just a few bruised knees and one or two scraped arms from briars that we'd encountered among the vines.

We spoke very little as we made our way down the canyon, wading back and forth across the river through water sometimes as deep as our waists. Our mood was alarmingly tense—so much so that the urgency to find food and fresh water became secondary to reaching a place of relative safety. Maybe such uneasiness was natural, considering where we'd just been, and what we'd just seen and possibly heard. I half expected a Gadianton to leap out from behind every boulder. Anyone might have spotted us from the ridges above. I'd be glad to reach the shelter of the jungle. And yet we eventually had to run into *someone*. How else would we find Joshua, Meagan, and the others?

After about an hour and a half, we sighted the canyon mouth, another hour further away. Beyond it lay a flat, forested valley with more jungled hills and distant mountains, kissed by low-hanging clouds. The weather was starting to drizzle.

"Do you recognize anything yet?" Micah asked Gid.

The Nephite shook his head. "I would still wager that we're in Zarahemla, but this is a region I've never visited."

We heard a high-pitched squawk from the sky. Harry's falcon soared out from behind a cliff ledge with something clasped in its feet. As Rafa flew over Harry, it dropped a dead rabbit onto the stones in front of him. My brother held out his arm for the bird to land.

"Good to see you again," he told the bird.

Gidgiddonihah recovered the rabbit and examined it. "Should provide a few bites for all of us," he said. "Nicely done."

"Hear that?" Harry said to Rafa. "Ya done good. Find us another one. Understand? Another one."

Rafa enthusiastically leaped back into the air and disappeared into the cliffs. Amazingly, the bird seemed to understand Harry's instructions perfectly.

Harry said to Gid, "As soon as we make some kind of camp, Becky and I will take another moment to inquire of the Lord using the seerstone. We'll see if any more can be learned about where we are or what direction we should travel."

Rebecca was content to walk near Pagag for much of the afternoon, asking questions like, "Did you like girls when you were my age?" and "What's your favorite color—blonde or brunette?" I was sure the lout would answer "brunette" since he spent most of his time ogling Mary, but fortunately he was sensitive enough not to hurt blonde-haired Becky's feelings and replied, "I have found myself susceptible to the charms of both."

At last Becky walked ahead to speak with Harry. This allowed me my first moment alone with Pagag outside the hearing of others. We were twenty yards behind the pack. Pagag hadn't let Mary out of his sights all day. As I watched him slosh through another shallow section of river, I felt sure the wheels in his mind were spinning—*scheming* how he might win her heart from my brother.

"So when do you plan to make a fool out of yourself again?" I inquired.

*That* broke his concentration. "Excuse me?"

"I'd just like to know so I can be there to watch."

He faced forward again, a little flustered and irritated. "And how have I made myself a fool?"

"You must think we're all blind," I replied. "Why *did* you come with us, Pagag?"

Calm and collected, he said, "Because I can help. And, I must admit, because I am infinitely curious about the lands and times that you and the others inhabit."

"Has absolutely nothing to do with that dark-eyed beauty between Harry and Rebecca, eh?"

He blushed like a stoplight. How I loved making a man squirm!

He ranted, "Are you—? Do you think—? Are you suggesting that I would offer my strength and skills solely for the benefit of a single woman?"

"*Benefit?*" I scoffed. "Just who do you think you are, Pagag?"

"The future king of a great people," he huffed. "And I certainly do not have to defend my actions to you." He quickened his pace to get away.

I called out, "Hey, Pagag."

He looked back at me resentfully.

I stopped for emphasis, and also so he couldn't claim to have misunderstood. "I'll tell you right now, if you try to come between Mary and my brother—if you try to stir up any contention among us whatsoever—you'll be dealing with me."

His eyebrows perked up in surprise. I think it was the first time in his life that he'd ever been threatened by a woman. He tried to laugh, but it sounded pathetic. However, he made no actual reply. Just turned around again to catch up with the others.

My words might have seemed pretty harsh considering that he was the son of the Brother of Jared. But sorry, I just didn't see it that way.

People couldn't hang on to their parents' coattails. Eventually they had to stand up on their own, be counted for who they were. And frankly, I was considerably less than impressed with this particular Jaredite.

I glanced up at the afternoon sun, half eclipsed behind the cliffs.

I stopped walking, my eyes blinking.

Something moved. I thought I saw a shape dash through a spike of sunlight. I squinted, shielding my eyes with my hand. I watched for several seconds, until the bright sun left a glowing red blob on my retina, but nothing else moved. I looked ahead at the others, wondering if I should sound some kind of alarm. I decided, out of pride, to wait until I saw something else. After my words to Pagag, I didn't want to appear paranoid or frightened. Fact was, my brain was still imagining Gadiantons behind every bush and boulder.

We soon reached the shelter of the forest. A camp was struck at a place where the stream from the canyon drained into a somewhat larger river, flowing north. Rafa returned with a second rabbit, but it appeared that she'd decided to have a portion of it for herself. I didn't consider myself a picky eater, but honestly, these scrawny critters didn't look that appetizing. Besides, I was too impatient to wait for the bunnies to be skinned and cooked.

I turned to Gid. "You know this country, right? Did you ever find yourself forced to survive in a place like this? What did you eat?"

Gid's mind was way ahead of me. He was already looking at the various trees in the forest. After locating a small palm a few yards from camp, he rapped it with his knuckles. "This should feed us all."

"A tree?" I asked.

"But it doesn't have any coconuts," said Rebecca.

"It's not a coconut palm," said Gid. "Have you not eaten heart of palm? You're in for a treat." He began hacking at the bark with his Roman sword and said to Harry, "Start chopping about three feet below me."

*Heart of palm.* I'd heard of that. Might have even tried some at a Sizzler salad bar once. Even so, I was still hoping for something better.

"Does any fruit grow in places like this?" I asked.

Gid paused, "Of course." He pointed through the woods. "There may be berries or cactus fruit along the base of that hill. Eat nothing before I've had a look at it. We don't need you poisoning yourself or giving yourself, uh, a frequent reason to visit the bushes."

I smiled as Gid looked a little embarrassed.

As I started toward the base of the hill, Gid told Pagag, "Go with her."

"It's not necessary," I responded.

"No one goes off by themselves," Gid stressed.

"How about Micah?"

Gid shook his head. "Micah will make the fire."

Pagag looked even less enthused. "What about Jesse? I could help you cut down—"

"Go *with her*," Gid repeated sternly.

Pagag sighed in irritation, but made no more argument. I headed into the woods, unconcerned with whether he was following or not. We'd walked almost a hundred yards in silence when I finally glanced back. He was only two steps behind me. I decided I might as well broach a subject. "So how long have you known Mary and Rebecca?"

"I don't wish to speak," he said flatly. "Let's find your fruit."

"Sor-*ry*," I said, emphasizing the last syllable. "Just trying to make some friendly conversation."

"I know how you make conversation. And it is not very friendly."

"I apologize for being so blunt before. But you have to understand. I love my brother very much. And you have no idea what he went through to find Mary and be reunited with her."

He paused a moment, then said thoughtfully, "I do not doubt what *any* man would go through to try and be with Mary. But I do have serious doubts about your impartiality in determining what is best for her."

I gave him a narrow glance. "Oh, is that so? And you think if I were impartial I'd choose *you* for her over my brother?"

He made a little hiss and looked away, as if the answer to this question was so obvious that it wasn't worth discussing.

I decided to take the challenge. "Well, then, let's see what I have to go on so far. First of all, I know that when I met you, you were mashing Mary to the ground—"

"I wasn't 'mashing' her. I was *protecting* her. You *know* that. Harry and the others are wearing the trappings of King Nimrod's soldiers."

"Secondly, you had the nerve to make overtures to Mary, fully knowing that we are on a desperate mission to save people's lives."

To that he had no quick reply. Surprisingly, his expression sagged with guilt. "I realize now that I made a mistake. It was a rash moment of bravado, and you were right to call it selfish. I promise you that such a moment will not recur—at least not until Joshua and your other loved ones are safe. But I do *not* promise that afterwards I will not again attempt to make my feelings known, or that I will not again present myself as a superior candidate for Mary's affections."

"And why is that?" I scoffed. "Because you're going to be a *king?*"

"Well . . . yes!" he responded, but then he shrank a little, even looking somewhat self-conscious and meek. "But not only that. For *many* more reasons than that. In my tribe I could have any woman that I desire."

I half closed my eyes and sent him a doubtful look. "Oh *really?*"

"Yes. But I do *not* choose any woman. I do not *feel* for other women as I do for Mary. She is . . . unique. Gentle, yet as strong as iron. Fragile, but with more resolute conviction than any woman I have ever met. No woman would make a better mother for my children. Or a better wife for me."

I made a *tsk-tsk* with my tongue. "Sounds like you have it pretty bad. That's very sad for you. Because you forgot one thing. *Loyalty.* No one is more loyal than Mary Symeon. You don't stand a chance, Pagag. Give it up. Give up now before you cause yourself anymore pain. She'd never waver in her dedication to Harry. And if you knew Mary, you'd know that was true."

Pagag mulled this over. Finally, he nodded sullenly. "Unfortunately, I believe you are right. So I'm left with only one alternative."

"Oh yeah? What, pray tell, is that?"

"If I cannot convince Mary . . ." He paused and chose another way to state it. "I sense that your brother is an honest man."

"I won't argue with that."

"He is a man of integrity who would not deliberately stand in the way of another's happiness."

I continued to listen, though somewhat nervously.

"Therefore," he concluded, "over the course of however long we are together on this journey, I must convince Harry that he cannot love Mary the way that I love her. That he could never make her as happy. I will convince him that he must abandon his object to marry her. If he is as honest as I suspect, I believe he will do so of his own accord—of his own free will and choice. Remember my words, Steffanie. It will happen."

I realized my jaw was dangling. I shut it tightly and turned away. I couldn't help but recall Harry's statements soon after we'd been spewed from that geyser into 3000 BC, right after I told him how I'd dumped my fiancé, Mike. I remembered that Harry had hinted of some lingering doubts about his feelings toward Mary. He'd wondered if what he felt for her was obligation more than love. At least I *think* that was how he put it. The conversation seemed so long ago. Mary had never faltered in her love for Harry—not even once. Not since the day he brought her home from ancient Israel. Harry, on the other hand—perhaps because he was so sure of her love—had allowed himself to question his love for *her*. But even Harry had admitted that those doubts were silly. And certainly such doubts had all evaporated over the past few days—especially the last twelve hours. Or had they?

Suddenly I liked Pagag even less, if that was possible. I feared—I definitely feared—that the Jaredite may have found a chink in the armor of Harry and Mary's romance.

*No,* I told myself. I was being ridiculous. It wasn't true. I was misjudging the situation horribly. Over the years I'd come to accept the future matrimony of Mary and Harry as surely as the smell of maple syrup on Sunday morning, or the invariable rising of the sun. Certainly it seemed more natural and inevitable than my own matrimonial plans with Michael Collins. In fact, such a marriage was *perfect.* They were perfect for each *other!* The very idea of some other future reality was repugnant to me. And now Pagag was over there grinning to himself. He read my reaction too easily. Now he *knew* he'd found a possible chink—because of *me!* I felt strangely like I'd just betrayed my own brother.

We continued to walk in silence. But in my head a funny little idea started to form. As the Grinch might say, "A nasty, awful, wonderful idea!" The solution to this problem was abominably simple. In order for Pagag to abandon his silly quest to win Mary's

heart, he only needed a distraction. And what was the best distraction
for a man? Why, another female, of course! But where would I find
such a female? Hmmm.

Guess I'd have to volunteer for the task myself. It was a dirty job,
but *somebody* had to do it. Frankly, I couldn't imagine a better candidate. Oh now, don't think I was being conceited. I wasn't trying to
compare myself to Mary. She and I were altogether different. Far be it
from me to categorize myself, but if pressed, I suppose I'd have classified myself as . . . the *exotic* type. Blonde and blue-eyed. Tall and
athletic. At least I was tall enough that I could have kissed him
without having to be lifted. (Spit and rinse out my mouth with lye at
the very thought!)

But all of this was beside the point. I really only had one objective, and that was to discombobulate his male brain and evaporate all
interest in Mary. After the mission was accomplished I would, unfortunately, have no alternative but to tell Pagag the truth. I would have
to inform him—quite delicately—that I was about as attracted to
him as I was to an Australian cane toad. This should let him down
softly enough. I know it was a very cruel plan. But what other option
was there? Mary and Harry were *meant* to be together. Goodness,
even their *names* rhymed! This strategy seemed to me the best way to
insure that the universe remained in balance.

In the midst of my devious ponderings I heard Pagag suddenly
announce, "I wonder if *these* are edible."

I childishly resented that he'd spotted them first. But just as Gid
had predicted, there was a bush loaded with rich, burgundy-colored
berries along the base of the thickly jungled hillside.

In my first feeble effort to woo this Jaredite, I decided to pay him
a compliment. "Wow. You have good eyes."

Pagag plucked a berry and drew it toward his mouth. Maybe I
should have just let him eat it, but considering my new objective, I
said, "Wait! Gid gave us a warning. I wouldn't want you to . . .
become sick."

Pagag smiled mischievously, then he popped the berry in and
started chewing. I suppose if the dunghead *deliberately* poisoned
himself that might have been okay. Heck, I'd have been off the
hook!

But Pagag's expression brightened. He declared, "It's very good. Sweet like a cherry. Here." He plucked another and held it toward me. "Try one."

Oh, what a choice moment! Let him hand-feed me a piece of fruit. Was there anything more seductive? Sorry. This game of winning his affections just wasn't worth risking a bout of diarrhea.

"I'll wait for Gid's assessment," I said.

He shrugged. "As you please." He ate it, licked his fingers, and started searching about for something that would help us carry the bounty back to camp. He indicated some nearby plants with large leaves shaped like elephant ears. "Break off a few of those," he told me. "We'll roll them into cones and fill them to the top."

I hesitated, which I guess was my natural response whenever a guy gave me orders. But allowing my contrary nature to prevail wasn't going to help me reach my goal. Besides, men liked obedience, right? Thus, I approached the elephant-ear leaves. I pulled one down to eye level to break the stem. Then I froze like an iceberg.

Staring back at me from behind the leaf was a *face!* A *man!* His complexion was dark, and his eyes and mouth were circled by glittering gold and raven-black paint. His teeth were *also* painted—alternately red and black. Gripped in his right hand was an axe with the sharpest obsidian blade I'd ever seen, semi-transparent at the edge. He'd been *hiding* here—waiting for the perfect moment to strike. He promptly raised the axe to strike downward.

I gasped and stumbled backwards. Instincts kicked in, and the moment I hit the ground I immediately twisted onto my shoulder, anticipating the strike. The axe blade sliced into the soil. I scrambled furiously away, fully knowing that his next attack would not be so carelessly executed, but also knowing it was *impossible* to crawl away fast enough!

A crushing pain inflamed my left hand. But not from an axe. From a human foot! *Pagag* had stepped on my hand as he sprang to contend with my attacker. As I rolled over to look, I heard a shatter. Slivers of black glass from the attacker's obsidian axe rained around me as it met Pagag's bronze sword.

In the next swipe it was all over. The attacker crumbled, not making a single sound as Pagag delivered his death stroke. My blood was pumping feverishly; my thoughts were in a whirlwind. I could hear the hammering of my heart over the splash of a small waterfall nearby. Maybe the excitement had also blurred my vision slightly, because when Pagag reached down to help me, I winced thinking that his hand might have been something else striking at me.

He finally grabbed both of my shoulders, hoisting me up. After I found my balance, I shook him off me and took a step toward the attacker's dead body. His eyes were wide and staring. The man had a shrewish face. The gold and black paint (*war*paint, I guessed) was striped across his forehead like some kind of patriotic flag. He wore thick arm and leg bands beaded with turquoise stones and other materials. On his chest was a heavy vest adorned in feathers the same color as the stripes on his face. However, his cloth and leather armor had been no match for the lethal edge of Pagag's sword.

"Are you all right?" asked Pagag.

"Of *course* I'm all right!" I snapped, though my lungs were still straining for oxygen.

"He must have heard us coming and concealed himself," said Pagag. "Do you have any idea who—?"

Instead of waiting to hear his question, I took off like a rocket, up the ravine and back toward our campsite. Everyone had to be warned. Where there was one attacker, there were sure to be others.

"*Wait!*" Pagag screeched through his teeth.

But I didn't wait. Adrenaline powered my legs. I smashed through the undergrowth. We'd wandered farther from camp than I'd realized—four or five hundred yards. I heard Pagag running behind me. I glanced back and realized he was almost on top of me. Those Jaredite legs were pretty swift. He gripped my shoulder to slow me down. I'd had just about enough of him. I whipped around and slugged him in the face. So much for my game of flirtation. But as the knuckles of my left fist struck his cheek, the wrist buckled. Pain flashed down my arm and up my spine, shocking my brain like a finger in a light socket. For the first time I realized my hand was injured. That Jaredite oaf. When he'd stepped on my hand, he'd *broken it!*

Despite my injury, Pagag still staggered from the punch. Instead of continuing to run, I nearly blacked out from pain. Pagag caught me. He pressed his palm over my mouth and said in a desperate whisper, "Are you completely witless? You want us to die? You're making more noise than a rhinoceros herd! *Stop! Think!*"

My pain subsided enough to grasp the wisdom of his words. I was only making myself a moving target. Pagag gripped my uninjured hand and led me through the forest. He was now hunched down, moving more stealthily. I tried to brace my injured wrist in my armpit, but the pain continued to pulse as if someone was stabbing it with a hot poker.

Twenty yards from the campsite, Pagag hunkered down in the brush. We listened. I'd expected to hear chopping, voices—anything. We heard nothing. Peering through the foliage, we *saw* nothing either. Pagag tightened his grip on my wrist and we moved a little closer.

The campsite fell into full view—and it was empty. Not a soul in sight. I saw the palm tree they'd been chopping on. The milk-white wounds were still visible on the trunk. Something had interrupted their efforts. Pagag saw my lungs fill with air. His palm quickly pressed over my mouth again.

"Don't you do it," he said, whispering harshly.

I pushed him away and whispered just as harshly, "*Fine! I won't!*"

He was right, of course. Yelling out anyone's name would have been the stupidest thing I could have done. Obviously I still wasn't thinking clearly. This surprised me. Normally when my body was pumping adrenaline, my instincts were dead on. The pain was throwing me off. Or just the presence of this cretin, Pagag.

We finally worked up the nerve to walk out into the open. My first idea was that Gid and the others had seen enemies approaching and run off to hide. But as I looked around, I quickly realized this wasn't the case. I found Jesse's metal sword—abandoned behind a stone. I noticed where Micah had begun to build a fire. A few pieces of gathered wood lay nearby, but not in any neat pile. They were scattered as if dropped or thrown. Then I found the most disturbing article of all.

As I reached into a clump of grass, I raised up a translucent white stone. It was the seerstone that Harry had always kept in his pocket. Slivers of ice shot up my spine. Harry would have never left that stone. He'd surely taken it out to make further inquiries of the Lord.

Whatever had occurred here, it had taken place so fast that he hadn't found time to put it back into the pocket of his cloak.

"What *happened?*" I asked. I'd tried to keep my voice low, but there was a definite vein of panic in it.

Pagag continued searching the ground for additional clues. He looked no less stumped or alarmed than I was. A thunderous wave of desperation washed over me. The feeling was more intense than any pain in my hand. In the last fifteen minutes—twenty at the most—every member of our party seemed to have vanished into thin air.

## NOTES TO CHAPTER 1

Archeological research supports the idea of ceremonial caves on cliff walls hundreds of feet in the air. In 1997, Italian archeologist Giuseppe Orefici headed up a team that surveyed several sites on the canyon walls above the La Venta River in Chiapas, Mexico. In one cave, located 600 feet up the nearly vertical cliff, his team found a ceremonial altar, textiles, pottery, tools, and the skeletons of children whose skulls had been fractured as part of a ritual sacrifice. The archeologists believed these "cave dwellers" to be the ancestors of the Zoque Indians who presently inhabit this region of southern Mexico.

In many ancient American cultures it is reported that priests would often purchase or abduct small children from their mothers to sacrifice to their rain god, Plaula or Chac. If the child cried hysterically during the journey to the place of sacrifice, this was viewed as a good omen, and a sign of a good harvest in the coming season ("Search for the Lost Cave People," transcript, www.pbs.org/wgbh/nova/transcripts/2507cavepeople.html).

The practice of Gadianton robbers taking refuge in the wilderness or in difficult mountain terrain as a means of self-preservation is well established in the Book of Mormon (Hel. 2:11; 3 Ne. 1:7). The Nephites often sent their armies in pursuit of Gadianton robbers and other wicked dissenters, which may have motivated them to establish exactly the kind of cave retreats that archeologists are now discovering. Over time, such retreats may have become sacred or revered by later generations, who continued to use them as ceremonial centers. Many of these kinds of caves are still used today by the Mesoamerican natives for rituals that are dedicated to the old Mesoamerican gods. Such rituals can be quite complex, and may include incense burning and animal sacrifice (Timothy J. Knab, *A War of Witches: Journey into the Underworld of Contemporary Aztecs* [N.Y.: Harper Collins, 1995]).

In his own research, the author has observed that modern archeologists and anthropologists, when reporting on the evidence of human sacrifice among ancient peoples, often refuse to pass judgment on such practices. In many cases scholars will openly request that readers or viewers lay aside modern prejudices and try to contemplate such practices with an "open mind" against the backdrop of the culture wherein such rituals took place. In others words, though such practices may seem barbaric to the modern mind, a scholar may propose that it would be amiss to pin a negative label on the ancients, who considered such ceremonies normal and even beneficial.

However, to most civilized societies such practices are now, and have always been, evidence of serious internal corruption and apostasy. From a gospel perspective, human sacrifice and other satanic rituals need never be classified as anything but acts of incomprehensible evil.

# CHAPTER 2

## Joshua

It was difficult to look into my father's eyes. Yet all he could do was look into mine. Look and weep, his tears cutting paths along his cheeks, grinding deeper paths along the surface of my soul.

They kept him and Marcos as prisoners in a dark and humid tent for an entire afternoon. It was several hours before my men found me to notify me that some very unusual prisoners had been captured—men I might wish to interrogate personally. When I saw them, I experienced a strange and harrowing rush of emotions. My heart leapt and withered all at the same instant. I had imagined this moment—*dreamed* of it—for many long years. But now that it was here, I felt unexpectedly awkward.

Immediately I commanded that their bonds be cut. My men watched in consternation as I accompanied Marcos and my father into my tent. We also brought their backpacks and other belongings. I could tell that their captors had rifled through at least one of their packs—an offense that I would inquire about later, meting out the appropriate punishment. But first I saw to it that their thirst was quenched. I also ordered that food should be brought.

Plainly my father and Marcos had not aged as I had. Their appearance was the same as when I'd last seen them at my boyhood home in Provo, Utah. However, as the minutes passed, I watched those missing years compound in the lines of my father's face. He seemed to grow old right before my eyes. I knew it was because of his grief, his mortification, upon gazing at me. The last time he'd seen me, I was a boy of twelve years. But those innocent days were gone. Seeing the pain in his face made my whole body ache with regret.

Marcos wore a similar expression of shock, though without the tears. I sensed that his overriding response was marked by anger rather than pain. In fact, if I'd still been twelve years old, I think he might have taken me over his knee. But over the course of several minutes I noticed that his emotions made a kind of transformation—from anger, to sorrow, and finally, to pity.

As my stewards laid down our plates of corn gruel, pheasant, chilies, and spiced beans, I said to my father and Marcos, "Why don't you eat? You both must be very hungry."

The sound of my voice prompted Marcos to finally choose a question from the long list assuredly whirling in his mind. The same questions were probably on my father's tongue, but he wasn't yet ready to voice them. For him the shock was still too great.

"What," Marcos began, almost breathlessly, "*happened?*"

I opened my mouth, but I could only shake my head, unable to find a starting place.

He asked another question, more specific. "How old are you, Joshua?"

"I am . . ." I looked at my father but quickly turned away when he met my gaze. ". . . nineteen."

Silence persisted. No one had touched their food.

Suddenly Marcos erupted with a flurry of questions. "How did this happen? Where have you been? How did you get here?"

"I . . . have been here for five years," I replied. "I mean to say, I have been five years among the Nephites."

They digested this, then Marcos asked, "And the first two?"

"The first two . . ." I felt peculiar—almost lightheaded—as if I were listening to someone else's voice answer these questions. I began again, stumbling, "The first *part* of the first two years . . . What I mean is, the first few weeks after my sister and I were kidnapped, I was with Mary in the land of Israel. It was 1840, I think. Or 1841. My memory is a little hazy. But soon thereafter we were in the land of Babylon and Salem in 3000 BC."

Silence prevailed again.

My father finally spoke, but only a single word, pronounced with urgency. "Rebecca?"

I shook my head, a cyclone of guilt swelling up inside me. The last time that I had seen my sister, she was . . . she was not breathing.

It was my fault. She'd been shocked by a lightning bolt—a bolt created by the evil sword that I held in my hands. I knew that Harry and Pagag and other righteous men were gathered around her, but . . . For seven years I had not dared to think of it. I had blocked it out— shut the door of my mind upon it, as if shutting out a furious hurricane. How could I tell my father what I had last seen? I utterly refused, especially when deep in my heart I still nurtured a vague glimmer of hope that perhaps . . . miraculously . . .

"She is not here," I reported. "I do not know where she is. Or Mary and the others. I last saw them in the land of Salem. For seven years I have not set eyes upon anyone that I once knew. We were separated in the wilderness."

"Separated *how?*" Marcos persisted.

I shuddered outwardly. Marcos waited patiently as another volcano of memories from that terrible time erupted inside me. I drew a deep, staggered breath and said, "It was the sword. Of Akish."

"Sword of *Akish?*" my father repeated in alarm. "The sword destroyed by your Uncle Jim?"

I nodded. "But not destroyed in centuries past. Todd Finlay— who kidnapped us—was looking for it. In our travels we came face to face with the swordmaker himself—Akish the sorcerer."

My father absorbed this, then asked, "Where would you have met such a man as Akish?"

"He was—It was—" I floundered a bit, straining to figure out how I could keep this story from provoking greater confusion. I began again. "The sword accidentally came into our hands when we were in the land of Babylon. Akish searched for it and eventually confronted us near the city of Salem. It was Akish who caused my separation from the others. He pulled me into a kind of time warp. The warp was created by the sword itself. He took me back to his own land of Morōn, among the Jaredites. This is where I resided for the next two years."

Marcos made sure he had it straight. "You lived for two years among the Jaredites in the Kingdom of Akish?"

"Yes. As Akish's prisoner. His slave. I won't recount what I endured . . . or the horrors I witnessed . . ."

A fresh tear tumbled down my father's cheek. His reaction made me sit up straight. I needed no sympathy from anyone.

I continued, "After two years my imprisonment ended at the hands of a very unlikely rescuer: Akish's wife—or rather, his *first* wife, the sorceress, Queen Asherah. She had somehow laid her hands on Akish's sword and used it to exact revenge on her husband for the death of her son, whom Akish had starved in the same dungeon where I was imprisoned. She also sought vengeance for the murder of her father, the former king, whom Akish had beheaded as he was giving audience to his people. I was set free along with many other prisoners and enemies of Akish. With a slash of the sword, the Queen cut another rift in the fabric of time. I was told that I would be transported to the place I most desired. I tell you now that my greatest desire—my *only* desire—was to go home. But instead I was sent here, among the Nephites of Desolation. Such are the twisted promises of sorcery and witchcraft. Coming here had once been my greatest desire, and the sword remembered."

"Where is this sword now?" asked Marcos.

I shrugged awkwardly. "Still with the people of Akish, I suppose. I do not doubt that from there it will play out its history until the day when Uncle Jim destroys it."

Marcos looked me up and down, taking in my blue warrior cloak with its long sleeves and my three-layered skirt of green kingfisher, gold parrot, and red spoonbill feathers. He also studied the fox-ear hood that hung over my forehead—the symbol of my rank. "But you're a *Captain?*" he noted. "How in the world did you ever become a leader of the Nephite armies?"

"It happened on account of the soldiers who found me in the wilderness, half-starved and living like an animal. At first they made sport of me, and I think they would have killed me if their commander—a Nephite named Cumenihah—had not taken pity. He brought me back to his headquarters at the city Jordan where I became his servant. During this time I also met Mormon, the chief captain of the Nephite armies. He gave his consent that I should begin my training as a warrior. A year later, when I was fifteen, I earned my eagle shield and was permitted to fight in my first battle. It was a battle that we lost. Jordan was overrun. But when the commander of my cohort was killed, I rallied those who had survived, along with several hundred survivors of other units. We escaped toward Cumorah, cutting our way through several thousand Lamanite and Gadianton troops. They hailed me as 'Little Mormon.' I guess Mormon's career also began at age fifteen. Because of the men's enthusiasm, and because we'd lost a great number of officers in the battle of Jordan, I was promoted to captain."

My father spoke, his voice still subdued. "Have you told anyone?"

"Told them what?"

"Who you really are. Have you told them your history? Where you're from?"

I raised my eyebrows and shook my head. Then I peeked through the doorway of my tent to make sure none of my guards or officers had overheard. "Of course not. Over the past seven years one thing I *have* learned is how to survive. If I were to tell such a story, they would burn me at the stake as a lunatic. Many Nephites are not . . . as I once imagined."

"What about Mormon or Moroni?" asked Marcos. "Surely they are righteous men who would not burn you as a lunatic for confessing such things."

I snorted and rolled my eyes. "They have never asked me about my origins, and I have never revealed it. Besides, I do not know them *that* well. Certainly not well enough to confess to them that I am a fugitive from another century."

"You're not a fugitive," said my father sternly. "You're just a boy."

I bristled. "I'm not a boy any longer."

"And these men are prophets of God!" he countered. "You must tell them who you really are. This is a conversation that must take place as soon as possible."

The sting of my father's reprimand cut me deeply. It had been a while since *anyone* beyond the high commanders of the Nephite army had ordered me to do *anything*. Yet he was my father. This softened an otherwise harsh response. I said, "That would be impossible. I command the warriors of the Fox Division—nearly ten thousand men. We are at war, Father. We fight for our very existence against enemies who surround us on all sides. I am assigned to watch the hills and plains to the north of Cumorah. Besides, I couldn't say where General Mormon was right now. Anywhere from Shim to Ogath. And Moroni hasn't been seen at Cumorah for months. He went to the Lamanite capital on a mission of peace. No one has heard from him since."

I watched my father's face redden. He practically exploded as he said, "*You don't belong here, Joshua!*" As suddenly as his anger flared, it ebbed away. He leaned forward, grabbing my arm, eyes filling with weary frustration. "Don't you understand, Joshua? Have you forgotten everything that you've been taught? This is the final struggle. The Nephites are facing destruction. Don't you see what's going to happen? Can't you foresee your own fate if you stay? This is not your world, Son! It's *not your world!*"

I pulled away from my father's grasp. Then I stood up and began pacing furiously, shaking my head. "It's not true what you say. The situation is not the same. Fate *has* changed the outcome of things. *I* changed them. But not just me. *Many* things have changed. Do you remember the battle of Jordan that I mentioned? If it wasn't for my actions and those of others, I believe hundreds of additional men would have died. These are men who have lived to fight another day. Perhaps they *should* have died that day—were *meant* to die. But they didn't. The Lamanites and the armies of Teotihuacán have launched five separate assaults against Cumorah in the past four years, learning our defenses, testing our mettle. I have played a part in turning back each one of those attacks. I do not say this to boast. I credit my men for what was accomplished, but—"

"Joshua, *listen* to yourself!" Marcos interrupted. "Do you hear what you're saying? You think you can change the outcome of what's written in the Book of Mormon? You think you can change an event whose outcome was decreed by God?"

"How do *you* know what God has decreed?" I snapped. "You speak of the Book of Mormon like it was written at the dawn of time. I tell you that such a book does not *exist*, Marcos! At least not today. Not in any finished form. You're trying to prove your point by using words from a record that isn't yet completed. And I say to you that the words that refer to our destruction at Cumorah never *will* be written." I turned to my father. "As you said, this is not my world. I'm here by a miracle that no one could have foreseen."

"*Everything* is foreseen, Joshua," said Father. "God foresees it."

I came to one knee before him, desperate to make him understand. "History is not set in stone. Don't you see? It can be changed. The outcome of things can be altered. I am living proof of that. My accomplishments are proof of it. Do you want to hear more of what I have done? Do you want to hear how I commanded my men in battle against twenty thousand Lightning Warriors of the Gadiantons and nearly drove them into the sea? Do you want to hear how we captured five thousand Lamanites in the land of Antum and forced them to help us build our strongest fortifications? Do you want to hear how I am hailed as a hero by nearly every Nephite man, woman, and child in the vicinity of Cumorah? I have become nearly as famous as General Mormon himself. I am the 'boy-captain' who brings victory and success to all he touches! They see me as a kind of savior, Father. Because of the things I have done, there is more hope burning in their breasts than they have felt in many years. Do you think any of these things are reported in the same Book of Mormon that we read together when I was a child? Sometimes hope is all that people need. Hope can change *everything*."

My father was shaking his head slowly, eyes searing into mine. "No, Joshua. Hope is *not* all that people need. Especially if that hope is rooted in the strength of men. Men need *faith*. The kind of faith that inspires repentance and compassion. The kind that turns men back to God. Have you seen your Nephite warriors exercise this kind of faith?"

I hesitated, but then I nodded staunchly. "Yes, I have seen it."

Marcos didn't buy it. "You said a moment ago that many Nephites are not how you once imagined. What did you mean?"

"I meant . . ." I squirmed a little and again started pacing. "I meant that their faith is growing. I *see* it growing. But you have to understand, these are a people who have teetered on the brink of destruction for almost a generation. You cannot expect them to have the same kind of Sunday School faith and compassion as a gathering of Saints on Temple Square. There is much kinship rivalry. Much bitterness and hatred. But I know that Mormon and Moroni are *pillars* of faith. The people look to them, and these two men never cease to direct our eyes to God. I believe the Nephites *are* looking heavenward more and more. It will just take time."

"Time may have run out, Son," said Father solemnly. "Joshua, I love you. It wouldn't matter to me if you were nineteen or a *hundred* and nineteen. I would sacrifice all that I possess for you. Yes, I admit, none of the events that you report are mentioned in the Book of Mormon. But neither are they contradicted. No detail you have mentioned would convince me that history will play out any differently than what will be written and passed down to our generation. I confess I don't know all things. But I know what I feel in my heart. What do you feel in *your* heart, Joshua? What do you hear the Spirit whisper when you pray?"

I stood up straight. I stiffened my jaw and somehow managed to gaze back into my father's eyes as I replied, "I hear the anthems of victory. I hear them loud and clear."

They both stared at me, doubt evident in their eyes.

Finally, Marcos said, "I don't know how you could possibly judge the faith of the Nephites, Joshua, when you're not in the practice of exercising faith within yourself."

I stomped up to Marcos, my nostrils flaring. "How dare you think you can judge me, Marcos Alberto Sanchez. The Nephite with a Mexican name. I could never understand you—never comprehend what you stood for. Those are *your people* out there, Marcos! *Your people* standing watch, patrolling for spies—fighting for their lives against an enemy who seeks to cut out their hearts and feed the flesh to their war god. You have the proudest heritage of any man on earth. Yet you chose a cushy life in the twenty-first century with satellite television and microwave popcorn. Those are noble men out there. Honorable men. Your blood and kin. Where's your honor, Marcos? Where's your nobility?"

My father stood, his temper inflamed like a lion. "You have no idea what you're talking about, Joshua Plimpton!"

Still my eyes did not waver from Marcos. He glared back at me. I was encouraged to see that my words had gotten a rise from him. He looked as though he might strike me. But with Marcos the fuse was always slow burning, and in a tone that seemed characteristic of this slow-burning fuse, he said, "My people. What do you know of 'my people,' Joshua? My people lived three and a half centuries ago. They lived in Zarahemla. But they *rejected* their religion, moved to the land northward and were destroyed. *That's* the heritage of my people. A heritage of shame. One that I've tried to suffocate and put behind me. For all I know, Teotihuacán was built right upon the ruins of

Jacobugath. I may share as much ancestry and blood with the Gadianton armies that you war against as I do with the Nephites of Cumorah."

I didn't even pause as I retorted, "You and I both know that's not true. You think I don't remember? You went *back* to your people in the north. You were a missionary among them for four years. No, Marcos. You can't wriggle out of it so easily. Your people are *Nephites!*"

He leaned right up to my face. "My people are the people of God, Joshua. No matter the race, no matter the origin of their blood, and no matter the century. I fight for the causes of the Lord's Kingdom. And I feel no loyalty for a people who trample His commandments under their feet—and who've chosen a course hell-bent on annihilation!"

"Stop this!" my father pleaded. "Both of you—stop!"

Marcos and I continued to glower at one another. Finally I said, "Fortunately, we are led by a man who thinks differently. A general who loves his people no matter what their faults and flaws. That, I believe, is true honor. But I can see by the look in your eyes that you don't understand a word that I'm saying."

I'd clearly touched a nerve. Still, I'd had enough of him. I turned to my father. "You should rest now. Both of you. We should all get some sleep."

With that I left the tent and walked out into the night. I couldn't remember the last time my thoughts had felt so scrambled. Several of my officers and guards were standing nearby, including Kigron, my second in command; Ammonchi, my secretary and banner chief; and Nompak, my bodyguard and "Snake Seeker," or anti-sorcery advisor. I felt sure they'd overheard at least some of our conversation—the *louder* portions. They were all looking at me with peculiar expressions.

I said to Kigron, "My father and cousin will sleep in my tent. What other arrangements can be made for me?"

Kigron was a large and able man who'd been with me since the battle of Jordan. A deep scar was cut down the middle of his chin, a souvenir received from a copper axe head at the battle of Boaz, which was before my time. My tone with him was a little gruffer than I'd intended. However, Kigron was unruffled and replied, "You can have *my* tent, Captain Josh. It has already been purged of sorceries. I will sleep with the other officers."

I paused to look at him, then I made a succinct nod. "Very good."

I spotted Kigron's tent and started toward it. I could feel the eyes of my men on my back, but I said nothing more to them tonight. *Let them spread their rumors,* I said to myself. I doubted if I could have stopped it anyway. *"Ah, so the boy-captain has a father!"* they would whisper among themselves. I wasn't sure if this revelation boded well for me. Part of my mystique was the mystery of my origins. Having a father sort of took the shine off the enigma. Maybe I was just being paranoid. And yet I had every reason to fear at least *some* of the men in this army.

Not *all* soldiers and people of Nephi viewed me with reverence. There were a few—and I feared the number was growing—who were jealous of how swiftly I'd moved up the ranks. Others believed I was manipulating the people, seeking for greater power than Mormon himself, or Zenephi, our chief judge. Zenephi's son, Shem, seemed to believe this nonsense more than anyone. Shem led his own army of ten thousand nearer the slopes of Cumorah. It had come to my ears that Shem—or those in his command—were spreading a vicious lie that I was a Gadianton in disguise—a spy of Teotihuacán—and that I would show my spots only when the consequences would be most devastating to the Nephites. Sorceries and assassinations had become so rampant among the Nephites that such rumors were easily believed. I had no doubt that the numbers of those who wanted to see my head on a pike were growing daily.

And yet, at the moment, my greater concern was not what my men thought of me. It was what I thought of myself. Shame was burning in my stomach like acid. I realized I had been breathing the atmosphere of intrigue for so long, I hardly knew the difference between truth and lies. Deceit was like a disease in the ranks of Cumorah's soldiers, and I had inevitably become infected. I'd just lied through my teeth to my own father!

But how many things had I lied about? Did I lie about the Nephites turning their gaze back toward God? No, I still believed they would. I *had* to believe it. A month ago Mormon had given a passionate and tearful address to all his officers, pleading for us to remember our noble history—a heritage rooted in Christian faith. Yes, afterwards there came the usual grumblings about how the old man was growing ever more maudlin and senile. But surely *some* had been moved. If a few key individuals would convert, the rest would surely domino.

No, the spiritual potential of the Nephites had not been a lie. The most boldfaced lie was when I told my father that I heard the anthems of victory in my prayers. In all truthfulness, I heard *nothing* in my prayers. Perhaps because I wasn't praying at *all*. I had never sought to know the whisperings of the Spirit on this subject, or on *any* subject, for longer than I could recall. I couldn't remember the last time I'd been on my knees. I remembered praying like crazy when I was first cast into Akish's dungeon. I pleaded with God for forgiveness for stealing Akish's sword, for giving in to its satanic enticings. I'd prayed constantly for the arrival of my father, or Harry, or Gidgiddonihah, or Apollus, or *anyone* who might deliver me from my misery. Later I prayed simply that God would let me die. None of my prayers were answered. I felt forgotten by heaven, by everyone I'd ever loved, and by time itself. When I finally was delivered from that dungeon, it was by the hand of an evil sorceress. My rescue was not the result of any uttered prayer. It was a consequence of a wicked woman's lust for revenge.

I felt sure that in some way I had committed an unpardonable sin. Perhaps listening to the sword was in some fashion the same as denying the Holy Ghost. My father once taught me that denial of the Holy Ghost was the only sin one could commit wherein there was no forgiveness—either in this life or the next. Surely I had committed it.

For many years I'd experienced the most horrendous dreams. Sometimes I swore that Satan himself was in those dreams, either taunting me for my sins, tempting me to join his ranks, or some combination of both horrors. Such dreams, I was certain, were part of the torments of a damned soul. All I had left in this world was to pursue the twisted desire that I'd nurtured as a boy—that of saving the Nephite nation from destruction. And since fate had so conveniently placed me in a position to bring about this very desire, I pursued it with all the passion of my heart that I could summon.

As I entered Kigron's tent and lay down upon his mats and blankets, I heard Nompak and his guards taking up their usual positions outside. Normally their presence was a great comfort to me, but not tonight. I felt an unusual desire to be completely alone—miles away from any other living soul.

It occurred to me that I hadn't asked my father a single question about my mother. Then I chided myself. If my father hadn't changed, neither had she. A familiar anguish pressed inside my chest as I let her image drift through my thoughts. Oh, how I missed her! How I missed them *all!* Suddenly I felt awful to have left my father's presence. A tear escaped my eye. I wiped it away quickly. Even in the privacy of this tent I was still a captain in the Nephite army.

And captains did not weep.

## NOTES TO CHAPTER 2

A brief history of the Book of Mormon figure Akish is as follows: His services were first employed by Jared, son of King Omer, at the suggestion of his daughter. This daughter, aware of the existence of secret plans of old, felt Akish would be the ideal person to help her father obtain supremacy over her grandfather's kingdom. She offered *herself* as Akish's reward if he brought her father the head of King Omer. Omer, however, was warned in a dream and escaped with his family and followers.

Jared was subsequently crowned king in his father's absence, and Akish received Jared's daughter to wife. However, it was then that Akish's true ambitions were revealed. Using those who had sworn an oath of allegiance to him, he murdered Jared and took the kingdom for himself.

Internal conflicts soon developed. Akish imprisoned one of his own sons and had him starved to death. A civil war erupted between Akish and his remaining sons that lasted many years, until all his subjects were completely destroyed, save thirty souls. Omer then rightfully reclaimed his kingdom. Ether does not mention the death of Akish, though we may assume that he was among the victims of this massive civil war (see Ether 8–9).

Much dramatic license has been taken with the character of Akish in the Tennis Shoes Adventure series. The concept of the accursed sword and Akish's sorceries across the spectrum of time are, of course, entirely fictional. However, Akish, son of Kimnor, remains one of the most evil figures in history. He is credited as the founder of secret combinations in the New World, which Moroni later tells us were the cause of destruction not only among the Jaredites, but among the Nephites. The Book of Mormon suggests that a record containing the dark oaths that Akish employed was brought across the ocean with the other Jaredite records. Specifically, the Book of Mormon states that these records contained an "account" of evil men of the past who used secret combinations to gain power and glory.

One might wonder why the Jaredites—or any righteous men— would preserve such a record. After all, Alma specifically commanded his son Helaman to withhold from the people of his day an apparent section of the twenty-four plates of Ether that documented satanic oaths, covenants, and ceremonies. Helaman was also commanded to suppress any accounts of the "signs and wonders" that accompanied such rituals. Alma feared that if such information got out, the temptation to engage in these practices might be too great for some Nephites and cause the people to fall into darkness and be destroyed (Alma 37:21–27).

In fairness to the Jaredites, it's possible that their leaders may have wished to preserve such things so that righteous leaders could recognize evil when it started to appear in their ranks. Any such records would probably have been kept in the custody of kings or prophets, and would not have been distributed among the general populace. Even in the case of Akish, we are not told that he actually used these records as his source of evil inspiration. The oaths may have been given to him directly by the adversary, just as he gave them directly to Cain. In any case, suppressing such information seems to be futile. Moroni tells us that these oaths and rituals are to be had among all peoples of the earth (Ether 8:20).

In 1988 the prophet Ezra Taft Benson stated, "I testify that wickedness is rapidly expanding in every segment of our society. It is more highly organized, more cleverly disguised, and more powerfully promoted than ever before. Secret combinations lusting for power, gain, and glory are flourishing. A secret combination that seeks to overthrow the freedom of all lands, nations, and countries is increasing its evil influence and control over America and the entire world" (*Ensign,* Nov. 1988, 86).

Other Church leaders have also testified that we need not look too hard to see evidence of secret combinations in today's world. Many point to obvious culprits like devil worshippers, members of organized crime, terrorists, or street gangs. But in truth, anyone can corrupt their soul with "Gadianton" aspirations. Anyone who knowingly supports or encourages those who lie, cheat, or steal, or anyone who commits secret acts of evil to obtain power over others, qualifies as a potential Gadianton. We are well advised to ask ourselves, with reference to specific political, religious, or business authorities, whether we offer support or look the other way when such parties commit immoral or unethical acts. The Lord warns those who follow such a course:

"Yea, even at this time ye are ripening, because of your murders and your fornication and wickedness, for everlasting destruction; yea, and except ye repent it will come unto you soon" (Hel. 8:26).

# CHAPTER 3

## Apollus

I am Apollus Brutus Severillus, Centurion of the 17th Cohort of the Fifth Legion of Rome, born in the eight hundred and fifth year since the founding of that great empire, or, as it is known in the Christian era, 52 AD. Let me say, however, that I am confident that I have wandered as far from the seven hills of my capital city as any Roman in the breadth of its history.

It exercises my patience that I must summarize the events that brought us to the place where I must again take up my tale. Nevertheless, I acknowledge that some may have forgotten the various entanglements of our journey, so temporarily I'll restrain that impatience. Forgive me however, if, for the sake of brevity, I bypass many details. Next time I will ask that the reader be better prepared by reviewing all the significant events before undertaking a new—

\* \* \*

*Meagan*

*Wait a second. Are you chastising the readers?*

I just think that if one plans to read a sequel, one ought to go back and—

*Apollus, don't chastise the audience. Trust me. Not a good idea. I ask the reader to please forgive my Roman's rather abrupt personality. He really is a sweet and gentle guy when you get to know him. Right, Apollus?*

Yes, of course.

*You rolled your eyes.*

Is that what I did?

*There's no call for sarcasm.*

May I go on with my summary?

*By all means. Continue. Just don't threaten to beat up the reader.*

I didn't threat—! Rrrr, never mind. I will begin my summary, fully expecting multiple interruptions from the doughnut gallery.

*You mean . . . peanut gallery?*

Yes, as you say.

When I rode my motorcycle to the home of Jim and Sabrina Hawkins in Provo, Utah, to warn them of the threat posed by Todd Finlay, I did not expect events to spin so rapidly beyond my control. It was hastily decided that Meagan and I, along with her present suitor, Ryan Champion, would ride to Frost Cave in the land of Wyoming. Our goal was to thwart Finlay's plan to steal the children away to an unknown century as he sought to recover his beloved sword. Along the highway we found the Jewish maiden, Mary Symeon. Eventually we also recaptured young Rebecca. But Finlay retained Master Joshua and led us on a chase through the catacombs of the earth until we reached the chamber with the silver pillar of light and power.

Unfortunately, our misfortunes only multiplied at this location. A tremor set off by an eruption within the silver pillar made the rocky shelf collapse, causing Ryan and Meagan to fall into a watery torrent. This river carried them, along with me, into the bowels of the earth, entirely separating us from the others for what proved to be an indeterminable span of time.

Somehow in the midst of this underground torrent Ryan, Meagan, and I were transported to the land of a people whom Meagan called Lamanites, though many of them called themselves the "Lamaya" or "People of the Water-Lilies." She also identified the era as the latter part of the fourth century AD, or very near the time period when the record called the Book of Mormon draws to a close.

Our first acquaintance in this land was a young warrior named Lamanai or Eagle-Sky-Jaguar. Lamanai was the son of a Lamanite King who had been executed by his conquerors. Lamanai had managed to survive to his nineteenth year with the help of a village shaman who kept the boy's true identity hidden. Lamanai interpreted our miraculous emergence from the waters of a jungle pool as a heavenly portent. He convinced himself that we were gods, come to help him reclaim his father's throne. At that time the Lamayan capital at Tikal was in the hands of invaders from a northern kingdom called Teotihuacán. On its throne was a prince of Teotihuacán named Blue Crocodile, though the actual conqueror was a ruthless military commander known as Fireborn.

*You think people care about all these names? I'm getting a headache trying to follow it all. And I was there!*

And you, I presume, could recount it better?

*Oh, may I?*

Well, truthfully, I was—

*Why, thank you, Apollus!*
*While we were residing at Lamanai's village of Seibalche, we heard rumors of a Nephite prisoner named Moroni who was being held at Tikal. This prisoner's execution was supposed to take place in three days! A rescue party was organized featuring Ryan, Apollus, Prince Lamanai, and sixty-two other loyal warriors. Yours truly, however, was left behind. The others traveled to Tikal and stormed—*

We stormed the prisoner compound at the temple of Venus in the dark of night, liberating not only Moroni, but another Nephite officer named Gilgal, as well as a spirited young woman named Tz'ikin. Tz'ikin had been imprisoned for an assassination attempt against General Fireborn.

Our escape from Tikal was precipitated by the acquisition of six "horses." I emphasize the term because they were not like any horses I'd ever ridden before. Our arrival back at Seibalche coincided with the arrival of twenty-thousand Lightning Troops of Fireborn. By a miracle, I found Meagan in the jungle unharmed, her life saved by a tamed panther—a black jaguar named Huracan—whose paw swipe had left scars in Fireborn's face. Afterwards we steered our horses northwest toward a land and hill known as Cumorah. It was here that the people called Nephites had been gathering for several years, preparing for war.

I believe that's all. I shall now continue from this point. Or was there something I missed?

*You interrupted me.*

Forgive me. As you sometimes say, I was "on a roll."

*Forget it. By all means, continue. You're actually doing a fine job.*

Yes, I know.

After our escape from Seibalche, the eight of us traveled for more than a week on horseback toward the land of Cumorah. These eight included me, Meagan, Ryan Champion, Prince Lamanai, Moroni, Gilgal, Jacobah, and Tz'ikin. A Lamanite named Antionum had remained behind to inform the elders of Seibalche, as well as the general countryside, that Prince Lamanai was on his way to Cumorah to forge an alliance with the Nephite nation. Together, Moroni and Lamanai hoped to defeat Fireborn and the invaders from Teotihuacán.

Over the next nine days we traveled over a hundred Roman miles, steering clear of the main highways, concerned that some of Fireborn's men might have gotten ahead of us. We encountered only the occasional shaman priest, or witch doctor of the forest—men like Lamanai's late stepfather, Kanalha, smelling of copal incense, wearing capes of black-dyed cloth and jaguar skins, and wearing hoods that shadowed their sagging faces. But these never caused us trouble. We also avoided settlements. Moroni feared that my physical appearance, as well as that of Ryan and Meagan, would draw suspicion from local garrisons. There was also the concern that Moroni and Gilgal might be identified as Nephites. Few racial differences existed between Nephites and Lamanites, but there were many variances in appearance based on custom. Nephites did not flatten an infant's forehead with boards. Nor did they have the same braids and hairstyles, tattoos and piercings. For this reason Moroni and Gilgal stood out dramatically. Thus, we contented ourselves with traveling incognito.

Another distinguished member of our company was Huracan, the jaguar. We never saw her during the day, but at night she often prowled into our camp, appearing as if from a mist of smoke, like the she-wolf of Mars. And just as the wolf was a sacred protector to Romulus and Remus, I believed Huracan was *our* protector, never too far away to offer aid if required. The horses were ordinarily the first to inform us of the jaguar's approach. They could smell her from some distance and would become agitated. As the days passed, the horses grew more accustomed to her presence, but never entirely. The only member of our company whom Huracan did not take to was Gilgal. But in truth, the feeling was mutual. There was a slight altercation on the first night of Huracan's appearance wherein Gilgal grabbed up his javelin to destroy her. The cat reared back on its haunches, and I think she would have torn out Gilgal's throat if I had not come between them. Afterwards the Nephite mourned that he would have liked to obtain the animal's rare black hide with its fire-orange tail. This desire offended me deeply. Gilgal was coarse, profane, and ill-mannered—a very different human being from his companion, Moroni. But Gilgal was an able fighting man. As a matter of habit I valued this attribute more than any other, though in his particular case I was prepared to make an exception. I suspected that Moroni also valued him for his battle skills. On the other hand, Moroni seemed to value every man, no matter his faults. Nevertheless, I believe he would have mourned Gilgal's death a great deal less than he mourned the death of his other companions at Tikal.

As for Huracan's miraculous behavior, I'd begun to believe that she had a keen ability to comprehend much of human speech. Or at least to comprehend the speech of Meagan, Ryan, and myself. Strangely, I also felt I understood *Huracan*—her expressions, snarls . . .

Perhaps I sound foolish to mention such things. Suffice it to say that I'd started to conclude that the unique ability to speak and be understood in divergent tongues while traveling in time applied not only to people, but also to certain beasts. I confess I'd grown rather attached to this feline, just as any other loyal comrade. Meagan's feelings were probably more poignant than my own.

And speaking of my attachment to felines, I suppose I should remark somewhat upon my rather tempestuous relationship with Meagan. One need not assume that tempestuous has entirely negative connotations. There is often great power in a tempest, and captivating beauty in a storm. But regrettably there is also a certain degree of . . . inconvenience.

*What a fascinating analogy, Apollus! Whatever do you mean? I can't wait to hear.*

I'm sure you can't. But if your curiosity will indulge me one more moment, I think I will first report upon the developing relationship between Ryan and Tz'ikin.

*That should be interesting, hearing it from you. Do you think you could make it sound the least bit intriguing or romantic?*

That would not be my object. I will simply report what I observed those first nine days.

In all sincerity, I did not think there could be an odder couple than Ryan and Tz'ikin: Ryan, the naïve and impetuous youth from the twenty-first century with no practical training whatsoever in weapons or warfare, and Tz'ikin, the would-be assassin from the Lacandon mountains of third-century Zarahemla. The reason for her hatred of the Lamanite commander, Fireborn, was unknown. There were many mysteries about this woman that we had yet to learn. She reminded me of a wounded leopard, silent and wary, yet ready to strike out viciously if another beast drew too close. Despite the dangers, Ryan Champion had made several overtures of friendship, though Tz'ikin had hardly reciprocated. Or perhaps she failed to notice his efforts. In any case, Meagan felt a strange compulsion to play matchmaker.

On the fourth night of our travels I overheard her speaking with Tz'ikin. Meagan was tying off her hammock for the night while Tz'ikin carved designs on her new dart-thrower weapon, or atlatl.

Meagan broached the subject by saying, "I think Ryan is sort of sweet on you."

The phrase was unusual to Tz'ikin, but she apparently understood the meaning—and quickly dismissed it. "I doubt that very much. But if it's true, I thank you for the warning."

"Warning?" said Meagan in surprise.

"I will take adequate measures. He should be made aware that I sleep with a knife in my fist. And that I also have other means of protection."

Meagan laughed awkwardly. "I think you misunderstand. Ryan is harmless. A perfect gentleman. I don't think I've ever met a kinder, more respectful young man."

I ground my teeth a little at that. Meagan and I had had an argument earlier that day over—how had Meagan put it?—my "arrogant, antiquated personality." Mentioning Ryan's name alongside a stack of compliments burned beneath my flesh like the flames of Prometheus. However, she paid me no mind, which meant that either she hadn't seen me nearby, or chose to ignore my presence.

"So why have you told me this?" Tz'ikin asked Meagan.

Meagan floundered. "Well, I—I just—I wasn't sure if you had noticed."

"And what would I do if I *had* noticed?"

"I guess . . . I don't know. I just thought maybe on this long journey it would be nice . . . I mean, it might make it a little easier if you had a friend."

"A *friend?*" asked Tz'ikin, seemingly baffled.

"You know. Someone to talk to."

I continued to fasten and bind the cane wood of my new forearm shield; though at this remark I confess I rolled my eyes. It had always amused me—and fascinated me—that a woman of the twenty-first century might think that a relationship between a man and woman could involve talking, and *nothing more*. It seemed a beautiful, childlike thing. Still, I found it difficult to believe that Meagan was so naïve as to think a severe and hardened girl such as Tz'ikin could ever comprehend such a relationship. It occurred to me that Meagan's innocence in this area may have been one of the things that I found so appealing.

Tz'ikin naturally interpreted her words as euphemisms.

"So you think I should 'talk' to Ryan?" she asked bluntly. "You think he and I would make a good match?"

Meagan tried to rein back a bit. "Gracious! I'm not talking about *matches!* Just *friendship.* Haven't you ever had a boy for a friend?"

The girl really didn't understand her. "Men and women are not friends. You're speaking nonsense."

"Actually, they can make very *good* friends," Meagan insisted. "Especially one like Ryan."

"In my village," said Tz'ikin, "if a man and woman were to speak apart from others, they would be forced to marry. Otherwise the woman would be shunned and cursed. Or, if it was thought she had been violated . . . the consequences would be death." There was a dark bitterness to Tz'ikin's tone.

"That's awful," said Meagan uncomfortably, and probably blushing, though I couldn't tell from where I was sitting. At last she was beginning to recognize how strange her words sounded in the ears of this feminine warrior. Earlier Gilgal had insinuated that the reason Tz'ikin was so intent upon assassinating Fireborn was because the commander from Teotihuacán had taken certain "liberties" when his army had passed through her mountains. But these were only rumors that Tz'ikin had neither denied nor confirmed.

"I'll say again," Meagan maintained, "it would be hard to find a better friend than Ryan."

Tz'ikin became thoughtful, and then she narrowed one eye at Meagan and said, "You should not try to massage your own guilt through me, Meagan Ix-Chel."

Ix-Chel was an appellation Meagan had received from Lamanai when he'd first mistaken her for the Lamanite goddess of the moon. She'd probably heard the term from Jacobah, who stubbornly maintained a worshipful attitude toward us despite our efforts to discourage him. From Tz'ikin the term was plainly mocking.

She continued, "I am aware that you have already spurned Ryan in favor of Apollus. Do not think I will trouble myself to ease your remorse."

Meagan gaped at her, dumbfounded. At last she got to her feet. "You know, Tz'ikin, *I* might make a pretty good friend as well, if you ever allowed it." She left Tz'ikin alone by their hammocks.

Tz'ikin looked at the ground. I thought perhaps I saw a twinge of regret in her features, but with Tz'ikin it was nearly impossible to read her emotions. She looked up at me, realizing I'd overheard the conversation. Abruptly, she also left the area.

Actually, I thought that the warrioress had brought up a worthy point. Not the guilt part. I don't think Meagan was motivated by this. But I was pleased that Tz'ikin had reminded her that she had chosen me over Ryan. It was a fact that Meagan frequently and conveniently seemed to forget. I wondered if she remembered that she had made any choice *at all!*

Despite everything that was said, Tz'ikin, to some degree, took Meagan up on her suggestion. I noticed she and Ryan speaking together quite often after that. That is, Ryan did most of the talking, speaking of gospel subjects and his future plans for serving a Christian mission. Perhaps young Ryan felt Tz'ikin would become his first convert. She seemed to listen intently. But perhaps just out of politeness. She seemed to me a far distant prospect for conversion, enmeshed as she was in so many complex traditions and beliefs that incidentally seemed to have much in common with ancient rites and superstitions of the twenty-first century tribal peoples of southern Mexico. On the other hand, not so long ago I would have also counted myself as an unlikely prospect for Christianity. At least the girl appeared to be listening.

Since there were eight of us and six horses, Tz'ikin had ordinarily been content to walk. Because our horses refused to travel faster than a steady gait, this hardly seemed to matter. But a few days after Meagan's conversation with Tz'ikin, I noticed her riding behind Ryan on his horse. Assuredly, their friendship was deepening.

As for Meagan and myself, I wasn't altogether certain where our "relationship" stood. And this despite the fact that she had approached me several times to seek clarity on the matter, as females are wont to do. In each instance I felt that I had made myself quite plain. I informed her that I had very deep feelings for her, and that because of this I considered that she was mine and ought to behave as such. But each time I explained this—in small words I might add, so that I was not misunderstood—she became as contentious as one of the Furiae and would not speak to me for the rest of the day. I had no idea how I had made her angry. In fact, on the morning before we reached the Fishing River, or River Sidon, she had not spoken to me for two entire days! Naturally, I felt I should deprecate myself and see if it were possible to end this silliness.

As soon as I convinced my obdurate horse to ride alongside her mount, I said, "Apparently I have offended you somehow. Is that correct?"

"I can always count on your infinite powers of observation, Apollus," she replied.

"Has your anger quelled sufficiently enough that you might explain?"

She looked forward and said, "I guess that's the trouble. The fact that I have to explain it to you."

"Perhaps if I had an oracle to read your thoughts, I could discern them for myself. But since I have no oracle, I am dependent upon your explanation."

I saw a flash of irritation, but then she gave up with a long sigh. "What's going to happen to us, Apollus? How do you see us ten years from now?"

"I thought I had already elaborated upon this. You will belong to me. You belong to me already. I see us with five or ten strong and healthy children."

"Okay, there's one example. What if I don't *want* five or ten children?"

"Oh, but you will," I assured her. "No self-respecting Roman would ever settle for a scrawny family. And don't think I haven't observed that your people are any different. Why, I've seen some Christian Mormon households with as many as—"

She interrupted. "I'm not saying that I don't want a big family. That's not what I mean. What I'm saying is . . ." She strained to find the right words. "What if I don't feel the same as you about something? About *anything*? What if I ever looked at an issue entirely differently than you do? Could you respect that?"

I made a low groan. "You are a curious creature, Meagan Sorenson. Wasn't it just two weeks ago that you informed me that all two people needed was love? That it did not matter that they might have an origin in different cultures? Or even that they had come from different centuries? Now why have you suddenly made this so complex and abstruse?"

"Like you said, I'm a curious creature," she replied. "But maybe you hit the nail on the head. Yes, all two people need is love. But what *is* love to you, Apollus? Because to me it sounds an awful lot like slavery."

"*Slavery!*" I exclaimed. Jacobah and Lamanai riding just ahead glanced back, so I lowered my voice. "What are you talking about? You think marriage to me would be as the life of a slave?"

"Could you ever see me as an equal?"

"Equal in what way? You are a woman. I am a man. We are two different beings. By its very nature what you say makes no sense."

"So I would just become your personal property, is that it?"

"Of course. That is the law, is it not?"

Her eyes widened. I don't think she had expected such a blunt reply. "You're *nuts!* What law are you *talking* about?"

"The law as it has always been. The law of Rome. The law of every land and people that I have ever encountered. Are you telling me that in your land it is different?"

"*Totally* different! Do you mean that in Rome a wife is a man's *personal property?*"

"Naturally! Why would such a concept seem so alien to you? A woman must *always* be owned. From birth by her father. In marriage by her husband. In widowhood by her sons. How could a nation ever hope to survive without this understanding? There would be chaos! I do not believe that in your land it is any different. Would it be so horrifying to have me as your master and steward?"

Meagan suddenly looked ill. "I think I'm going to throw up."

Fortunately, her threat to vomit never materialized, as our conversation was interrupted by Moroni. He called for several of us to join him at the head of our column. I opened my mouth to make some final remark to Meagan, but then I closed it again. Such a remark might have sounded like an apology. But what would I have been apologizing for? I had said nothing that should have been upsetting. Should I have apologized for the very nature of the universe? I spurred my horse forward and left her to stew over my words, confident that she would shortly come to her senses.

As Gilgal, Lamanai, and I rode forward, the trees opened up and we caught sight of the gleaming waters of an eastern vein of the River Sidon. As the river made a wide bend toward a canyon gap, we could see the hovels of a village on our side of the banks.

Moroni pointed toward the village. "That's the settlement of Korihab, if I remember correctly from our deerskin maps that were confiscated at Tikal. It's time to trade our horses for dugouts—at least for the next four or five days, until we reach the lower drainage. We'll then proceed westward on foot."

To me this was not unwelcome news. It would be a happy relief to bid farewell to my shabby steed. I reminded Moroni that this might be a good opportunity to replenish our store of supplies. All of us were growing weary of trail vegetables and the stews of iguana and armadillo. Besides this, gathering such things in the wilds wasted several hours of each day that could be better spent traveling or improving our armaments.

I said to Moroni, "Perhaps while you bargain for boats, Lamanai and I can visit the local market."

Moroni nodded. "We'll separate here. Meet us at the riverbank. By then I pray we will have a buyer for the horses. Conduct your business hastily. Speak to as few villagers as possible. Gilgal, you should go with them."

"Agreed," said Gilgal.

We trotted past Ryan and Tz'ikin, who rode together on the rear-most beast. They would have been the last people in our column except for Jacobah, who walked flank with an obsidian sword and a javelin with a halberd-sized flint warhead, never straying far from Ryan's side.

"Do we really have to sell the horses?" Ryan inquired.

"Unless they learn to swim," I replied. "Since they refuse to gallop, I hardly think swimming is likely."

His motive for asking was only too obvious. It would be his final day of riding with his arms around Tz'ikin's waist.

Before we entered the woods I noticed two more forest shamans poised at the edge of the trees to our right, watching us, their faces blackened and further hidden by the hoods of their cloaks. I'd never seen two of them together before. Perhaps this should have provoked curiosity, but I ignored them. We directed our mounts toward the eastern end of the village.

Upon reaching the first hovels of Korihab, we dismounted. Our weapons were kept close at hand, though directed downward to lessen any threatening appearance. I wore my new forearm shield on my left arm and balanced my unstrung bow on my right shoulder. On my left hip was a quiver with a dozen new arrows and behind my left shoulder I carried my new obsidian-edged sword. I was particularly proud of the sword. I had made some interesting modifications in its design. The edges were composed of broken lancetips that we'd found in abandoned settlements. Thus, my blades were considerably thicker than the usual variety, tapering quite gradually to a glistening sharp edge. This made it more susceptible to chipping if I knocked it about, and perhaps it would decrease its overall lifespan, but while in use it was as formidable a weapon as I could craft. I'd also thickened the hilt, though I left the hole at the back for a leather wrist strap, which I found to be an interesting variation to European weapons. I further augmented its design with a narrow, plunging stone tip—a standard three inches in length for quick thrust and retrieval. I doubted I could have come much closer to duplicating at least the balance and weight of a Roman broadsword. Now if only I had my old form-fitting armor, horsehair helmet, and metal greaves. Instead I had to settle for a quilted-cotton mantle with a reinforced plant-fiber lining. Moroni had tutored me in its construction, again using abandoned materials from villages he said had once belonged to Nephites. I agreed with Moroni that the mantle would deflect most arrows from a distance, but I had serious doubts about its effectiveness at closer range. For that I would have to depend upon my forearm shield. I will say, though, that the mantle was surprisingly cool in this sticky environ-ment—a feature that would not have been the case with Roman armor. Moroni had equipped us all with similar uniforms. To the people of Korihab this likely gave us the same appearance as profes-sional soldiers. But soldiers from whose army?

Korihab was a dismal setting. If anything, it was even more shabby and decayed than other settlements along our trail, many of which had been abandoned over the decades by other tribes. The local populace appeared out of place, like rodents or wild animals who'd taken up residence in the cracks and crevasses of dilapidated structures. I was reminded of the Syrians and Samaritans who laid claim to the villages of Galilean Jews after they'd been slaughtered or forced to flee to Jerusalem during the early years of the Roman War. This observation was more or less confirmed by Gilgal's next statement.

"Squatters," he said, spitting into the street. "This is a *Nephite* village. Stolen, like all the others, from my people when I was a boy. Typical of what the Lamanites have done with our land."

Lamanai overheard his remark. Gilgal had undoubtedly *meant* for him to overhear it. After all, Lamanai's father, Jaguar-Paw, had helped draft the treaty of 350 AD, which had forced the Nephites to abandon nearly all lands south of Cumorah, including their beloved Zarahemla. The comment was meant as a stab, but perhaps also as a reminder of the price Gilgal expected Lamanai to pay if the Nephites helped him reclaim his throne. Gilgal wanted the Lamanites *out* of Zarahemla. He expected Lamanai to let his people go home.

Lamanai replied with a mixture of insult *and* diplomacy. "Yes, Lamanite buildings *do* tend to last a bit longer. It will be a great day when your people can return here, and mine can be encouraged to build decent new cities of their own."

Gilgal never knew quite how to reply to such statements. The words burned, but Gilgal's desires had been assured. Eagle-Sky-Jaguar was a clever young man. *Too* clever, in my opinion. I was never certain what went on in his ambitious mind. Was he sincere in his promise to Moroni to join forces with the Nephites and fight with them as equals? Lamanai seemed to be a man of contradictions. He'd been visibly moved on the day we'd healed the stricken people of his village. He did not seem to question the power of Jesus Christ. But there was something else about him that I couldn't quite grasp. It may have been simpler than I was willing to admit. His head might have been swollen with the worst case of vainglory that I'd ever beheld. Yes, he'd seen miracles. Yes, he'd witnessed the power of God's true priesthood. And yes, he'd made an alliance with the son of his father's greatest enemy. Yet none of this seemed remarkable to him. Like Alexander of Macedonia, he might have believed the universe was naturally aligning itself for his sole benefit. Indeed, I wondered if he felt that anything that did *not* fall into this alignment would be sorely cursed. Even if the objectors had been the gods themselves.

There were many eyes upon us as we approached the market plaza. Or more accurately, they were gaping at our horses. When we'd first encountered horses outside Tikal, Moroni admitted that he had never seen one before. Many of these people appeared possessed of the same curiosity. But there was also a palpable tension in the air. An old man scowled. Others drew back. A mother gripped the arm of her child, dragging him away as he tried to touch my horse's neck. Was this tension caused by the presence of the horses or by us?

The marketplace had been laid out under a shady canopy of cypresses in the village center. Goods were heaped into baskets or spilled out across blankets of checkerboard cloth. We stopped at a meager stall with a canvas awning. A sinewy Lamanite with a receding hairline stood up to greet us. His wife and a young boy—age eleven or twelve—were in the background grinding maize kernels. Like the other villagers, the merchant looked over our horses. But unlike the others, he seemed more fascinated by *us* than by our mode of transportation.

"We'd like a sack of these," said Lamanai, pointing at a basket of dried white beans. "And maize, well ground. Some of this dried fruit. And some salt."

The man nodded. "What have you to trade?"

Gilgal and Lamanai turned to me. I pulled out a jewelry trinket that had belonged to Meagan—a silver necklace with a teardrop-shaped charm that showed a young woman before the spires of a temple—the one in Salt Lake City, I believe. Meagan had offered it to me several days earlier just in case such a moment as this arose. The offer had surprised me, but she replied that it really wasn't that valuable in her century, and would be easy to replace. Yet as I tried to dangle it from my palm for dramatic effect, the merchant's attention remained fixed on Lamanai.

He asked the prince, "Where are you from, traveler?"

"From the east," said Lamanai vaguely. "And we are in a hurry."

The man signaled to his wife to begin filling the sacks. I raised up the trinket to again start the bargaining, but the merchant wasn't finished with his questions.

"What is your name?" he inquired of Lamanai.

The prince narrowed one eye. "Do you always interrogate your customers so boldly?"

The merchant shrugged. "Not always. But it's plain that you have journeyed some distance. We don't get many overland travelers in Korihab. Most come by river."

"Then we are pleased that we could make this day different from most other days," said Lamanai.

The merchant proceeded to tie off the sack of beans. "The day before yesterday was very different as well. We heard strange rumors."

"What rumors?" asked Gilgal.

But the merchant was not interested in talking to Gilgal. He did not even glance at the Nephite, but answered directly to Lamanai. "Rumors of an agitator from Tikal. A man who claims to be an heir to the throne of Great-Jaguar-Paw. They say his lies are stirring up many people in the south."

Gilgal and I looked around, assessing the environs. Indeed, many of the people in the market had paused to watch us, whispering to one another outside our hearing. I cursed inwardly. Our worst fears had been realized. With all of our loitering, making weapons, and scavenging for food and supplies, some of our enemies had gotten ahead of us.

"Interesting," Lamanai replied to the merchant. "And what makes you so sure that these rumors aren't lies?"

The merchant hesitated. He displayed a glimmer of vulnerability. "Because the lineage of Jaguar-Paw is become as the morning mist, burned off by the sun. All his heirs were murdered by the armies of Lord Fireborn."

Lamanai's gaze locked into the eyes of the merchant. "Well, then, if this is true, why should it stir up so many of our people?"

"Because," said the man quietly, sounding almost entranced, "some would wish with all their hearts that such a thing could not be."

"What else was reported about this man?" Lamanai inquired.

"That he may be traveling with Nephites." The merchant glanced at Gilgal, and then, with puzzlement, he glanced at me. Obviously my own nationality was more difficult to place. "Also that he may be traveling with . . . horses."

I decided to speak. "Who is spreading this rumor?"

The man leaned around the tent canvas and took in the market street in both directions. Then he answered softly, but again only to Lamanai, "It is spread by the Lightning Warriors of Fireborn."

I stepped closer. "Where are these warriors now?"

He finally looked at me squarely. "They arrived two days ago in long battle dugouts. The dugouts are amassed a short distance to the south, but as far as I know they have not yet carried them downstream. They have left many spies in the city. And lookouts are camped along the river, watching to see what travelers might arrive."

"Why would they *carry* their dugouts downstream?" I asked.

"Korihab is the last market settlement before the gorge," he explained. "River traffic stops here. Boats are carried to the bottom on foot. Some carry their own; others hire porters. It is a trip that takes several hours. But for you . . ."

"For us *what?*" asked Lamanai.

"For you this trip would be impossible to make unnoticed," said the merchant.

My eyes scanned the ridgeline north of the city. "What if we took our horses over the ridge by another way? Can we purchase boats at the bottom of the gorge?"

He seemed amused at my ignorance. "There are no dugouts for sale at the bottom of the gorge. The canoe makers and merchants are *here*, in Korihab. I know of no other trail to the bottom but the one cut directly along the gorge, above the current. Otherwise you must travel two days east, where it is rumored that a larger army from Tikal may be gathering. It is along the trail above the gorge where a number of the men of Fireborn have made their encampment."

One might have guessed my next question. "What if we floated directly down river?"

The merchant snorted once in laughter. "You would all be killed. Your dugout would be destroyed."

The boy of eleven or twelve ceased grinding maize and said, "Some have done it."

The merchant brushed this off. "You may ignore him. My son is very—"

The boy interrupted, "But the rainy season has only just begun. You told me that while the river is still low you wouldn't fear such a journey."

The merchant appeared embarrassed. "I'm afraid those were the boastful words of a proud father."

"But is the boy right?" I asked. "Have some done it successfully?"

He seemed frustrated that I still pursued this subject. "You would all drown. Or be smashed by the rocks." He again looked to Lamanai. "And if you are . . . if you are the person who some say . . . for you to die before you can reclaim the throne of Jaguar-Paw would strangle the hopes and dreams of many."

As the merchant spoke, I watched the village pathway behind us. The two forest shamans we'd seen earlier were making their way toward us, but not in a manner I might have presumed for simple priests. Their arms were hidden under their cloaks. Something else protruded from beneath one cloak. The closer he drew, the more certain I became that it was the end of a bow. Not a crude *hunter's* bow, but the longbow of a warrior. The blood rushed from my heart to my limbs—my senses snapped to alertness. Gilgal signaled to me. I looked toward the opposite end of the plaza. To my surprise *another* shaman was also wending his way surreptitiously in our direction.

The sacks of supplies were presented to us, tied together with a rope so that I might carry the bundle over my shoulder. Again I held out Meagan's necklace, but the merchant rejected it.

"The supplies are a gift." He, too, had noticed the approaching men. He said hastily to Lamanai, "You must leave quickly. Cross the river. Go west. You will find many allies among the people of the Earth-Stone in the new lands won by Jaguar-Paw." He glanced at Gilgal, who knew full well that he was referring to Zarahemla, or those lands his people had lost.

Prince Lamanai appeared to be the only one who hadn't yet noticed the approaching threat. Either that or he'd deliberately chosen to disregard it. The young man put his hand on the merchant's neck, like a kindly benefactor. "I will consider your advice. What is your name that I may remember it?"

"We have to go," I declared.

Carefully, I turned my back to string my bow. Gilgal filled his hands with a javelin.

"Sadok-Mo," the merchant replied nervously to Lamanai. "Please run swiftly. May the Hero Twins spirit you to safety."

Calmly, Lamanai replied, "And may you always be nourished by Lord Chac." He glanced at me and added as an afterthought, "And by the Messiah Jesus."

Sadok-Mo raised an eyebrow, but he wasn't about to let the utterance of a Nephite deity spoil this moment. He'd just met the Prince of Tikal—a man he obviously considered a potential *human* deity.

I now counted five cloaked shamans in the market plaza. Two appeared to be taking up attack positions. And then, in a blinding flash, I saw the sun reflect off an obsidian arrowhead. The nearest shaman threw off his cloak, revealing the bright, feathered garb of a Fireborn lightning warrior.

"Weapon!" I cried, and ducked to load my *own* arrow.

But Fireborn's soldier was not aiming at me. He knew his target. The arrow sailed through the air toward the Prince of Tikal. Lamanai, however—with a motion as adroit as a leopard—stepped behind the head of his horse. This was precisely where the arrow struck—piercing his mare's neck and causing the beast to shriek and rear back on her haunches. It was her last explosion of energy. As the mare twisted in midair, I realized she was about to collapse—right on top of Gilgal! By providence the horse itself saved Gilgal's life, clipping him in the chin with her hoof. Gilgal was knocked backwards. But as he fell, he was nearly killed by *another* obstacle—the discharging arrow from my bow!

The missile slipped between his arm and chest, cutting a hissing path across the square until it hit its intended target. I felt shameless satisfaction that our attacker was slain in the same manner as the murdered horse—by an arrow in the throat. But now there were more arrows whistling around us—as well as atlatl darts. I raised the shield on my forearm to deflect one dart. Another pierced the canvas of the merchant's tent. He and his family lay flat behind their piles of goods, looking terrified. I hoisted Gilgal to his feet as he clasped his injured jaw.

"Leave the horses!" I shouted. "Make for the river!"

We began to run. I glanced in both directions, realizing the number of warriors had swelled to eight or nine.

I called to Lamanai, "How many pursuers do you think may have overtaken us?"

"Unknown," he replied. "Possibly *all* of them. They may have used the river."

Frustrated, I asked, "Why didn't *we* use the river?"

"It would have forced us to travel back toward Tikal, into the heart of Fireborn's domain."

Several darts screamed past both of my ears. Again I raised my shield and caught an arrow in its wood. I thought of Meagan, Moroni, and the others. Were they also under attack? The dangers of the river gorge had completely fled my mind. I now feared the possibility that we might not reach the river at all.

## NOTES TO CHAPTER 3

The political scenario of fourth-century Mesoamerica used in *Warriors of Cumorah* and *Kingdoms and Conquerors* is based on the framework of research that has come forth in the last two decades. For example, there is evidence to suggest that Teotihuacán became the ruling power in Tikal in AD 378, installing a foreign Ahau (Lord or King) to replace Tikal's king, Great-Jaguar-Paw (or Great-Jaguar-Claw), whose death is recorded that same year (Peter D. Harrison, *The Lords of Tikal: Rulers of an Ancient Maya City* [New York: Thames and Hudson, 1999], 79–80). It should be noted that the name Teotihuacán is a Náhuatl name ("Place of the Gods") that was given to this city centuries after its demise and may not have been its name during those centuries when the kingdom flourished. The author uses the name in this book for convenience and to help readers make the geographical association.

This novel takes the liberty of mingling historical figures recorded on various stone monuments of the time period (i.e., Fire-born, Spearthrower Owl, Lord Blue Crocodile), scriptural figures mentioned in the Book of Mormon (Mormon, Moroni, and others), and fictional characters from the author's imagination (Lamanai,

Tz'ikin, etc.). The object is to paint a plausible picture for how the political landscape was laid out at the time of the Nephite nation's demise in about AD 385.

The author has stated before that it seems remarkable how neatly the destruction of the Nephites and the battle at Cumorah fit into the historical framework laid out by modern scholars and archeologists. This novel bases its setting upon Book of Mormon geography as supported by many LDS scholars, who place the Hill Cumorah in the Tuxtla Mountains, northwest of the Isthmus of Tehuantepec, in the state of Veracruz, Mexico. Since this location sits directly between the ancient kingdoms of Teotihuacán and Tikal, and since this entire region is reputed to have experienced much warfare and intrigue in the latter part of the fourth century, it may offer Latter-day Saints helpful insights for why a battle of extermination would have been conducted against Mormon and his people. The scriptures, of course, already explain this from a spiritual perspective. However, the Lord often uses earthly dynamics to carry out spiritual consequences, just as with Nebuchadnezzar, who was often referred to by the chroniclers of the Old Testament as an instrument of God's wrath when he destroyed Jerusalem. Simply stated, the corrupt and weakened Nephite nation would have been "in the way" of Teotihuacán's continuing campaign of expansion and conquest. Couple this with the ripened hatred of the Lamanites—that is, the peoples of the Yucatan and Chiapas regions of Mexico and Guatemala—and fatal results should have been expected.

In this chapter the author describes Nephites and Lamanites as having very few physical or racial differences. This may conflict with the viewpoint of many Latter-day Saints who presume that the "skin of blackness" placed upon the Lamanites in the sixth century BC (see 2 Ne. 5:21) prevailed until the fourth century AD. However, after the visitation of the Savior in AD 34, these two races appear to have united. The designation of "Lamanites," or indeed *any* manner of "–ites," entirely disappeared for two hundred years (see 4 Ne.1:17). When these label distinctions were again adopted by the people in approximately AD 231, it appears to have had less to do with physical differences, as it had to do with an individual's faith or belief. The scriptures tell us that the designation of "Nephite" was adopted by those who maintained a "true belief in Christ," while the distinction of "Lamanite" was taken on by those who had "rejected the gospel" (see 4 Ne. 1:35–38). From time to time some Latter-day Saints have pursued the idea of searching for remote "white-skinned" Indian tribes with the object of holding them up as evidence of a surviving Nephite bloodline. If, after the Savior's visit, there were few physical differences between Nephites and Lamanites, it would make such a pursuit meaningless. Nephites and Lamanites would have been, in many respects, racially equivalent; the most visible differences may have been primarily cultural.

This chapter makes reference to "branches" of the River Sidon. Sidon is the name of the major river in the Book of Mormon that runs, for the most part, north to south. The city of Zarahemla was built on its banks. The Book of Mormon also names other cities and landmarks associated with this river. In Hebrew, the word Sidon is translated "Fishery" or "Place of Fish." Evidence suggests that the ancient peoples of Mesoamerica may have used a single name— "Xocalha (showk-al-ha)"—to refer to the entire drainage from the Guatemalan highlands that emptied into the Gulf of Mexico. Xocalha is also translated as "Fishing Waters" or "Place of Fish," offering a possible correlation with the Book of Mormon. The naming of drainage systems by a singular designation, rather than giving names to individual streams and branches, is also consistent with continuing Maya custom (Alan C. Christensen, PhD, personal conversation with author, Brigham Young University, 24 March, 2004). If this is true, it would partially resolve the occasional dispute between LDS scholars, some who wish to designate the Sidon as the Grijalva (San Miguel) River which flows through Chiapas as the River Sidon, and others who designate the Sidon as the Usumicinta River which runs from Guatemala northward through much of southern Yucatan. Both are major rivers, but curiously, their headwaters begin within fifty miles of one another in the Guatemala highlands. Also, both rivers empty into the same delta in the state of Tabasco on the coast of the Gulf of Mexico. Simply put, *both* rivers and all their branches and tributaries may be the ancient waters known as the River Sidon.

The treaty referred to in this chapter wherein the Nephites lost the land of Zarahemla to the Lamanites and the robbers of

Gadianton is mentioned in Mormon 2:28–29. In these verses it appears that the robbers of Gadianton are an independent political force—one that participates in treaties. Mormon could have used the term "robbers of Gadianton" to refer to any of the peoples or tribes of invaders from the north. To him this term would have been accurate enough since the north had long possessed a reputation of being a haven for dissenters and secret combinations. Readers of the Book of Mormon will recall that the dissenter King Jacob took his followers and fled north. It was here that he founded the city of Jacobugath (see 3 Ne. 7:9–14). But the wicked reputation of the northern lands goes back even further. Enemies of the Nephites often attempted to flee northward, perhaps because they might join others with similar anti-Nephite or anti-Christian sentiments. Consider the case of the dissenter Morianton, whose flight northward was cut short by Teancum (Alma 50:28–35), or the missionary journey to the land northward by the brothers Nephi and Lehi, whose preachings were utterly rejected (Hel. 7:1–3).

Teotihuacán would have been part of this land northward. In fact, some Book of Mormon geographers have placed Teotihuacán and Jacobugath in the same location. (See Joseph L. Allen, PhD, *A Proposed Map of the Book of Mormon*). Jacobugath is reported to have been destroyed just prior to the arrival of the Savior, but because of its reputation it may have been reconstructed later by followers of secret combinations.

According to a growing number of LDS scholars, the land of Zarahemla would have been located in the Chiapas depression of southern Mexico, southeast of the Isthmus of Tehuantepec (see John Sorenson, PhD, *An Ancient American Setting for the Book of Mormon;* see also John L. Hilton and Janet F. Hilton, "A Correlation of the Sidon River and the Lands of Manti and Zarahemla with the Southern End of the Rio Grijalva," F.A.R.M.S., 1992, 142–162). The Nephites' desire to regain these lands was undoubtedly a motivating factor behind their invasion against the Lamanites from the land of Desolation in AD 363. Mormon reports this as a fatal mistake, believing that so long as his people waged a war of self-defense, the Lord would protect them. It was when the Nephites became the aggressors that the Lord's protection was withdrawn (Morm. 4:1–8).

# CHAPTER 4

## Jim

"*Keep digging!*" I yelled at the men who were arriving from the roadway below. "Quickly! *Please!*"

The time pillar of Frost Cave had literally transported us into a hillside of solid ground! At first only my face and one arm were exposed from the short vertical ridge. My screams had alerted men from the roadway—part of a caravan of some sort. Fortunately, gratefully, they responded quickly. Five of them were now pressed around me, frantically scraping at the soil, sand, and rocks that still encased half my body. More were getting their fingers into the fray. I still could not pull free. But the terror I felt was not for myself.

"Please hurry!" I pleaded. "There are two of us! My sister is behind me!"

The men in ancient mantles paused in their digging. If they were not surprised enough by the sight of a face and arm jutting out of a dirt wall, the news of *another* person behind me filled them with genuine fear.

"No! I beg you! Don't stop! She may be suffocating! *Keep digging!*"

Many appeared ready to turn tail, as if fleeing from a rising corpse—but this feeling was dispersed by a man standing ten feet behind the others.

"Continue!" he ordered them.

I'd hardly noticed him before, except to wonder why he wasn't digging along with everyone else. I vaguely noted that he was older. A tightly curled beard covered his chest. A sleeveless blue robe hung around his shoulders. Maybe he was too feeble to help, or he was unaccustomed to menial labor—even to save someone's life! Yet it was only because of him that anyone was helping at *all!*

"Do as he says," he continued urgently. "Dig! *Dig!*"

With dread crushing my heart, I tossed away handful after handful of soil with my free arm. My buried hand continued to grip my sister's arm. Her muscle was flexed—a positive sign—but time was running out.

A second old man, similarly dressed in blue, stood just left of the first. His beard and hair looked identical, twisted into countless ringlets, but his face was sharper, more birdlike.

"Did someone . . . *bury* you here?" he inquired incredulously.

The soil did not appear significantly disturbed. To them it might have seemed like fossils coming to life—like allosaurs at Dinosaur National Monument struggling to free themselves from the stony hillside. But if not buried alive, what other explanation was there for our predicament?

"Yes," I panted.

"By whom?"

"Bandits! Robbers!"

I'd say whatever I thought might shut him up—allow me to concentrate. My left leg broke free. I released my sister's forearm and withdrew my right arm from the hole—just to be sure I could pull it out. Then I plunged my hand back into the gap to find my sister's forearm again. Her muscle was no longer flexed. Panic overtook me. Gritting my teeth, I belted out a cry from the pit of my stomach. In that burst of strength my body wrenched free of the hillside. Parts of the exposed hole looked like a plaster mold. My arms and clothes were caked with dirt and mud. The backpack was still on my shoulders. As I stripped it off, the Dacron straps tore apart. This surprised me—but I had no time to think about it. I stabbed my fingers back into the dirt, heaving aside great clumps of soil. The ground partially caved in and covered our progress.

"Help me!" I cried. "She's in here! She's dying!"

Eight people were now digging alongside me. Dirt was flying everywhere. I aimed my efforts toward the place where I was sure I'd find Jenny's head and face. Someone unearthed one of her legs. It was directed upward. My sister was upside down. It was also limp—no movement.

Behind me someone said, "Surely she's already expired."

Those words affected the men like a douse of cold water. All at once they stopped digging and backed away. The man who'd pulled out her leg looked pleadingly at the two old men in bright blue robes, his face screwed up in disgust, hands held out from his body, as if he'd just been smeared in manure or anthrax.

"*What's wrong?*" I demanded. "Don't stop! She's almost out! She's not dead! *Help me!*"

The first old man with a rounder face pointed at two others. "Shalman, Aram—those not of Israel—*keep digging.*" He looked at the person who'd unearthed the leg. "Hosea, you must continue. You're already defiled."

I ignored their insanity, continuing to dig furiously, even if I had to do it alone. "*Jenny!*" I shouted. "Jenny, hang on! Almost there! You're almost free!"

I found a lock of hair—the strands woven evenly through layers of soil, like roots of grass, or little blonde capillaries. My teeth were gritted like iron, my mouth tasted of dirt, and tears cut muddy lines down my cheeks as I pulled away a clump to reveal her face—eyes shut, mouth open.

She wasn't breathing.

"*Jenny!*" I shrieked again.

The other three men—the last of those still willing to help—had freed up her torso and limbs; I managed to get my hands around her torso. I feared her backpack would prevent me from pulling her loose. With all my strength I leaned back and pushed with my ankles. She was hoisted free. The pack ripped away from her shoulders, as if the straps had disintegrated. Half the shelf collapsed around us as I dragged her body away from the cliff face and laid her on level ground. The others, including the two old, bearded men, wore expressions of deep sorrow—pity mingled with wonder. They were awestruck that I still believed she might be alive.

Her mouth was clogged with dirt. I turned her head to the side, stuck my fingers in, and cleaned her mouth out. My limbs were trembling as I fought down the dread, yet I kept my concentration. I scooped out all of the mud and gunk from around her tongue, careful not to shove any of it deeper down her throat.

"I think the airway is clear," I announced, not that anyone may have understood why this was important.

A hand came to rest on my shoulder. "You must not overexert yourself," said the second old man with a bird-like nose. "Your sister is passed."

I shook him off harshly. "Get away!"

I wasn't trying to sound angry. I just needed him to give her more room. Okay, maybe I *was* angry—angry that most of the men had stopped digging at the most critical moment. Not that it mattered now. I laid my ear against her heart. No heartbeat. Pressing my palms to her chest, I attempted to resurrect a pulse. After a half dozen compressions, I plugged her nose and blew air into her lungs. The crowd became invisible to me; all voices and sounds went silent.

After three more compressions, I grabbed the wrist of the one called Aram—a dark-complexioned young man with frizzy black hair. "See what I'm doing? Repeat it!"

His lip curled up, confused. He glanced at the two old men, who neither consented nor shook their heads, just gawked.

"*Just do it!*" I yanked Aram's hands and placed them, palms down, against my sister's chest. "Like this."

I demonstrated thrice more, then blew more life-sustaining oxygen into her lungs. Aram made a genuine attempt to imitate my actions. I showed him the technique once more, then focused all my attention on the mouth-to-mouth. Not a word was uttered from the audience.

It seemed like an hour passed, though it was probably only a minute. A dark feeling engulfed me. Was Jenny really dead?

"Please, Heavenly Father!" I said aloud.

*My oil!* Where had I placed my anointing oil?

Just then I heard a gasp. Aram flung himself away, stricken with surprise. Simultaneously, a gasp erupted from the onlookers—no less dramatic than the one from Jenny's throat. She rolled onto her side, coughing and wheezing, knees curled into her belly. She vomited onto the sand, her last meal mixed with mud. I cleared more dirt from her lips and eyes. Finally, I looked at all the men who surrounded us. Their expressions were pale. Several mumbled prayers. The face of the first old man in the blue mantle shone like mother-of-pearl. His gray-flecked eyebrows bristled with wonder. The second old man's black eyes were opened to their widest degree.

For the first time, my gaze took in the gathering more closely. It was now easy to distinguish those who were "of Israel" and those who were not. Men of Israel were dressed in sleeveless robes like the older men, but creamy-white instead of robin's-egg blue. That is, they were creamy white except for the ones whose knees and arms were now stained with dirt. Each of their mantles was fastened from sandal to throat with little golden hooks. Without exception, everyone wore thick, black beards, neatly groomed and sprinkled with silver dust, and showing hundreds of little curls. The locks of their sideburns and long hair hung around their shoulders like bells. Complexions were dark and lustrous, as if anointed with cosmetic oils. They looked quite different from any other Israelites I'd encountered. Most wore jeweled rings, but no one's fingers glittered more brightly than those of the two old patriarchs, every knuckle adorned with gems.

I glanced over their caravan on the roadway below. The train comprised at least twenty camels and half as many mules, all loaded down with luggage and bundles. Several mules supported expensive-looking palanquins, or litters, shining with blue, gold, and copper paint. The landscape around us was thirsty and desolate. Balding white hills jutted up from a plain of crimson and yellow bedrock. However, the ruggedness of the terrain did not prevent these well-dressed men from traveling in style.

I decided that those who'd stuck it out with me to the end and helped free Jennifer from the hillside were servants or hirelings. Their light brown tunics were simple, but clean. Or they *had* been clean. More servants watched from the trail. In all, I guessed there were fifty sets of eyes glued to what was happening.

I noticed a smaller group of men on the hillside above us who looked different from the rest—wild and untamed: ragged beards, bodies swathed in sackcloth and animal skins. I didn't think they were associated with the caravan. People of the desert, I presumed. Nomads or Bedouin with faces licked by the sun's fiery tongue. They'd played no part in our rescue, but appeared no less astonished.

I wanted badly to ask the Israelites our location, what year it was, where their caravan had come from, and where it was headed. However, I simply said, "Thank you—everyone." They continued gaping as if I was some kind of mad magician or sorcerer. I felt no need to trump that viewpoint by asking questions that would reveal that I was a visitor out of time.

Jenny, however, practiced no such restraint. Her eyelids fluttered open. After focusing on my face, she asked in a tone of alarm, "Where are we?"

The onlookers thought nothing of it, passing the odd question off as a symptom of delirium.

I heard the one called Hosea, who'd freed Jennifer's leg, say to the old man with the round face, "Father, the woman is alive. I have not touched a corpse. I am still purified, yes? I can still participate in the ceremonies of the festival?"

The old man's gaze did not budge from me and Jenny. He started to nod to his son. But then the second old man said to the first, "You shouldn't be so sure, Barak. The woman had no life in her. I saw it with my own eyes."

"This may be true," said Barak. He opened up his palms toward me with considerable pomp, as if he was the emcee of a magic act. "This man . . . has performed a *miracle!*"

I shook my head. "No. No miracles. Just technique. And *faith.*" I changed the subject abruptly. "We need to get her out of the sun."

"Of course," said Barak. "And you'll both need water." He clapped his hands. "Shalman, see to it. And Gazabar, see that my tent is erected."

Another young man in a white mantle approached Barak. "Would you have all of us raise our tents, father?"

"Yes, Eli," he replied. "We will take our rest here for the Sabbath."

The other old man broke in. "But we'd planned to spend the Sabbath in Jericho. We've already paid for lodging."

"Jericho and Jerusalem can wait." Barak stepped closer to me. "Forgive me for not insisting upon more diligence from my men. For many it is their first pilgrimage and well . . . I'm afraid I did not believe there was any hope, and I did not want any others to be defiled. I am Barak of Babylonia."

"I'm Jim of . . . Jericho." Why did I say that? I felt I had to say something. Maybe, like him, I just wanted my name and hometown to have the same first letter alliteration. "My sister is named—"

"Jen-nee," he said before I could finish. "Yes, I heard you before. This is my brother, Mordecai."

Mordecai nodded obligatorily.

Barak called out, "Aram, help him to carry the woman! We must see to her needs before the Sabbath!"

Unlike the others who were afraid to touch her when they thought she was dead, Aram was more fearful of touching her after she had returned to *life*. Nevertheless, the two of us, plus several others who joined the effort en route, helped Jenny down the hill.

My mind sifted through all that I had heard. So they were Jews. Jews on a pilgrimage to Jerusalem. I presumed that meant one of the Jewish feasts. Passover or the Feast of Tabernacles or one of the other festivals whose names, for the moment, I couldn't recall. As for the year, it could have been anywhere from 500 BC to 70 AD—the time span of the second Jewish Temple. This was the only era wherein I could imagine Babylonian Jews making pilgrimages to Jerusalem.

By the time Barak's men had erected the tent, Jenny was substantially recovered, though still weak and distressed by her ordeal. I overheard people mumbling in astonishment about my supposed miracle—how I had raised my sister from the dead. I wanted desperately to set them straight, but how would I go about it? To these people CPR and mouth-to-mouth resuscitation would have looked exactly like an occult ritual—as if breathing a spirit back into a deceased soul.

We learned that there were a few women among the caravan—the wives of Barak and Mordecai and those of their various sons. Several came forward with damp cloths to wash our faces. They also brought two sets of clean clothing. Barak insisted that we exchange them for our soil-encrusted wardrobes. There was a general urgency to complete these kindnesses before the setting of the sun.

"Thank you again," I said to Barak, my heart nearly overflowing. "I don't know what to say."

"I hope that you will say much indeed," said Barak, "after you have changed."

Curiously, the dirt was so ingrained in the fibers of my shirt, my pants—and even my shoes—that they were hardly recognizable as clothing. As I took off each item, it veritably fell apart in my hands. The same thing happened to Jenny. I'd never experienced anything like this in all our incidents of time travel. Then again, I'd never materialized directly inside a mound of dirt before. Most distressing of all, our back-packs were also ruined—along with every single article inside. After we got down to the caravan, I watched several of the desert nomads rifling through our things. The material of the packs, the clothing and food—all of it was filthy and decayed. It was as if our packs had been moldering in that hillside for a generation. Even my new set of aluminum cooking pans and utensils crumbled and fell apart in the hands of the nomads. It seemed as though the molecules of our inanimate belongings—metal, cloth, plastic, rubber, etc.—had perfectly intermixed with the soil of the hill, corroding each and every element. This also explained why the straps of our packs had so easily torn. Only living tissue seemed to escape this corruption. Because of the way we'd been transported, I realized that we'd come into this world with utterly no worldly possessions, much the same as newborn babes.

After cleaning up a bit and adorning ourselves in our new Babylonian-Jewish apparel, I made a comfortable place in the corner of Barak's tent for Jennifer to continue her recovery. Some padding was laid down for her, much like a portable mattress, with something like dried beans or tiny beads sewn inside the layers, while the cover was overlaid with soft fur.

"How are you feeling?" I asked my sister.

"Better." She tried to sit up but abandoned the attempt and lay down again. "Okay, only a *little* better. Still a little dizzy." Her tone changed and her expression became very serious. "Jim, we need to speak. I have something I have to tell you."

"About what?"

"About something I saw."

I drew my eyebrows together. "Saw?"

"Yes," she replied. "When I was unconscious."

I pulled a face. "You saw something when you were unconscious? You mean when you were . . . *dead?*"

She opened her mouth to answer, but right then we heard Barak's voice outside the tent. He entered two seconds later, followed by his brother, Mordecai, whose pointed, almost horse-shaped head and close-set eyes surveyed us with considerable suspicion. My sister had shut her mouth. It appeared that I wasn't going to hear any description of what she'd seen anytime soon.

"The sun is now setting," said Barak. "And you both appear to have substantially recovered from your ordeal."

"Yes," I said. "But my sister needs more rest."

Barak nodded. "She will have it. We will stay here overnight. And all day tomorrow, for the Sabbath."

Mordecai made a whistling sound and shook his head at his brother. "I am not so sure that this decision has been wise."

"Mordecai, Mordecai," said Barak. "Must I also debate this matter with you?"

"We are barely within the borders of Rome," said Mordecai. "This may not be a safe place for spending the Sabbath."

"At this time of year, with the roads so traveled with pilgrims, there seems little danger," said Barak.

"But the festival—?"

"—will not begin until the day after tomorrow. We will miss nothing. And who knows but what the things we have witnessed are not as significant as the celebration of Israel's deliverance from bondage."

Passover. Those words told me that the season was Passover, when Jews the world over journeyed to Jerusalem in remembrance of their emancipation from Egypt. Mordecai's statement about being "barely within the borders of Rome" told me much as well. Just as with my last visit to this part of the world, Judea was under Roman occupation. We were near the easternmost border of their empire. It was also clear that Jerusalem and Rome were not at war, otherwise this road would not have been laden with pilgrims. Thus, the time period was earlier than 70 AD.

Barak now looked at me with a great, glowing expression, like a man eager to hear news of wondrous things. "Now at last we have an opportunity to learn more about our new friend."

"Yes," said Mordecai, "such as how he and his sister came to be buried alive in a hillside on the plains of Moab."

Barak narrowed his gaze at Mordecai disapprovingly. "Jim has already told us how it happened. He said it was bandits." He turned back to me. "You must forgive my brother. He is, by nature, a most careful man."

"A trait which, by your own admission, has saved us more than once," Mordecai reminded him.

Barak waved this off. "Now you must tell us, Jim: Are you the man of wonders whom we have heard so much about, even as far away as the realms of Babylonia?"

I gaped at him dumbly, "Am I . . . ? What was that again?"

"We have heard there are many strange happenings in Israel. It was for this reason that so many of our family members decided this year to make the holy pilgrimage. There is much talk of healings and miracles and the advent of One who will at last break the yoke of the Edomite and restore Israel to its rightful glory. I have fasted much that I might learn the truth of these things soon upon arriving so that my heart would be prepared for what is to come. Now it appears that my prayers are answered even before we have reached the gates of the Holy City."

I looked at Jenny, whose brow, like mine, was furrowed in deep confusion. And yet her eyes were sparkling. Man of miracles. *No,* I thought. I was jumping to conclusions. Yet I could feel my heart pounding in my chest. I trembled even to consider the possibility.

Mordecai responded to Barak, "My dear brother! You have let yourself become too carried away with this subject. Our guest has said that he is from Jericho. The One that we have heard about is said to be a Galilean."

"But have we not also heard that there are miracle men in the wilderness of Jericho?"

"That man, or so we heard in Philadelphia, is likely the same man who was executed by the Tetrarch. You are mixing and mingling your rumors, dear Barak."

John the Baptist. He was, I felt sure, referring to John the Baptist. John was beheaded by Herod. With each sentence that these men uttered the possibility was becoming more and more incredible. *"Please,"* I said. My voice was a little sterner than I'd intended. The men looked at me curiously.

"Please," I said more diplomatically. "Tell me more about what you heard in Babylonia. What did you hear about a Galilean?"

"Ah, where to begin?" mused Barak. "We have heard so much. We have heard that all of Israel is ebullient with hope, breathless with anticipation. We heard that the Galilean is a newly arisen warrior of the party of the Zealots."

I raised an eyebrow. My heart sank slightly. It was starting to sound nothing like what I'd thought. Certainly this didn't describe the same Galilean that I'd expected.

But Mordecai became scolding of this brother, "Barak Ben Uzziel, be careful of your words . . ."

Barak's eyes widened. He hissed like a teapot. "Nonsense! I am not afraid of speaking openly. We are not in the bosom of Roman authority—not yet. And we are certainly not among the Romans or their spies."

"Are you certain?" Mordecai eyes flashed from me to Jenny. "How do we know that these are not loyal subjects of Caesar and the Legate?"

They stared at us—Mordecai with suspicion and Barak with patient confidence—waiting for a confirmation or denial.

"No," I assured them. "We are not Romans or spies. We—"

"Then what kind of names are Jim and Jen-ee?" Mordecai insisted. "Not Hebrew, I can assure you. They sound very Latin."

"They do? I mean, *no!* They're not Lat—"

"Tell him, Jim," urged Barak. "Tell him that you are of the Covenant. Mordecai has not been to the festival of the Paschal lamb since he was a child. Whereas I was here a mere nine years ago. And I know that the scattered and returning children of Abraham show many complexions—far more than my less-traveled brother might think."

I thought about this, then I made my shoulders a little straighter. "Yes. I am of the Covenant."

"What tribe?" challenged Mordecai.

"E-Ephraim," I said, taking pleasant refuge in my patriarchal blessing.

"Ahhh," they both responded simultaneously.

"There you see?" Barak slapped his brother's knee. "Ephraimites always were a motley group."

I felt like we were straying from the desired subject. "What else did you hear about the Galilean?"

Barak leaned a little closer, his voice almost conspiratorial. "We have heard that He is gathering his army even now. A thousand men. *Tens* of thousands. And that He will soon make himself known—first to those at Jerusalem, and then to the world." He leaned closer still. "Or perhaps, if deemed worthy, the coming Messiah might first reveal His intentions to two tired old men of Babylonia—men with influence in the synagogues of the Chaldees who would be more than willing to offer their services when the time was ripe."

I perceived that he wanted me to reveal some sort of secret. Something beyond the hearing of eavesdroppers outside his tent. "Uh, I'm not sure that I—"

Barak could no longer contain himself. "Tell us, Jim! Tell us if the long-awaited day is at hand!"

My eyes widened. "Long-awaited day? I don't quite know what you're referring to—"

Jennifer spoke up. "Gathering an army? You heard that this man from Galilee was gathering an army? That doesn't sound right. Are you sure, perhaps, that you haven't mixed up a few more rumors?"

Barak gaped at us. Our words had rankled him. I think it was our sincerity—our innocence—that had taken him aback. He realized that we genuinely didn't seem to know what he was talking about. The color in his face darkened and the veins seemed to bulge beneath the flesh of his cheeks. He asked me pointedly, "Are you not this man? Have you heard none of these things that I am declaring? Are you not at the very least one of this man's disciples?"

"Disciples of a Zealot warrior? I'm afraid . . . No."

He sat back, disappointed and somewhat embarrassed. "I don't understand it. I saw the miracle—*your* miracle—with my own two eyes. I would swear by the holy vestments of the High Priest that you raised this woman from the dead. These are said to be signs of His holy calling: wonders and miracles. Evidences of power from on high."

"Barak, Barak," Mordecai interrupted, his voice tired and petulant. "You are making a fool of yourself. What we witnessed earlier was but a magician's trick, like one of the carnival priests of Marduk. Nothing more."

"But he is of *Israel!*" Barak argued.

"So are some of the charlatans of the Chaldean court," said Mordecai.

I broke in, "I already told you. What I did for my sister was no miracle. No magic was used whatsoever. It's just a technique. Anyone can do it, if they know how it's done. But you may be mistaken if you think I know nothing of a certain man from Galilee. I may know more than you could have ever expected. But you must tell us everything that you've heard—nothing withheld. First of all, who told you about this man of Galilee? Where did they say He was from? I mean, more *specifically?* Did they mention a certain village? Has anyone told you where this man is at the present time? Or where He is going? And perhaps most importantly of all, has anyone mentioned His name?"

Mordecai replied, "To name the source of tidings about this man would be like naming the source of the east wind. He is mentioned in every synagogue. His doings are recounted in every marketplace and caravanserai. They breathe of Him in their little houses in Anaharath and Megiddo, Moreshethgath and Gedor, Rimmon and Chorazin. Farmers speak of Him across their fields, nobles and kings in the courts of Jerusalem and Galilee. He is spoken of among shepherds and sandalmakers, dyers and weavers, Publicans and lepers. Even among the beggars and pickpockets of Alexandria and Caesarea are they said to fight and quarrel late into the night about the various signs of His coming. Of late in Judea the people are *drunk* with their hopes of the Messiah, more than at any time in living memory. And not just the people of Judea, but *all* of Jewry throughout the known world—from the forests of the Rhine to the rivers of Ethiopia. But I, for one, will not be a party to this foolishness. *Bah!* We have been so *often* deceived! Always the tender hopes of the Jews are shattered, and usually by the fists of foreign kings. I am not so old that I have forgotten the massacres that took place under the deception of Judah the Zealot— another false messiah, and another *Galilean,* I might add!"

Barak smiled. His brother's negativity hadn't affected him in the least. He said to me, "My brother has been too long in the company of the Cynics of Greece and Persia. He would strangle our hopes before they can even bloom. But you can hardly blame him. What he says is true. There *have* been many deceivers. But I swear to you by the Temple's golden lintels that this time it is different. Jim, you asked where He is, this man of Galilee. That is why I was so anxious to speak to you, because it was said by several travelers whom we have met going east that He and His followers are right at this very minute in the valley of Jericho, and that there is an active movement even now to gather swords and arms to the city of Jerusalem, where it is only proper that a conflict of this magnitude should begin."

Again I was confused. "I'm sorry. This movement isn't like anything that the man I'm thinking of would be involved in. He's not the kind to orchestrate a revolt or rebellion."

"Not the *kind?*" said Mordecai. "Then he is surely not the Messiah. For it is written that the Messiah will crush the heathen conquerors and that later His powers will spread and conquer the whole earth."

"Are you sure that's how it's written?" asked Jenny.

Mordecai pursed his lips, mildly insulted.

Before he could respond, I asked, "Hasn't anyone mentioned this man's name?"

"Yes, they have mentioned it," said Mordecai.

His brother cut him off. "They have *mentioned* it, but we do not repeat it too often or too loudly." He moved to the flap of his tent and pulled it shut. "This is in case it becomes too commonly spoken and reaches the ears of those who might reveal Him before His moment of triumph. And we have been given to understand that in some circles He uses an alias, such as a name like yours or mine."

"You see?" Mordecai pointed a critical finger at his brother. "The true Messiah would have nothing to fear by His oft-repeated name. When He comes, no power on earth can stop Him. This I have heard since I was a small child."

"You forget the practical nature of God's word and prophecy, my brother," said Barak. "There is no wisdom in uprooting the tree before the fruit has fully ripened."

"But will you tell His name to us?" I asked, lowering my own voice in hopes of earning their trust.

The light was dancing in Barak's eyes. He leaned very close to me and whispered, "Yeshua."

A warm rush of blood surged through me. It was the correct name—the original Hebrew form of "Jesus."

But then Barak added, "Yeshua Ben Abba."

They studied me for a reaction. Even Mordecai, despite his cynical exterior, waited to see if I might smile or nod or somehow confirm that the name was accurate.

Jennifer repeated, "Yeshua *Ben Abba?*"

Yeshua, son of Abba. That's what it meant. I didn't need a Hebrew dictionary to know that. I knew because of our gift—the gift that had always accompanied me when traveling in time. Abba meant father, but it was also a proper name. Jesus was not the son of Abba. He was the son of Joseph—or at least that's how He would have been known to His countrymen. Was Barak in error? Was this just another example of mixing and mingling rumors?

I asked pointedly, "Don't you mean Yeshua Ben Joseph?"

The brothers looked at each other. They made small shrugs and shook their heads.

"This is not the name that we have heard," said Barak. "But perhaps we heard it wrong."

"We did *not* hear it wrong," said Mordecai. "It may have been *told* to us wrong. But the man from Galilee was said to be the son of Abba. Yeshua is a common name. My own *son* is Yeshua. If it was Yeshua Ben Yoseph we would have been *told* it was Yeshua Ben Yoseph."

Then I thought about it . . . *Yeshua Ben Abba. . . . Jesus, the Son of the Father.* Gracious! Maybe this was a more accurate name for Jesus Christ than I could have imagined!

But Barak had grown impatient with names. "It does not matter!" he quipped. "Jim was about to tell us what he knows of this man, *whatever* His name may be. At least we can be sure that it is Yeshua. Tell us, Jim. Tell us what may await us this Paschal season when it is said that a perfect red heifer is to be sacrificed on Olivet at the Miphkad Altar—the first such heifer, it is said, to be born in Israel in a generation!"

Though I wasn't sure what he meant by the part about a red heifer, and though much of what these men repeated had clearly been filtered and twisted by the rumor mill, it was apparent enough that there was an unprecedented spirit of expectation throughout the land. If such feelings had engulfed the minds of two pilgrims from Babylon, I could only imagine how it had affected the inhabitants of Judea and Jerusalem. Again I looked at my sister. Curiously, I saw the same expectation in her eyes, but also a keen distress. I could tell she still wanted to tell me about what she had "seen" while unconscious.

But I could also perceive another question on her lips. I could almost guess it without hearing it. It was certainly the same question that was on my own mind, though I wasn't sure I could have formed it in a single sentence.

Primarily it was *why?*—Why were we here? For what purpose had the Lord sent us to this place and time? God knew that we were searching for our children. Were they here in Israel? Was this to be the location of our reunion? I had never known the Lord to allow something to happen without a very specific objective. My heart burned within me as I pondered what it was that the Lord might want us to witness in this place. Even so, at the same time that I found this thought exhilarating, it was also terribly intimidating. One question still pulsed in my brain: How, in the end, would it bring my family back together and aid us in our quest to return to the twenty-first century?

Barak was still waiting for my answer.

I began haltingly and said, "I think . . . there may be *much* that I can tell you. Greater things than you can possibly imagine. You may be right. Extraordinary events may be about to take place. I wish I could be sure this Yeshua was the same person that . . . I'm a little confused by a few of the things you've said. And yet I think the truth may be revealed to all of us shortly. I'm no less anxious than you are to go to Jerusalem and learn for myself. Maybe we can learn of these things together. If you will have us, I would be most honored if my sister and I could remain with you for the Sabbath, and then journey with your caravan to the Holy City."

Barak smiled widely and took my hand with fatherly warmth. "The honor would be all ours, I assure you!" His eyes widened at Mordecai, hinting that his brother might make the same overture.

Mordecai forced a smile, but then the smile seemed to broaden, and with what seemed like genuine cordiality he said, "Yes, Jim. Welcome to our little band of pilgrims."

I glanced at Jenny, expecting to see approval in her expression. It must have pleased her to know that we would be traveling to Jerusalem in the safety and security of a large caravan. But instead, her eyes seemed filled with greater distress—even fear.

I would hear the reason soon enough, as she described to me the terrible vision in her mind. Soon I would learn of a purpose for our visit beyond anything I could have expected, and with a greater potential for tragic consequences than I'd ever experienced before.

## Notes to Chapter 4

The springtime Passover festival in ancient Jerusalem has only one modern equivalent—the Islamic "Haj" or journey to Mecca that is required of all Moslems at least once in their lives. Some might compare it to the bi-annual trek that some Latter-day Saints make to Salt Lake City for general conference, but actually this would not compare sufficiently in religious significance. Only in Jerusalem, at the House of the Lord where resided the authority of the Levitical Priesthood, could a faithful Jew offer a worthy sacrifice and be cleansed from sin. Even in AD 34 there were hundreds of thousands—perhaps *millions*—of Jews living throughout the Mediterranean and beyond. This included Babylon, where Jews had resided since the time of the Prophet Lehi and the destruction of the First Temple (in the fifth century BC). Although all faithful Jews retained the basic customs and practices of their religion, they also naturally adopted many of the customs of their various homelands, including clothing, language, education, etc. Therefore, at Passover, Jerusalem truly was one of the most cosmopolitan cities on earth. In the first century AD it is estimated that this city, whose normal population was probably under a million, swelled to nearly *three* million. (For details on how this estimate was reached, see Bruce R. McConkie, *The Mortal Messiah*, Vol.1, 163.)

Judah the Galilean is often referred to as the founder of the Zealot movement in ancient Israel. This movement vigorously sought to overthrow the authority of Rome (see Josephus, *Wars*, 2:118). Many were fooled into believing that Judah was the promised Messiah who would usher in a new era of Jewish sovereignty over the earth. His revolt took place in about 6 BC in response to the new census tax placed upon Jews (and apparently upon denizens in all other provinces of the Roman empire) by Caesar Augustus. Many historians, including LDS General Authorities, have suggested that this was likely the same census associated with the birth of Christ, wherein Joseph and Mary were required to go to the village of their nativity. This suggests that Jesus Christ may have been born between 6 and 4 BC (see McConkie, *The Mortal Messiah,* Vol. 1, 349–350).

The revolt of Judah the Galilean is also referred to in Acts 5:37. It ended with the execution of many thousands of his followers, including two thousand who were crucified at Jerusalem. It seems ironic that a charismatic leader mistakenly identified as the Jewish Messiah would arise during the same time as the Savior's birth. This means that it's possible that all of the furor surrounding Judah the Galilean's rise to prominence may have diverted attention from the far more significant events taking place in the tiny village of Bethlehem. Such a diversion may well have pleased the adversary. A few may have even associated certain signs of the Messiah's advent, including the new star in the heavens, with *Judah* rather than Jesus Christ.

The ritual of the red heifer sacrifice is a phenomenon not often discussed, though its symbolic relationship to the Savior's Atonement may be more notable than any other ritual of the Law of Moses. The full details of its performance are found in Numbers 19:2–10, but some of the essential details are as follow. It was a sin offering performed very rarely—only when there was to be found a heifer whose coat was entirely red, no spots, white hairs, or any other impurities. The occurrence of such a specimen is extremely rare, even today. Unlike all other sacrifices, the red heifer sacrifice was performed *outside* the walls of the Holy Temple, precisely two thousand cubits east of the Sanctuary (approx. 4.5 miles), on the slopes of the Mount of Olives, upon a special altar permanently erected for just this purpose. This was known as the Mihkpad ("appointed") Altar. Also significant is the fact that this sacrifice purified the sins of *all* (unlike other sacrifices wherein only the sins of those presenting the offering were purified). However, it should be noted that the one who *performed* the sacrifice became unclean "until evening." The significance of these details, along with other details of the red heifer sacrifice, will be discussed at a future time.

# CHAPTER 5

## Ryan

Hey, I'd love to talk all about how wild it was being on an adventure in ancient America with Moroni and a Roman centurion, and how my parents must have flipped out wondering if they'd ever see me again, but now wasn't the time. At the moment we were right at the edge of death—a rather common state of affairs in this land. I was sure in the past few weeks I'd come face-to-face with the Grim Reaper more times than Dirk Pitt (That guy from Clive Cussler novels? Kind of a secret agent who—NEVER MIND!)

Apollus, Lamanai, and Gilgal had cruised into town to purchase supplies. The rest of us had gone directly to the riverbanks to do some horse trading—literally. Moroni had succeeded in trading three of our steeds for two wooden canoes, but not without provoking serious consequences. See, the way I figured it, a few of the river people—Lamanites—were quite literally on the lookout for any wingnut who might come riding up on a couple of trusty steeds. Well, those wingnuts were us, and it wasn't five minutes after we made our bargain that attackers started storming out of the woodwork. One "sticker" (my word for arrows) flew past my nose and zipped into the surface of the river like a torpedo.

Moroni cried, "Into the dugouts!"

Meagan stopped and shrieked, "What about Apollus?"

Moroni answered, "Pray that God will bring them in time."

I grabbed Tz'ikin's hand and drew her toward the first canoe while Meagan and Moroni dove into the other with most of our gear and weapons. Jacobah might have more easily jumped into the second canoe with Moroni and Meagan, but true to his role of serving as my official bodyguard every minute of the day, he grabbed the rim of our canoe and rolled inside. Another sticker thudded the side of the dugout and imbedded itself in the wood.

Just then I looked toward the village and spotted Apollus, Lamanai, and Gilgal—the latter who appeared to be in some kind of pain. They were speeding toward the waterfront like there was a cyclone at their backs.

Meagan stood in the canoe and shouted, "Come on! Come on!"

Moroni pulled her back down.

I looked behind us and saw three other canoes—all filled with Fireborn's furiously rowing assassins. A short distance behind them were three more canoes. And then, from around the curve in the river upstream, appeared three—four—five—six *more.* In each canoe one man stood at the nose with a sticker ready to launch as soon as he got in range. Where in Timbuktu had all these attackers come from? I braced myself for what was coming, swallowing all my natural fears, replacing those emotions with a razor-edged survival instinct.

In all the fuss I recalled something that the squat little boat merchant had said to Moroni—something about hiring porters to carry our canoes downstream. A peculiar concept, I'd thought. I'd sorta figgered the point of a canoe was to let it *float.* But that was when all Hades broke loose. Now, as I looked ahead to where the river was pulled into the canyon, that little conversation was starting to bother me. The canyon had high, sheer banks of pale yellow mud and stone. Once we started into it, there would be no getting out of the river.

Apollus was confronted by a warrior on shore. The dude stepped out in front of him with a copper-pointed spear twice the length of Apollus's new obsidian sword. Not that this was any real concern for the centurion. When Apollus raised his black stone blades to meet the long wooden weapon, the Lamanite spear was chopped in two. Apollus disposed of his opponent handily. The sight of this newly slain Lamanite hardly fazed me. Over the past few weeks I'd witnessed so many men fall in combat that I think my senses were starting to numb.

Apollus, Gilgal, and Lamanai splashed into the river to reach us. The water was up to their waists by the time Tz'ikin and I hoisted

Gilgal into our canoe. Apollus and Lamanai climbed into the boat with Moroni and Meagan.

I shouted at our new passenger, "Grab an oar!"

There were four, square-shaped paddles on board, which wasn't exactly a match for the dozen rowers powering the enemies' canoes. They were gaining rapidly. It also didn't help that Gilgal was still favoring his jaw, which looked very swollen. His mouth was bleeding. Something must have hit him hard. I think he might've lost a couple of teeth.

Jacobah yelled at him, "Row, Gilgal! You must bear your pain!"

Attackers on shore were scurrying along the bank, firing their weapons. Stickers were streaking all around us.

"Here!" shouted Apollus.

From the other canoe he began throwing us several of the shields and weapons we'd all been carving and constructing during our journey. In her drive for vengeance, Tz'ikin ignored the shield thrown to her and grabbed up her atlatl and darts. She stood on her feet and launched a missile toward shore. One of the Lamanite bowmen folded up like a lawn chair. But before Tz'ikin could load another dart, I heard the horrible hiss and thunk as a sticker impacted her in the upper arm, directly under her shoulder. She let out an ear-splitting yelp. Tz'ikin was *hit!* Her knees buckled and she crumbled into the canoe. Her atlatl dropped into the water and promptly disappeared into the deep blue (or puke green, in this case).

"Tz'ikin!" I called out.

I was about to go to her aid, but Jacobah shouted at me harshly, "Keep rowing! Don't stop!"

I pulled at the water with every muscle. I saw that Apollus had laid his own oar aside long enough to load his bow and fire. He let one fly into the cluster of Lamanites who'd fired at Tz'ikin, and he hit one bloke in the chest. But another assassin quickly stepped up and took his place.

Tz'ikin laid on her side in the bottom of the boat, grasping at the arrow shaft with her other hand. The black feathers stood straight up into the air. The sticker had gone deep into the muscle of her bicep. If it had gone in just two inches higher, the padding of her cotton vest might have deflected it. There were no groans or tears from Tz'ikin. She just clenched those teeth and shut her eyes.

I heard Apollus in the other boat say to Moroni, "There's turbulent water ahead. Possibly waterfalls."

Moroni said, "I know."

Apollus seemed surprised by the calm reply. He added, "If we don't find a place to go ashore, our dugouts may be destroyed."

Moroni said, "I know that too. But I cannot see that we have any other choice."

There was always a quiet power about Moroni that I don't know if I can adequately explain, but it made me feel better even when he was acknowledging potential disaster.

Stickers started flying at us from the other boats. I watched them whizzing toward us, dread coiling in my stomach. Luckily, most fell short or missed us badly. Our pursuers were trailing us by about seventy-five yards. Many of the assassins on shore were persistently following us along the bank. But it was our good fortune that a tangle of thatched huts, trees, and other obstacles were slowing them down. Soon they'd be faced by a rocky ridge; this would cut them off entirely. I could feel the current becoming stronger, but no way did I stop rowing, despite the fact that my shoulder muscles felt like they were on fire. I began saying a prayer in my heart—for strength, for courage, and for anything else the Lord thought I might stand in need of about now.

As the river curved around a little more, I made out what looked like foaming white water up ahead. And I was beginning to hear a disturbing sound—like a low growl, getting louder.

Meagan, who was beside us in the other canoe, said, "They've stopped rowing."

I turned to look back. The three closest canoes had noticed the last place with a wide enough sandbank for parking and were eagerly paddling toward shore. The other dugouts looked like they were tossing in the towel as well.

Meagan observed, "I think they're giving up."

Apollus said, "Giving up? I'd say they *succeeded*. They were *forcing* us downriver. Driving us like sheep."

A shiver inched its way up my back. The walls on either side of us had grown to twenty feet high. The top edges were overgrown with tangled roots from the forest trees, but none of those roots hung down far enough, or looked sturdy enough, for climbing. A little farther on and the canyon walls appeared to be *twice* as high. Right now we weren't going anywhere but forward. Even the skinny-legged herons perched on the narrow ledges along the river's edge seemed to be watching us with eyes of pity.

I pulled in my oar and went to Tz'ikin, trying to support her head and back. Even lifting her up a little bit sent a spasm of pain through her arm.

"Sorry. I'm sorry," I said.

Moroni's canoe was beside us, about two meters away. Those guys had also stopped rowing, giving themselves over to the current.

Meagan asked, "How is she?" She sounded a little winded from rowing, and her voice sounded emotional as she saw the pain in Tz'ikin's face.

"Why not . . . ask *me?*" Tz'ikin replied through her clenched teeth. "I'm . . . not dead."

A feeling of urgency came over me. That sticker had to be removed—and quickly—or it would only tear up her arm muscles even worse.

I looked up at Moroni and Apollus and asked, "What should I do?"

Apollus leaned out and grabbed the rim of our canoe, pulling our boats more tightly together. Moroni studied the wound as closely as he could. He leaned his head to the left and seemed to be judging the sticker's angle and depth.

Finally he said, "You'll have to push it through."

I raised my eyebrows. "Push it *through?*"

Apollus nodded. "He's right. It's almost all the way through as it is. If you try to pull it out, the wound may open too widely; we may not be able to stop the bleeding. Much safer to push the arrow out the backside of her shoulder, clip off the tip, and then yank it back."

I swallowed uneasily and looked down at Tz'ikin. She hesitated, and then she bravely sent me a nod. I watched a pool of sweat break out on her forehead just at the thought of the pain I was about to inflict.

Moroni peered off at the approaching rapids and added, "Do it quickly before this water becomes any more turbulent."

My fist carefully wrapped around the protruding shaft. I looked again at Tz'ikin's face. Her jaw was tightly set. Almost as an afterthought, I dug into a pocket of my cloak and pulled out what remained of my brown leather wallet. I'd purchased the thing three years back on a family vacation in Nogoles, Mexico. Since I'd arrived in this land it had gotten wet and mud-slicked so many times that I'd thrown away nearly everything inside it—all but my driver's license. Maybe I'd hung onto the wallet for just this moment. I held it toward her mouth and said, "Bite on this."

She accepted it and pinched her eyes shut.

One sharp shove—that's all it took—and the black stone arrowhead pierced through the flesh on the backside of her shoulder. The wallet dropped from her mouth. Tz'ikin fainted. Who could blame her? I felt queasy inside, reminded again why I had no interest in the medical profession. I quickly shook off my revulsion and used my knife to cut off the arrowhead. I then yanked on the shaft and removed the sticker from her arm before she might reawaken.

There was a lot of blood. I tried to apply pressure to the wound while Meagan provided me with a long strip of cloth from material she'd scavenged along the trail and stored inside her pack. Jacobah aided me as I wrapped it tightly around her shoulder and arm and tied it off.

Tz'ikin tried to wake up once, but then her eyes rolled back as she appeared to faint a second time. I slapped her cheeks—though I tried to be gentle.

"Tz'ikin. *Tz'ikin!*"

I felt it was very important to keep her conscious. The rapids were drawing closer. If we happened to overturn, she'd drown for sure if I didn't keep her awake. My yelling only seemed to rouse her partially. To my relief, the cloth dressing seemed to be helping; the bleeding had slowed down. I could hear the roar of water more loudly than ever, though the worst of it remained invisible somewhere downstream. Our canoe started to wobble as it was sucked into the first chute of rapids.

I yelled again, "*Tz'ikin!*"

She replied groggily, "I'm fine," though she didn't open her eyes.

Jacobah and the occupants of the other boat began grabbing up oars again, eyes peeled forward. Carefully, I laid Tz'ikin in the bottom of our canoe and got back in rowing position, wiping my bloody hand on my cotton vest. I also retrieved my poor leather wallet, now embossed with a deep circle of bite marks.

The drums inside my chest were really starting to thump. Something bad was around the next bend. No doubt about it. Waterfalls flashed in my thoughts—Yellowstone, Niagara, Yosemite . . . and the one from that movie, *Fellowship of the Ring,* that carried Boromir's body down into the mist. That's what I imagined was about to appear as I stared ahead at the river current. The swirling green water had turned almost black—just the color you'd expect from a body of water possessed by a powerful desire to kill you.

Seconds later the current drew us into its first big dip, tossing my stomach forward. Gilgal made a grunt—the first sound he'd made since climbing into the canoe. I wasn't sure if he could even talk. Maybe his jaw was broken. As I was helping Tz'ikin, he'd borrowed some material from Meagan and made a kind of sling for his head. Maybe I should have been grateful the dude was helping to row at all. Despite his swollen face, he looked one hundred percent dedicated to fighting the river.

And if we didn't have enough trouble, I suddenly heard more stickers whooshing over our heads. As I looked up at the ledge on our right, I saw a whole flock of Lamanite troops—maybe a hundred men. A trail up there ran alongside the river, likely the same trail that porters used when carrying canoes downstream. To be sure, this new group of attackers had been posted here all along, just lying in wait.

One man stood out more than all the others. Right away I felt like I could feel an aura of evil around him. First impression: the dude was on fire, as if he'd been doused in kerosene and somebody had laid a torch to his feet. I quickly realized it was just his uniform—feathers of gold, red, orange, and purple, fanning up from his head and shoulders, legs and arms.

Meagan gasped, "It's Fireborn!"

So this was him—the notorious warrior-general from Teotihuacán. The appearance of his face seemed to add to the illusion that he was on fire. Man, I mean, it was *gross* looking. The skin was all shriveled and stiff, and I swore I could see veins of dried blood. But there were circles cut around his mouth and eyes. A mask? Yes, he was wearing a *mask* of some kind of animal leather. Lamanai spoke, his voice bitter with emotion, and the reality became even more abominable than I could have guessed.

With seething hatred, he uttered, "It's my *father!*"

I looked at Lamanai, baffled by the statement. Then I looked back at Fireborn, whose eyes were indeed fixed on the Prince of Tikal. His statement seemed weird. I *knew* that Fireborn was not Lamanai's father. In fact, Fireborn had *murdered* Lamanai's father. So what did he mean by—?

Then *boom*—it hit me, and my guts twisted like I'd swallowed a ball of knotted snakes. The chin, the cheeks, the forehead—it was all there in the features of that mask. The bird-like nose was especially pronounced, and maybe this was what Lamanai recognized. Fireborn was *literally* wearing the face of Jaguar-Paw, the former king of the Lamanites. The human skin had somehow been preserved and formed so it fit tightly over Fireborn's own flesh, like a leather mask. Meagan had told us that Fireborn's real face had been severely injured by a swipe from Huracan's claws. Was this mask meant to cover the scar? Or did he wear it as an intentional insult—a brutal way of communicating to Lamanai that Eagle-Sky-Jaguar had no more authority here, but that all the power of his father's lineage had passed on to the kingdom at Teotihuacán.

Even Tz'ikin's eyes had opened wide to behold the warrior-general's grotesque image. Her sickly pale features darkened with hatred. Even with intense pain in her shoulder, I saw her try to reach for a bow. But her wound was too much. She gave up the effort with excruciating regret. Lamanai, however, had no injuries to impair his aim. He stood up, and with a furious cry, he fired a sticker toward his enemy's heart. A gaggle of men immediately jumped in front of Fireborn's body. Instead of hitting Fireborn, the sticker pierced the chest of one of his bodyguards. The sight of Prince Lamanai rising to his feet was a cue for the warriors to rain down the heaviest barrage of missiles yet.

Apollus pulled Lamanai back down into the boat. Moroni and Meagan had also ducked as low into the canoe as possible, throwing their shields over their heads. I curled into a crescent over the top of Tz'ikin, making myself the smallest target possible, and then I held up my shield. Stickers rained all around us, splashing into the water or thudding against the wood of our shields and canoes. As the barrage tapered off, I peeked out from behind my shield. The river's current had finally carried us out of range. Stickers had turned the exterior of our canoes into porcupines. Two more arrows had struck my shield and were still vibrating. Moroni had a sticker protruding from his back. Yet he wasn't wounded. The missile was imbedded in the material of his cotton vest, but the arrowhead hadn't pierced his flesh. Stickers were also stuck in the quilted material of Jacobah and Meagan's cotton outfits. The padded "armor" constructed by Moroni had saved their lives.

I glanced back at Fireborn's ledge. Many of the Lightning Warriors had departed to pursue us by following along the trail. The terrain forced the trail to curve back into the forest, away from the river, so I wasn't sure how easy it would be for them to keep up. Fireborn remained standing on that ledge until we were out of sight. Lamanai continued spewing venom, assuring us that he would feed Fireborn's heart to the volcano, blot out his name and memory above and below the clouds, and other odd-sounding curses.

The roar of the current was starting to sound like a hyperactive crowd at Lavell Edwards Stadium. The roller-coaster ride was about to begin. Somehow Moroni and Apollus's canoe had gotten ahead of ours, so they were the first to hit white water. Their boat twisted around till it was facing backwards. Looking farther up ahead, I began to perceive a drop off, but not a waterfall—more like a plunge through a gauntlet of Class V rapids. The river, which had been eighty feet wide, scrunched to about half that. The pressure as it squeezed through the canyon gap looked like a dam break. My proudly earned merit badge for canoeing on the Bear River definitely hadn't prepared me for this.

Our boat hit the same whirlpool as Moroni and Apollus. I fought to keep our angle straight, but the river was too strong; we twisted backwards exactly the way that they had. In our plight, I lost sight of the other canoe. The river was spinning us like a windmill—and the worst rapids were still to come!

We hit a boulder. Our canoe instantly half-filled with water. The current pulled us around to face forward, then we plunged into another shoot. Tz'ikin hardly reacted, even though she was soaked—out cold. Gilgal stabbed his oar against the next boulder to keep us from being crushed, but an instant later his oar snapped in two! Jacobah and I were now the only ones controlling the boat—or *pretending* to control it.

Just then our canoe went over a drop. The front end dove right into a churning pool. The water curled over the top of us, like a surfer sliding through a pipeline. We hit something hard and the back end of the canoe was kicked upward. The four of us and all our weapons were thrown into the drink. I thought I heard Jacobah call my name, and then my feet flipped past my eyes in a blur of mist and spray. I believe I somersaulted twice before the rapids fully engulfed me. I started panicking, thinking of Tz'ikin. I had to find her—grab onto her—before she drowned. There was a body on my right—Gilgal. He groped around until he'd seized my neck, trying to use me like a life preserver. Somehow the current wrenched us apart, dragging us in separate directions. I was sucked into some kind of hydraulic vacuum. I wasn't going downstream at all. So this was what river runners meant by getting "Maytagged." My sandals were stripped right off my feet. My cotton mantle became saturated; the weight of it keeping me submerged. As I fought for air, I realized something was caught in the vacuum with me—another body. I latched onto its waist. Somehow, our combined weight broke us free of the vacuum. Again the current carried us down river.

As my head broke surface, I saw to my relief that I was holding Tz'ikin. Her eyes were closed, lips pale. She was coughing up water. "Hang on!" I managed to yell before I was sucked under again. I had one arm across her chest and I used my other arm to try and swim. The current pulled us into another somersault, but I refused to let go of Tz'ikin. As a result, I scraped against something very sharp under the surface. My cotton mantle was ripped away from my back, exposing my skin. Then the rocks *really* did a number on me—grinding away at my flesh. Still, I maintained my grip and struggled to hoist Tz'ikin upward so she could breathe.

To my right I glimpsed something jutting out of the water. I caught it in the crook of my elbow. A tree branch! Or more specifically, a tree *root*. Again I was able to draw air into my lungs. Tz'ikin was conscious. She looked around as if realizing for the first time that we'd been thrown from the canoe. She grabbed at another dangling root with her uninjured arm, and it was good that she did, because the current could have easily yanked her away from me. We were only about five yards from the east bank. The steepest canyon walls were behind us. The river's edge was lined with jungle. Yet the white water went on; I couldn't see the end of it because the river made another bend, then dropped over more cascades. I couldn't see our canoe, or the canoe of Moroni.

The tree I'd latched onto must have fallen into the water many years ago, along with several other trees lying farther downstream. Water sprayed in our faces, and waves washed over our heads every few seconds. I felt if I could just pull us toward the bank a couple more feet, there was an area that looked calm enough that we might swim to shore. Trouble was, between the two of us, we had only two good arms. Obviously I had to use one of mine just to hold Tz'ikin.

I yelled over the rush of current, "We need to pull ourselves along this tree! I need your help! Is your left arm strong enough?"

She answered without hesitation. "Yes!"

"Are you sure?" If she was wrong, we'd both drown.

She replied, "Are *you?*"

"Okay. We need to coordinate. We can't let go at the same time. Our arms need to work as one person."

She nodded. I tightened my grip as she reached toward the next branch farther in. She caught it in the crook of her elbow, just as I'd done. Then came the scary part. I had to let go. For several seconds I'd be entirely dependent upon her strength as the river whipped me around close enough to grasp the next branch nearer to shore.

I asked, "Ready?"

Again she nodded. *Here goes nuthin'.* I released the root. The current tried with all its might to tear me away from Tz'ikin. But I hung on and found a grip as water rushed over my face. Somehow I pulled myself close enough to hook my elbow, like before, but the position wasn't as good, and the branch didn't feel as sturdy. The next handhold was merely a broken nub. I could only hope the current wasn't quite as strong a few feet farther in.

I said, "Okay! Now!"

She let go. The current flipped her around. I tried with all my might to maneuver her close enough to grab that nub. Then my branch snapped. We were pulled underwater, once again at the river's mercy.

Before my head went under I heard Tz'ikin yell, "Swim!"

No need. I was already swimming with my free arm. Somebody up there must have liked us, because I managed to catch hold of the next uprooted tree downstream. This time we were on the side that faced upriver. At last I was able to breathe deeply. I continued pulling us shoreward with my free arm. Moments later I could feel mossy stones under my feet, along the bank. I hoisted the two of us to safety.

For several minutes we lay there with our legs dangling in the current, allowing our lungs to catch up to our hearts. My arm continued to tightly hold Tz'ikin's waist.

She grunted, "You can . . . let go!"

I must have been hindering her ability to breathe. I released her and rolled onto my back. Mistake! *Arghhhh!* For the first time I felt the deep gashes cut by that rock. My layered cotton pullover had been torn off one shoulder. It now looked like the frock of a caveman. And of course, I had no shoes.

The dressing for Tz'ikin's injured shoulder was clinging by a thread. I could see both the sticker's entrance and exit wounds. The flesh was white and pink. Fortunately, there was very little bleeding. Or maybe she'd already lost so much blood that there wasn't much left. I removed the material for the dressing and squeezed out the water, then I retied it around her upper arm. I couldn't imagine anything more germ-ridden than water from that river, but this was the best I could do.

I got up on my knees and tried to see downstream. Still no sign of anyone. As I stared into the trees behind me, I could see part of the trail used by the porters—the same one the Lamanite assassins were likely standing on when they were firing at us upriver. We were quite a ways downstream from those guys now. Or so I hoped. Still, any minute I was sure they'd come charging along, eager to reach the bottom of the gorge to see how many of us had survived.

I said to Tz'ikin, "We're exposed here. We need to move into the trees."

Her eyes were closed; I thought she'd fainted again. But then she nodded and tried to sit up. I helped her, wincing a little from the pain in my back. *The two of us are quite a pair,* I thought. We climbed up the bank and slipped into a shadowy nook. There was plenty of surrounding ground cover—ferns and shrubs, all thick with leaves. I finally felt somewhat hidden and safe. But what about Meagan and Apollus and Moroni and the others? I shivered to imagine that some might have drowned. What if *all* of them had drowned? What if Tz'ikin and I were completely alone? The thought filled me with desperate energy.

I told Tz'ikin, "We can't rest here long. We gotta get downstream—see what happened to the others."

"You go," said Tz'ikin. "I'll wait."

"I'm not gonna leave you here alone. Fireborn and his assassins might come down that trail any second."

Her eyes opened again. "Fireborn," she whispered malevolently. "I must . . . I must . . ."

"You must *nothing.*" I couldn't believe after everything, she still had aspirations of killing him. "What do you think you're gonna do? *Bleed* on him?"

Her eyes closed again, and her body relaxed. She confessed, "I don't think I can go farther. Not for . . . for a while."

"We'll rest a few minutes. Then I'll carry you."

She looked at my face, her eyes filled with a curious intensity. "In the river . . . you hung on to me. You saved my life."

Her tone was so matter-of-fact, so lacking in emotion that I crinkled up a corner of my mouth. "You make it sound like I did something rather weird."

"It *was.* You might have drowned. You should have let go."

"You really believe that?"

"Anyone else would have."

I shook my head. "I couldn't have lived with myself. I had to at least try. We were lucky. The Lord was watching out for us. Consider it payback for all the 'He-woman' stuff you did for me at Tikal."

She studied me a moment longer, then declared, "You are a strange man, Ryan Champion."

"Is that a good thing or a bad thing?"

She paused, then answered as if pondering the question very seriously. "I'm not sure."

"You'll let me know when you decide, right?"

She said, "Turn around. I wish to see your wounds."

I did as she requested and displayed the cuts on my back.

She declared, "The cuts are deep. You're bleeding."

"I'm not surprised. It stings like a son-of-a-gun."

She closed her eyes. "You'll live."

"Oh, you think so?"

"Yes."

"I'm glad to know it."

"But you should apply a poultice. Juice of ylin bark, root of
cypress bush, wax salve, yolk of duck's egg . . ."

"Hmm. I'm all out of 'ylin' juice, cypress roots, and duck eggs at
the moment. But I'm pleased to hear your concern. Honestly, I think
*you're* the one who needs that poultice. As your wound heals, that
shoulder will hurt like somebody stabbed it with a hot poker."

She said, "I can endure pain," as if I'd insulted her.

"You know, you don't always have to be tough as nails. You can
admit when it hurts."

"I didn't say it didn't hurt. Just that I can take it."

"I meant no offense."

Again she stared at me. Her eyes finally softened—a look I was
beginning to think I'd never see. "Thank you . . . for hanging on."

"You're welcome."

"And for your kindness . . . the past while. It's been . . . pleasant."

I raised my eyebrow. "Wow. Pleasant, eh? That may be the
kindest thing you've ever said to me. I felt like during our long rides I
was pretty much doing all the talking."

"Yes. But I was listening."

"Oh?" I sat beside her. "So what did you think? Maybe you'll be
my first convert. Eh?"

"Convert?"

"To the gospel. Are you sure you were listening?"

"Yes . . . mostly." She tried to laugh a little, but it was too painful
for her.

I observed, "You seem to know a lot about poultices. Was your
father a doctor?"

She replied, "A sorcerer."

"Like a shaman? Like Lamanai's stepfather?"

She shook her head. "Like a witch."

*That* made me sit back a bit. "I see. Was he . . . Are your people . . . Gadianton robbers?"

She looked puzzled. "I don't know . . . what that is." Slightly offended, she added, "But the Lacandon do not rob."

"Good to hear."

"Unless the person *deserves* to be robbed."

I blinked my eyes dumbly, then said, "Well, I'm just glad to know that you were listening to me *part* of the time."

She was quiet for a moment, then she said something unexpected. "It must have disappointed you greatly to have Meagan . . . reject your affections."

*That* was weird. "Why would you say that?"

She looked away. "If you want her back, I can help you."

"Huh?"

"I know ways a man can capture a woman's heart. *Secret* ways."

I screwed up my face in befuddlement, then shook my head firmly. "I'm not interested in any of that. Meagan's a wonderful person. Beautiful. Smart. Doesn't take any guff. But . . . I don't think she has the corner on those things."

I was looking at her intently, studying the strong lines of her face and cheek bones. Tz'ikin truly had the features of a feminine warrior, but those eyes were also a little hypnotizing. I shook it off. Heaven willing, I'd soon be a missionary. And this girl could, in a way, be considered my first investigator.

I'd hoped my comment might draw a smile. Instead she shut her eyelids and stiffened from a sudden jolt of pain.

I said, "Easy now. You rest. Catch your breath. Try not to move your arm."

I looked at her again. She appeared to be already asleep. Quickest any girl had ever taken my advice. Again I looked around. My nerves were suddenly on edge again. How long could we afford to wait here? The others might need serious help. Maybe Tz'ikin had been right—I should leave her here and try to find the others—verify that they were alive. I hated feeling such indecision. I had to make up my mind.

Then my mind was made up *for* me. I heard voices. Just as I'd feared, the Lightning Warriors of Fireborn were coming toward us at a run, eager to either confirm that everyone in the canoes were dead, or else to finish us off. That settled it. For the moment, I was staying put.

Then again, what if they attacked Moroni and Apollus without warning? I had to find them, let them know, give them some time to prepare or hide. I could see the assassins now. There were seven of them, weapons and spears bristling at every angle. If I tried to flee now, I'd become their newest object for target practice. All I could do was pray.

I scrunched down in the ferns as they rushed by, their eyes scanning the banks of the river. Tz'ikin made a noise—just a low groan— but I crawled back to her with my finger to my lips. Not that she opened her eyes to see it.

I whispered, "Stay quiet."

I remained still. The warriors' footsteps seemed to be fading away. I raised my head and caught a glimpse of their backs as they disappeared behind some foliage down the trail. But something was different. I tried to count the men. I could now only see snatches of feathered leggings and leather armor through the trees, but it seemed to me that there were *fewer* of them. I could only verify five. Had two men broken away from the group? An awful feeling percolated inside me. There was no way they could have heard us . . . was there? Tz'ikin's groan was barely audible even to *me,* six feet away. If we'd been heard, wouldn't it have stopped the whole patrol? Maybe two of the men had gone back. *Arrgh!* I was just being paranoid.

Then I heard the rustle of leaves. My muscles stiffened. The noise came from somewhere to the south, yet I couldn't tell quite where. I opened my ears, listening hard, but the only thing audible right now was the thump-thump of my heart. Then I heard another sound— fainter than before. The quietest snap of a twig. This was bad. *Way* bad. Whoever had made that sound knew we were in here. They were creeping toward us. But the funny thing was, I'd heard the *second* sound from the north. This meant at least one assassin had peeled off from the patrol after he got ahead of us.

To my left lay a hand-sized rock, half submerged in dirt. I reached out. *Dang!* Stupid thing wouldn't budge. Like an iceberg, there was a lot more under the surface. I heard more rustling from the foliage ahead of Tz'ikin. She didn't react. She appeared entirely unconscious. I stared into the greenery, muscles ready to spring.

The leaves moved. A face started to emerge. Midnight black with—

*Wait!* It was an *animal! Huracan!* But the jaguar was in an attack stance, fangs bared. *She was leaping!*

I shielded my face. "Huracan, it's *me!*"

But the massive black shadow jumped right over the top of me. I heard a sound, like a scream, but also like someone gurgling water.

I whirled around and saw that Huracan had found a target—a Lightning Warrior! He'd been creeping up after all, but from the other direction. The jaguar's jaws were clenched around his throat, neck already broken. Then I realized the second assassin was *right beside me!*—four feet to my left!—spear drawn back. He'd surely been in the act of thrusting that spear point toward my spine just as Huracan had leapt, but then his eyes turned to watch his partner being torn apart.

At that instant I used the only weapon in my arsenal—a kick-boxing roundhouse to the head. My kick connected perfectly. The warrior dropped his spear and staggered back, eyes wide with surprise. However, the tough ol' hombre didn't go down. I watched him reach for the obsidian-edged club behind his shoulder, but before he could draw it, I threw a twisting punch right into bridge of his nose. I'd never actually thrown a punch at someone's face before—not without a boxing glove on my hand. The warrior wasn't expecting this move either. In fact, I don't think fistfighting was a common thing among Nephites and Lamanites. Again, he staggered back, screeching bizarrely, and throwing his hands up over his nose as it started bleeding like a sieve. My opponent was nowhere near defeated. He might have drawn that club and taken my head off. But I'd won the game of intimidation. After I sent him a subtle gesture that urged him to come back for more, he turned and started scurrying back toward the trail, still screeching like a stuck pig. The sound didn't last long. Huracan pounced and brought him down like a gazelle.

I turned away. It wasn't necessary to see what happened from there. Besides, my knuckles hurt like nobody's business. I shook it off and went to Tz'ikin, who was now awake and alert. Amazing what a little extra adrenaline had done for her. However, I feared every Lamanite within ten miles had heard that warrior's peculiar screaming.

I said, "We better get out of here. How do you feel? Can you walk?"

She nodded and tried to stand. Her injured arm looked as lifeless as a spaghetti noodle. I helped her to her feet. The second assassin's spear lay close by. I picked it up and handed it to her.

"Lean on this a sec."

I went over to the dead body of the first assassin. His eyes were opened wide and full of terror. No time to be squeamish. We needed weapons. He had a bow, but that gadget would be useless to me. Even if I could use it, the bowstring appeared to have snapped in the fracas. Instead, I took the saw-toothed sword off his back. As an afterthought, I also stripped off his sandals. It felt strange and gross to be removing shoes from a dead man. But it's not as if he'd have any further use for them. I tied them quickly around my ankles and calves.

Tz'kin said, "Perhaps Fireborn himself will come down the trail."

"Forget about it," I said bluntly. "Your assassin days are over for a while."

As I started to stand up straight, the back of my hand brushed a furry head. I jumped a little. It was Huracan. She gazed up at me with calm, seemingly reassuring eyes. Blood covered her teeth and chin. Her flaming yellow tail gyrated back and forth. I wondered if I'd ever get used to this animal's presence. So magnificent and frightening. With some hesitation, I reached out and touched her head.

I said, "I'm grateful to you."

Tz'ikin watched us. For a moment she ignored her pain and said, "I've never known an animal to behave toward people as this one behaves toward you."

"Just me?"

"No. You, Apollus, and Meagan."

I feebly brushed off her observation. "I think it's *all* of us."

Yet she was right. Apollus had told me his theory a few nights before—that the jaguar could understand our words. Honestly, I was starting to believe it.

Tz'ikin continued, "To my people the balam is a sacred crea-ture—a god who will one day have power to bring death to all earthly creatures. This balam seems to feel your power, as if you are one to be obeyed."

"Don't start that again," I said. "We're not gods. If anything, its behavior is a blessing from the one *true* God." As if to contradict what I'd just said, I crouched down, looked into Huracan's face, and spoke to her directly. I might have been more discreet, but I didn't think there was time to mess around. "The others—we have to find them. Can you lead us to them?"

I had a feeling she'd seen everything that had happened on the river. She studied me for a moment, then glanced to the right and left. Without further delay, Huracan started off into the forest.

Tz'ikin looked after her in amazement, then back at me.

I pointed upward and again stressed, "Not my doing. *His.*"

She narrowed her eyes. I wasn't sure what she was thinking. Finally, she handed me back the spear and said, "My arm is injured, not my legs."

She tried to lead the way, but her balance was wobbly and it was clear that she was about to stumble. I caught her before she fell. As I held her in my arms, I said, "Whether your legs are injured or not, I'll still have to carry you for a while."

She wasn't very heavy. Still, how far could I realistically carry her? I prayed hard that I'd have the strength to do so just as far as neces-sary, then I followed in the jaguar's footsteps.

Huracan did not stick to the main trail. She led us straight into the thickest part of the jungle where the trees were a hundred feet high, swelling above us like broccoli heads, and blanketing the forest floor in perpetual dusk. Mossy vines hung around us like cobwebs, all of them dripping with humidity. And this was even *before* the after-noon rains.

Without warning we were inside a cloudburst. Rainwater collected on the leaves and bromeliads until many tree trunks and branches overflowed, dangling waterfalls all around us like horses' tails. The downpour lasted thirty minutes, when suddenly beams of sunlight burned holes in the canopy. A few minutes later, the forest was thick with mist.

After half an hour my arms felt like they were being stretched on a rack. I was certain that I couldn't carry Tz'ikin much farther. My silent prayers for strength became more vigorous than ever. Also, I was beginning to doubt Huracan's inner compass. But to the creature's credit, we saw no other Lamanite patrols. We crossed a rocky knoll with chasms and boulders that caused my legs the greatest challenge yet. I finally had to set Tzi'kin down and rest. I also used the time to make a sling for her arm using some of the shreds of my upper cloak.

After I was finished, I took in my work and asked her, "How's that?"

"Better," she replied.

I slapped my neck and killed a nasty-looking fly before it could suck me dry, then I lifted her into my arms one more time. We quickly moved on. After a few minutes we reached the top of the knoll and found ourselves overlooking a humid rainforest with misty clouds moving through the trees like rivers of cotton. In the distance I could see a bend of the river, reflecting like molten gold. The sight was so stirring that I couldn't help but pause to gape. Then I heard a low growl in Huracan's throat. The jaguar was staring eastward, where there was an open plain between two lines of trees. The mist remained very white and soupy in that direction; nevertheless something about that open plain had aroused the balam's ire.

Tz'ikin said to me, "I'd like to try and stand."

I set her down, then I squinted hard to see if I could figure out what had upset Huracan.

Finally, I saw it. The mist had burned off just enough that an image began to emerge—a very disturbing image. There were hundreds of men camping on that plain. In fact, there were *thousands*. The tents stretched deep into the woods. I couldn't even perceive where the Lamanite encampment ended. It almost appeared as if Fireborn had brought his entire *army!*

As soon as I caught my breath, I said, "All that just to capture *us?*"

Tz'ikin had seen it now. She said, "I suspect those warriors are headed to the same place as you."

"Cumorah?"

She nodded. "Especially if they've figured out Lamanai's intentions. Fireborn will never allow Eagle-Sky-Jaguar to unite with the Nephites—not if he can stop it."

Mystified, I continued to gape at the mass of warriors. Then, in a flash, I came to my senses. "Scenic rest stop over. Let's get to the river."

As I tried to lift Tz'ikin, she put out her arm. "I will walk for a while."

"You sure? I'm not sure how far you'll get."

Stubbornly, she ignored me and started following the jaguar.

Huracan led us across the knoll and back into the forest. A short time later we emerged from a cluster of foliage to find ourselves on a flat shelf overlooking a calmer stretch of the mighty Sidon, though I could still hear the roar of rapids somewhere up above. And lo and behold—beneath an umbrella of trees directly across from us I spotted a dugout canoe on the bank. In fact, I saw *two* canoes, and the unmistakable strawberry-blonde hair of Meagan Sorenson.

She was with two other people. One was Lamanai—I recognized those arm and leg tattoos even from a quarter mile away. The other, I could swear, was Gilgal. He was sitting on the ground with something tied around his jaw. So Gilgal hadn't drowned. But where were Jacobah and the others? My stomach twisted. Was it possible that these were the only ones who'd scored a victory against the river? No way. That would mean *Moroni* had drowned. And that was simply impossible.

I wanted to call out to the people below, but I didn't dare. Again I looked upriver. It was getting late. The basin and surrounding lands were illuminated by a ruddy haze. However, it seemed to me that the section of river below us was *not* the place where porters from Korihab would have plopped a customer's canoe back into the water. More likely that would have been at the bottom of the rapids, which I guessed was a couple of bends upstream.

Just then, I heard Moroni's voice. "Ryan! Tz'ikin!"

I turned to see them all emerge from the woods—Moroni, Apollus, and my dog-faithful bodyguard, Jacobah. Only Jacobah looked the worse for wear, mantle torn and scratches on his face and arms.

He clasped my shoulders. "Ryan Xbalanque, you are alive!" He went to embrace me, but I immediately yelped. As he saw my back, he apologized profusely.

Moroni suddenly leaped toward Tz'ikin, catching her just before she collapsed. Now that we were reunited, her mind decided she no longer had to be tough. She'd gone limp from blood loss and strain. I joined Moroni and put my arm around her waist for support. Moroni examined her wound.

Apollus said, "We were afraid we'd have to search the riverbanks for you all the way back to Korihab."

With urgency I told them, "There are thousands of Fireborn's warriors camped to the east of here. We could see the whole *herd* of them from the top of that knoll."

Moroni nodded. "I feared as much. The great march against the Nephites at Cumorah has finally begun."

Apollus said, "As we were floating farther downriver, we could see many men pouring from the woods to reach the base of the falls."

I asked in surprise, "So there *were* waterfalls at the end of the rapids?"

Apollus clarified, "Well, not exactly. But it was very steep. Difficult to navigate."

I asked admiringly, "You made it all the way down without getting tossed into the drink? I'm impressed."

Moroni said, "We were fortunate. The dugout nearly overturned many times."

I doubted if fortune or luck had anything to do with it. It occurred to me that maybe I'd chosen the wrong canoe to ride in. Should have known the Lord would keep Moroni afloat. The son of Mormon still had gold plates to deposit. It occurred to me that next time I ought to stick to him like glue. Then I felt ungrateful. I was here. I was alive. We may have gotten a little wet and beaten up, but the Lord had ultimately delivered us, just as He had delivered them.

Jacobah said, "Apollus and the others pulled Gilgal and me from the water. They also overturned our capsized dugout, though it was badly damaged. It may not travel much farther."

Moroni said, "It will travel as far as we need it."

"But everyone made it." I felt overflowing with relief.

Huracan snarled again. She didn't seem to approve of our pausing to chat.

Apollus said, "The lioness is right. We must get back on the water tonight. The men at the porter's dock will tell Fireborn's warriors that we survived. They'll be pursuing us without delay."

Tz'ikin tried to sit down, as if she hadn't heard a word Apollus said.

I raised her back up and again lifted her into my arms.

Moroni tried to relieve me of my burden. "Let me. You're wounded."

"I'll be all right."

Jacobah had a second look at my back. "Your cuts should be dressed."

Again I insisted, "I'm fine. I've brought our favorite assassin this far. Might as well carry her the rest of the way."

Huracan started following along the shelf, determined, if necessary, to go on without us. No rest for the weary, I thought. We followed her toward the temporary encampment of Meagan and the others. Next stop: the Lacandon mountains.

The homeland of Tz'ikin.


## NOTES TO CHAPTER 5

It is worth again detailing the role that Fire-born, or Siyah K'ak, may have played in Mesoamerican history (compare with the Chapter 14 notes in *Warriors of Cumorah*). "Fire-is-born" is an actual person mentioned in several places on stone stelae and artifacts discovered at Tikal and other sites in lowland Guatemala. Because his name is associated with art and iconography that resembles other art and iconography of the same time period at Teotihuacán in central Mexico (also known as *Tollan* in Nahuatl or "Place of Cattails") he is said to have been a warrior-general from Teotihuacán who conquered much of the Maya region in the name of a king named Spearthrower Owl or "Atlatl Cuaac." The date given for this political takeover at Tikal is AD 378. Fire-born's arrival and the death of Tikal's ruler, Jaguar-Paw (or "Jaguar-Claw"), are recorded on the same date, which strongly hints that the former king was executed and that the transition of power was propelled by violence. These events, of course, took place only seven years before the destruction of the Nephites at Cumorah.

Fire-born installed a possible son of Spearthrower Owl, Nun-Yax-Ayin ("Blue Crocodile" or "First Crocodile"), as the Ahau or "Lord" of Tikal to rule in his father's name. Fire-born then continued as a figure of authority in this region, presumably expanding and consolidating Spearthrower Owl's empire. Because these Guatemalan lowlands, which spread west to Chiapas, Mexico (Zarahemla), have been proposed by many LDS scholars to be the heart of Lamanite territory (Joseph Allen, *Exploring the Lands of the Book of Mormon;* see also John Sorenson, *An Ancient American Approach to the Book of Mormon*), it has been speculated that Fire-born *may* have been involved in the campaign against the Nephites in AD 385.

Teotihuacán, because it is situated north of the lands that have been proposed as Bountiful and Zarahemla, is presumed to have been a kingdom founded by descendants and adherents of the Gadianton cult. The scenario that Gadianton and Lamanite armies commanded by men who espoused Gadianton philosophies were responsible for the Nephite downfall seems to fit Mormon and Moroni's descriptions of the final war in the Book of Mormon, particularly when they ultimately credit secret combinations as having been the major cause of their nation's demise (Hel. 2:13; Ether 8:21; Morm. 2:27–28). For a detailed secular account of Fire-born's role in fourth-century Mesoamerica, see David Stewart, "The Arrival of Strangers: Teotihuacan and Tollan in Classic Maya History," P.A.R.I. Online Publications: Newsletter 25, July 1998.

A detailed catalogue on how to treat native ailments in Mesoamerica was compiled shortly after the arrival of the Spaniards. The recipe for a poultice to help in the healing of wounds as described in this chapter was taken from this document (Martín De la Cruz, *An Aztec Herbal: The Classic Codex of 1552,* trans. by William Gates [New York: Dover Publications, Inc., 1939, reprint 2000]).

# CHAPTER 6

## Steffanie

My heart was still hammering, as if trying to break free of my chest. Harry, Micah, Mary, Jesse, Gidgiddonihah, and Rebecca had somehow vanished into thin air. To my dismay, I'd also found the seerstone. For me this was proof that Harry and Gid had been taken against their will. But *where?*

They couldn't have gone far. A mile at the most. I was also infinitely curious why the men of our group hadn't put up much of a fight—Gid in particular! I'd have expected to find several corpses in his wake. But there were no bodies, and no blood. It was as if they'd just thrown up their hands and consented to become prisoners—no questions asked! Again I was tempted to scream out their names, but I stopped myself. As Pagag had been forced to remind me, this would have also alerted the enemy that more potential prisoners had been left behind.

Pagag continued frantically trying to glean clues from the footprints. He finally raised his eyes and pointed toward the pine-forested hills to the southeast. "The aggressors came from in there. Dozens of them. Maybe over a hundred—moving swiftly, like an army on the march."

"But it was less than twenty minutes ago!" I said. "Where did they go?"

He motioned for me to lower my voice, then he turned and peered into the thick, shadowy forest spreading northward over a range of low hills. "They went in that direction."

Still nursing my throbbing hand, I started marching in the same direction. I slipped the seerstone into a pocket of my mantle and filled my hand with Jesse's abandoned bronze sword.

"Wait!" Pagag whispered through his teeth. His frustration with me seemed to be mounting. "Are you always so impetuous and reckless? We should not follow them directly. There may be scouts or stragglers, like the warrior who attacked us. We will take a parallel course. But first you will show me that hand."

I bared my own teeth, *so* wanting to ignore him and continue on. This desire was tempered as I recalled that I was attempting to woo this beast away from Mary Symeon. Or maybe I backed down simply because, yes, I *had* been acting recklessly. Somehow Pagag was keeping a cooler head, which annoyed me to no end. To my credit, at least I recognized this and paused. He came and lifted my hand to get a closer look. It was also the first time *I'd* studied the injury. My wrist looked swollen and my pinky finger was oddly bent. I couldn't move it.

"You broke it," I informed him.

"Perhaps," he admitted. "But only to save your life. It should be tied in a splint. But not here. Let's get out of the open."

Just then we heard a bird cry overhead. I looked up and saw Harry's falcon, Rafa. He circled us several times. The bird's behavior was a little unusual, as if he wasn't sure that he recognized us. Or as if he didn't fully trust us.

"Rafa!" I called, though not at the top of my lungs. Pagag still thought it was too loud and sent me a searing glance.

The falcon circled one more time. At last he landed on a broken limb a few yards in front of us and made several more chirps in agitation.

I spoke directly to Rafa. "You saw it, didn't you? You saw what happened?"

Another high-pitched squawk. It was incredible, but it seemed to me that the bird had actually said yes.

"Are they all right?" I asked Rafa.

Pagag's expression was dubious. "You are interrogating a falcon?"

I looked at Pagag in confusion. "You mean you didn't understand that? It didn't just seem to you as if the bird said yes'"

"It chirped," said Pagag, scoffing. "It did not speak."

But in response to my second question Rafa became more agitated than ever, flapping his wings, shaking his beak, and making several more furious squawks.

"I think they're all alive," I said, as if translating directly from "bird" language. "But Rafa is terribly worried."

Pagag widened his eyes in amazement. Rafa's reaction, right on cue with my question, was difficult to dismiss. "You understand what the bird is saying?"

"Sort of," I said. "Not really. I mean, he's not speaking in words, exactly. But he *is* communicating."

Again I was surprised that Pagag couldn't comprehend it. To me it was quite plain, almost as if the same miracle that allowed me to understand Pagag was also allowing me to understand Rafa. As I thought about it, this explained so much that had happened over the years with other adventures. It explained why young Harry had been so successful at guiding the mammoth, Rachel, despite his lack of training. It explained why Melody was so devotedly attached to her dog, Pill. Melody often said that she felt she could understand her dog's every need, and felt the dog could also understand *her* needs. Honestly, I felt a little ridiculous that it had taken so long for this to register with me. Then again, the theory *didn't* explain why that stupid elephant back in Mardon's camp in Shinar had continued to bolt even after Harry had ordered it to halt. But I guess, like people, animals didn't always feel a forthright obligation to obey.

But if animals could understand time travelers, why couldn't Pagag understand Rafa? I could only assume that since Pagag and Rafa were from the same century, the miracle didn't apply to them.

"This is astounding," said Pagag. "Does the bird know where they are?"

I repeated the question. "Rafa, where are they?"

To that the falcon again took to the air, flying toward the north.

"Wait!" said Pagag. "Call it back! Call it back!"

I thought about giving Pagag the same dirty look that he'd given me for raising his voice. Instead, I held out my arm to the bird. "Rafa!"

Suddenly I realized how stupid this was. My arm had no sleeve. Those falcon claws were like steak knives. As Rafa glided back toward me, I quickly raised up a broken stick that Micah had gathered for firewood. Just before he landed, I said, "Not the arm! The branch!"

The falcon caught the stick in its talons, flapping its wings for balance. The perch I'd provided was not very steady.

"Ask how many enemies are with them," said Pagag.

I repeated the question. The bird gaped at me. Finally he made several ear-piercing cries. I narrowed my eyes in puzzlement.

"Well?" asked Pagag.

"I don't think a bird communicates like us. In numbers, I mean. Or maybe they *do* communicate in numbers, but . . ."

Pagag became impatient. "Did it tell you anything *helpful?*"

"I think he said 'many colors.'"

"Many *colors?*"

"Mostly I think he was saying it was a silly question and 'why were we just standing here?'"

Pagag tucked in his chin in surprise. We'd just been scolded by a bird.

"Ask it this," said Pagag. "Ask it to guide us to where the others are being taken. But tell it to warn us if there are spies or assassins lying in wait."

I repeated the statement. Rafa made a final ear-piercing squawk and launched back into the air. As we watched him fly over the trees, Pagag asked, "Did it say yes?"

I nodded, but I also smiled.

"What's funny?"

"I think a better translation would be, '*Duh!*' In other words, *obviously* he will do those things."

Pagag noted the falcon's direction once more, and then quickly tied the leather scabbard of Jesse's sword around my waist. Then he took hold of my uninjured wrist and led me into the trees. I didn't appreciate his assumption that he could just drag me along, but I didn't resist either. Obviously his ego required that I play the part of a compliant female, so I would do my best.

For the next hour, as we endeavored to keep the bird in our sights, Pagag seemed to totally forget the fact that I was still in pain. Each time Rafa disappeared toward the north and flew back to find us, he was gone longer. I wasn't sure if this was because the army that had captured Harry and the others was moving faster, or if Rafa was somehow being delayed. Maybe the bird had found a way of communicating with

Harry or Gid. But if that was true, why would the falcon never fly close enough to us to relay any messages? Rafa's interest was solely in whether or not we were following.

Daylight was waning. Now and then we'd catch a glimpse of a pale orange sunset through the tangled branches of the trees. The pain in my hand subsided for a while. I think this was because my brain went into some kind of defense mode, realizing that no relief would be soon in coming. However, as darkness deepened, the throbbing became worse than ever. Still, I refused to complain. Men did *not* like women who complained. If Pagag had so quickly forgotten my injury, it wasn't going to do me any good to whine about it.

Just before the bright red sphere sank completely behind the hills, we reached a steep gully, utterly impassible without climbing. With my hand the way it was, I definitely wasn't going to do any climbing. We'd have to find a way around it. It had been quite a while since we'd sighted Rafa. Perhaps it was simply too dark for him to return. Wherever Harry, Mary, Becky, and the rest had gone, we weren't going to catch up to them tonight.

At last Mr. Sadistic decided to inquire, "How is your hand?"

"Fine," I said, though I was gritting my teeth as I said it. I tried hard to suppress it, but I think there was murder in my eyes. I'd had quite enough. I didn't care about my stupid plan anymore. I was in too much pain.

In a rare burst of compassion, he said, "I'm very sorry to have put you through this before taking care of your injury. I'd hoped that with the aid of the falcon we might catch up to the others before we lost daylight. I think we can now conclude that this will not happen tonight."

"You are so wise." I don't think I did very well at masking the sarcasm.

His eyes drooped with guilt. He reached for my hand. "Let me see it again."

I drew it back. "Never mind."

"Please. I can still help you."

"Not necessary."

He stepped closer.

"Don't touch me!" I snapped.

Despite my objection, the ogre managed to grab my elbow. His hold was so firm that I didn't dare pull away, fearing I might lose my arm in the attempt. The truth was, my hand was hurting so badly I was terrified that I might actually start *crying*. Maybe this would have melted Pagag's typical male callousness. But try as I might, there were certain things that my pride would not allow me to do in front of a man. Especially in front of a jerk like him.

After examining my hand in the dimming light, and especially my pinky, he said, "I will have to set the bone in your smallest finger before I apply the splint."

"Don't even think about it," I snapped. "If you even *attempt* to— AHHHGGG!"

He *yanked* it! The moron had brutally pulled my finger straight with no warning whatsoever. I heard it crack as the bone went into place. My reaction? I couldn't stop myself. It was like a knee-jerk reflex. I cocked my uninjured fist and smashed it into his nostrils. It was the second time I'd thrown a punch at this Jaredite, but this time my wrist didn't buckle. Pagag staggered back, holding his nose. My plan to win over this young man's heart was obviously coming along brilliantly.

And then, just like the weak-kneed, soggy-bottom sop that I guess I really was deep down, tears started gushing from my eyes and sobs retched out of my throat. My strength left me, and I plopped onto the ground, holding up my hand like a dead fish.

Pagag's nose was bleeding. He pinched it with his fingers and said in a nasally voice. "It's all right. I deserved that. I promise you, it would have hurt worse if I had given you warning."

I didn't respond, just hugged my arm and continued to weep. Pagag came closer again—more tentatively—afraid that I might wallop him again. But I didn't have any more energy to lash out. Nor did I prevent him from reexamining my hand. Pagag reached for his waist pouch and pulled out some gauzy cloth, almost like something right out of a modern-day first-aid kit, except the cloth was dusky colored. He also reached for a nearby bush and cut several stiff, straight branches. But before he began to wrap the splint, he found something else in his pouch. It looked like a leaf, tightly rolled and dried until it was about the size of a piece of Chiclets gum.

"I want you to chew on this," he said. "Chew it until it becomes a paste in your mouth, then put it under your tongue and leave it there."

"Why?" I asked.

"It will help with the pain."

"I don't need a painkiller."

"If you don't, you may not sleep. And tonight you will need your rest. Tomorrow you must be very alert and strong."

I glanced again at the leaf wad. Then, without a second thought, I snatched it up and tossed it into my mouth. As I chewed I said, "So you carry painkillers wherever you go? Are you some kind of junkie?"

I wasn't sure if the word would translate, but it did. "Of course not," he responded. "My mother harvests the leaves and dries them. They are for pain. I have four such leaves. I have carried them a long time."

He took my arm and proceeded to make his splint. Moments later my fingers were tightly wrapped and tied against the wood; my wrist and forearm became arrow-straight. He also made a sling so that I could support the arm against my chest. All the while he was doing this I could feel the painkiller start to take effect. The hum of cicadas and other night insects began to take on an eerie, electrical, reverberating quality. The medicine worked surprisingly fast. Soon I felt no pain whatsoever. In fact, it felt as if my whole body was going numb. I definitely couldn't feel my tongue. Afterwards Pagag undid the woolen cape from around his shoulders and laid it around mine.

"It may get chilly tonight. I'm sorry that I have nothing for us to eat."

"That's okay," I said, my voice somewhat slurred, but my mood significantly improved. "I'm not so hungry anymore."

He smiled. "I wish I could say you'll feel that way in the morning. I am told that when the effect wears off, one's appetite is doubly voracious."

"You mean you've never chewed one yourself?"

"No," he admitted. "They are mostly for women. For childbirth. My mother is a midwife."

"Well, thank your dear ol' mother for me, will ya?" I said jovially. "'Cause at the moment I'm feeling rather happy to be a woman."

"Yes, well . . ." Pagag looked around. "I'll stamp down some of this grass. This ground ought to stay fairly dry. I suppose we should try and get some sleep."

"Oh, what for?" I asked. "I'm not tired. Are you tired? 'Cause I'm not tired."

"You will be shortly. Trust me."

"I don't think so," I said, my voice more slurred than before. "Besides, I have a few things I want to tell you, Mr. Pagag."

"You might want to refrain. You may regret the things you say."

"I don't think so," I insisted. "I don't think I could regret *anything* I have to say to you."

Suddenly I remembered myself. What was I doing? I was trying to woo him. This was no time to tell him how I really felt. *Be charming,* I told myself. *Charming.*

"Scratch that," I said. "I'm gonna be charming. I'm not gonna tell you you're a jerk. Not even that you're the biggest jerk I ever met. 'Cause that wouldn't be nice. And I'm gonna be nice. You'll like me better if I'm nice, right?"

"Well, I—I think that . . . might make a difference, yes—"

I narrowed my eyes and splurted out, "Then why can't you be nice? What's wrong with you, Mr. Pig-ug? You should be ashamed of yourself. Why can't you find your own wubbin?"

"You mean woman?"

"That's what I said. Wa's wrong with your ears? Don't you know what a woman is? *I'm* a woman."

"Yes I . . . I noticed."

"Only a cretin of the worst kind would steal another man's woman. If you try it, I'm gonna have to slobber you."

"Excuse me?"

"Slobber. Slaughter." I tried to concentrate. "*Clobber* you! I'll beat you to a pulp. That pretty face of yours will look like a mushy when I'm done with you."

He leaned closer and grinned in a way that was mildly mischievous. "I see. So you think I have a pretty face, eh?"

"What do ya mean? Prettiest face I ever saw. If I didn't hate you so much I'd eat you like a cone cream . . . thing. But I hate you. You hear me? Hate you worser than abby-noddy."

He was smiling the way someone might smile at a toddler covered with chocolate cake. I wished I had the strength and coordination to wipe that grin off his mug for good.

He asked, still grinning, "And why do you hate me so much, Steffanie?"

"I just told you, Mr. Pa-gag-me-with-a-spoon. Have you listened to a thing I heard? You think you're God's gift to gifts. But you're not. You hear? Just a pretty boy. That's all you are."

His grin wilted. "I guess we . . . we made a very bad first impression on each other, didn't we? I'm sorry about that."

"You shub-be," I said. Or I *think* that's what I said. I must confess my memory of some of my statements is a little foggy. Honestly, I wish I could forget it *all*. I continued, "But it wouldna matter, Mr. Piggly-pig-a-pig-gag. No impression would be different making. You're still jes' a pretty boy. Pretty, pretty, pretty. Sooooo pretty. So, so, so, so, soooooo—"

"Maybe you should lay down now, Steffanie."

"I'm not finished. –Purrrr-retty. Purrrrr-erfect. Purrrrr-snickety. Purrrr-ogative—"

"I'll lie over here."

"Purrrr-pendicular—"

"If the pain starts to return in the night—although I doubt that it will—I will give you another leaf. But now that there are only three left, we may want to be sparing."

"Purrrr-ple. Purple people eater picked a peck-a pickled purrr-rurrr-rurrr . . ."

I think at that point my head hit the ground, softened only by Pagag's palm. And that's the last thing I remember of our first day back in the world of the Nephites.

* * *

Boy, he wasn't kiddin' about the voracious appetite! When I woke up the next morning I could've eaten a horse. But on top of the intense hunger, I also had a marching band playing bazookas on my brain. My stomach was making noises like a toilet with faulty plumbing. I wouldn't have thought it was possible to be hungry *and* nauseous, but I was. And this was all on top of the fact that my hand was throbbing again.

"What *happened* to me?" I managed to say with my eyes tightly shut against the sunlight.

Pagag was returning from somewhere. I heard him drop something heavy onto the ground by my head. I felt the vibration in both of my temples.

"You slept soundly," he reported. "I'm very glad. We may have a long walk today, and you'll need your strength. I found food."

*That* opened my eyes. I looked at the thing he'd dropped. It was like a block of smooth white wood. He also spread out several elephant-ear-sized leaves as a makeshift mat. On this mat he laid out a mound of burgundy-colored berries, just like the ones we'd found the day before, and some mini-sized bananas, along with other fruit that looked like mangos, but smaller.

I decided to take the risk of getting poisoned and scooped up a handful of berries, gobbling down several bites before even registering the flavor. The skin was bitter, like chokecherries, but the juice was very sweet. After several more handfuls, the fingers of my right hand looked as purple as the berries. No doubt my lips and tongue looked the same. With my mouth full I glanced at Pagag. He was watching me with a queer expression. *Boy,* if I was still trying to attract this guy I was, without a doubt, breaking every rule in the proverbial book. A girl should never let a guy watch her eat. And eat like a hog? That was just, shall we say, *not done.* I switched to a mango, which might at least look a little more dignified. I also demanded a sip of water from Pagag's freshly filled water pouch. As I guzzled, he set about cutting off chunks of the white block of wood.

"Eat this," he suggested. "It seems to be the most filling. It's the inner meat of the same tree that Gid and Harry were cutting down yesterday. Quite good."

Didn't need to ask me twice. And it *was* good. Not that I was too particular. Honestly, *none* of it would have tasted as good as an all-American bacon cheeseburger.

"How is the pain in your hand?" Pagag inquired. "If you only chew half a leaf, you should still be able to travel."

"*No!*" I said firmly. "Don't ever give me that stuff again. The hangover isn't worth it. I'd rather endure the pain."

Pagag nodded. "I understand. It *does* provoke some interesting conversation."

I wasn't even going to acknowledge that crack. I refused to look at him. In reality, this might have been the main reason I rejected a second leaf. I was deathly afraid of another episode of "foot-in-mouth" disease. My face burned just *thinking* about some of the stupid things I'd said last night. And those were just the statements I *remembered!* If this Jaredite was any kind of gentleman, he would attribute it all to the medicine. Then again, I doubted if he was a gentleman. In my personal prayers that morning I might have even put in a silent request that he forget about every word I had said.

It was time to confess—no girl had ever done a more deplorable job at attracting a male. I might have done better by *deliberately* acting like a geek! It was almost as if I'd forgotten how it was done: a little flirt, a little hint, a well-timed smile, striking an occasional irresistible pose. My gracious! This wasn't exactly *brain surgery!*

Oh, what was the point? Why was I wasting any energy at all on this pathetic exercise? If the villains who took Harry and Mary managed to do them harm . . . I was sickened just thinking of it. Then again, it was almost as if fate had *purposefully* set things up to accomplish my devious mission. Maybe I was *supposed* to do this to Pagag—strictly to protect Harry and Mary. The circumstances of this situation couldn't have been planned any better if we'd been stranded together on a deserted island. And yet, truth be told, if I didn't start making serious progress in my plans to secure Pagag's affections, soon I wouldn't be able to face myself in the mirror and call myself a female.

Pagag bundled up the rest of the food. Afterwards, he reached under my arm and helped me to stand. My first instinct, of course, was to push him away. But not this time. From now on I would encourage all acts of chivalry. Besides, I was still a bit woozy from Pagag's painkiller. And chivalry or not, I had to face the facts: I *did* have an injury and I *was* dependent upon him for the moment. After I came to my feet I even managed to say—in a voice as sincere as I could possibly muster—"Thank you, Pagag. I want you to know, I do appreciate all the kindness that you've shown me."

"Of course you do," he replied with a shrug, and walked on ahead without giving the matter a second thought.

If he'd glanced back he might have seen me briefly twist my face into a snarl and raise up my right hand as if to claw his eyes out. Luckily, he did not glance back.

We continued to follow the ravine in a northwest direction. There was no sign of Rafa that morning. I was concerned that something might have happened to him. What if Harry's captors had figured out what the falcon was doing and shot it out of the sky? To complicate matters, I didn't think we took the best route around the ravine. We ended up veering almost directly west for several miles and crossed between a pair of hills covered with short, scrubby trees. To me it no longer looked like a logical path that an army would have followed. Pagag also couldn't find anymore footprints.

Around noon he began scolding himself. "I was too dependent upon that bird. I should have followed ground signs. It might have been slower, but I would not have lost the trail."

I decided to withhold my opinion, which I'm sure he appreciated. The after-effects of the medicine had mostly worn off, and my hand no longer throbbed unless I bumped it against something, which actually occurred more often than I cared to admit. Still, Pagag's splint and sling held up exceptionally well. I even took a moment to tell him so—a compliment that he also received without a second thought—even though what I *really* wanted to do was remind him that he was the one who'd caused the injury in the first place.

In the early afternoon we began to smell smoke. I looked to the north, but skies appeared clear—perhaps only a slight, blue-gray haze. I said to Pagag, "The Nephites and Lamanites burn their fields before planting. It enriches the soil. There may be farms over there. Or a village."

We altered course slightly and went directly north to where the landscape was more level. Our first hint that the source of the smoky smell was *not* a farmer's field came as we passed the charred remains of a hut in the woods.

I turned to Pagag, "The warriors who took Harry and Mary—do you think they—?"

Pagag shook his head. "This fire is three days old. Or close to it. Those soldiers could not have been responsible, unless . . ."

"Unless what?"

"Let's go on," said Pagag. I noticed that he drew his bronze sword and kept it at the ready.

I drew my own sword—or rather *Jesse's* sword. After all, I still had one good arm—my *fighting* arm. We passed a second hut with a burned roof. This time I gasped in dread. A man's body was visible near the doorway. One more step and my heart clenched again. There was also the body of a *woman!* But these people hadn't been killed by fire. There were terrible wounds. *Unspeakable* wounds. I saw no evidence that any one of them had resisted. They were cut down like stalks of corn. The man looked older. Not a soldier; just a humble farmer.

"Who would do this?" I asked, my voice quivering. "Who would kill a farmer or murder a woman?"

Pagag didn't speak. He urged us forward. We finally came to the village center, or what *had* been a village center. All the buildings were destroyed. The smell of smoke was pervasive. Smoke—and death. Our arrival startled several animals that fled into the trees. Coyotes, I suspected, or smaller carnivores. There were also numerous black vultures with misshapen red, leathery heads and bloody beaks. Our presence didn't disturb them at all. They fed on corpses. I didn't count the bodies. Nor did I look closely at any faces. What if I had spotted a child? I didn't think I could have handled it. The odor was overpowering. My lungs and stomach couldn't take anymore. I tugged on Pagag's cloak, indicating that I needed to leave before I lost my breakfast, and before my indignation caused my mind to self-combust.

Only after we were a hundred yards away from the carnage did I try to speak. But as I prepared to unload my feelings of revulsion on Pagag, he raised up his palm and pressed two fingers against my lips—a gesture that in Jaredite unmistakably meant to "shut up."

He'd heard something. A cold feeling pricked over every inch of my flesh. Yet I heard nothing at all.

"Over here," Pagag whispered. He led me toward the west, his body bent low and his footsteps careful to avoid cracking a twig.

I was a little confused. My ears still hadn't registered anything out of the ordinary. Pagag paused several times, as though he was *still* hearing some disturbing noises. As soon as he was confident that he'd pinpointed the exact source, he set aside our bundles of food and started creeping forward on his forearms. Needless to say, I wasn't about to crawl with my injured hand. I remained behind and watched him. He continued toward a nest of leafy plants mingled with brush that was situated fifty feet farther on, and then he disappeared like a snake into the grass. Being the impetuous soul that I am, I followed after him, my posture bent as low as possible, until I'd reached the place where he'd slithered into the undergrowth.

Finally, I started to hear voices, though very faint. They were barely audible even now. Wow, I was very impressed with Pagag's sense of hearing. The voices were definitely *human* voices, but I couldn't make out any words. Several men were whispering, perhaps just thirty feet beyond where I was crouched.

I tried not to breathe, which in retrospect is the worst thing a person can do in a situation like this. By *not* breathing you actually make far more noise, because eventually your lungs *will* force you to take in air. When that moment came, it sounded like the quick suction of a vacuum cleaner. All whispering promptly ceased.

*Ohhh boy,* I thought. They'd heard me. *Stupid, vapid, brainless female!* Why hadn't I just stayed put near the supplies like my instincts had advised me? I recognized a very real flaw in my personality. One might think this a terribly strange moment for such an epiphany, but I had it nonetheless. My obsessive competitiveness made me incapable of trusting any man to do a job on his own. *There!* I'd confessed it. I might have even been proud of this revelation. That is, if the very weakness to which I was confessing wasn't about to cause me the same violent and untimely death as the villagers.

A twig cracked. I turned my head slowly and looked up. My eyes met the face of another warrior—one who looked just like the one who'd attacked us the day before. The same gold and black stripes crossed his forehead and the bridge of his nose. The man gaped at me for several seconds, as if surprised to see a woman, or perhaps merely surprised to see a *blonde*-headed woman with a shiny metal sword. Finally, his puffy lips stretched into a grin, revealing two rows of checkerboard-painted teeth.

I straightened my posture and held out my sword threateningly, though with my left arm bound up as it was, I doubted if my pose was all too fear inspiring.

He glanced back and said to some unseen person or persons, "Come and see what *I've* found!"

Three more men stepped into view, all flashing the same Mardi Gras makeup and brandishing flint-edged swords. One man also wielded a kind of spear or trident with several flint points. I started to back away, but they swiftly encircled me, smiling wickedly.

"Where did you come from, woman?" asked the first warrior, who was considerably more portly than the others.

"What is that weapon?" asked another.

"Don't come any closer," I warned. "I know how to use this."

They looked at each other and enjoyed a laugh.

The fat one said, "So tall. And she has *fire.* Not like these Lamanite wenches."

"Slay her," said a third man—the one with the trident. "We must get back to the pit."

"What's the rush?" said the fat man. He narrowed his eyes at me and asked, "Are you alone?"

"No, I am not," I said. "My army of a hundred men is just entering the village. The village you burned."

It was a lame lie, and lamely delivered. I think the part they found most humorous was the idea that a woman could be the leader of a hundred-man army.

"Let's have a look at that pretty weapon," said the second man, who also had gold stripes down his sleek mane of black hair.

He came forward with a complete lack of caution, apparently thinking I was no threat whatsoever, and tried to grasp my wrist. In reply, I thrust my blade into the flesh of his bicep and drew it back. At first he looked utterly aghast, as if I'd insulted his sense of decency and good manners rather than almost severing his arm at the shoulder. Finally his teeth clenched with ruthless enmity. The other three men also seemed to lose interest in whatever unseemly intentions they may have had. They mutually decided I was better dead than anything else. The wounded man faded back to nurse his injury while the other three closed in.

The fat man said, "You like to play with sharp things, eh? Very good. We like to play with them too."

The one who carried the trident made a ghastly grin. As he raised his weapon and drew it back—the center point aimed between my eyes—I had the most irritating realization: I needed help. I know that sounds lame, but no matter how bad things ever got, I'd always felt that I could somehow change the dynamics. I could take care of myself. But not this time. Without help, I was about to die. *Anytime, Pagag,* I thought to myself. If this oafish Jaredite was going to save the day, now was his opportunity. It crossed my mind that he had *deliberately* abandoned me to my death.

Then, as if struck by lightning, my attacker's head bent grotesquely backward. His feet came several inches off the ground and then he toppled over like a bowling pin. I thought I might have heard a thunk, but whatever had hit him was very small and moving very fast. He lay on the ground, convulsing like a fish that had been knocked with a club.

Pagag burst from the brush. I was bewildered to see that he'd slipped his sword back into its sheath. The Jaredite appeared unarmed except . . . except for a strip of leather in his right hand. The leather was packed with a stone. It was a sling. Pagag had just pulled a David and Goliath!

"No one move," he threatened. "It is not necessary for anyone else to die."

Despite the warning, the fat man raised his flint-toothed sword high and charged at Pagag like a freight train. The Jaredite's leather sling whipped around twice and released. I heard another sickening thunk. The fat warrior crumbled and slid until he was two yards from the tips of Pagag's sandals.

By the time the other two attackers looked up from the quivering body, Pagag had loaded another stone. He whipped it around confidently, filling the air with a musical twang.

In a voice almost pleading, Pagag said, "I do not wish to kill anyone else. It grieves me that you would die so unprepared to meet your God. I advise you to flee—*swiftly!*"

They gaped in disbelief.

"Do it *now!*" barked Pagag.

The man that I'd stabbed in the arm was first to heed the advice. The other snorted a time or two, then scurried after his comrade. Both men vanished into the forest to the east.

I gaped at Pagag in awe. Or something *like* awe. If anything it was a bit *more* than awe. His prowess, his skills, his deadly quick reflexes. I realized my heart was still pounding, but not just with the adrenaline of our confrontation. What would you call this emotion? I think what I felt was . . . *safe*. That sounds lame. I guess for so long I'd taken on the pressure of being defender and protector. It seemed quite a while since I'd been on the *receiving* end. What's more, I rather *enjoyed* it. It wasn't so bad letting someone else be the powerful one. I especially enjoyed—I must confess—watching those rodents scurry away merely at the sound of Pagag's commanding voice.

And yet I couldn't feel this way. Whatever virtues he possessed, they were far outweighed by his flaws. But it was no doubt further evidence of the personality deficiencies within *me* that I still felt the irrepressible need to criticize the man who'd just saved my life for the second time. "What are you *doing?* They will inform others! Soon we'll have their whole brigade on top of us!"

"You believe I should have killed them?"

"Well, I—" I glanced at the two dead men. Suddenly I felt queasy. No, I did *not* wish he'd killed the other men. Then, to my utter surprise, I started shaking. Was this some kind of delayed reaction? It certainly wasn't the first violence that I'd ever witnessed. There were those Roman soldiers at the inn in Judea. And the Shinarians I'd fought atop the Tower of Babel. This was totally bizarre. I was almost acting like . . . like a *woman!* Yes, Pagag had done right. So *what* if ten thousand men converged on us? How easy it was to forget that we were in God's able hands, not our own!

Pagag was already at my side, gently supporting my back. "It's all right," he said soothingly. "You have not been harmed."

I looked into his face. Those radiant, marine-colored eyes pierced into mine. I felt . . . I wasn't sure. A little faint. All I knew for certain was that I desperately wanted someone to stop the shaking. Oh, this was almost gross! I wanted to be *held!*

Pagag must have sensed this, because his arms suddenly enfolded me. I buried my face into his shoulder. I couldn't believe how good it felt, like the embrace of a father. No, more like a brother. A bishop? Maybe a boyfriend. None of those seemed accurate. It was sort of a shock. Being in his arms felt like all those things at once. Never in my life had I felt a sensation like this. It was like . . . being home.

Again I looked into his eyes. Was it my imagination? Or did his face have a look of shock much like what I felt?

*Uggghh!* What was *wrong* with me? I'd always been able to count on my own strength and abilities. Why was I feeling this way? Perhaps because I'd never before found myself alone with someone who was more capable of protecting me than I was of protecting myself.

Thank goodness something shattered the moment. We heard a faint cry—like a child's cry—somewhere to the west.

"Take my hand," said Pagag.

Almost deliriously, I gave it to him. He led me around the thicket of undergrowth.

"Those men were guarding something before they heard you," said Pagag. "It's over here."

We continued some distance farther until we found ourselves at the edge of a muddy pit, about eight feet deep and eight feet around. It looked like it had once been some kind of trap, perhaps for cougars or jaguars. But right now it imprisoned an altogether different prey. Nine pairs of eyes stared up at us from the mud. They were children—ranging in age from two to about nine. Their bodies were covered in mud and filth. One boy, maybe eight, clutched a two-year-old little girl in his arms. My heart turned to water as I registered that these were certainly survivors from the attack on the village. I also knew that every child had probably lost parents and many other loved ones. Their faces were blanched with terror, like animals awaiting certain death. Immediately my emotions took over and encircled my heart. I felt a peculiar, strangling-type of feeling in my chest—pity and love and anger.

Pagag got down on his knees, leaning over the pit. "We've come to get you out of here. We're not going to harm you."

None of them believed him. Even as tightly crammed as they were, they shrank away from him, pressing against the pit's far wall. Several started crying.

I leaned over the edge as well, and my emotions overflowed. "He's telling you the truth. The men who were guarding you are dead, or else they've run away. We won't hurt you. We'll protect you. Please. Let us lift you out of this hole."

Pagag reached down. I did the same with my uninjured right hand, but no one made any move like they were about to reach back.

An older boy, about nine, wheezed to his companions in a thirsty voice, "They are the ones who were coming back for us!—the ones who took the others! They will kill us! They will feed us to their devils!"

The words ripped me up inside. I thought back on what I'd seen in that horrible, gruesome cave in the cliffs. This is what the child had meant. The poor boy was afraid he and the others were about to be sacrificed. They were afraid they'd all become like one of those tiny skulls!

"I swear to you," I said, my voice almost breathless in my determination to convince them, "we are *not* the ones who were coming back. We would never hurt you in any way. We want to *save* you. Please allow us to help you."

There was a long pause as they continued to study our faces. Then a young girl, perhaps four or five—still too young to believe any adult might deliberately want to harm her—came tentatively forward and reached upward toward my hand. Despite all the grime that covered her from top to bottom, her complexion was like a little angel. But she was too short. She couldn't reach my fingertips.

"*Please,*" I begged the older children, "someone lift her up."

At last the second-oldest boy stepped forward and raised up the little girl, possibly because he decided whatever we might do couldn't be any worse than the consequences of remaining where they were without food or water. I grasped the child's wrist. Even as awkward as it was using only one hand, she seemed so light that I hoisted her out with relative ease. Without encouragement, she threw her arms around my neck and held me tightly. I returned her embrace with all my energy. A tear escaped my eye. The horror of it was too much to take in—what these men had done to these innocent souls. There wasn't a millstone heavy enough to hang around their necks or an ocean deep enough to drown them! I wanted to see the girl's face, wipe some of the mud from her angelic cheeks, but she wouldn't let go. So I just continued to embrace her, and rock her, and cry.

I heard Pagag say, "Raise up the youngest ones toward me first."

He lifted out the two-year-old girl and four-year-old boy. They weren't wearing a stitch of clothing—only layers of filth. All of them had chapped lips and sunburned faces. The two-year-old was so lethargic that she couldn't cry anymore for the pain of thirst.

As Pagag was in the process of extracting several more children from the pit, I said to him, "Your water pouch—give them your water pouch."

After they'd been helped out of the hole, the oldest children tried to hoard the water and slake their thirst ahead of the others, but I managed to keep them at bay until the little ones had taken several gulps. I was so worried about the two-year-old—worried that she would not have the strength or will to drink. But as soon as the liquid touched her lips, she guzzled it eagerly. So voraciously, in fact, that I had to tell her to slow down.

Unfortunately, only five of the children had taken a drink before the water pouch was completely empty. I'd spotted a stream running through the village. It had flowed from the west. We walked a short distance west and managed to locate it quite easily. Gratefully, the area was upstream from the massacre. Downstream water might have been too contaminated for consumption. The children drank to their heart's content. I helped the youngest ones to wash the mud and grime from their bodies while the oldest took care to do the same. In all there were four boys and five girls. The boys were aged nine, seven, five, and four, while the girls were eight, five, four, three, and two. We didn't ask them their names right away, only ages. I hoped there would be plenty of time later to learn their names. Right now they were all in equal need of love and comfort and aid.

Pagag collected our foodstuffs. His heart-of-palm might have fed the two of us for days. As it was, that block only lasted about fifteen minutes. He'd also found several blankets of multicolored material, though I didn't ask where. He used the blankets to wrap up the ones who had no clothing. Later he made the material into actual garments by cutting head and arm holes and tying strips about the children's waists.

At last some of them appeared as if they might be able to talk.

Pagag said to the oldest boy, "You mentioned other children. Do you know what happened to them?"

"There were others," said the boy, his body starting to shake. I put my arm around him and held him until he had the courage to continue. Finally, he added, "They took them away."

"Took them where?" I asked urgently.

"Secret places," he replied. "You cannot find them."

"Who are the savages who attacked your village and put you into that pit?" Pagag demanded

"Nephites," he declared.

The word hit me like a blow to the stomach. "*Nephites?* Nephites did this? Are you sure?"

He nodded resolutely. The other children cowered at the word, much the same way that the little children of Rome might have cowered when they heard "Huns." Or the children of 1940s Europe when they heard "Nazis." Or those of early Mormon converts when they heard "mob."

"Then," I asked tentatively, "are you . . . Lamanites?"

The oldest girl nodded. "We are Lamaya. The people of the Earth-stone."

I wasn't sure what she meant by that last part. Possibly she was distinguishing her people as a specific branch or tribe of Lamanites.

Pagag asked, "The men that I killed—the ones who were guarding you—were they also Nephites?"

The children nodded.

Pagag turned to me and said in a lowered voice, "I thought Gidgiddonihah mentioned that *he* was a Nephite."

I turned back to the children, "Were they *Gadianton* Nephites?"

They looked around at one another. No one seemed to recognize that word.

I changed the question slightly, "Were they *wicked* Nephites?"

"*All* Nephites are wicked," said the oldest boy coldly, teeth clenched so hard I thought the enamel might crack.

The intensity in his frame caused me to widen my eyes. I had a feeling this hatred had existed long before his village was burned, well before his parents were slain. Pagag touched my shoulder and motioned that I should join him a short distance away, beyond the hearing of the children.

After I followed him, he said in a serious tone, "From Gidgiddonihah's words I had concluded that Nephites were a noble people. Tell me the truth."

"They *are*," I defended. "Or at least they *were*. I suppose it depends on the century."

"In what century were they so vile as to slaughter innocent men and women, and to butcher children for Satanic rituals?"

I thought a moment, then I raised my eyes as the answer resonated inside me. "Toward the end."

"End of what?" asked Pagag.

"End of . . . their nation. *Oh, my word!* I think I know what time period this is!" Suddenly my elation sank to the dregs. "Oh, no!"

"What's wrong?"

"If this is the century I *think* it is, it would mean that the Nephites are just as corrupt—perhaps *more* corrupt—than the Lamanites."

My face must have blanched at this thought, because Pagag asked me, "Why does this prospect fill you with such fear?"

"Because it means that we're alone. It means we may have no friends here. No refuge or place of safety. Anybody we meet is just as apt to kill us as anyone else. Oh, Pagag, you have no idea how hideous, how *terrible* this is. What it means is, I'm no longer sure what we should do."

"That hardly makes our circumstances any different than they were when we woke up this morning. Come, let's—"

He stopped as he looked back toward the children in puzzlement. They were crossing the stream, as if trying to get away from us.

"Hey!" I called out. I took off after them. "Where are you going?"

It didn't take much effort to overtake them—not with the older ones carrying the younger ones in their arms. Fortunately all nine seemed determined to stick together.

After catching up with them, I said, "Please! We're trying to help you! Why are you running away?"

"We must leave here," said the oldest girl. "The Nephites will return."

"But where will you go?" asked Pagag. "Do any of you have relatives that we can take you to? Perhaps in other villages?"

None of the children seemed to have an answer to that. It even caused one boy and girl to start weeping again. I wondered if they were old enough to even know how to reach nearby villages where they might possibly have relatives. Once more my heart was wrenched in sympathy. It was up to us to decide which way we should travel. In the end we determined to go northwest, in basically the same direction that we'd been traveling to follow Harry. Of course, every time I thought about Mary, Becky, and the rest, my emotions became frazzled all over again. I was sure there were moments in our past adventures when I felt just as insecure, just as frightened for the lives of loved ones as I felt now, but I couldn't recall any such moments right now. In the midst of this, I realized how overwhelmingly grateful I felt for Pagag, for his indomitable energy and strength.

Pagag. This was *another* issue that was driving me crazy. I had to remind myself over and over that he was the enemy—an enemy who was attempting to tear my family apart. Okay, maybe that was overstating it. He was only trying to tear Harry and Mary apart. But there was that brief moment—right after he'd saved my life for the second time . . . when I looked at him and felt . . . What the freak-fest was *wrong* with me? I couldn't think about this! So much else demanded my attention. I needed to concentrate on these children.

We finally learned their names. In reality, only the oldest two boys and the oldest girl had permanent names. The others all went by pet names, so to speak. In other words, they hadn't received their "adult" name. Such names were presented only when a child reached seven or eight years. They were given in some kind of official naming ceremony with elders or shamans. The other names were created by loving parents in hopes that their baby survived the precariousness of childhood.

The oldest boys were Chitam-Tok and Zoram-Pakal, although they seemed perfectly happy if I just called them Tok and Pakal ("Zoram" was the only "Book-of Mormonish" sounding name of the lot, though for Pakal his first name was more of a surname, or tribal name.) The girl was Jūn-Kala, whom I called simply Kala. The five-year-old boy's pet name was Bird-Bringer, which made no sense to me, though I didn't ask for an explanation. The four-year-old boy was Monkey-Swing, which made *perfect* sense, as he was the most rambunctious of the lot. Tok's five-year-old sister was White-Petal. The four-year-old girl was Eye-Pleasure. The three-year-old girl, whom I had first helped from the hole was Many-Kisses—a name I liked very much—while her younger sister, the two-year-old, was Laughing-Smiling. I liked this name the very best, though I realized it might take some time before such a name would again describe her personality.

I admit we didn't make it very far that day. The children were still very weak. Despite my splint, I carried Laughing-Smiling the entire distance. Pagag, on the other hand, had the exhausting task of carrying both Many-Kisses *and* Eye-Pleasure. We traveled until we arrived at the crumbling remains of a stone structure many centuries old. It was on the edge of a low bluff and seemed like a relatively safe place to camp, offering a decent view of the valley to the north and south.

Pagag searched for more food, aided by Tok and Pakal. They returned an hour later with a wild turkey (again the handiwork of Pagag and his sling) many armfuls of burgundy-colored berries, cactus fruit, and pale mushrooms that grew like a fungus on the bark of large trees. (Then again, mushrooms *are* a fungus, right?)

The oldest boy, Tok, seemed to have been born for the job of de-feathering and cleaning turkeys. He was finished in minutes. We made a small fire in the corner of the ruins, cooking only thin strips of meat threaded on green sticks. As the sun began to set, turning the clouds to the west into a massive tangerine-colored cauldron, Many-Kisses looked up at me with her enormous brown eyes and said, "Are you going to be my new mother?"

I hugged her tightly, trying hard not to cry. "I don't know, little one. But I promise you—" I looked at all the children. "—I promise *each* of you—we will do everything we can to protect you until you're safe in the hands of people who will love you."

Monkey-Swing and Eye-Pleasure smiled widely, while others looked guardedly hopeful. Some looked as though they wouldn't have cared one way or the other.

It was only a few minutes after filling their bellies that everyone curled up together and fell asleep. Jūn-Kala and White-Petal fell asleep sobbing quietly. I heard one of the older boys—I think Zoram-Pakal—whispering prayers to an object that had been hanging around his neck—a clay figurine of some sort. Laughing-Smiling dropped into a deep slumber in my arms. As I rocked her, I began gently singing the song "Butterfly Kisses." Pagag stared at me from across the fire. He kept right on staring until I had finished singing.

His ogling was making me uncomfortable.

"*What?*" I demanded.

He became self-conscious, fumbling as he said, "I-I just—I was just listening to your song. You have a very . . . soothing voice."

"Thank you," I said. I decided, in light of my objectives, that I would milk the compliment a bit. "My choir director in church told me I had potential. She said I should take private voice lessons, but I was always too busy."

"You don't need any lessons," said Pagag. "It is your sacred gift, and needs no improvement."

"Thanks," I said. "That's a kind thing to say. But I think any gift or talent can be improved."

He fidgeted some more, then he said, "I want to apologize, Steffanie. For my behavior, I mean. You were right before. My reasons for coming here were . . . not altogether altruistic."

"No problem," I said, waving it off. "Apology accepted. You've certainly proven your worth."

He rambled on, "I also want to apologize for the way I have treated *you*. I have not been very civilized."

"It's fine. Don't worry about it—"

He interrupted. "But *mostly* . . . mostly, Steffanie, I want to apologize to you for . . . my misjudgment . . . of you. I did not realize how . . ."

I raised my eyebrows, waiting.

". . . how *good* you were."

"Okay," I said, a little self-consciously. "Always good to be good."

This was a surprise. I seemed to be gaining favor in his eyes despite my earlier blunders and the shattering of every rule of feminine flirtation. Strangely, I didn't feel like gloating. My plan had been that as soon as I saw the least progress in my objectives that I'd capitalize on it by turning up the charm even further. I didn't feel like doing this either. Or maybe I *did,* but . . . I guess I didn't feel as "in control" as I was hoping. Instead, I felt terribly self-conscious. I was afraid I might even be blushing. I wanted to see a mirror. Fortunately there was no mirror within at least a millennium. One look at myself and I'd have certainly screamed and fainted.

*Oh, brother!* This was all wrong! *Snap out of it, sister,* I told myself. He was a jerk! *Jerk* with a capital "J," remember? Besides that, he was a *Jaredite.* Twenty-first century women did not fall for Bronze-Age bozos. Of course there was always Melody and Marcos. And Harry and Mary. But those relationships were different. *Very* different. Soon Pagag would be back with his family, preparing to journey across the ocean. Nothing would change this. It was in the Book of Mormon, for criminy sake!

*Remember the goal,* I told myself. The goal was simply to get this guy out of our lives so he could go back to his happy world in the third millennium BC and never bother us again. Somehow I had to get my head on straight. And *fast.*

I suddenly realized there was an awkward silence between us. Actually, it wasn't difficult to dispel. I yanked my mind back to reality by looking at the sleeping toddler in my arms.

"Oh, Pagag," I mourned, "what are we going to do? All of these children . . ."

"We must find another village. One where more persons live who belong to the kinship you call Lamanites."

"Yes. But what if the village won't take them in?" Anxiety was percolating inside me. "We don't have *time* for this, Pagag! We still have to find Rebecca and my brother. What if we've lost them entirely? I feel certain now that they're in the hands of wicked Nephites."

"You do?"

"Yes. But a different army from the one that attacked that village."

"Or it's the *same* army," Pagag countered, "except that it back-tracked. When these Nephites captured Gid, Micah, Harry and the rest, they might have been on their way *back*—returning from caves of sacrifice like the one in those cliffs."

"Well, then," I said, "they obviously decided not to return to fetch their nine remaining victims. And they completely left out to dry the four men who were guarding them. Why would they do this?"

"I suspect something happened. Something that made them march back to their own territory sooner than planned. Maybe they desired to take Harry and the others to their leaders."

I pondered this, and said, "If the army that kidnapped Harry and the others was Nephite, it might explain something else."

"What would it explain?"

"Well,"—I strained to piece it together in my mind—"the thing that confused me yesterday was that Gid, Harry, Micah, and Jesse would just *let* themselves be captured. They went without a fight. I think when these men identified themselves as Nephites, it surprised them—especially Gid—and put them off their guard. After all, Gid is *one* of them. He might have felt that being taken prisoner was all a big misunderstanding—one that might be quickly resolved as soon as they explained themselves, maybe to some higher-up Nephite commander. As a precaution, though, they weren't about to tell them about you or me. Gid would have professed up and down that he was a Nephite and therefore on their side. Harry wouldn't have realized what century it was right away. He wouldn't have grasped how vile these men actually were. As I mentioned earlier, Nephites weren't *always* despicable murderers like the ones who attacked that village. In Gidgiddonihah's day they were righteous and God-fearing."

Pagag grunted. "Well, it appears that today they are as bad as—or *worse* than—the soldiers of King Nimrod. It is truly a dark time when a people once righteous turn to wickedness. The judgments of God will be upon them."

I nodded, not bothering to explain how accurate he was. Nor did I express to him my concern that we might be right in the middle of it—right in the middle of the final conflict between two mighty nations. I wasn't sure just how close we were to the Nephite destruction at Cumorah, date-wise *or* geographically, but one thing seemed certain. If this was indeed the era where the Lord had chosen to bring us—the world where Joshua had become lost in time—before this was over it was possible that we might gain a lesson in corruption and wickedness beyond anything that we had yet endured.

NOTES TO CHAPTER 6

The practice of changing a person's name as they grow older or at certain phases of life, as described for the Lamanite children in this chapter, is common in many Native North American and Mesoamerican cultures. Among the Aztecs, for example, a child was given their first name a month or so after their birth with the assistance of a community's astrologer or shaman, and that name might be changed several times throughout their lives according to significant accomplishments, noteworthy events in their community's history, ranks obtained, or for other reasons. Among many tribes of Mesoamerica, naming a child was a very careful and sacred undertaking, and was often attended with fasting, prayer, and other rituals so that the most appropriate name was selected (Bray, Warick, *Everyday Life of the Aztecs* [London: B.T. Bratsford Ltd.], 1968).

# CHAPTER 7

## Marcos

After Josh—or rather *Captain* Josh—left me and his father alone in his tent, we sat in silence a long moment. Garth's shock over seeing his son and listening to his words was no less than I would have expected. He bowed his head and wept. "I've lost my son. I've lost my boy."

Not only was he missing seven years of Joshua's life—the years when a boy becomes a man—but I knew that he also feared he may have lost his son to the same darkness that presently had a stranglehold on the Nephite nation.

I stewed over the things Joshua had said. He'd accused me of cowardice and betrayal, saying I would not fight for my people, the Nephites. Even as a child I knew he did not approve of my life choices, implying that I was foolish—even weak—for wanting to live in the twenty-first century. He seemed to care nothing for my reasons, all of which related to Melody, the love of my life. Her fragile health demanded that I remain in the future. I'd assumed that Josh would understand this as he matured. It now appeared that his disapproval had only intensified.

And yet, to my unexpected distress, his words reverberated inside me. I scolded myself. Feelings of culpability were ridiculous. I'd done all that I could for my people. I'd served them as a missionary for four years, all the while putting off my personal desire and ambition to reunite with Melody. I confess, realizing the present condition of the Nephite nation, it was hard not to feel as if all my efforts to preach salvation to them had been for naught, even if such efforts were more than three centuries past. But should I have blamed myself that their nation had finally succumbed to avarice and pride? What could I have done differently? What could *anyone* have done?

Yet I did feel guilt. Joshua declared that Mormon had not given up on his people. Mormon had known the fate of the Nephites all of his life. He'd read the prophecies. The words were confirmed to him by the Spirit. Even so, he continued his labors as their general and prophet. He would love them and serve them to his dying breath. I had to confess, a thick vein of that love was also rooted in me. I wished there was something I could do to change the course of events. But for now I would not dwell upon my own feelings. Rather, I sought more than all else to comfort Garth.

"We should eat," I told him. "There's much food here."

He shook his head. "You eat. I can't."

"Garth—" I waited until he looked at me before I continued. "—your son is alive. As long as he's alive, there's hope for his heart and soul. I don't believe he's as hardened as he makes himself out to be. It's a mask that he's been forced to wear for many years."

Garth looked away again. "I've read that verse of scripture a hundred times, and never imagined the connection . . ."

I squinted in confusion. "What are you talking about?"

Languidly, Garth reached for his backpack. He found a side pocket and pulled out his dog-eared triple combination. Seconds later, he'd opened to Mormon, chapter 6, verse 14. I knew the content of that chapter. It spoke of the aftermath of the great battle at Cumorah. The verse in question listed many of the war commanders who had fallen.

Garth read: *"And Lamah had fallen with his ten thousand; and Gilgal had fallen with his ten thousand; and Limhah had fallen with his ten thousand; and Jeneum had fallen with his ten thousand; and Cumenihah, and Moronihah, and Antionum, and Shiblom, and Shem, and Josh—"*

He stopped on that name. My heart stuttered inside me. I took the scriptures from Garth's hand so that I might read it myself. As I did so, Garth finished the verse from memory.

*". . . and Josh had fallen with their ten thousand each."*

I read it a second time. And then a third. The name was there. A Nephite captain named Josh. I looked up at Garth, still unable to speak.

Again, Garth repeated the lament: "I've lost him, Marcos. I've lost my son."

"No!" My lungs felt devoid of breath. "That can't be what it means. It is not referring to your son. There must be another Nephite captain by that name."

He spoke listlessly. "I wouldn't dare to hope so. And the scriptures do not lie."

Again I shook my head. "There must be an explanation. Another possibility."

Garth didn't reply. The man appeared completely drained of hope, as pale as the inside of a seashell. I couldn't stand to see this. It didn't feel right. I looked again at the verses in question. I tried to imagine the circumstances under which they were written, and again I came at him with a similar logic. "These verses were written in mourning, Garth. They were not written for historical accuracy."

Garth would hear none of this. "No, Marcos. I appreciate your efforts to . . . to comfort me. But those verses were written by a prophet of God."

I persisted, offering a counter interpretation: "A prophet who said that the Book of Mormon might contain the mistakes of men."

He stopped me again. "No. You can't say that. Moroni said he knew of no fault in the record—"

"Is it a 'fault' if Mormon, while recounting the destruction of his people, makes an error regarding the fate of one of his captains? I would not call this a fault. The Book of Mormon was written by men. Inspired, yes. Perfect, no. And this may be nothing more than a simple error in record keeping."

He looked up at me with sad eyes, but behind them I also thought I saw the vaguest glimmer of hope.

I grabbed hold of that and continued. "With all that we've experienced—all the miracles and complexities of time travel—you cannot discount possibilities that are beyond our understanding. You cannot give up hope."

He continued to look into my eyes. At last, he took my hand. He held it tightly. Then he brought forth his other hand, laid it over the top, and held it tighter still. His eyes remained moist, but it seemed to me the fires of hope were faintly burning.

He smiled wanly. "Thank you, Marcos."

Garth never acknowledged that I might be right. But at least my words gave him enough peace of mind that he managed to sleep a little. Neither of us had felt inclined to eat. Refusing to waste good food, I gave our meal to several large, shorthaired, long-snouted dogs that were tied up a short distance from our tent. Guard dogs, I presumed, or else hunting dogs, perhaps for tracking spies and deserters.

Afterwards I lay uneasily on the floor of the tent. A strange feeling circulated inside me that went beyond the other stresses of the day. I felt, even though Joshua had rescued us, we were not altogether out of danger. I couldn't pinpoint a reason for this. I tried to blame it on the curious stares I received from sentries as I fed our meal to the hounds. Or perhaps it was the fact that—except for Joshua—no one had spoken a single word to us. There was more darkness in this place than the darkness of night. I sensed a most disturbing spirit—one that I hadn't sensed in a long while. Not since Jacobugath, in the palace of my father. I remembered that I had always felt this blackness in the presence of Balam, my father's assassin and occult advisor. I can give it no other description than the spirit of evil. Evil itself seemed to be lurking in this army camp. Because of it, I found it very difficult to close my eyes.

In the darkness I managed to fish out of my backpack something that even Garth was not aware that I had brought. It was a firearm—a Glock 30, .45-caliber handgun. I did not inform Garth that I had it; I felt sure that he would disapprove. Garth Plimpton was a man of uncompromising peace. I'd heard him once proclaim that he had never been forced to end the life of a single soul in all of his exploits as a time-voyager. God had protected him; there was no cause for arming himself with guns or other weapons. I, however, had a different outlook. I had sworn an oath that I would protect my loved ones and the people of God's covenant. Therefore, I felt justified in bringing it along, secretly hoping that I would never have to use it. Nevertheless, I brought no additional ammunition—only the ten rounds already in the clip.

With the Glock by my hand I managed a few hours of guarded slumber. But sometime in the wee hours of morning, I was awakened by a curious sound. My eyes opened and turned toward the right side of the tent—the west side—where the light of the moon gave the trees of the forest a faint silhouette against the tent's rough maguey-fiber canvas. For a scant instant after my eyes had opened, I saw movement. It was only for a split second, but I perceived amidst the other silhouettes of trees and foliage that a human shape slipped into the darker shadows on the south side of the tent. Immediately, I felt for the gun.

For several minutes I waited. At first there was no additional sign of movement; not a sound beyond the steady buzz of morning cicadas and the distant roar of howler monkeys as they anticipated the coming dawn. Yet I knew that something was there—just behind the thin canvas wall on the south—just beyond the place where Garth lay sleeping in the captain's hammock that had been originally set out for his son. Who or what was standing on the other side of that wall? I knew that the sentries were all positioned on the northern side of our tent, on either side of the opening. I had only seen that lone vague silhouette, and yet all my senses shouted that something deadly was lurking behind that canvas.

I heard a small rip—like the sound of a knife plunging through woven material. As I heard the whisper of tearing fabric, I raised the gun and pulled the trigger. But I did not fire into the center of the canvas. Instead I fired high, toward the peak. My intention was not to kill—only to frighten. At that I succeeded because the ripping ceased and I heard a pair of feet scuttling quickly away.

The blast of my handgun resonated across the encampment. I heard Garth come to his feet and a clamor of voices.

From the darkness, Garth spoke to me. "Marcos, what have you done?"

"I think I just saved your life."

Within moments I could see the light of oil lanterns on their way toward the tent. Several of Joshua's men burst through the entrance, finding me and Garth on our feet.

"What has happened?" The inquirer was a man with a nasty scar down the center of his chin. "What made that sound?"

The gun was still in my hands. At the moment I didn't trust anyone. For all I knew, the assassin who'd tried to cut through that canvas had backtracked and was now one of the men standing in our entranceway.

I showed them the Glock. "It's called a gun. I would not advise any of you to come closer. This is what made that hole in the canvas."

In the lamplight they could easily see the bullet hole. They could also see where the assassin's blade had sliced a wide opening, almost to the ground.

I addressed the Nephite officers. "Where's Joshua? I want to speak with your captain."

At that instant Captain Josh pushed through his men and came before us into the center of the tent. "What's this about?"

He glared at me as he took in the gun. He also noticed the damage in the maguey fabric.

My tone to Joshua was bold. "I believe I prevented a murder. My own. And that of your father. An intruder tried to cut his way in."

Joshua stepped closer to examine the bullet hole. Then he turned brusquely to the man with the scarred chin. "Kigron, where were the guards?"

Kigron answered. "Nompak and your other bodyguards were moved to your location."

Josh clenched his fists. "Then who was guarding this tent?"

Another man with long black hair stepped forward. "Gabriel and Urihab, and whoever else was in their detail."

"It was Urihab's hour of the watch." A puffy-faced man had spoken, no doubt the one called Gabriel, attempting hastily to cover his hind end.

All eyes turned toward a lanky warrior who stood just outside of the tent.

Urihab made no effort to deny blame. "It's true. It was my watch. But I saw nothing. And I heard nothing before the thunderclap made by this man's silver weapon."

I had my own suspicions that Urihab had fallen asleep, but I did not say it.

Kigron may have drawn the same conclusion. He announced the consequences of his dereliction. "Bind his arms! He will be interrogated and flogged!"

"But I am innocent! I did not see anything!" Urihab's pleas didn't stop several men from hauling him away.

Joshua spoke to his father. "Are you all right?"

Garth nodded. "Yes."

"Did you see anyone's face?"

"No. I was asleep. The gunshot awakened me."

Josh turned back to me.

I answered before he could ask. "No. I saw no one's face. But . . ."

"Yes?"

I tried to concentrate—tried to remember. There was something about the human silhouette that I had seen. Something about the shape of his head. The image was too vague. I couldn't come up with any words to describe it. Shaking my head, I said to Joshua, "It's nothing. I saw only a shadow. But I don't think the intruder was looking for me or your father. I believe he was looking for you."

At that the man named Nompak stepped forward. "He's right, Captain. None but the senior officers would have known that you were not sleeping in your tent." He referred to me. "This man has thwarted an assassination attempt on your life. There is no doubt that he saved the life of your father."

Joshua stared at me. I saw a flash of gratitude in his eyes, but then he turned away and examined the bullet hole in the canvas, poking his finger through it. "You aimed high."

I wasn't sure I heard him correctly. "Pardon?"

Josh turned around. "You deliberately aimed high. Why did you miss?"

I scowled. "It is not my habit to kill everything that moves, Joshua Plimpton."

Joshua stiffened. His officers were also gaping in surprise. I realized I had spoken foolishly. His comment may not have been meant as an insult, just as an inquiry. But now I had insulted him in front of his men.

Joshua stepped forward and held out his hand. "Give me the gun."

My chest sank. I would have done anything to help him save face with his officers. I would have bowed down on my knees before him, but I wasn't about to give up my firearm. In this place, among these people, I felt as though my life was as fleeting as a gossamer breeze without it.

My grip on the pistol tightened. "I will not."

The tension thickened. I could have cut it with a sword. Several of Josh's men started to slowly ready their weapons, but no one drew nearer. They had heard the gun's explosion. They saw the hole in the canvas. Despite the fact that none had ever seen a gun, they knew instinctively that it could blow their heads off.

Joshua clenched his jaw and hissed, "You still don't understand, do you, Marcos? This is my encampment! I am in command. I order you to give me that gun."

I shook my head. "It's you who doesn't understand. I brought this weapon to protect my life, and the life of your father. This pistol is the only insurance I have of returning home to my wife, Melody, and my son, Carter."

I'd mentioned people whom Josh had once loved in hope that it might ignite some spark of compassion. His face was crimson with fury. It seemed an act of heaven when our standoff was interrupted by the voice of another of Joshua's officers, a short man with gray-streaked hair and a dour face. "Captain Josh!"

I felt sure Joshua was grateful for the interruption, yet he turned grudgingly to his officer. "What is it Ammonchi?"

"Our tracking hounds. They're dead. All three."

This news was distressing, but it wasn't immediately clear what it had to do with matters at hand, as was evident in Joshua's exasperated reply. "Why do you rush in here with this news?"

The warrior named Gabriel understood immediately. "Because that man gave the hounds your food—your meal from last night." His knobby finger was aimed at my throat.

Joshua faced me. "You fed the dogs with the food delivered to my tent?"

"Yes. We weren't hungry. I saw the hounds and thought—"

"*Poisoned!*" The declaration had been made by Nompak. Apparently he was some kind of security guard. He was a strange-looking Nephite with a long, skinny neck that seemed disproportionate to his muscular trunk and bird-thin legs. I'd also noticed that his eyes were discolored. In fact, they had *no* color—no pigment at all. Just black pupils and gray irises inside an egg-white ball. If he hadn't been making eye contact with those around him, I might have presumed he was blind.

Expressions of outrage followed Nompak's declaration, some that I judged sincere, and others . . . I wasn't quite sure. But when their accusations began to be directed at me, I shook my head in astonishment. How was it that Joshua had surrounded himself with such imbeciles?

Ammonchi leveled the first accusation. "The man called Marcos slipped something into the food! He tried to poison Captain Josh!"

Other voices were quick to follow. "He killed the dogs so they could not track him!"

It was immediately apparent that Joshua was not buying this. Hate me, Joshua might. But he at least had the wherewithal to dismiss such a theory out of hand. But only after Joshua's expression revealed his doubt did his men also seem willing to dismiss it.

Kigron proffered the most obvious theory. "No, it could not have been Marcos. It would have to have been poisoned before it arrived at the captain's tent."

Muscles stiffened as the men realized what this meant. Someone whispered the word, "Treachery!"

"There is a villain among us!" This exclamation had come from Nompak. "A traitor who would murder our captain!"

Everyone looked at each other's faces with doubt and suspicion.

Kigron turned back to me. "Who is the assassin? Who was outside the tent?"

I shook my head. "I saw no one. He ran away."

"Then he is not among us," said Ammonchi.

"He fled the encampment," said someone else.

There erupted such a flurry of outrage and speculation that it became difficult to hear one voice over another. I searched the faces of Joshua's men, wondering if I might glean something from any of the men's expressions. I tried to remember everything about the shadow that I had seen through the fabric—the height, body shape, or some feature of his silhouetted face. There was only that dim image of something strange about the top of his head. I simply had not seen enough to draw any conclusions. The behavior I witnessed now made it evident that cageyness and distrust were epidemic here. Each officer seemed afraid of the other. The assassin who'd tried to cut his way into the tent would not have known that Josh was sleeping elsewhere. This, at least, seemed to clear most of the higher ranking officers of wrongdoing. But what about the poisoned food? I watched Joshua. Every muscle in his body was rigid. Yet he appeared uncertain, indecisive. It seemed this young captain had never faced anything like this before.

Finally Joshua raised his hands. "Silence! Everyone! I want my tent cleared of all but my Snake Seeker, Banner Chief, and Head Jaguar Knight! Guards will return to their posts. All other Jaguar Knights and officers will awaken their contingents and make ready for the day. It's nearly dawn. *Out!*"

The tent was cleared within seconds—all but Nompak, Ammonchi, and Kigron. Garth and I looked at one another, wondering if we had also been dismissed. Joshua's father seemed to have recovered some animation in his features. Amazing what an immediate crisis can do to restore energy and vitality. But as Garth took a step toward the tent door, Joshua stopped him.

"No, Father. You and Marcos remain."

Joshua paced in the midst of his head officers as Garth and I looked on.

Kigron asked a question of Ammonchi. "Who prepared and delivered the captain's meal yesterday?"

Ammonchi shrugged. "Gimnah, as usual. I will arrest him."

Joshua protested. "No. Gimnah is a good man. Question him. Find out who was helping him."

Ammonchi was apparently the Banner Chief. I guessed this was like a personal secretary. He was an older Nephite with what seemed like a permanent expression of grief. I guessed that he provided to Joshua much advice on how to command troops. I couldn't help but wonder if an old warrior like Ammonchi resented having to serve a young captain like Josh.

Nompak, the Snake Seeker, offered a solution. "I will appoint a taster. You will eat nothing before it has been sampled by others."

Snake Seeker was an interesting title. Nompak was a security guard to be sure, but my impression was that his position involved more. I wondered if he was almost like an "anti-sorcerer." Maybe he was a sorcerer himself, trying to defend his leader against other sorcerers. Tonight's pandemonium seemed a direct result of his failures. I could see the remorse in his face. But was it remorse or something else? Could it have been disappointment?

Joshua nodded absently to Nompak. "Good."

Kigron spoke next. "But would the man who poisoned the food be the same man who tried to cut through the tent?"

It seemed a worthwhile question from Josh's second-in-command. Or was this simply part of the Head Jaguar Knight's ruse to direct attention away from himself? I shut my eyes and tried to shake off the frustration. Josh was in quite a predicament. They might *all* be his enemies. I could think of nothing more terrible for a military leader than wondering if all of his allies are false.

"For now we must assume there is only one assassin." This was from Ammonchi.

Josh bristled at this suggestion. "We will assume *nothing!*"

His officers were surprised by the outburst. Josh appeared exhausted. He dismissed his men with a wave. "Go. Start your investigations. Make ready for the day."

Kigron made a tentative inquiry. "Will you go to the earthworks at Archeantus as planned?"

"No." Joshua looked over at his father, who had remained silent during the entire exchange.

Garth looked tired and worn, but there was nothing but empathy in his eyes.

Josh looked back at Kigron, a new resolve—perhaps even a growing enlightenment—burning in his heart. "I will go to Cumorah. I will seek an audience with General Mormon."

\* \* \*

Joshua

There were heated protests when I announced my plan to seek an audience with our chief commander, Mormon. Kigron reminded me that leaving my post with so many rumors of a gathering Lamanite army might cause the Nephite leadership—especially our oft-vindictive chief judge, Zenephi—to revoke my command. Ammonchi worried that my men might view my decision to leave in the face of two assassination attempts as an act of cowardice. I told them that my decision was final, and I informed Kigron to take command until my return in a few days. Nompak and Ammonchi would accompany me with one hundred of our elite Jaguar Knights to the city of Zenephi at the base of Cumorah. Beyond that, I offered no explanation for my actions. Perhaps because I *had* no explanation.

I had no clear reason in my mind for why I wanted to speak with Mormon. Was I seeking advice? What would I say in his presence? Would I confess my true identity, as my father had urged? I highly doubted it. Mormon was a reasonable man. A spiritual man. But he would never allow a lunatic to command one of his armies. I'd become a lowly water carrier in the blink of an eye. Advice. Yes, I could definitely use his advice. A year ago, when I was in council with the other captains, Mormon had placed his hand on my shoulder and said, *"You are very young to be commanding ten thousand men, Captain Josh. I was once where you are now. Know that if you ever need my advice or counsel, I will provide it."* I sensed something unusual in his eyes. I wasn't sure what it meant. Only that it was a serious offer. Now I wondered if it had meant something more.

In any case, I'd never sought an audience with him prior to now. I was a proud, young cuss—that was certain. I'd been determined to succeed without his aid or anyone else's. Now such a meeting with the chiefest of chief captains of the Nephite armies seemed long overdue.

I decided that I would also have Marcos and my father accompany us. I'd considered leaving them in Kigron's care. Kigron was my oldest friend among the Nephites and I trusted him fully, but in the end I decided against it. It went against my instincts as a leader. Their presence seemed to erode the morale of my men—especially the presence of Marcos. Then again . . . maybe it was *instinct* that told me to bring them along. Or the whisperings of something else—perhaps a voice I hadn't heard in a long, long time.

I briefly separated myself from Marcos and my father while I donned the regalia of my office as Fox Captain, including headdress and other adornments. I insisted that my officers do the same. If we were to be received at army headquarters at Zenephi, we should look official. During my preparations, Nompak remained close by with a dozen of my most skilled bodyguards. I sensed that he felt ashamed for not having foreseen the assassination attempts. It was true that my life had not been saved by any forethought on his part, but by sheer luck—and Marcos's pistol. Nompak seemed determined to make up for his failure.

He reported to me about my cook. "Gimnah wishes to resign as your meal preparer. He accepts all blame for what happened and confesses that there *were* several occasions when your food was unguarded."

"No," I repeated. "I won't accept his resignation. I do not blame him."

"This would be against my advice," said Nompak.

"Yes, yes," I said tiredly. "But instead of his dismissal, I want to increase the security available to him when preparing the meals of all officers and knights."

Nompak made an impatient grimace. "I fear you do not yet comprehend the danger, Captain. All your routines must change. There are more ways to commit murder than you know, and many among the Nephites who have studied each and every method. The evil winds might bring the 'shadow of death' to your tent. It is created from the dust of bat droppings, gathered in secret caves. When inhaled, this dust will snuff out your life in a few days' time. You may find a tiny black leaf stuck to your shoulder blade or the back of your arm, smeared with a poison that will strangle your lungs. Or you may feel a prick, ever so slight, in the skin of your neck or leg as you pass through the midst of your men. All of these methods could kill you in a matter of hours, and the murderer might never be found. It's your lack of caution that makes you vulnerable."

"I can't live in paranoia," I responded soberly. "I can't behave as if I'm afraid to leave my own tent. I'm the commander of an army."

"No other Nephite captain practices such an open rapport with his men. They know to maintain a safe distance—physically and . . . emotionally."

"I realize that," I replied. "But I want my men to trust me—to know that I would not have them do anything that I wouldn't be willing to do myself. It's not my personality to keep them at arm's length."

"Then you must *change* your personality," urged Nompak. "I do not mean to offend you. I seek only your safety."

I sighed in aggravation. "Thank you, Snake Seeker. I will think on this, and I will try to heed your advice."

"Then also heed *this* advice. Do not take your father and this man, Marcos, with you to Zenephi."

"Why not?"

"Use your powers of reason, Captain Josh. There were no attempts on your life before the arrival of your father and this man. And in both instances, Marcos was directly or indirectly involved. We do not know that he didn't cut the tent canvas with his own blade, or create the lightning from his thunder weapon when no one was standing outside. We do not even know that he did not poison the food himself."

"That's ridiculous," I scoffed. "Why poison the food after I'd already gone to bed?"

Nompak looked down deferentially. "Last night there were some who overheard portions of your conversation with Marcos and your father. It is said that they tried to convince you to relinquish your command and return to your homeland. Is it possible that Marcos would stage these events as a way to manipulate your decisions? Might he have fed poisoned food to dogs as a means to provoke you to abandon your army?"

I gaped at Nompak, then shook my head vigorously. "No. Marcos wouldn't do that. He has no *reason* to make—He would *never* pretend to . . ."

Nompak's question had thrown me for a loop.

My Snake Seeker pressed the matter further. "How can you trust a man who behaves toward you with such insolence? *You!* A Fox Commander in the Nephite army! I fear news of his refusal to hand over the thunder weapon will spread quickly among the warriors. His presence cannot benefit you in any way. How well do you really know him?"

"I've known Marcos all my life," I responded. "Or *nearly* all of it. He's a decent person. Just . . . misguided."

"Misguided in what way? Has he ever practiced the dark arts?"

"No, he . . ." Then I realized Marcos *had* practiced such things, being a former Gadianton. But that was long ago, before his conversion. Before he fell in love with Melody. Before *everything*.

"You hesitate to answer," noted Nompak.

"I *don't* hesitate," I said with irritation. "Nompak, I'll heed your advice on all other points. But my father and Marcos *will* accompany us to Cumorah."

Nompak frowned heavily. "If you do not heed my most *strenuous* advice, how can you expect me to serve you with efficacy? Again, I do not mean to offend—"

"You're coming very close," I said with a tone of warning. "I've made my decision."

That finished the discussion. Nompak and I rejoined Ammonchi and the assembled Jaguar Knights at the edge of the encampment. The sun was shooting rays of morning light across the rolling grasses and scattered forests of the Nephite borderlands. About a dozen servants and carriers were also among the gathering, including my cook, Gimnah, who looked down at the ground in remorse.

Marcos and my father were waiting as well. I noticed that Marcos had changed into the cloak of a Nephite warrior. My father still wore his modern-day jeans and a fresh corduroy shirt. Both were also wearing their twenty-first-century travel packs, and beneath his left arm, I noticed that Marcos was also wearing a shoulder holster for his pistol.

As I arrived, I looked into my father's eyes. They were still filled with pain, but they also had a warm, reassuring glint. I couldn't resist taking his hands as he reached out toward me. I think he realized that embracing me in front of the men would not have been wise, but this simple gesture still gave me a great deal of strength, so much that I almost forgot myself. Abruptly, I straightened my spine and shouted, "Let's move out!"

"Wait," said my father. "What about a prayer?"

The assembled warriors gawked. I heard sniggers among them.

I leaned close to him and whispered, "These are Jaguar Knights. It is not their custom to—"

My father, unfazed, interrupted and said, "No man is too 'elite' for prayer."

His eyes were burning into mine. I gaped a moment; then in a flash, I roused my faculties and announced, "Bow your heads, men! All of you! We're going to have a prayer!"

There was stirring. There were grumbles. Even a few scornful chuckles.

I knew that my Banner Chief, Ammonchi, was no less astonished by the idea as the Knights. However, he quickly barked, "You heard your captain! Bow your heads, you curs! Any man who fails to join in the praying will be severely *flogged!*"

The grumbling ceased. Now it was Marcos quietly chuckling. But the men did as commanded. Heads were bowed. Some even seemed to recall the custom of folding one's arms. For many of these warriors, I wondered if it was the first time they'd ever prayed.

I turned to my father and nodded my consent for him to say it. I could tell that he felt a bit awkward. Not about saying the prayer. I think it was the idea of praying with men who'd just been threatened to pray or be flogged. However, he bowed his head.

*"Father in Heaven, we come before Thee in humility, asking for Thy blessings on this journey. Please watch over us, protect us, and keep us from harm or evil. And especially, Father, watch over my son, Joshua, the captain of these men. Preserve his life, if it be Thy will. Preserve . . . his life . . ."*

He paused. I thought he'd lost his words. Then he recommenced:

*"And if it be Thy will, make it so that we may again be reunited as a family."* Another pause, then: *"Let us receive wise and inspired counsel from Thy servant, Mormon. Let us hear counsel that will bless the lives of each of these men here present. Grant unto them, O Father, a deeper—a more profound—understanding of Thy matchless powers, and Thy infinite mercies. Fill them with an understanding that may save their lives . . . and save their souls. Father, soften their hearts. Enlighten their minds. And plant within them a seed of faith that may grow and flourish. Watch over those who will command in Joshua's absence. And this we ask, in the name of Thy beloved Son, Jesus Christ. Amen."*

"Amen," I said in response.

I heard a few scattered "Amens" among the troops. Some faces flashed resentment. I ignored this and sent my father a sincerely grateful smile. It was so good to hear him pray. There was something healing and soothing about the sound of his voice. The prayer stirred up precious memories from long ago. The feeling was so over-whelming I feared I might shed a tear right there in front of my men. Fortunately, I regained my self-control. Nevertheless, I caught more than a few strange looks from the troops. I observed doubt in some of their faces. Doubt or disapproval. Either way, I had never seen such looks before today.

I drew a deep breath and roared, "All right then! Everyone still alive? Nobody keeled over dead, did they?"

There was light laughter. The ice was broken a bit.

"*Good!*" I barked. "Let's move out!"

Our train of men began marching toward Cumorah. The road was clogged with mud. To the west stretched the marshlands of Ripliancum. Nompak arranged it so that Marcos, my father, Ammonchi, and I walked at the head of the column. Ten Jaguar Knights—chosen for their exceptional skills and prowess—marched on either side of us. Another ten were positioned just ahead. Three more marched a hundred yards up the trail, keeping careful watch of anything out of the ordinary that might reveal itself.

Marcos asked Ammonchi, "How far is it to our destination?"

Ammonchi made a slight scowl, communicating that he did not favor speaking with the former Gadianton. Finally, he replied, "Nine hours."

"We'll be there by nightfall," I added.

My father asked, "What exactly is our destination?"

"Army headquarters at Zenephi," I replied.

"Is that a city?" asked Marcos.

"It's our present capital, named for our chief judge."

"*Current* chief judge?" asked my father.

I nodded. "Zenephi was—is—a war hero to this people. He fought in Mormon's army long before my time, and was chief captain of the army after Mormon went into . . . temporary retirement. When Mormon reclaimed his command, the counsel made Zenephi the chief judge."

My father pondered this. He spoke the name again, as if carefully tasting each syllable. "*Zenephi.* I've read the name before. I believe he was mentioned in the second-to-last chapter of Moroni. And if I remember right, the reference did not place him in the most favorable light."

Ammonchi shot my father a puzzled and suspicious look.

I leaned close to my dad and whispered, "Father, please don't say such things. It provokes . . . questions."

"Sorry," he said regretfully.

Nompak's colorless eyes scanned the surrounding hills, as if he expected enemies to appear at any instant, or some disagreeable event to suddenly erupt. An hour into our march the column was alerted by a disturbance in the tall grass a short distance to the east. A covey of wood partridges took flight, agitated. Many warriors paused, including Nompak. Most dismissed it as a phenomenon of nature, but Nompak became—if it were possible—more wary than before.

He approached me and said, "Captain Josh, we may wish to consider taking the overland road around the east side of Cumorah."

I pulled in my chin in dismay. "What for? That would cost an extra day."

My Snake Seeker considered his next words carefully. "Your original plan for this day, Captain Josh, was to inspect your fortification lines near Archeantus, along the northern perimeter."

"That's right," I confirmed. "So?"

"This plan would have brought you down this very road—at least for another hour."

"Yes. At which point we would have veered north."

"Many have known this plan for a week."

"So what's your point?" I asked patiently.

"I fear we may be vulnerable to ambush."

"From *who?*" Marcos inquired. I realized he'd made it a point to overhear every word my Snake Seeker had spoken.

"I cannot be certain," said Nompak.

"From Lightning Warriors of Teotihuacán?" I asked. "From Lamanites?"

"Or from . . . other factions," said Nompak.

I scoffed. "You mean from *Nephite* assassins? Oh, come now. We have over a hundred men. Who would attack us?"

"There are reports," said Nompak, "that Wolf Witches are very active in this region."

I nodded. "I've heard the same reports. But those vermin are always scurrying about."

Marcos inquired, "Wolf Witches?"

"Disaffected Nephites," Nompak explained. "Men who disagree with the present course of our leaders. They do not support Mormon's policy of self-defense. They favor an all-out attack against Lamanite strongholds—"

"Which would be *suicide*," I said dismissively. "The cause of the Wolf Witches is ludicrous. They hold their meetings in secret caves or hidden places, plotting ways to overthrow Captain Mormon and our chief judge."

"Their numbers are said to have tripled in the past year," Nompak continued to Marcos. "They send bands with painted faces into our former territories to the south, attacking Lamanite settlements—killing men, women, and children. Some believe this is a deliberate provocation of a Lamanite invasion. They *want* a final showdown—believe it will awaken the Nephite leadership from their stupor of—"

"So what does this have to do with our situation?" I asked petulantly.

"I have sometimes wondered," said Nompak, "if there are officers in the regular army who sympathize—and even contribute—to their cause."

"Officers in *my* division?" I blurted out, as if the very idea was nonsense.

Marcos glared at me with exasperation. "You've had two attempts on your life in the past twenty-four hours. Perhaps you should listen to your Snake Seeker."

I struggled to calm myself. It was at moments like this that I feared my weakness as a military leader became obvious. I simply could not accept the idea that anyone might have it in for me. Again, it was my idiotic pride. Wasn't I the young warrior whom Mormon himself had promoted to captain? Wasn't I the boy-genius who'd proven himself an unconquerable battle commander? Why would *any* Nephite want to betray me? Among the Nephites, heroes were hard to come by, and I knew that many had allowed me to fill that role in their eyes. I confess, the attention was very flattering, and it might have dimmed my wits, dulled my natural instincts. Nompak wasn't the first to caution me about moving so freely among my troops, or for the casual, personable manner that I adopted when addressing them.

But despite Nompak's warnings, we passed the fork where we would have turned northward uneventfully. My Snake Seeker seemed to relax.

My father said to me in a low voice, "Have you thought about what you're going to say to Mormon?"

I glanced about before answering. Only Marcos seemed to be eavesdropping, which I decided to tolerate.

"No," I replied. "I mean, *yes*. I will tell him what happened last night. I will seek his advice."

Marcos commented, "Then you *do* believe the villain is likely one of your own men."

I gritted my teeth and said to Marcos, "Keep your voice down."

"I thought I was," said Marcos.

"Of *course* I suspect it," I admitted. "I'm not a complete imbecile."

"That's not what I meant, Josh," my father interjected. "I had hoped, Son, that you might talk to him about . . . other things. Those things that we—"

At that instant one of the bodyguards three yards to my left let out a wretched cry. A lone arrow had flown from the brush and struck him in the abdomen. He dropped to his knees, then fell forward onto his face.

Instinctively, I dropped flat against the roadway. To my right, I saw Marcos drop to one knee. He pulled the gun from his shoulder holster and gripped it tightly in both hands . . .

\* \* \*

## Marcos

I carefully aimed the pistol into the brush, ready to defend Joshua and his father against any object that moved.

Nompak shouted to my left. "Surround the captain!"

Immediately my line of fire was blocked as every uninjured warrior on either side surrounded us in a phalanx, their spears directed outward. Cooks and supply carriers dropped to the ground and took shelter behind their tumpline packs. Bowmen lined themselves along the roadway to our left. Many were already firing into the thick tangle of trees and grasses, though I couldn't spot any particular target.

"Pursue the assassin!" This command was Ammonchi's.

Every warrior except those who immediately surrounded Josh, Garth, and myself charged into the brush. As I stood up tall, I found myself facing Ammonchi. He looked at the gun in my hands. He then looked straight into my eyes. He seemed to vacillate, as if he hated to confess that my skills, or this weapon, might serve a useful purpose.

Finally, he said, "Go with us! Help us apprehend the assassin!"

I hesitated, then nodded. Something about this felt strange. But I did not want to give offense the first time my services had been so boldly requested. Swallowing my misgivings, I crossed the road, leaping over the body of the slain bodyguard, and followed after Ammonchi and the other warriors who were thirsty for blood and revenge. After I'd covered about two hundred yards of ground, I paused and looked about. I was amidst thick brush and grasses as high as my hips. Many of the other Jaguar Warriors, including Ammonchi, had also paused, eyes fiercely scanning the brushlands. Finally, someone shouted, "Over there!" The culprit had been spotted. I ran toward the cry and stumbled upon an open area that offered me a wide view of an elevated terrain to the southwest.

The assassin was standing there, about two hundred meters distant, glaring back at us. He was alone, out in the open. A bow in his hands confirmed his guilt. He looked winded. Obviously he'd been running hard from the scene of the crime. I wondered why he'd stopped, and why he'd paused at a place where he was so plainly visible to his pursuers.

These facts didn't seem to bother any other warriors. Arrows were launched toward the knoll, despite the assassin being well out of range. Other warriors were charging ahead, each one eager to claim the prize of slaying Captain Josh's assailant.

I might have raised my firearm, but something stopped me. I couldn't bring myself to take action. Then suddenly it was too late. The assailant turned and fled toward the south. Ammonchi's seventy-five Jaguars Knights remained hot on his tail, the Banner Chief shouting "After him!" at the top of his voice.

I held my ground. This entire scene bothered me immensely. A suffocating chill seized my chest. I realized that the lone assassin may have *deliberately* paused on that rise. I was now convinced that he'd *wanted* us to chase him!

With my jugular relentlessly pulsing, I ran with all speed back toward the roadway. When Joshua and his remaining contingent of warriors came into view, I realized my instincts were right. Garth, Nompak, and the twenty remaining warriors were under siege.

A horde of men wearing black and yellow face paint was rushing upon them, shooting arrows and hurling spears. At least five of Joshua's defenders had fallen, wounded. Nompak and a dozen other Jaguar Knights were firing back, but the raiders were too numerous—over a hundred. Within seconds the first wave of attackers would reach them, obsidian clubs raised to strike.

I screamed like a howler monkey and started running full tilt. I aimed my pistol into the air and fired. The blast got everyone's attention, but the attackers' charge did not falter. Finally, I aimed my weapon at the lead raider—a man whose axe was poised to strike. His target: the neck of a Jaguar Knight he'd already knocked to the ground. A second blast rang out. By the grace of providence my aim was true; the attacker crumbled. Two more raiders tripped over the fallen man.

I'd nearly reached Joshua and the others. Nompak was trying to shield Joshua with his own body. Joshua, armed with a broad-tipped spear, boldly pushed Nompak aside to meet the oncoming surge. Even Garth had somehow laid hands upon a short obsidian sword, ready to defend himself if necessary.

The painted raiders had heard the discharge of my weapon and watched their comrade fall. Some had stopped their charge, now looking at me gravely. I watched another man hammer his way through until he was but a few short steps from Garth. The warrior's obsidian sword was longer than a baseball bat, and twice its girth. Garth raised his shorter weapon to meet the charge, but I knew he could never withstand that first blow. Again I fired. My bullet cut down the adversary, who tripped and rolled until he came to rest at Garth's feet. Garth looked up at me. I could see his gratitude, but his face was also marked by grief. Garth never gloried in death—even the death of a man who was about to slay him.

The enemy advance was broken. Many of the raiders glared at me with terror-filled expressions. Those at the rear of the charge had seen their fill and turned in retreat, fading back into the dense and tangled brush. The assault was pared down to about twenty determined fighters. My gunfire had reinvigorated Josh's body-guards. They fought with terrible fury. Arrows quickly slew about half of those who remained, while the other half clashed with the defenders. Joshua was among those engaged in armed combat.

As I entered the knot of fighting, one raging assailant broke through and confronted Joshua face on. This raider was the largest and most aggressive warrior of the group—undoubtedly their paragon. His face was painted like the others and he wore a double topknot in his hair. I raised my weapon, but as the two men circled, I couldn't find a clear shot. However, the young captain was getting along surprisingly well. Josh's spear had been knocked away, but he'd managed to retrieve a battle-axe from a fallen knight. With this axe he shattered the stone tip of his opponent's spear. The man now fought by swinging the broken shaft. At last Joshua caught the warrior after he'd missed a swipe, landing a decisive strike on the raider's forearm, surely snapping the bone. The paragon grunted and dropped what remained of his weapon. Joshua was unrelenting. His axe also struck the man's upper thigh, causing him to fold over, reeling in agony.

I realized there were no further attackers. All had fled or perished. At least five of Joshua's bodyguards were dead. Two others were badly wounded. We'd also lost several supply carriers in the crossfire. Joshua did not finish off his opponent. He chose to let him live. Even as the man writhed in pain, the captain began his interrogation.

"Who is your commander? Who planned this raid?"

The wounded paragon spat at Joshua. "I curse you! I will betray no one!"

Josh replied with succinctness. "Then you will die."

The paragon's voice twisted into a savage growl. "So kill me! Why are you waiting, you coward?"

As I looked southward I saw that Ammonchi and the bulk of the Jaguar contingent were returning from their goose chase with the lone assassin. Of a surety they had heard the gunfire. Their pace quickened as they saw the carnage.

Nompak placed his sandal on the paragon's wounded arm. Another bodyguard pinned the raider's unhurt arm to prevent him from pushing Nompak away.

Nompak began his interrogation. "Is this solely the work of Wolf Witches? Or are you in league with Nephite officers?"

When the man hesitated to answer, Nompak ground his sandal into the wound, causing the man to wail.

"I will betray no one!" His voice screeched with agony.

Garth started forward, presumably to put an end to the torture. Joshua also stayed Nompak's actions by placing a hand on his Snake Seeker's back. I was ready to interfere as well, but Ammonchi vigorously pushed his way through to where the attacker lay.

The Banner Chief addressed Nompak and Josh. "What happened here?"

"Can't you see for yourself?" Nompak indicated the bodies of the dead. "Was it your infernal idea to call away three-fourths of our garrison in pursuit of a single attacker?"

Ammonchi bristled. "I gave the order, yes. The assassin was slain."

Nompak screamed into Ammonchi's face. "And while you were slaying your lone assassin, we were ambushed by an army of more than a hundred Wolf Witches!"

I did not take my eyes off the wounded paragon. I watched to see if he would look up at Ammonchi—betray some hint of recognition. If so, the traitor would be revealed. And yet it seemed to me that Ammonchi was already guilty. What experienced officer would fall for such a foolish trap? Either Joshua was surrounded by incompetents, or something far more sinister was at work here. The wounded man barely glanced at Ammonchi. He was either extraordinarily disciplined—even as he faced his own execution—or he had never met the man who'd enlisted his services. I suppose another alternative would have been that Ammonchi was innocent. This was hard to accept. Then again, even I had been momentarily deceived, caught up in the heat of the chase.

Ammonchi spoke contritely. "I am deeply sorry, Captain Josh. I should have foreseen the ambush."

Nompak wasn't ready to accept an apology. "Your sorrow is meaningless! If your captain had been slain, his blood would be on your hands!"

Ammonchi bristled again, this time directly challenging Nompak. "Are you making an accusation, Snake Seeker?"

Instead of answering, Nompak grabbed hold of the wounded warrior's topknot and forced him to look directly into Ammonchi's face. "Do you know this man? Is he one of your kind? A fellow conspirator?"

More loudly than ever, the paragon replied, "*I will betray no one!*"

Ammonchi trembled with ire. But amazingly, he contained his passions and turned again to Joshua, dropping to one knee. "If the captain believes that I am guilty of any crime, I will resign this moment."

"He should resign and face punishment even if he is *not* guilty!" charged Nompak. "For sheer stupidity!"

"Silence!" snapped Joshua. "If you are guilty, Ammonchi, you will face more than resignation. You will face execution. I will decide on this matter later. Until then, we cannot linger here. The Wolf Witches may return, this time in greater numbers. Reassemble the ranks. We will move out immediately."

Garth spoke. "What will be done with the wounded man?"

Nompak grabbed up his knife. "He is of no further use. I will take care of him."

Garth's lungs filled with air to protest, but Joshua saved him the breath.

"No," Josh commanded. "Bind his wounds. We'll bring him to Zenephi. I will interrogate him again before Mormon and our Chief Judge."

The Snake Seeker shook his head. "He will slow us down. His wounds are deep. He will surely bleed to death before we arrive."

"We'll take that chance."

Ammonchi also tried to dissuade the captain. "It's useless. He is a Wolf Witch. They are sworn by a blood oath to secrecy or death. You'll get no more information from this one."

"I have given my order." Joshua turned to walk away.

"Wait," I said suddenly.

Joshua and the others turned back.

I continued to study the paragon's features. There was something about him—something about that double topknot . . . Of *course!*

"That's it!" I said. "The shadow I saw last night—the shape of the silhouette outside the tent." I spoke directly to the wounded man. "It was you, wasn't it? You're the one who tried to cut his way through the canvas."

Joshua and the others were surprised, but they shook it off and watched the paragon's reaction. There was a fatal hesitation. Then he said one final time through his checkerboard-painted teeth: "I-will-betray-NO ONE!"

Joshua stepped closer and glowered down on him. "Who sent you to my tent?"

The man answered nothing. He looked away.

Joshua hissed at him. "Don't turn your head from me!" He stepped forward, a terrible intensity in his frame. Garth read the intensity and reached out to stop him.

"Joshua, don't!" Garth's voice was desperate.

Joshua railed at the man even as his father held him back. "Who are you working for? *TELL ME!* Who hired you to kill me? *Give me a name!*"

Garth pleaded with Joshua. "A name will not help you, son. Nothing this man says will help you if you cannot receive the light and mercy of God! *Please,* Josh!" With tear-filled eyes, he spoke one final, desperate phrase. "You are not one of them!"

Joshua found his father's face. He snapped out of his fit of rage. He even looked surprised at himself, and a little shaken. Then once again his eyes became laser beams. He pointed at the Wolf Witch one last time. "We will continue these questions in the presence of Captain Mormon."

Joshua's eyes swept over us all once more. Nompak and Ammonchi appeared astonished by Josh's intensity, but they also seemed to approve. Finally, the captain turned and walked away, growling at several gawking men. "What are you gaping at? *Regroup! Let's move out!*"

Nompak had been right about the paragon's wounds. The Wolf Witch did not survive the journey. Despite a carefully applied dressing by Joshua's medic, he died four hours later from blood loss. Nothing more came out of his mouth that might have helped identify his co-conspirators.

The skirmish on the road to Cumorah had left everyone deeply distrustful. Nompak and Ammonchi avoided each other like polar magnets, refusing even to look in one another's eyes. Few words were exchanged among any of us for the remainder of our journey.

I checked the clip of my pistol. Only six bullets left. I prayed to God that I would never have to use them even as I slipped the weapon carefully back into my shoulder holster. I also grabbed up the long obsidian club/sword from the body of the man who'd nearly slain Garth. If today's events were any indicator of the future, I feared I would have to resurrect my skills with these ancient tools of death, defending myself and my companions with all the fervor of my soul.

## NOTES TO CHAPTER 7

The concept of "Wolf Witches" is a fictional device created by the author, though the idea of conspiracy and intrigue among the Nephites at this time period is consistent with Mormon's descriptions of widespread corruption.

The brutal methods that Nompak describes to Joshua of assassination and murder are based on techniques still practiced in some rural communities of Mexico and Central America. Non-LDS anthropologist Timothy J. Knab, in his book, *A War of Witches,* documents a blood feud between the villagers of San Martín in the highlands of southern Mexico wherein dozens of people were murdered over the course of several decades of the twentieth century using sorceries that date back to pre-Columbian times.

For example, the murder technique known as the "shadow of death" is achieved by placing amounts of dried bat dung inside the home or vehicle of the intended victim. The dust, when breathed over a period of days, causes sickness and finally death. Only certain species of bat can produce this lethal dung, and it can only be found in certain caves, which are known to experienced witches. These individuals then pass on this information to future generations of acolytes.

Another technique, called the "flower of death," is more complex. A certain black leaf is harvested, and on the smooth side of this leaf—the only surface that can be touched—a mixture of resin and clay is painted. On the other side a small wad of ground obsidian is mixed with the plant poison and fixed with glue made from the pseudobulb of a local orchid. It is placed upon the skin of the intended victim, perhaps with an embrace or a pat on the back, and preferably affixed to the nape of the neck. Even if the victim discovers the attached leaf before the toxins take effect, the person realizes that a witch is out to get them. At that point the power of suggestion and fear is often so strong that it can produce the same result, and the victim dies (Timothy J. Knab, *A War of Witches: A Journey into the Underworld of the Contemporary Aztecs* [New York: Harper Collins Publishers, 1995], 8–9).

Other methods of murder and sorcery are documented among numerous branches of the modern Aztecs and Mayans, intertwined with the complex mystical symbolism of their ancient religions. Few details are given here for the same reasons as expressed by Alma to his son Helaman in Alma 37:27–29.

One shouldn't assume that all Mesoamerican natives support or practice such sorceries. As with most cultures, the majority eschews them, but there's no denying that in many communities ancient mysticism and superstition are deeply rooted in the people's psyche and dramatically affect their daily lives. The scriptures tell us that secret combinations of evil are to be had among all peoples (Ether 8:20). Techniques may vary according to tradition and environment, but the basic objective of seeking power and gain remains the same. As with all forms of evil, the only truly effective and definitive defense against them lies in utilizing the power of God and the gospel of Jesus Christ (3 Ne. 5:1–6).

# CHAPTER 8

## Jenny

*The brothers Barak and Mordecai finally left our tent to participate in prayers welcoming the Sabbath. Jim and I were left alone to continue recovering from events on the hillside. I'd left Jim with a doosey of a cliffhanger the whole time the two Babylonian patriarchs were in our presence. No sooner had they left than Jim brought up the subject again.*

*"What were you about to tell me before? You said something about seeing a vision while unconscious?"*

*"Did I say a 'vision?'" I was still trying to get my head around it.*

*"Was it something different? Are you telling me you had a near-death experience?"*

*"I-I don't know exactly."*

*"Did you see angels? Did someone tell you not to 'go toward the light'?"*

*"No," I said with irritation. "If you'll be quiet I'll tell you. It wasn't a near-death experience. At least not like any near-death experience I've ever heard about. I think it was more like . . . a vision."*

*"Vision of what?"*

*I felt a coldness settle over my flesh, sprouting goose bumps on my arms. Jim saw the change and grabbed my hand.*

*"Take it easy," he said. "Just start at the beginning."*

*"I think it was more like a revelation. But there were images. Horrible images."*

*"Sounds more like a nightmare."*

*"No," I replied. "I saw my family. Something terrible had happened. Something worse than I could have ever expected."*

*Jim listened carefully, making no more comments.*

*"I felt so helpless, Jim. Like there was nothing that I could do to prevent an awful catastrophe from taking place. But then ideas flowed into my mind. I'm sure of it. I felt* hope.*"*

*"I'm still not following very well," Jim confessed. "What kind of cata- strophe?"*

*"I don't know," I said, fighting back tears. "But I felt as though all of them—Garth, Becky—and especially Joshua—were on the brink of destruction. It may have involved your family as well."*

*"My family?"*

*"Though I'm not as sure about that. And the only hope of saving them rested with one person. That person was* here—*in this place and time."*

*"Who? Do you mean . . . the Savior?"*

*"No," I replied. "I mean, yes. The Savior is* always *involved whenever we're at the brink of destruction. He's* always *the One who ultimately saves us. But in this vision I was told that saving my family depended upon someone else as well."*

*"Someone who lives in this era?"*

*"Yes."*

*Jim sighed in frustration. "Are you sure this was a vision? Because maybe it was just a . . . strange, jumbled dream like people have when they're sick or traumatized—"*

*"No," I said emphatically. "It was* real, *Jim. I don't care what you call it—vision or . . . But there's more to it. I was told, before this person could save my family, we would have to save* them.*"*

*He sat back in astonishment. "Save them from* what?*"*

*I squinted, trying to remember. The memory wasn't there. I felt sure this knowledge or inspiration had not been given to me. Finally, I said, "I feel the Lord may have only given me the most important detail."*

*"Which detail was that?"*

*Fretfully, I replied, "That we have to find someone and save them so that they can save my children and my husband!"*

*"All right," said Jim, trying to be calm. "Don't be impatient. I'm just trying to understand."*

*"I'm sorry." I felt emotionally taxed to the last farthing.*

*Jim put his arm around me. "It's okay. It's just . . . It seems so vague. What does this person look like? A man or a woman?"*

*"I'm not sure, but . . . it's someone with a great deal of power."*

*"You mean strength?"*

*"No. Not that kind of power."*

*"Spiritual power?"*

*I pondered that. "Not exactly. . ."*

*"Political power?"*

*I nodded. "Yes, but . . ."*

*"But what?"*

*"Oh, Jim. I know I'm driving you crazy. But it's not exactly political power. More like . . . influence."*

*"So the person we have to find has a lot of influence," Jim repeated for clarification.*

*"Yes," I said simply, though my voice didn't have a lot of conviction.*

*Jim stared at me a moment, then straightened up, determined to give it a positive spin, as my brother always did when he felt he had all the available facts. "Okay, then. A person with great influence. Seems reasonable enough. If that's what you saw in your vision, then I'm sure the Lord will help us to find this person. Might they be in Jerusalem? Do you have any objection to traveling with Barak's caravan?"*

*I nodded. "I think this is a good decision. Yes, I do believe we may meet this person in Jerusalem. It seems . . . right."*

*My brother smiled at me, his expression solemn. "Okay then. We'll cling to that. And there's no reason to stress ourselves. If we remain faithful, the Lord will guide us. We'll pray in earnest, Jenny. We'll do what we know is right and hold to the belief that God will grant us more insight as we need it. He's never left us helpless before."*

*My eyes filled with tears. "Thank you, Jim."*

*He hugged me more tightly.*

*But despite his calm assurance, his unwavering confidence, it was still hard for me to settle down and relax. I think I was just overly exhausted. So much so I could hardly see straight. And honestly, there were many wonderful things to focus on, too. It didn't take much effort to see how blessed we really were—how lucky that Barak and his men had appeared when they did to dig us out of that hillside, and how fortunate we were to be in their care. Clearly, the Lord was still very much in control of our destiny.*

*However, we'd learned many confusing things from Barak and Mordecai. I wasn't sure of anything, not even the time period. Who in the world was Yeshua Ben Abba? He sounded more like a criminal. Definitely not a Teacher of Righteousness.*

*Jim left me alone to fall asleep. I secretly hoped I might have another vision to explain the first one, but it must have been the sleep of the dead, because I didn't even remember dreaming.*

*When I awoke, it was morning. With my Babylonian mantle bundled around me, I went to the tent door. Not many people were stirring. It was, after all, the Sabbath. I was impressed that a caravan would be so faithful. I wondered how many traveling Latter-day Saints of the modern day would have been willing to wait in a motel room all day long to keep the Sabbath.*

*Yet the camp wasn't entirely devoid of activity. I could hear conversation and laughter in several tents. The servants and camel drivers were caring for the animals. I recognized Jim among them, helping Shalman and Aram attach feeding bags to the mules' snouts. I'd been told these two Syrians had been indispensable in bringing about my revival yesterday. My brother saw me and smiled widely.*

*"Morning!" he said. "I'm glad you're awake. You've been invited to breakfast with the women."*

*He indicated the tent wherein resided Hephizibah, the dignified, silver-haired wife of Barak, and also Hananeel, who was the wife of one of their sons. I liked this idea very much; it would give me a chance to thank them for yesterday's kindnesses.*

*"Naturally, I'll be having breakfast with the men," said Jim.*

*Hephizibah and Hananeel emerged to confirm the invitation. As I walked toward their tent, the Syrian named Aram sent me a wide grin, revealing some teeth black with decay. He looked as proud as a peacock. Before I slipped inside, he mumbled to his fellow servants, "She looks well, yes? Her heart began beating again under my very hands!"*

*His companions scoffed and minimized his contribution to the miracle, to which Aram replied, "You should show more respect. Someday I may bring you back to life."*

*Another woman named Marantha was also inside. She was Hephizibah's daughter, perhaps eighteen or nineteen, and unmarried. All of them wore mantles with many layers of colorful silk. Hephizibah wore a violet head covering, while the other two had white head coverings with golden trim. Everything smelled of soft perfumes.*

"How you are feeling, my dear?" asked Hephizibah.

"Much better," I replied. "I slept well. Thank you for everything you did for me."

"I hope you're hungry," said Marantha.

She brought forth a basket covered in delicate linen. Underneath were flatcakes speckled with reddish spice. Before we ate, we prayed, washed our hands in special basins, and poured the water outside onto the parched earth. The cakes tasted wonderful, and they were warm!

"They were baked yesterday," Marantha explained, "but reheated this morning in a brazier. Don't worry. The coals from last night were still hot."

I guessed she said this in case I was concerned about some Sabbath Day rule violation. We also dined on sweet cakes, made sweeter by dipping them in honey, figs, and a creamy white "spread" that had the consistency of yogurt, but tasted like cheese. Our drink was pomegranate juice. I imagined it would taste very syrupy and bitter, but it was quite delicious, mingled with other juices as well. I confess, I was feeling rather famished, so I probably ate more than I should have, much to the delight of my three companions.

As breakfast ended Hananeel asked to brush my hair. They seemed fascinated by its color and softness. I nodded, afraid that if I refused, she'd be greatly insulted. But I learned that "brushing" one's hair in ancient Babylon involved more than just straightening. Hananeel produced a pretty ceramic vial and poured several teaspoons of ointment over my scalp. It smelled very strong—of flowers and animal fats and a hint of sugars, like fruit syrup. Thank goodness I didn't have allergies. Hananeel went right to work combing it in.

Marantha started to speak and stopped herself. She'd had a question all during breakfast, but didn't quite have the courage to ask. Finally, she worked up the nerve. "What is it like . . . to die?"

"Pardon?" I said.

"What do you feel? When you're dead, I mean? Is it all darkness, as taught by the Sadducees? Or is there a world beyond, as taught by the Pharisees?"

Hephizibah drew a breath as if to scold her daughter, but she refrained, perhaps because she, too, was terribly curious to hear my answer.

*I smiled warmly and replied, "I can't remember very much of what happened yesterday. But I don't believe I died in the way you think. I was unconscious. That's all."*

*"They said you had no heartbeat," Marantha protested. "Without a heartbeat you cannot be alive."*

*"Then," I conceded, "I'd have to say I don't remember." I certainly wasn't going to mention my "vision."*

*Marantha turned to her mother and said with resoluteness, "Then I must favor the interpretation of the Sadducees."*

*"Oh no," I said, shaking my head. "I'm not sure exactly what the Sadducees teach, but if they believe there's no life beyond this one, I'd have to go with the Pharisees, at least on that point."*

*"But you said you can't remember," said Hananeel.*

*I paused, then said, "I know this because of other things."*

*"What things?" asked Marantha.*

*"Things . . . I have been taught. And also things I have seen for myself."*

*Marantha wasn't satisfied. "Taught by whom? What have you seen?"*

*"You seem very interested in the subject of death," I commented, trying to soften her eagerness.*

*"You must forgive her," said Hephizibah. "It has been a very difficult year for my youngest. Last winter her heart was broken by the death of her betrothed—a young man of nobility at Shushan, taken suddenly by a fever."*

*I turned back to Marantha and said with sympathy, "I'm very sorry."*

*She blinked a few times, eyes becoming moist, but she appeared no less determined to hear my answer.*

*I sighed and said, "It would be difficult to explain if you have not experienced these things for yourself. But the true Messiah has taught—or will teach—that there is a world beyond this one. There you will have the opportunity to be reunited with those you love. I hope in your life you will see and hear many things that will help you come to this knowledge for yourself."*

*"Do you think I may see and hear these things in Jerusalem?"*

*I stammered, "I . . . I'm not sure . . . "*

*"My father hopes we may meet the true Messiah there. A man named Yeshua Ben Abba. So you have met this man? Is he truly the Messiah?"*

*I shook my head. "No. I have never met anyone named* Ben Abba. *But I have met a man named Yeshua. And yes, I believe He is the Messiah. In fact, I* know *it."*

*The women were wide-eyed. Marantha, almost breathless, said to me, "Will we meet this Yeshua in Jerusalem?"*

*"I wish I knew," I replied.*

*"Then where did you meet Him?" asked Hananeel.*

*Again, I was very careful. "I met Him many years ago, in a place far from here."*

*"Well," said Marantha, "if I see Him in Jerusalem, I will walk right up to Him and ask Him to* prove *that He is the Messiah. Then I will decide for myself. And if He cannot promise me that I will see my beloved Dalphon in some heavenly paradise, I will know that He is yet another pretender."*

*Her tears finally flowed, with her mother and sister-in-law trying to comfort her while I sat there feeling awkward, my hair heavy with ointments.*

*I glanced outside and noticed more Bedouins and horses in the hills above us. Maybe such people* always *loitered near caravan camps. Still, these men seemed unusually restless, pacing, staring, as if trying to get another look at the woman who'd been raised from the dead. They made me nervous.*

*Marantha asked more questions—this time about my home and family and the bandits who'd buried us in the hillside. I tried to give short and simple answers, but she was hardly ever satisfied. I was just on the verge of telling them about my life among the Nephites, and the births of Joshua and Rebecca, when I heard the clatter of horse hoofs.*

*At first I thought the Bedouins had ridden into camp, but as Hananeel opened the tent flap wider, it was clear from the raised dust that more than just a few horses had arrived. My heart faltered, afraid we were about to become the victims of highway robbery. Sticking my head out, I watched several horses gather around the tent where Jim was breakfasting with the Jewish patriarchs and their sons. I guess-timated about fifty horsemen. No one had yet drawn any weapons. This was comforting, because our visitors looked much better armed than the caravaneers. One horseman with a long curved sword trotted past our tent, causing Hananeel to pull the flap closed.*

*I opened it again, but made the gap much thinner. Barak, Mordecai, and Jim were now standing in the middle of the horsemen. The sons of Barak and Mordecai were complaining loudly. No violence had broken out, but it seemed on the brink. Who were these men? What were they demanding?*

*I started to exit the tent. Hephizibah and the other women tried to stop me.*

*"Please," I begged them. "I must see what's happening."*

*Reluctantly, they let me go. As I hurried past our mules and camels, I heard one rider explain to Barak, "Our master insists that we bring the miracle worker. If you hand him over willingly, we will not rob your caravan. Otherwise we are instructed to plunder everything, just as we have done to countless others on this road."*

*One of Barak's more spirited sons said in protest, "The Sicarii will now even plunder pilgrims on their way to festival? And on the Sabbath? Reprehensible!"*

*The lead rider rode up to the young loudmouth. He was a rough-looking chap with a twisted nose, broken so many times he almost appeared to have two noses.*

*He said to the young man in a low, snarling voice, "We rob from the rich and give to the poor—all in preparation for the day of Israel's redemption."*

*Another horseman noticed my approach. He pointed at me and said excitedly, "There she is! She is the one who was raised from the dead!" I recognized him as one of the Bedouins pacing on the hillside.*

*All eyes were gaping at me. I hadn't been the object of so much attention since I was Prom Queen at Cody High School.*

*Jim asked the lead horsemen with the crooked nose, "Who is your master?"*

*"Yeshua Bar Abba," he replied. "He awaits us at his headquarters near Jericho."*

*Barak and Mordecai's eyes lit up. They could hardly believe their ears. I heard astonished whispers as the name was repeated up and down the caravan—"Yeshua! Yeshua! The Messiah!" The patriarchs looked at Jim, seemingly stunned that it was less than twelve hours ago that we'd been discussing this very name.*

*Barak requested confirmation. "Is this the same Yeshua whose name is spoken all the way to the banks of the Tigris? The same who will deliver Jerusalem from bondage?"*

*"The very same," another rider shamelessly proclaimed.*

*I decided it was time to say something. "What does this man want with my brother?"*

*The lead rider's horse snorted, as if in disapproval of my boldness.*

*"That is for Bar Abba to say," replied the horseman with a similar snort.*

*Barak spoke to Jim. "You must go with them. Because of your gifts, you are being granted a great honor! And to think we were witnesses of your miracle!"*

*Mordecai asked the rider, "We would greatly like to meet your master, Yeshua Ben Abba. Is it possible that we—"*

*The horseman interrupted. "Soon all of Judea will meet him. But right now we are in haste." Another rider came forward on a horse. In his hand were the reins of a* second *horse, this time with no passenger on its back. The lead horseman turned back to Jim. "Will you come willingly or must we bind you?"*

*Jim looked greatly perturbed. I felt sure that this Yeshua Ben Abba, or Bar Abba, or whatever his name was, could not* possibly *be any kind of messiah. Nonetheless, my brother realized he had no choice.*

*"Where is the horse for my sister?" he demanded.*

*"We were not told to bring anyone else," the horseman replied.*

*"I'm not going without her," said Jim.*

*The lead horsemen stewed over this.*

*Another rider declared, "Bar Abba may wish to see the woman whose life was restored."*

*"We did not bring another horse," said a third rider.*

*"She'll ride with me," said Jim.*

*The leader made his decision. "Agreed. She'll ride with you. Take your mount. Hurry!"*

*All of the horsemen with their shabby cloaks and shiny swords were looking nervously up and down the highway beside our camp. This confirmed what I suspected. They were criminals. That is to say, they were Jewish rebels. Just as I'd guessed last night, Yeshua Bar Abba was a Zealot, and his men were deathly afraid of being spotted by soldiers.*

*I climbed onto the saddle blanket behind Jim. The rider did not let go of our reins as he turned his mount with the rest of the rebels and kicked his horse into a run. I locked my arms around Jim's waist and hung on for dear life. Our horse wasn't very large. She was red in color and appeared as if she wasn't very well fed. I was afraid she wouldn't be able to carry two people. But what she lacked in girth she made up for in stamina. We kept up with the other riders just fine.*

*I counted fifty-three of them. Fifty-three horsemen. That's how many this Yeshua Bar Abba decided to send after us. Some were the Bedouins who'd been loitering in the hills. Perhaps they weren't homeless Bedouins after all. I thought I had the chain of events pretty well figured out. Certain of the men who'd watched Jim resuscitate me had reported what they saw to this Bar Abba fellow, who then organized the kidnapping. They must have wanted Jim pretty badly. Coming out in the open must have been risky for Zealots. But we weren't in the open for long. Our gang of riders quickly galloped over a hill and into an area of rough country without trails. It wasn't until we were well out of sight of the highway that our horses slowed to a trot.*

*Jim turned to the leader of the horsemen. "What's your name?"*

*"Heli," the man with the mangled nose said stoically.*

*"Well, Heli, I should tell you—what happened yesterday with my sister was nothing miraculous. I'm afraid your master is going to be very disappointed."*

*Heli's expression darkened. He leaned close to Jim and said, "You are right. That would disappoint him. For your sake I hope that you are only being modest. If Yeshua discovers that there is no magic in you, he will have no further use for you. Or your sister. I assume that you understand."*

*We understood. Nothing like a veiled death threat to brighten our morning. It was also a conversation killer, because we spoke to none of them for the next several hours.*

*The day was not particularly warm—even here in the desert. I assumed this was because of the season. But the sun was still bright. I hid my pale, Anglo-Saxon skin as much as I could under my head covering.*

*Some time later the land became more fertile. We crossed the River Jordan at a wide and shallow place north of a main caravan crossing. I heard one horseman comment that the water was "deep"—which I assumed meant deeper than usual. But since it barely reached our mare's belly, we got through with only minimal mud splatters on our Babylonian clothes. From there we traveled south along the river, bypassing numerous date palm plantations.*

At last we arrived at a walled villa near the banks of the river, somewhat hidden by high bushes and trees. The original owner must have been quite rich, but presently the place looked pretty ragged. The grape vines were untrimmed, full of weeds and thistles. So were the vegetable and flower beds. The ground was covered with shriveled dates, unharvested from the previous season. A lookout on the villa's wall spotted us from afar. The gate was hastily opened and then speedily closed behind us.

It wasn't exactly the setting I'd imagined for these rebels. I thought we might be headed for some flea-infested cave. There were about twenty other horses in a stable and corral to our left. There might have been one hundred more rebels inside the property. Dozens of faces watched us dismount. This once-beautiful villa was definitely showing signs of its occupation. Garbage, broken furniture, and pottery vessels were lying about. Part of the stable area had been converted into a weapons dispensary, with broken swords and armor lying about, some awaiting repair, but most discarded. I saw Roman helmets, breastplates, and bucklers among the heaps, either stolen or stripped from dead soldiers. Many of the men were armed with homemade weapons or farm tools that had been converted into implements of death. Somehow Bar Abba and his cohorts had made this villa their base of operations. I didn't want to think about what might have become of the original occupants.

The Zealots themselves were a motley group. Some looked like hardened warriors; others were hardly older than boys. Some looked like they belonged in a barroom or back alley, but others wore clean mantles, and had well-groomed hair and oiled beards. I wanted to sympathize with them. After all, they were freedom fighters—they wanted to free their nation from the yoke of Roman oppression. My own country had been born of the same passion and desire. But I couldn't shake the general creepiness that I felt in their presence—something that hinted that their cause was not wholly pure or noble. All of them glared at us as we were escorted across the stone portico and inside the entranceway of the main building. Several grunted or made huffing noises. They surely must have heard rumors of Jim, the miracle worker, but few seemed impressed by what they saw as he entered their domain.

We entered a large foyer with several burley-looking men seated upon a scattering of ornate but mud-stained couches and chairs. They arose as we entered, but one in particular had a presence that immediately identified *him as the man in charge. He was a large man, skin burned dark by the sun, and muscles nearly as defined as a professional bodybuilder. His hair and beard looked wind-tossed, but his teeth flashed out milk white between his lips in an expression that was either a smile or a snarl. I couldn't tell. I suppose he was handsome in a John Wayne or Harrison Ford kind of way, but there was also something about him that reminded me of a rodent. His beady eyes were alert and bright, and couldn't seem to focus on any one thing for more than a few seconds before they again flitted about, rechecking his surroundings, fore and aft.*

*Heli introduced us. "This is the man from the road to Betharamphtha. And this is the woman who was unearthed and restored to life."*

*"Pleased to meet you!" said the muscle man. "I am Yeshua Bar Abba. Is it true what is reported by my spies on the eastern highways? Are you a man of miracles? Did you breathe the breath of life back into this woman after she'd lain in the grave?"*

*The story had apparently been embellished a little by the Bedouins. But why else would I have been lying in the ground if it wasn't my grave? I looked at Jim's face. Recalling Heli's death threat, I wondered what he would say. I held my breath, knowing my brother wasn't about to lie.*

*He answered very delicately. "I did . . . restore her. But not by super-natural means."*

*"Oh?" said Bar Abba, and he looked suspiciously from Heli to the face of the Bedouin who'd first identified me back at the caravan. "What is this that he says, Punan?"*

*If Bar Abba found out this Punan had caused him to go to all this trouble over false information, it seemed certain his life wasn't worth much more than ours.*

*Punan said in defense, "It was supernatural! I saw it in person! The woman—his sister—was dead of poisoning or suffocation. Her body was already stiff with rigor. And this man—her brother—put his lips to her mouth and blew the breath of life into her lungs. Not only my eyes saw it, but those of Tabor and Azekah and fifty more besides."*

*Bar Abba turned back to Jim. "If not by means that are supernatural, by what means did you do this thing?"*

*Jim searched for a reply.*

*Bar Abba pressed him. "Did you indeed breathe your breath into this woman's mouth?"*

*"Yes," said Jim. "But—"*

*No one heard the "but." Just the "yes," and our escorts immediately started going "Ah ha!" and "From his own lips!" and "It is as I said!"*

*Bar Abba grinned widely, again flashing those teeth. "What is your name, miracle worker?"*

*"James," he replied. I knew his real name was Jamie, but perhaps he was trying to sound biblical. Then Jim boldly changed the subject. "I wish to know why you have brought us here."*

*"Why, to be my guest!" Bar Abba announced. "I am anxious to learn more about you, James. Very anxious indeed. It is undoubtedly the will of God Himself that brings you to us."*

*"Your men brought us," Jim corrected. "Against our will."*

*Everyone in the room—that is, everyone besides Jim and Bar Abba—squirmed nervously because of Jim's curtness. Bar Abba only looked confused. Then he suddenly let out a guffaw that sounded more like the honk of a taxi cab and put his arm around Jim's neck. Up to now my own presence had been virtually ignored.*

*"You must be hungry after your long ride. Are you hungry, James? What about your sister? Is she hungry?"*

Hello! *I was standing right there. He could have asked me directly.*

*Bar Abba started leading my brother into the next room. I think Jim would have resisted, but the whole gathering was pressing around them and following along. It appeared that I would be left behind. I saw several persons lingering behind with me—staring at me the way a dog might stare at a Thanksgiving turkey. These men looked a little too lonely, if you know what I mean. Hastily, I followed Jim and the others.*

*The next room was a dining room, though at present there was no real furniture. Just blankets and mats of all colors, and a spread of platters and goblets and bowls. There was also quite a bit of food, but it wasn't exactly the gourmet fare we'd enjoyed this morning. It was mostly meat—two large lamb roasts, several whole ducks, and other meat I didn't recognize and probably didn't want to know. I might have thought it was laid out for us, but the roasts were half-eaten and much of the duck meat had been torn away, revealing bare leg bones and ribs. It must have been leftovers from the night before. Dirty plates and half-filled goblets of wine lined the edges of the walls.*

*Jim was seated in front of a half-eaten lamb roast. Bar Abba used his knife and personally cut him off a slice. Jim looked around for me and urged me over, probably in an effort to keep me closer. I sat on his left.*

*Jim spoke to Bar Abba. "I'm not hungry. Big breakfast. And I'm still waiting for an answer to my question."*

*Bar Abba put his knife away and folded his arms. "I see that you are a man who does not like to waste time. Very well. Though I am surprised that you have not surmised the reason already. Do you not know who I am?"*

*Jim was reluctant to reply. Finally, he said, "I am told that you are a Zealot—a rebel who would like to free Israel from the Romans."*

*"You have heard well," he said. "But not only from the Romans. I wish to free Israel from all oppressors—the Edomites whom the heathens have made our rulers, and also those betrayers of the House of Hanan who stand betwixt the people and their God. Is this all that you have heard?—a report that I am a Sicarii rebel?"*

*"I heard that some people . . . think you're some kind of messiah."*

*He gaped at Jim, but with a sly smile on his face. A few of the rabble who were seated around us started to chuckle. The laughter increased until everyone, including Bar Abba, was also laughing.*

*After it died down, Bar Abba clapped his hands once and declared to Jim, "And so it is true, James the Miracle Worker!"*

*Bar Abba looked like he was about to say something more, but I interrupted: "We wondered if there might also be another person in the land who people say is the Messiah. A Messiah whose first name is also Yeshua."*

*There were a few more splutters of laughter, but when they realized that Bar Abba did not find the comment humorous, the splutters died away quickly, replaced by whispers and grumbling.*

*Bar Abba pointed a stocky finger toward me and said in a patronizing tone, "Do not confuse the speeches of fanatics for the actions of patriots. Messiah, messiah! There are always a dozen men in Israel who claim to be messiahs. But it is not in the waters of baptism that we will find our savior. It is at the edge of a blade!"*

*Mutters of approval followed this declaration. I began to feel very anxious. Why were we wasting our time talking with these hoodlums? If I could have whispered in Jim's ear, I think I would have tried to convince him to rise up with me and make a mad dash for the door.*

*"Once again," asked Jim, "what does all this have to do with us?"*

*Bar Abba's expression became pensive, as if his eyes were trying to peer into Jim's soul. "I will answer this," he began. "But before I will do so, I* must tell you what my 'eyes and ears' are doing at this very moment across the countryside of Judea. They are spreading the story of you, James. Of your miracle on the Betharamphtha road. By now my eyes and ears will have reached Jerusalem. They are noising it in every tanner's shop and tavern that I will soon be arriving. And at my side will be the voice of one who cries in the wilderness—a man of miracles who proclaims that the Day of Judgment is soon at hand. That man is you, James."

My brother's face went pale. He stared at Bar Abba for what seemed like an eternity. Bar Abba let him stare, determined that it would be Jim who spoke the next words—no matter how long it took. The entire gathering was waiting and watching with the same determination.

Finally Jim stammered out, "I-I don't know . . . know what . . . I don't think you understand what you're saying."

"Ah, but I do understand," said Bar Abba. "My father was a most distinguished Rabbi in Galilee. From his lips were uttered the prophecies of old from morn until eve until I could recite them in my sleep. I know what those fools—the Pharisees and the Sadducees—will expect. I know what they must say to the common people if they are to finally rise up against their taskmasters. They must confirm that the prophecies are fulfilled. They must confirm that every requirement of God's word is satisfied before they will proclaim that the Messiah has at last arrived to break the backs of the oppressors. You see, they are a most particular lot, and if but a single jot or tittle of the law is not met, they will reject in total all that I have to offer. For many months I have been searching for my forerunner, ever since the Roman procurator slew so many of my comrades inside the Temple precincts at the Feast of Tabernacles. I knew that he must be a prophet, a man of the desert, someone who could work wonders before the eyes of many witnesses. I also knew that he would reveal himself before the Paschal Feast. And finally, I knew that when he appeared, I would learn of it and have him speedily brought to my presence." The Zealot leaned back, looking thoroughly satisfied. "So my friend, my ally, my Elias, I have told you. Now I hope you are beginning to understand the role that you are destined to play in the history of the world."

Jim was still looking stunned. But not so stunned that he couldn't shake his head slowly and say, "You've made a big mistake. You don't understand. I'm no one's forerunner. I'm not the person you think I am."

There was muttering among Bar Abba's men.

*Bar Abba leaned forward again and the voices went silent. He brushed away Jim's response. "This is no surprise. I am not alarmed that you do not recognize who you are. I knew that it might take some time to convince you. Do not worry. We have all the day long to discuss it. But let me assure you, my friend, I have made no mistake. I've waited far too long for this day—and for the days which are to come. You are my Elias, James. You are the Forerunner."*

*"Forerunner for what?" Jim spluttered. "For telling the people of Judea that you are the Messiah?"*

*"Yes!" he declared without compunction. "And for telling the people that now is the time to unite! We must unite under a banner of power and strength—that of Yeshua Bar Abba, son of the plains of Geneseret, disciple of the Arbel cliff! You must tell them that they must take up their rakes and shears and pruning hooks and whatever else they can find and at last wage a war of liberation against the Romans and the Edomites!"*

*My brother continued shaking his head. "I can't do that. I won't do that. At the risk of losing my life, I must tell you the truth. I am not who you think I am. What happened in the desert was misinterpreted by those who were watching. I am not a man of mir—!"*

*"Say no more!" Bar Abba snapped with so much ferocity that Jim immediately shut his mouth. The Zealot's face was red with fury as he continued to study my brother. Then all at once, Bar Abba's muscles relaxed and he smiled. After a moment, he even laughed several times from the belly and said, opening his arms widely, "Forgive me, James. My manners are atrocious—no better than a fisherman. But I would not wish for you to speak unwisely before you have a full understanding of what is to come. You and I must continue this conversation, but not here in the midst of stale bread and greasy meat. Come with me to the upper room of this mansion where I have my offices. These are the same rooms where I have met with many of the nobles and priests of Jerusalem who support our cause. Come, Jim. You are not a prisoner here. No true patriot would ever suffer a slave to dwell in their midst. Come as my guest, and we will further discuss the intricacies of our new relationship."*

*Jim looked flustered. He didn't want to follow Bar Abba anywhere, and I didn't blame him. But again, Jim's eyes turned to me. "What about my sister?"*

*"Certainly!" said Bar Abba. "Both of you, come! And also you, Heli."*
*He turned to his men, "The rest of you, fill your bellies and sharpen your*
*swords. Tomorrow begins the first phase of our glorious revolution!"*

*A cheer was raised up, but not with as much enthusiasm as I think*
*Bar Abba would have hoped. Jim's behavior had dampened their mood a*
*bit. No doubt this was why Bar Abba wanted to get us alone and out of*
*their presence. Butterflies were fluttering like crazy inside my stomach. I*
*was afraid that once this man got us alone, we'd come face-to-face with an*
*altogether different personality.*

*My fears proved right.*

*As soon as the four of us entered the upstairs room that Bar Abba had*
*made into his office, he ordered Heli to shut the door. Heli did so and*
*stood there to bar the exit. Not a prisoner, eh? Apparently someone needed*
*to read the meaning of that word to Bar Abba from the dictionary.*

*The room was decorated in murals. There was a painting of the*
*cityscape of Rome, but also of the Jerusalem temple. This told me something*
*about the former occupants of this property. I could only conclude that they*
*were pro-Roman Jews whom Bar Abba had conveniently disposed of. The*
*Zealot leader invited us to sit on a wooden couch with many layers of*
*fabric cushioning. Bar Abba, though, did not sit. He paced back and*
*forth, and for a long time he wouldn't make eye contact with us at all.*

*He finally spoke as if he was speaking to himself, saying, "I am*
*running out of time. All my forces are gathered to Jerusalem for the feast.*
*The time is ripe. The people are waiting. Never has the populace been so*
*hungry, so expectant of the appearance of their Messiah. It all seems so*
*natural in the course of my own destiny. I cannot ignore that the hand of*
*God has carefully laid every stone of my pathway. But it does not really*
*matter what I believe. What matters is what the* people *believe. And*
*what my men believe. They need a messiah—someone to give them*
*courage and strength. Someone who will instill in them a will to fight—a*
*man who will lead them to victory." At last he turned to Jim. His hand*
*pointed toward a curtain that hid a closet or chamber of some sort. "I*
*want you to pull aside that curtain, James."*

*"What for?" Jim asked.*

*Bar Abba gaped at him. It was plain to see that he would explode*
*with anger if another one of his orders was questioned. Jim decided to do*
*as requested before being asked a second time.*

As the curtain was pulled back, I craned my neck to see what was inside. My eyebrows shot up high. The closet was stacked with treasure— gold and coins and jewels and statues and silver dishes and platters and every other conceivable kind of booty. I caught a whiff of cinnamon and myrrh. No doubt Bar Abba had collected all of this over many months— perhaps years—along the highways and byways of Judea. It reminded me of treasure troves from a pirate movie or a book about Arabian knights. I couldn't imagine how many innocent victims that booty represented. Not all Roman victims, either. Much of it was certainly from wealthy Jews like the former owners of this estate—anyone whose politics disagreed with Bar Abba's raiders. I might have guessed what our Zealot host was going to offer next.

"Feast your eyes on the decadence of Judea!" Bar Abba began. "Yet this is only a small sample of the riches hoarded by the emissaries of our heathen Emperor and the corrupted priests of Hanan. And it is only a small portion of the wealth that we will enjoy as instigators of the new order. Go on, James. Choose a golden vessel for yourself. That vessel at your feet with the rubies in the rim is enough to make you a rich man all of your days. But remember, for those who follow me, such is only the beginning. Soon you will have portion in the riches of the whole earth. Riches and power surpassing Tiberius, Alexander, and the pharaohs combined! All you must do is play your part, James. If you are indeed capable of miracles, so be it. But if you are not, it doesn't much matter— so long as the people *believe it*. And *so long as you point to me*, Yeshua Bar Abba, *as the messiah of the Jewish nation*. It is only a small thing, but it will lead to incomparable greatness. What do you say to that, my noble friend?"

Jim continued to face the closet full of plunder. "I say . . ." He turned and faced Bar Abba. "I say no. I won't do it. I can't do it—because I don't believe it. It's not true. I won't be a liar for any man and lose my soul."

Bar Abba's face was emotionless for several seconds. He seemed to be wondering if there was something he might have missed. More words he might say. Something else he could offer. Perhaps there was some nuance of his request that he hadn't made clear. As the weight of Jim's rejection settled in, his face filled with disbelief. I don't think he'd ever met anyone who could turn down an offer like the one he'd just proposed. A moment *later the frustration was visible in his eyes, soon overtaken by scintillating anger. Heli's hand moved to his sword. His eyes watched his master, waiting for the word—some signal that he should carry out his solemn duty and kill us in cold blood.* I swallowed hard. I could feel my heartbeat pulsing in my throat.

"I am . . . very disappointed," Bar Abba said, his voice low and full of poison.

Heli drew his sword. I wanted to move closer to Jim, but Bar Abba stood between us.

The Zealot continued speaking, his tone somewhat lighter. "Disappointed that you are not capable of seeing what I see. How is it that you cannot catch the vision of what I am proposing? Your accent bespeaks the purest of Hebrew dialects! How is it that you do not understand who I am?"

"We know *who you are.*" I almost looked around to see who had spoken. It took a second to realize it was *me*! I don't know where I found the courage, but I added, "And it's not the Messiah. *We* know *the* Messiah. The *real* Messiah. He's a man of peace and love. Not butchery and bloodshed. His name is Jesus of Nazareth."

Bar Abba blanched for an instant. But then he smiled again, shaking his head—not because he thought my words were funny, but out of a sheer unwillingness to comprehend how anyone could be so stupid and foolish as the two of us. His face sobered again and he said, "I weep for you. I weep for you *both.*" He said to Jim, "Are you also thus deceived to believe that something—anything—worthwhile or good can come out of a backwater like Nazareth of Galilee? It is a backwater even to *Galileans!*"

Jim nodded. "I do believe that this Jesus is the true Messiah."

Bar Abba continued pacing. "And you are both willing to give up your lives for this belief?"

With terror in our eyes, but conviction in our hearts, we nodded. "Yes."

Bar Abba, still shaking his head, began to draw his sword. Heli moved closer toward me, watching his master, eager for the gesture of consent. *So this is it,* I thought. *Like so many martyrs over the centuries who'd given their lives for their testimonies of Christ, Jim and I were about to face a similar fate.*

"Very well," said Bar Abba, his sword now fully drawn.

*I thought of my children. My husband. Tears filled my eyes. But despite the pain in my heart, I wasn't nearly as terrified as I thought I would be. I recalled the vision—the revelation that someone would appear to save my family—and to my surprise, I felt remarkably calm.*

Suddenly Bar Abba turned to Jim and asked, "But are you also willing to let your sister die for you?"

Bar Abba sent Heli a signal. The man with the broken nose lunged toward me, sword outstretched. I wrenched out a cry as he seized me around the neck. He held me there, but he didn't kill me right away. I felt the point of his blade pressing under my lowest rib. Jim tried to come to my aid, but Bar Abba stuck the tip of his sword against Jim's belly, stopping him. Both men were well trained in these weapons. It wasn't going to be one of those times when a lucky knockout blow or kick to the groin saved the day. I saw no chance of escape—not this time.

Tears leaped from my brother's eyes. "What do you mean 'let her die for me'?"

"Just as I said," Bar Abba explained. "I have no intention of killing you, James. One way or another, you will act as my forerunner. The scripture demands it. The people will demand it. However, for your present insolence, I will tragically be forced to take the life of your sister."

"Any man can play your charlatan," said Jim, his voice weak.

"Not anymore, they can't," said Bar Abba coldly. "Word has now spread abroad. Fate has chosen you."

"No," Jim pleaded, his voice breaking. "Don't do this. Please."

Bar Abba gave up his pretense of self-control and let his temper flare. "Oh, so now you plead with me? You plead with me after I have exhausted my breath pleading with you?"

"I don't care about my life," said Jim. "You can do with me as you like. But please—please don't hurt her."

"It's all right, Jim," I choked out. "It's all right!"

Bar Abba continued, "If you wish to save her life, I give you the power here and now. Go with me tomorrow to Jerusalem."

Jim dropped to his knees before Bar Abba and said helplessly. "I cannot say the things you want me to say."

Bar Abba pondered this a moment. Finally he blurted out, "All right then! Say nothing! Curse you both! You are worse than Essenes! You will go with me to Jerusalem, James, or your sister will perish this instant!"

*Jim's tears were still flowing, but he was thinking about it. Then slowly his head again started to shake.*

*But Bar Abba wasn't finished. "And if you do this, I will make you a promise. I have but one love in this world—Judea, my people of the House of Israel. If the people of Jerusalem reject me, if they would rather choose a Messiah of words over one of action, I will accede to their will. By the Temple's gold I swear an oath that I will fade away into utter obscurity. And you and your sister may go and freely lick the dust from the feet of whatever miserable messiah you happen to find among the scorpions of the desert."*

*I could see Jim's mind turning. He was trying to think—not an easy thing to do with a sword pricking your belly and another ready to plunge into your sister's ribs. My own mind remained surprisingly clear. Even with this brute's arm choking my neck, I could tell that Bar Abba's offer was a joke. He didn't love Judea. He loved himself. He had no intention of bowing to anyone's will. I was sure he would use my brother for whatever he needed, then kill us anyway. But there was vacillation in Jim's eyes.*

*My brother spoke. "If I do this—if I go to Jerusalem with you—will you set my sister free? This very minute?"*

*Bar Abba pursed his lips, as if he'd bitten into something sour. "Now what kind of an agreement is that? Is it sensible? Is it fair? You must earn your sister's life, James. I assure you, not a single yellow hair of her pretty head will be harmed if you will but journey with me to the Holy City."*

*I was shaking my head. I couldn't believe I was actually shaking my head. But Jim wasn't looking at me. He was looking at Bar Abba, and he said, "And you will not ask me to speak?"*

*"I will not ask you to speak," the Zealot repeated. "Not unless . . . you choose to speak of your own accord after seeing and hearing all that you will see and hear. This is my oath. Now I advise that you make your decision quickly."*

*The sword tip continued poking sharply into my flesh, surely penetrating the cloth of my mantle. I had the feeling Heli was going to be very disappointed if Jim agreed. Killing me was obviously nothing to him—like swatting a housefly.*

*"I'll go," said Jim with a heavy exhale.*

*Heli released me and pushed me toward my brother. Bar Abba lowered his sword and moved aside. I would have tripped and fallen, but*

*Jim caught me. He held me tightly. It wasn't until now that I realized I'd been shivering. My flesh was like ice. I think every drop of blood had gone out of my arms and legs.*

*"There, there," said Bar Abba, mocking us. "You see? I am not a heartless man. But merely a man of passion and conviction. It is my hope, James, that as you get to know me, you will come to understand the forces that guide me. I am, in my heart—as you will doubtless discover—the most peaceful man one can ever know. But alas, the days of peace are at an end. All right. That's enough. Heli, take her away."*

*Heli nodded and grabbed my shoulder. Violently, I shook him off me, indicating that I was willing to walk by myself.*

*"I thought you said Zealots didn't believe in keeping prisoners," I snarled.*

*"But we do enjoy the company of some guests longer than others," Heli replied in an oily tone.*

*"Where will you take her?" Jim demanded.*

*"You needn't worry. You will see her tomorrow. She will come with us to Jerusalem, but in Heli's tender care. You may not speak to her again until tomorrow at sundown. But if you disobey me, or if you say the wrong things . . ." He didn't bother to finish the sentence.*

*I turned to look at my brother before I was led off to another part of the villa. Tears remained in his eyes. Jim's face had a look of deep, anguished apology, terrified of what I might endure in the company of this orangutan.*

*But I wasn't afraid. I recognized now that it was all a matter of faith. Bar Abba and the others thought Jim was a man of miracles. Well, maybe they were right—though not in the way they might have expected. At the moment, we definitely needed some kind of miracle, and if anyone could bring about a miracle when it counted most, it was my brother, Jim.*

### NOTES TO CHAPTER 8

In this chapter the young Jewess, Marantha, mentions differences in belief between the two primary religious parties in Israel—the Pharisees and the Sadducees. These two groups had very different views of their religion, and were both condemned by Jesus Christ during His ministry, along with the Pharisaic "scribes," who were essentially legal specialists who interpreted the law of Moses to determine God's will in every situation, developing more than 600 specific commandments that are not found in the scriptures.

The Pharisees came mostly from lower, middle, and artisan classes in Israel and were considered more in touch with the common people since they lived among them and controlled the synagogues. The Sadducees were mostly from the aristocratic, or land-owning classes. They controlled the priesthood, temple rituals, and finances. The Pharisees believed in the law of Moses as the authority in every facet of life. They also believed in the soul, life after death, eternal rewards and punishments, and angels and demons. The Sadducees denied all of these things, believing that the law was fulfilled in temple worship. Both of these parties were major obstacles to reception of the gospel of Jesus Christ by the Jewish people. Some Pharisees, however, such as Nicodemus and (probably) Joseph of Arimathea, supported Jesus. To learn about the Lord's judgment upon them, see Matt. 23, Luke 11, and Mark 7. (For more information see Bible Dictionary/Pharisees/Sadducees, 750, 767.)

The Jewish historian Flavius Josephus (AD 37–AD 100) claimed that the roots of the Zealot or *Sicarii* movement began in 37 BC, on the very first day of Roman occupation, after the province was conquered by Pompey (*Antiquities*). One of the first major uprisings took place in AD 6–7 against the Roman procurator, Coponius, who wanted to take a census, which was considered tantamount to accepting the Roman occupation.

The program of the Zealots was simple—its members were required to unequivocally reject any ruler over Israel except God. They held the unshakable conviction that only if unconditional action were taken, and if total obedience were evident, would God then intervene and establish the Messianic age. Thus, they refused to pay taxes, harried and murdered government officials, and sought to eliminate the use of the Greek language as it was considered a symbol of pagan influence. To a Zealot, the worst thing for a Jew was to be a collaborator with Rome, and they frequently took revenge upon those who did. The Zealots (along with many other Jews) did not accept King Herod and his descendants as rulers. First, they would have considered them half-breed Idumeans and not pure Jews. Second, the Herodians got their authority from Rome and were therefore puppets of a foreign, pagan occupier. Finally, the Zealots, like most common Jews, despised the House of Hanan, or the current family appointed by Rome to act as High Priests in charge of the Temple. The House of Hanan, which included such infamous figures as Annas and Caiaphas, was guilty of many abuses of power, and was viewed in ancient Israel much like today's Mafia.

As portrayed in this chapter, the Zealots did not hesitate to use intrigue, violence, force, and deception to achieve their ends. They also felt it was better to commit suicide than submit to the will of their oppressors (*The Zondervan Pictorial Encyclopedia of the Bible* [Grand Rapids, MI: Zondervan Publishing House, 1976], 1036–1037). During the time when Jesus Christ and John the Baptist would have been ministering, there were at least six major Zealot insurrections, usually instigated in the regions surrounding the Sea of Galilee. Galilee was a hotbed of Zealot activity throughout Roman occupation, until the Jewish War of AD 70 crushed their rebellion for good. For three or four generations, Gamla in Galilee served as their base of operations. In turn, Gamla influenced the many villages around the Sea of Galilee, from which the disciples of Jesus were called. A hundred years before, when the Jewish sect known as the Hasmoneans were reconquering areas of Israel, those who went to the "frontier" of Galilee were those with deep religious and political convictions about the land of God and the worship of God. Their hearts and minds were open to the Zealot message, allowing the movement to increase in size and influence over the course of years without much interference from the government. By contrast, Galileans were also more open to the message of Jesus Christ, as is reflected by the fact that all but one of His original twelve Apostles were from Galilee.

Another stronghold of the Zealots was located on the opposite side of the Sea of Galilee from Gamla. In the Canyon of Pigeons, in the vertical cliffs of Mt. Arbel (which overshadows Magdala, home of Mary Magdalene), Zealot command posts and strongholds were established. This 1,500 foot cliff is visible from all parts of the Sea of Galilee and was a constant reminder of resistance to the Romans, their vassal, Herod the Great, and his descendant rulers. It's quite possible that when Jesus was teaching on the plain of Geneseret, located just below Arbel and saying, "Blessed are the peacemakers," the people could hear a faint clank-clank-clank of weapons being forged in the cliffs above for the coming confrontation with Rome.

There is no doubt that Jesus Christ was well-acquainted with the teachings of the Zealots. One of His chosen disciples, Simon, was a member of this party before his call to discipleship (Luke 6:15; Acts 1:13), and retained the designation after he joined the apostolic band. Some scholars believe that Judas Iscariot was also a Zealot. While some interpret Iscariot as meaning, "man of Kerioth," others believe it is a form of Skarioth, possibly taken to reflect the Latin, *Sicarii*. Judas, the lone member of the twelve who was a Judean, is sometimes associated directly with Jewish revolutionaries in Judea (Everett Ferguson, ed., *Encyclopedia of Early Christianity* [New York: Garland Publishing, Inc., 1990], 508–509).

Because it was common knowledge that Galilee was the center of Zealot activity, it would have been natural for Jews of that period to assume that Jesus Christ was somehow associated with this movement. Although the Savior, too, believed that the only ruler of Israel, and the only God worshipped in Israel, should be the Lord, it would have soon been evident to His listeners that He was firmly opposed to Zealot methodology and views. This fact would have quickly disappointed many listeners, who found the militant solution offered by men like Bar Abba much more appealing.

Note that "Bar" and "Ben" are interchangeable in meaning, the former meaning "son of" in Hebrew, and latter meaning "son of" in Aramaic. Abba in Hebrew means "Father." Therefore the full meaning of the name Bar Abba or Ben Abba would be "Son of the Father."

# CHAPTER 9

## Steffanie

At dawn I was awakened by a strange rumbling in the earth—very uniform—like the steady beat of drums. Pagag and I awoke at the same instant. We arose from the midst of the nine sleeping children we'd rescued from the pit, and went immediately to the edge of the ruins atop the jungled hill where we'd spent the night. As we peered over the crumbling wall and looked toward the south, the valley floor was buried beneath a veil of morning mist.

This mist weaved through and around every tall jungle tree, exposing only the very crowns. It climbed up the sides of the hills like cottony frosting. Closer to us the mist floated and danced the way dry ice vapors float on a Halloween cauldron, hiding every portion of visible ground. This made the rumbling ever more ominous since we had no way of viewing the source. Yet I did perceive a kind of shadow moving beneath the mist, almost like a dark lava stream oozing down from the hills and gathering onto the valley floor.

"Awaken the children," said Pagag, his voice full of alarm.

He didn't need to explain. I'd figured it out easily enough. There was an army headed toward us, and not a measly army of one hundred men. There were thousands of men moving beneath that mist.

"Tok! Pakal! Kala!" I yelled. "Wake up! We have to leave. We have to leave *now!*"

Most of them were still rubbing sleep out of their eyes as Pagag and I gathered the youngest children into our arms and herded the rest toward the opposite end of the ruins and down a pathway that led toward the bottom of the bluff. At one point Tok stopped as a fresh view of the southern valley opened up on our right. Some of the mist at the base of our hill had dissipated enough that I could clearly see the bodies of warriors moving among the trees, some pounding steadily on drums that hung at their waists.

"Tok, please!" I cried. "Keep moving!"

I was terrified that our hill was already surrounded. My memory of the exact moment that I'd awakened was rather foggy, but I was certain it coincided with the commencement of drums. There was apparently a widespread command that the drummers were to start pounding in unison, probably at dawn or some other moment where there was perceived to be a certain amount of light. The army itself, however, had likely started marching much earlier, possibly since long before sunup.

Laughing-Smiling started to fret in my arms, undoubtedly because she was hungry or thirsty. I didn't stop, just hugged her more tightly while whispering, "Shhh. It's all right, little one. It's all right."

As we reached the valley floor, both older boys paused again, peering into the trees, almost as if they recognized the shadows of the warriors. Then it hit me. This was not a *Nephite* army. It was *Lamanite.* It was Tok and Pakal's own people.

Still, this didn't change my opinion that we should run. These Lamanites may have been an entirely different tribe or kinship from the one to which these children belonged. Who was to say that warriors in this army would treat the children any differently than an army of Nephites? I just couldn't take that chance.

In an attempt to keep us out of sight, Pagag veered into a ravine with tall grasses. The dew quickly drenched my garments below the waist. Honestly, I couldn't see how keeping out of sight would make any difference so long as this baby kept crying. I pleaded with her, promising honey-sweets and bananas and whatever else I could think of. She just didn't understand. I heard the rustling of men moving through the forest on either side of the ravine, and the incessant beating of drums.

The ravine snaked around several turns. My sling had come loose—my injured arm fell free. *Great!* I hissed under my breath. This was all I needed. But at that instant a warrior leaped right into the middle of us from the shelf above. The children screeched and scrambled to back away. I was standing right beside him, still holding Laughing-Smiling with my good arm. The man's lethal attentions were riveted on Pagag. He started to raise his obsidian-edged club. But before he could even adopt a full attack posture, he got a taste of my elbow as I threw it into his mouth. The impact caused a quivering pain in my injured wrist, but the man went straight down, either disoriented or knocked out cold. We didn't stick around long enough to find out.

A short distance north the ravine spat us out onto flat ground. To one side was a thick copse of brush with elephant-ear-shaped leaves. I looked at Pagag. He read my thoughts. Our best course was probably to hide. Maybe if we stopped, Laughing-Smiling would quiet down. But it was *too late!* Agitated voices shouted to our left. Fifty yards away I could see several men pointing their bony fingers at us. Pagag moved as if he would lead us back into the ravine. Then he froze and seemed to make a final decision.

Pagag set down Eye-Pleasure and Many-Kisses and calmly said to me, "Gather the children more closely together."

"What are we going to do?" I asked desperately.

"Nothing," he replied. "Don't move. Don't speak. And bc calm."

I wanted to scream at him. What kind of knuckle-headed decision was that? Shouldn't we have at least *tried* to escape? The Lord only helped those who *acted!*

Against all my natural instincts, I did as Pagag ordered. I urged the children closer together and stood still as the warriors converged from two directions. My thoughts started to clear. My heartbeat began to slow, and a strange assurance settled over me. As the next events unfolded, I realized how inspired Pagag's decision had been.

Twenty men surrounded us, spears and swords at the ready. They said nothing, just gawked wide-eyed. Also arriving was the guy I'd elbowed in the mouth, now bleeding from a split lip. Our weapons were seized. Some of the men looked eager to tear us apart—particularly the guy I'd attacked. Others noted the nationality of the children and might have decided we were their kidnappers. But there were a few level-headed men in the bunch who quelled the tempers of the others. Most of these Lamanites seemed frightened or intimidated by us. Again I concluded it was our appearance, especially our hair color and height.

These men were dressed very differently from those we'd already encountered. No paint on their faces, but plenty of swirling black tattoos covering necks, arms, legs, backs, and chests. Whereas the Nephites had worn a kind of protective vest over hips and chest, there was no protective armor here. In fact, their wasn't much of *anything* covering their bodies beyond jewelry, feathered headbands, furry leggings and greaves, high-backed leather sandals, and the scantiest of loincloths. But they were armed to the teeth with spears, saw-toothed swords, colorful shields, dart-throwing atlatls, and longbows.

A man came forward to address us. He was the only one wearing fancy headgear—a kind of wooden mask with jaguar fur, tall feathers, and teeth that came over his forehead. Frankly, it didn't look much like it would protect the head from any kind of heavy blow—at least not a blow delivered by one of their gnarly club-swords. Was it only a symbol of his rank?

He snarled at Pagag. "Who are you? Are you Nephites?"

"No," Pagag replied calmly.

"Then what are you doing with these children? They are *Lamaya!*"

"Yes," said Pagag.

"We rescued them," I interrupted.

The Lamanite snapped at Pagag, "Silence your woman or I'll fill her mouth with the point of my spear!"

I gulped. The guy was serious and drew back his spear to prove it. I glued my lips shut.

Amazingly, Pagag maintained a passive demeanor. "The woman spoke correctly. We found these children in the hands of Nephites. Our intention was to deliver them into safe hands."

"He speaks the truth," said Chitam-Tok bravely.

"*Silence!*" the warrior shrieked at the boy. Again to Pagag: "What happened to the Nephites?"

"There were four," said Pagag. "They were posted as guards. I killed two and wounded a third. He and the remaining man fled."

The Lamanite glared at Pagag. He paced back and forth, apparently trying to decide what to say next. In the end he said nothing. He stepped away to consult two other men while the rest aimed spears at our throats. The consultation seemed to take forever. I couldn't hear their words. Laughing-Smiling was still crying. I bounced her in my arms, but I didn't dare even to say "shhh" in her ear.

Two of the men departed, pushing urgently through the swelling crowd. For forty-five minutes we stood there. Only the smaller children dared sit. My hand started aching so I gave Laughing-Smiling to Kala. Twice I grabbed Many-Kisses and Monkey-Swing to keep them close. The older boys finally helped.

At last an official entourage arrived wearing a half-dozen high, swinging, feathered headdresses. The most impressive was bright blue and carved into the shape of a fearsome beast, like some kind of dragon. It was framed along the top by triangular-shaped material covered in stone mosaics—turquoise, jade, and other gems. The design resembled a menacing pair of eyes. From a distance it might have given the soldiers of an army the impression that they were being closely watched. The entire thing was topped with lofty blue, red, and green feathers, fanning out like a peacock and sweeping all the way down his back. If this man wasn't a king, he was certainly a top general. As it turned out, he was a little of both.

The peacock-headed man looked us up and down. For an instant I registered the same surprise in his eyes as those who'd first surrounded us. He quickly shook that off, however, and turned to one of his entourage.

"Bring them to my post. Take the children to the rear." He turned and walked away with his men.

My heart tightened. I couldn't hold my tongue any longer. "Wait! What will you do with them?"

Upright spear shafts were thrown before me, like cell bars. These prevented me from lunging forward as warriors grabbed up the smaller children and hastened the others to their feet. Little Many-Kisses started to cry. She reached out toward me with tiny arms, but her pleas were ignored. A Lamanite soldier carted her off with the others.

Tears burst from my eyes. Within seconds the children were gone, and Pagag and I were being escorted behind the general's entourage. I glanced back many times seeking a glimpse of those nine precious souls that we'd saved from that pit. But the truth was, I never expected to see any of them again.

The general's "post" was a small hillock a short distance to the west. A shade awning had been raised. His job for now appeared to be admiring the troops as they marched through the forests on either side. I could also see lines of men along the slopes of the hills. As we passed through the endless human streams moving northward, I reevaluated my earlier estimate of tens of thousands of men. It was more like *hundreds* of thousands.

Our audience with the Lamanite general was immediate. He was a stern-faced man with heavy, dark eyebrows and eyes the color of black cherries. We stood directly under the awning while he walked around us, as if appraising a pair of horses for quality and breeding.

Finally, he introduced himself. "I am Sa'abkan, son of Aaron, king of the people of the Earth Stone, commander of the western armies of the Lamaya, loyal subject of Lord Blue Crocodile of Tikal."

He waited. He wanted a response of some kind, but after all the threats and spear-waving, we were more than a little hesitant to speak.

Finally, Pagag said, "I am Pagag, son of Mahonri of the Shemites, prince of the clan of Moriancumr."

He studied Pagag another moment, then said, "I do not know these people 'Shemites.' But Moriancumr—I have heard this name. Are your people from the mountains and coasts to the west?"

Pagag hesitated. "I . . . I'm not sure. I am a little disoriented on directions."

*Good answer,* I thought.

Sa'abkan gestured toward me. "And this woman? Is she yours?"

Pagag glanced at me, then shook his head. "No. She is her own."

Sa'abkan faced me. "Who are you?"

Apparently he wasn't expecting me to observe the same feminine rules about keeping silent. "I am Steffanie, daughter of Jim, of the clan of Hawkins." Maybe I should have stopped there, but I didn't know if I'd get another chance to talk, so I asked, "What have you done with the children? What will become of them?"

He studied me curiously, then replied, "They will not be harmed. They will be taken back to their own people."

"Who will care for them?"

His eyes narrowed. The question seemed to perturb him. "They will be cared for by our women. We do not torture and sacrifice our own children as the Nephites torture and sacrifice theirs. Did you find these children near the burned village to the south?"

Pagag nodded. "Yes."

"I am told that you rescued them from a band of Nephite savages—the same band, I presume, who have ravaged this region for months, destroying our homes, murdering our people, and sacrificing our children in the same secret mountain caves used by their ancestors. I am told that the children themselves confirmed your noble deeds."

"It was our privilege to help them," said Pagag. "Unfortunately, I spared two of the savages. This was before I realized the extent of their crimes and inhumanity."

Sa'abkan made a strange grin, then motioned to one of his men who, in turn, motioned to others. The onlookers parted and two warriors stepped beneath the awning. In their hands were a pair of rough brown sacks. The bottoms were moist with blood. As the men reached inside, they hoisted out two objects—objects with *hair.* I turned away quickly, but not quickly enough. I recognized the sallow faces, striped with gold and black paint. My squeamish reaction caused the warriors to chuckle. Sa'abkan also seemed amused by my revulsion. I suppose the people of this century had seen so much blood, it no longer affected them. I prayed that I would never become so accustomed to such horrid sights.

Sa'abkan asked Pagag, "Are these the men?"

"Yes," he confirmed.

"We filled twenty-one more sacks with similar contents in the last three days," said Sa'abkan. "The rest of them have fled north like the cowards that they are. Each of these will be removed from the sack and cast over the walls of the Nephite capital—just before we begin to make a bonfire of the remains of every man, woman, and child of the liar in the land of Desolation."

Yowls of approval went up from the ranks of Sa'abkan's officers and staff. We understood now why the Nephite army had abandoned those four guards. They'd undoubtedly seen this flood of oncoming Lamanites and turned tail for home.

I asked another question. "Are you preparing to attack the Nephites at Cumorah?"

"*Attack?*" Sa'abkan faced me, eyes sizzling. "We plan to *annihilate* them. We will make the name of our ancient betrayer a hiss on the wind. We will burn away all memory of the Nephites as the sun burns off the fog. For years we have prepared. All the Lamaya of the four directions—earth and sky, water and fire—are united. United even with the Lords of Teotihuacán. Swift messengers from Tikal have announced that the time is now. Fireborn and his armies march from the east with the people of the Water-Lilies. We march from the south with the people of the Earth-Stone. The Lightning Warriors of Spearthrower Owl march from the north. We march even as rivers begin to swell in the season of rains. For another month we will gather to Cumorah's plains. And then the final contest will commence, the final clash of steel and stone, thunder and fire. Every child of the liar will fall or confess the wrongs of his ancestors. They will welcome enslavement or die. They will deny the power of their magic, of their inheritance, and of their gods, or their blood will nourish the earth in the season of burning. At last, after so many centuries of warfare and weeping, there will be a millennium of peace in the One World."

The warriors pressing around us hooted after every phrase of Sa'abkan's speech. Even knowing the events of the Book of Mormon, I couldn't have grasped the full intensity of Lamanite hatred. Nor could I have grasped that so much of that hatred—based on the savagery I'd witnessed with my own eyes—was *understandable.*

Sa'abkan continued to examine us. Something about our appearance genuinely disturbed him, as it did many of the other officers. At last the reason for all the gaping eyes and gasping mouths was revealed.

"The messengers brought *other* news from Tikal: rumors of a pretender who claims to be a son of Great-Jaguar-Paw, former king of the Lamaya. Jaguar-Paw was my father's cousin and overlord. But the power of his dynasty was silenced by the Lords of Teotihuacán."

He studied us carefully for a reaction. We had none to give. What was he expecting?

He continued, "This pretender is said to travel with another charlatan—a white god of the Nephites called Aryin-Kukalcan. Also an underworld demoness called May-geen. She is said to have eyes like jade. Both are said to have hair the color of sunlight and maize." He looked again into my eyes and seemed disappointed that they were not jade-green, though I would have thought that blue was equally rare.

Again, no reaction appeared on my face, perhaps because it took several seconds for the information to click.

May-geen: Meagan. Aryin: Ryan.

Was it possible? The pronunciations were boogered a bit, but the coincidence was too remarkable: two white-skinned travelers with light-colored hair. A female with green eyes. I had no idea what "Kukalcan" meant. Many things remained confusing. Pagag's expression was blank. He'd either forgotten the names of who we were searching for, or he was exerting the same efforts as me to play ignorant.

"I do not take either of you for gods or demons," Sa'abkan concluded. "Gods do not arm themselves with mortal weapons." He waved a hand toward our armaments, which were currently heaped into a pile outside the awning. "Nor do they suffer mortal injuries." He indicated the splint on my hand. "Yet I find it very curious that your features so resemble the messenger's descriptions. I will not deny that my cousins, the people of the Water-Lilies, are often foolish and easily deceived. They will worship a cockroach if it manages to evade the stomp of their foot." A few in the audience sniggered. Sa'abkan concluded by asking, "Nevertheless, is it possible that you are familiar with these things?"

Pagag shrugged. "We are not. We are flesh and blood, as you have said. And we know nothing of a pretender or any of the others you mention."

Sa'abkan watched our eyes a moment longer, then asked, "Have you traveled here from the hotlands of the east?"

Pagag shook his head. "No. We have come from the south."

"And before that from the west," I interjected, hoping to connect up with what Sa'abkan had said earlier about Pagag possibly being from the western mountains and coasts.

"What has brought you through the country of wild beasts into the lands of Desolation?" Sa'abkan asked.

"Hunting," I replied. I vaguely remembered somewhere in the Book of Mormon that Nephites or Jaredites or *someone* had set aside

208                    CHRIS HEIMERDINGER

special wilderness areas for hunting game. Sa'abkan looked like he was going to pursue this question further—ask exactly *what* game we were hunting, or some other question I couldn't have answered, so I quickly diverted the subject. "However, several other members of our hunting party were captured by this same Nephite band that burned your villages. We were following them northward when we came across the nine children whose lives we saved. If our family members are still alive, we must pursue them and reclaim them."

"Are these others white skinned like you?" he asked.

"Yes," I answered simply. "Where I am from, this is a very common trait."

His demeanor changed. He looked more relaxed. I might have even thought he looked disappointed. I suppose it might have been quite a thrill to find a couple of gods running loose in the forest. Then I realized the cause of his disappointment was something else.

He asked again, "And you are sure that you have never heard of a man who claims to be a son of Jaguar-Paw?"

"No," said Pagag. "I regret we have never heard of such a man."

He sighed, finally nodding. "I believe you."

There was sadness in his voice. He seemed to wish that this so-called pretender might be real, but the subject was never brought up again.

"It appears that you and I are hunting the same enemy," said Sa'abkan. "The Lamaya have no quarrel with the peoples of the western mountains."

We waited a moment. Finally I asked, "Are we free to go?"

He nodded. "You are welcome to journey with my army to Jordan where we will join with the Lamaya warriors already stationed in that city. I will have one of my Hummingbird Captains serve as your escort. Perhaps at Jordan we may learn the fate of your family members."

Pagag looked at me for some sign of how I felt about the idea. Truthfully, I didn't know for sure. Not that such an escort would put us in any particular danger. I guess I was still wrestling with how I felt about Nephites or Lamanites. I wasn't certain whose side I should be on! Obviously I wanted to be on *Mormon's* side—Mormon or Moroni. I couldn't imagine that either of these prophets knew about a marauding band that routinely murdered Lamanite children. Or if they knew, they certainly wouldn't have sanctioned it. I shook my head at Pagag minutely to let him know that I did not wish to accompany Sa'abkan's army.

Pagag faced the Lamayan general and politely declined. "If you will allow it, we would like to pursue this band of Nephites on our own by a somewhat different path than the one taken by the main body of your forces."

Sa'abkan raised an eyebrow. "By what path will you travel?"

"I fear we made a mistake the day before yesterday," said Pagag. "We may have traveled too far west. We will cross over these hills to the east and travel northward through the next valley."

"What do you think you and an injured woman can do against this band of savages?" asked one of Sa'abkan's officers.

"Perhaps very little," Pagag replied. "But it may be to our advantage to travel in a manner that does not attract so much . . . attention." His eyes swept over the thousands of warriors who continued to march past the awning.

Sa'abkan became thoughtful, then said, "Our interest in seeing these Nephite marauders destroyed remains the same. If you will allow me, I will dispatch eight-hundred men to your services—an entire battalion. They will go with you in pursuit of your companions, and rejoin us later at Jordan."

Again Pagag looked at me. I could tell he was very tempted to accept the offer. Still, I shook my head. All I could see in my mind were horrible images of a battle wherein Harry, Mary, Becky, and the rest were deliberately executed as the Nephites panicked in the face of an attacking Lamanite battalion. Somehow I wanted to believe God might help us to rescue them without so much violence and bloodshed—and without the help of Lamanites.

I decided to speak. "Thank you, your Majesty. But we would prefer to go alone. As for the rest, we will leave that in the hands of our God."

Sa'abkan seemed surprised at my decision, but only shrugged. "As you please. Again, we thank you for saving our little ones."

I spoke again, hesitantly. "Is it possible, I mean, to see them once more? We never said good-bye. They have been through so much."

Sa'abkan bristled. "We have *all* been through 'so much.' My entire nation has been through 'so much.' The little ones are Lamaya. There is nothing they cannot endure."

I raised my eyebrows. I certainly wasn't meaning to offend him. I opened my mouth to say more, but Pagag gently squeezed my arm. Regrettably, I dropped the subject, though Sa'abkan certainly perceived my disappointment.

So that was that. Our weapons were returned. We were given a blue feather with a wooden token glued at the base that would supposedly grant us unmolested passage through the Lamanite ranks.

Pagag and I left the presence of Sa'abkan and his officers and began climbing the hills to the east. It was afternoon. The rains that arrived each day at this hour began to fall. I didn't even notice the rain clouds rolling in. They seemed to materialize out of nowhere, like something from Star Trek's transporter beam. We paused at the top of the hill where Pagag rewrapped the sling on my arm. As we turned back, we could still see the wide streams of Lamanite warriors moving northward. Drums continued booming throughout the ranks, urging marchers to keep pace. It was an incredible sight. A *harrowing* sight. Any self-respecting Nephite would have been utterly terrified.

I realized we'd forgotten to ask Sa'abkan a few crucial questions— like how far it was to Cumorah and how many days it would take to reach it. Worse yet, I wondered if I'd just made a monstrous mistake by rejecting his generous offer.

"Maybe I was wrong," I said to Pagag. "Maybe we should have agreed to let the Lamanites come with us. I know that you wanted to accept Sa'abkan's offer. It's just . . . they're *Lamanites!* They're on their way to kill Mormon and Moroni!"

"I will not question your judgment," he said simply. But then he fell silent, which told me that he was questioning my judgment. Finally, he said, "Those names. You recognized them, didn't you? The demoness and the fair-skinned god? Those were two of the ones that we came here to find, were they not?"

"Yes, I think so," I replied. "I guess I shouldn't be surprised that people who look like us would stand out and cause rumors. If my hunch is correct, Meagan and Ryan—and hopefully Apollus and the others—are headed toward the same place that we are: Cumorah."

"If so, it would reveal that God is truly guiding our steps. It appears that for a while longer we will have only each other for company."

I glanced at his face, unsure how he meant that. Was it with regret or friendliness? I almost suspected that he'd deliberately said it in a way that I wouldn't be able to decipher the intent. So I replied using the same sophomoric strategy.

"Yes," I said, keeping my tone neutral. "But I suppose I'll tolerate that a while longer."

Out of the corner of my eye I caught him staring—as if desperate for some hint of my meaning—but I faced forward and walked on ahead. So the game-playing hadn't ended. Just my tactics were changing. "Hard to get" and "feminine obtuseness" were much more my style. But what were my intentions if I won this insipid contest? What would I do with the prize? I supposed I wouldn't worry about that right now. I could always worry about it later. In my mind I was still shaking off the feelings I'd had the day before—the feelings when he had . . . held me. *BLAAAAA! Forget about it, girl! FORGET IT!*

Pagag looked as if he was about to say something more, but at that instant something wonderful appeared in the sky. A Peregrine falcon!—zipping towards us like a fighter jet and squawking like a banshee.

"Rafa!" I cried.

The bird passed between us, no less thrilled to see *us* than we were to see *him*. He made what looked like a flip-turn in mid-air and circled back around toward us. Then he opened his wings as brakes, flapped twice more, and landed on my shoulder. Fortunately the cloth of Pagag's sling gave my shoulder extra protection from those needle-point claws.

Rafa continued chattering. It was still remarkable to me that I understood most of what he was communicating. Not in "words." Falcons didn't use them. But in *feelings*. Rafa was thrilled and grateful and stressed and anxious.

"We thought we'd lost you," I said to him. "Thank you for coming back—for not giving up in your search for us."

"Ask if it has seen Harry and Gidgiddonihah," said Pagag.

He didn't realize that the falcon had already answered this. "Yes, he has. But he's worried. *Very* worried."

"How far away are they?" asked Pagag.

I posed the question, but again Rafa didn't give a direct answer. And like before, the message seemed more than a bit sarcastic.

I replied to Pagag, "He said, 'As far as it is.' Meaning, I suppose, that he doesn't see the point in answering such a question since it won't bring them any closer. He just wants us to get moving. He seems more frightened for their safety than ever before. But at least, if I understand him correctly, everyone is still alive."

"Is that all? Did it say anything else?"

Again playing Dr. Doolittle, I said to the bird, "Is there anything else we should know?"

With that, the bird made a final whistling cry and launched from my shoulder, flying off in the direction it wanted us to follow.

"I guess that was my answer," said Pagag.

"He did add a P.S.," I said with a chuckle. "It was directed at you."

"Oh?"

"He said, in essence, 'Don't let the man get lost again.' I think Rafa believes I ought to be the one responsible for keeping him in our sights."

Pagag gave Rafa a scowl as he circled back to make sure we were coming.

My stomach was still knotted with tension. I was feeling more than ever that we should have accepted Sa'abkan's help. Despite my distrust—and yes—despite my outright prejudice of Lamanites and their mission to destroy the Nephite nation, I realized that I needed to swallow all such resentment—at least for the time being. Rafa certainly wasn't going to appreciate the further delay, but I felt we needed to go back. Telling Pagag that I'd been wrong was no pleasure either, but it was the best decision for the lives of my family and friends, and I wasn't about to let pride get in the way.

So we would accept the help of the Lamanite warriors after all. I only wished I knew who to fear more—Lamanite soldiers or Nephite marauders. All things considered, I felt we might have been better off in a pool of sharks.

NOTES TO CHAPTER 9

Mormon and Moroni left us few details of what life was like for the Nephites before and after their destruction. They give us many indications of the corruption and wickedness that prevailed among them (see Morm. 4:10–12, 5:18), and a particularly interesting verse about their mental state of mind (see Morm. 2:12–15). But most of the details are histories of various battles and troop movements, spiritual laments, and doctrinal instruction. Mormon claims that he made a more complete account of events (specifically a more complete account of his people's wickedness) upon the plates of Nephi, but such details were not included in his abridgement (see Morm. 2:18).

Nevertheless, we do glean a great deal of information from what he wrote, including descriptions of geography and topography, the names of many Nephite cities and Nephite commanders, and the name of at least one Lamanite adversary. This man was Aaron. He was called a king, but he was also a military commander, as was the common practice of kings and lords in Mesoamerica. He is mentioned by name only twice (see Morm. 2:9, Moro. 9:17), though it is possible that he is also the Lamanite "king" mentioned in Morm. 3:4 who forewarns Mormon of an impending Lamanite invasion. It appears that Aaron is never mentioned beyond AD 362 and may not have been involved in the final battle wherein the Nephite nation was destroyed.

It is interesting to note that the epistle that Mormon wrote to his son Moroni, found in the second to last chapter of the Book of Mormon, likely speaks of events that took place several decades before the battle at Cumorah. Many have assumed that because this chapter is so close to the end of the record that it speaks of events surrounding the final episodes of the Nephite destruction, or even of events that took place *after* the battle at Cumorah. This is unlikely. First, it mentions fallen Nephite generals who are not named at the battle of Cumorah (see Moro. 9:2). Second, it mentions landmarks and troop movements that appear to have no relation to circumstances at Cumorah (see Moro. 9:16–17). Third, it mentions that Mormon has yet to deliver up the sacred records to Moroni (an event described in Morm. 6:6). Finally, it mentions King Aaron, whose name was associated with events that took place approximately forty years before events at Cumorah (see Morm. 2:9). It thus becomes more likely that Moroni decided to include this letter at the end of the record, not because it gives us an accurate sequence of events, but because it offers his fullest portrayal of the spiritual condition of the Nephites. It also provides a marvelous glimpse of the character of Mormon, his relationship with his son, Moroni, and his powerful testimony of the Savior.

In this book the fictional character Sa'abkan is the son of this King Aaron. The author's suggestion that Aaron was a subordinate king (Ahau) of a higher ruler at Tikal (Kalomté) is also speculation, though it would be similar to the kingship pattern established in Mosiah between King Lamoni and his father. A similar kingship pattern is also suggested by scholars who have described the political situation in Mesoamerica in the fourth century AD (see Peter D. Harrison, *The Lords of Tikal,* 1999).

The author distinguishes several "branches," or individual Lamanite tribes, in this book. Though the tribal names the author uses (Earth-Stone, Water-Lilies) are fictional, these are phrases commonly associated with ancient Mayan/Aztec symbolism. The idea that the Lamanite peoples were already factionalized, or broke into factions shortly after the destruction at Cumorah, is indicated by Book of Mormon text (see Morm. 8:8).

# CHAPTER 10

## Meagan

*My dreams were all filled with Caesar salads.*

*When one eats beans and tortillas day after day after day, supplemented by strange fresh meats from wild animals like boar and curassow, paca and spider monkey, one's body tends to crave chlorophyll—anything edible and green. Or at least tomatoes! I'd been taught once that the Indians of the New World* invented *tomatoes! (Cultivated?) So where the bloomers were they? Since we'd embarked on this journey I'd chowed down on some of the grossest things—vile stuff like snake and even toucan (yes, the same beautiful bird from the Fruit Loops box!). Truth be told, I devoured whatever the boys happened to hunt and kill and prepare—so long as it was prepared in such a way that I could no longer recognize what it was. I was ecstatic whenever we found wild fruits or vegetables—bananas, mangoes, blackberries, onions, avocados . . . Still, I'd have given my eyeteeth for a nice all-you-can-eat salad from Sizzler or Sweet Tomatoes.*

*We'd abandoned our canoes several days before and were again traveling overland. Apollus and Lamanai felt sure that we were finally well ahead of Fireborn's army. Nevertheless, they climbed trees every night before we settled into camp, or ascended to some high place so they could survey the surrounding landscape.*

*After living for so many days here in the fourth century* AD, *I felt like I was losing my sense of time. The Lamanite or "native" members of our expedition—Lamanai, Jacobah, and Tz'ikin—acted as if they had no concept of time whatsoever. To them every experience had a kind of rounded fullness—untainted by the hurrying, divided minutes or hours. Ah, maybe that doesn't make sense. I'll just say that sometimes I felt as if I were floating through time rather than living within it.*

*And let me also dispel one myth: the one about how it never gets cold in the jungle. There were nights when I was bundled up in my hammock wearing every stitch of clothes and wrapped up in two blankets and* still *the bitter north wind chilled me to the bone. But I must say, it wasn't the chill from the cold north wind that started to concern me most as our journey continued. It was the internal chill that had taken hold of many of the members in our expedition.*

*Maybe it was because we'd been forced to spend so much time together, or the fact that we all had such different personalities, but I noticed that as each day wore on, certain members of our expedition began to wear increasingly on each other's nerves.*

*Of course, there was the usual tension that existed between me and Apollus. But that kind of tension I sort of enjoyed. It may be awful of me to say, but I rather relished driving my Roman a little crazy. He certainly deserved it. Some days we were talking to each other, and some days we weren't. Some days we held hands and exchanged the occasional kiss, and some days we couldn't walk far enough apart. But no matter how often he did, or said, something stupid (which was virtually every day) he eventually, consistently, went out of his way to try and understand and make up for the foolish error of his ways.*

*Besides, watching him backpedal was sometimes deliciously funny. A few days after we began traveling into the Lacandon Mountains, I made some comment—out of hearing of Moroni and anyone else from the third century—that there might have been less trouble among Nephites and Lamanites if they'd elected a few female chief judges.*

*"Women are not disposed to politics," said Apollus. "They do not have the temperament for it."*

*"Excuse me?" I replied. "Not 'disposed?' What kind of temperament do you think is required?"*

*"A leader must be steady in mind," he declared. "And disinclined to be swayed by flattery and self-interest above the needs of the state."*

*"Oh, yes," I said sarcastically. "And there has never been a male tyrant swayed by self-interest. Nuh-uh. No way."*

*"I speak only in generalities," said Apollus. "I think history would confirm that for every Caligula, there are a hundred Messalinas."*

*"Messalinas?"*

*"Wife of Claudius Caesar. Executed for conspiring to murder him and for seducing half the Senate—"*

"I know *who she is,*" I said tartly. "But your analogy is screwed up. She wasn't a real leader. Just a hussy and a wanna-be. You really think half the world's wars would have been fought if women had been in charge? What a crock! I suppose you think I'm unsteady in mind and given to flattery and self-interest."

I could see the panic in his eyes, stuttering like Porky Pig as he tried to dig his way out of the pit—er, crater—he'd dug for himself. "I-I-I was not referring to you, Meagan Sorenson. I meant it as a broad, prevailing—My intent was certainly not to provoke umbrage."

"Well, 'provoking umbrage' seems to be your special talent. Gee, I'd hate to hear what you'd say if you were deliberately *trying to sound like a narrow-minded, egotistical chauvinist.*"

"But is it not discouraged by our religion to have a woman pursue a career of such high ambition?" he asked.

"Oh, you wish!" I declared. "We're taught that motherhood is our highest priority, but after that we can do whatever we like. Besides, I'm talking about intelligence—ability. And on that score I think men run a distant second. But of course I'm only speaking in 'broad, prevailing generalities.' Maybe I'll run for president someday! Could your ego handle that? What would you do then, Mr. Apollus Brutus 'the Conqueror' Severillus?"

"Well, I-I-I—I'd do—I'd have . . ." He heaved a sigh, then smiled in blissful defeat and replied, "I'd cast my ballot in your favor. Most assuredly."

I continued to scrutinize him with razor-thin eyes, then said, "Good answer."

But truly, it wasn't the frequent tension between me and Apollus that worried me most. It was the growing tension between others. Particularly between Lamanai and Moroni. In fact, between Lamanai and just about everyone else.

From the time that we'd departed Korihab and floated northward up the Sidon, I'd noticed Lamanai becoming more distant and somber. It took me a while to figure out why, but I finally put it together a few days after we left the river and began traveling westward toward the Lacandon Mountains.

It just seemed so natural for all of us to defer to Moroni as the expedition leader. He was, *after all*, Moroni!—son of the compiler of the Book of Mormon. He was the prophet/angel who would one day appear to

*Joseph Smith. But even knowing Moroni's future, there was simply a character and charisma about the man that made it easy to follow him to the ends of the earth. He had such a gentle strength, such a quiet confidence, that* anyone—*or at least anyone with a pure heart—naturally vacillated to his leadership.*

*It had started to become apparent that Lamanai resented the devotion we gave so freely to the son of Mormon. It's not that Lamanai ever really showed his resentment directly, or that he said anything derogatory. I just think the Prince of Tikal started to long for the kind of devotion he expected to receive from his subjects, the Lamanites, as soon as he reclaimed his throne. No one in our group really gave him the kind of respect or adoration that I think he felt he deserved. Not even Jacobah treated him as someone particularly extraordinary, maybe because of his attachment to Ryan. Apollus had described to me how a merchant in Korihab had practically fallen to his knees and worshipped the prince on the spot as a living deity when he discovered who Lamanai actually was.*

*Lamanai had witnessed every miracle that had taken place in his village of Seibalche. He'd seen the priesthood in action and he appeared to accept Ryan's proclamation that this power emanated solely from Jesus Christ. For a time, all of us—or at least Apollus, Ryan, and I—were convinced that he was developing a strong testimony of the gospel. Even Moroni seemed to have high hopes for this. He'd even gone so far as to invite Lamanai to be baptized. But Lamanai's response was that he preferred to wait.*

*"If I am baptized," he said, "I will do so in Tikal, before the eyes of all my people."*

*I supposed this made sense. It was a cultural thing, I guessed. Letting his people witness such an event would have had a tremendous impact. But it was that word "if" that bothered me. For the first time I realized that Lamanai might not be truly converted, or at the very least he was suffering serious doubts. But our conversation the night before we arrived at Tz'ikin's home village removed all doubt that Lamanai still faced serious spiritual challenges.*

*We camped that evening in the thick of an enchanting mountain forest near a small stream with turquoise-colored pools and bubbling waterfalls. Our campsite was dry, which was a nice change. All day long we'd trudged through mud the consistency of cold lentil soup.*

*Tonight we would sleep surrounded by a vegetal wall of mahogany, cedar, and sapodilla trees with nests of thick moss, brilliant scarlet and pink bromeliads, and elephant-ear leaves that were of a size fit for mastodons.*

*In less than an hour the boys returned with supper—a small brocket deer, slain by Gilgal's arrow. It was the first hunt Gilgal had participated in since the accident that had injured his jaw. Most nights he just stayed in camp, groaning and looking grumpy. It hurt him to open his mouth, which for the rest of us was a blessing. For some time now Moroni, Apollus, and Ryan had been helping him cut up his meat and food so fine he could swallow without having to chew. But over the last few days I'd noticed he was feeling better and speaking more often. Unfortunately, the horse's kick hadn't improved his personality, and most of what he said was in some way crude or obnoxious.*

*Tz'ikin and I laid a carpet of palm fronds around the fire and gathered clusters of red and black berries, and low-hanging cassava. Tz'ikin's arm was still in a sling from her arrow wound on the river, but this restriction hardly slowed her down, and every day she insisted on pulling her weight.*

*Just before dusk, Huracan was welcomed into our camp for a share of the day's bounty. This had become a wonderful nightly tradition. Even during those days when we'd traveled by canoe, Huracan had always managed to find our riverside camp and pop in just as the bright colors of the jungle were blending to gray and black. Tonight, like most nights, after receiving her portion of meat, she slid gracefully back into the forest. As little as she took of today's deer, it seemed certain that she'd killed her own game out in the woods and probably found it more appetizing. I was convinced that her appearance each evening was just her way of telling us that she was there, still concerned for our welfare, and ready to come to our aid if required.*

*After supper, the boys and Tz'ikin settled into their usual routine of making tools and weapons—fletching arrows using parrot, bluebird, and hawk feathers, and chipping flint and other stones for arrow and axe heads. Jacobah was also engaged in finishing new sandals for Ryan and Apollus from the hide of a boar that we'd eaten three nights before. Shortly thereafter the conversation turned religious, instigated by a direct question from Lamanai to Moroni:*

*"If you are a general and a leader among your people," asked Lamanai, "does your God tell you all that you must do to command them?"*

*I sensed that there might be a hidden agenda behind this question, but I couldn't have guessed what it was.*

*"Sometimes," Moroni answered. "When it is my stewardship. Or else I will seek counsel from my father."*

*"Did your God tell you to journey to Tikal to be imprisoned by Lord Blue Crocodile and Fireborn?"*

*It was a veiled insult. I knew it, and I'm sure Moroni knew it too, but he treated it as a serious question.*

*"My father and I both felt that it was the right course of action to seek a treaty with Blue Crocodile," Moroni replied. "Our God does not always forewarn of every impending danger, nor does the Spirit ever misguide. There is always a plan and a purpose."*

*"So, it is your belief that your imprisonment and suffering, and the death of nearly all of your men served a holier purpose?"*

*Moroni answered carefully. "Yes I do. And that purpose may be sitting right in front of me. It may be that forging a treaty with you—with Eagle-Sky-Jaguar, Prince of the Lamanites—is far more important than a treaty with Blue Crocodile of Tikal. If I had not come on this journey—if I had not been imprisoned and later rescued by you, Apollus, Ryan, Jacobah, and Antionum—perhaps such an opportunity would not have come to pass."*

*"And if, at the last," said Lamanai, "you do not succeed in establishing this treaty with Eagle-Sky-Jaguar, what will you then think of your God?"*

*All of us stopped doing what we were doing to hear Moroni's answer.*

*He straightened himself and said boldly, "I will think no less of my God. But I might mourn deeply for you. If you were to reject such a sacred opportunity for peace between our two nations, I believe one day you would have to answer to God for the choice that you have made."*

*The two men stared at one another for a long moment. I could feel the tension in the air thickening. At last Lamanai relented and looked away. He waved his hand past his ear, as if to dismiss the seriousness of his questions and dispel the dark mood it had provoked. "You will not mourn on my account, Moroni Iqui Mahucatah. We will have our treaty. There will be peace between our peoples. But I do not understand why your God will tell you the things that you must do, and yet He will not tell me. Am I not destined to be a great lord and king of my people? Why is it that this Holy Spirit will whisper His great wisdom and instructions to you, but not to me?"*

*"Have you prayed and asked for His instructions?" Moroni inquired.*

*Lamanai seemed surprised by this. "Why must one pray and ask to receive such wisdom? Does not your God know all things? Does He not know that I am the future Kalomté of my people and have great need of His instruction?"*

*"Yes," said Moroni. "The Lord of Heaven indeed knows all things. It is true that He knows our needs even before we ask—better even than we know them ourselves. But it is His will that we ask Him nonetheless, as an expression of humility and contrition, recognizing that it is by Him and through Him that all good things are obtained."*

*Lamanai considered this, then said, "In my father's kingdom, supplication to the gods was made by the priests in my father's behalf. It would not have been dignified for him to kneel and beseech the omnipotent Itzamna for blessings like a common beggar. A king has no time for such things, so the duty is relegated to lesser men."*

*"In the eyes of God," said Moroni, "all souls are equal, and each individual must work out their own salvation with fear and trembling."*

*Lamanai pulled in his chin, as if he found this point astonishing. "And you believe this? You believe that all human beings are equal before heaven's eyes? Kings and slaves? Women and malformed children? Teotihuacános and Lamayans?"*

*"Yes," said Moroni simply, but with sadness. All of us were beginning to realize—in some ways for the first time—just how deep-seated many of Lamanai's prejudices were.*

*The prince was looking down, shaking his head. "This does not make sense. The gods created the universe, and the universe is one of order—not chaos." He raised his eyes. "Do you mean to say that you believe you are the son of a great general and prophet of your people by mere chance, and not by the will of the gods? Do you mean to say that I was born of Great-Jaguar-Paw and destined to become Lord Kalomté of the Lamaya not because I am favored of other men?"*

*"I believe," said Moroni, his tone a little more bold, his mind as lucid as sunlight, "that it is by our actions in mortality—by our faith and*

*obedience to God's word—that we obtain favor from God. Not by our birth or station. Where much is given, much is required, and the judgments of our Lord Jesus Christ are always just."*

*Lamanai sat in silence, stewing, but with a strange slippery smirk on his face, as if he felt he finally had something up on the son of his father's old enemy, almost as if he believed he'd confirmed some kind of twisted superiority. I feared that the reason Moroni's words were not sinking in was simply because it was Moroni saying them. Lamanai's jealousy and resentment of Mormon's son was increasing by the day. We could all see it. I thought it might enforce Moroni's words if I said something supportive.*

*I added, "I believe the Savior takes into consideration all of a man's gifts—his blessings and opportunities—when He judges them. If a person is born of righteous parents, having everything he could ever need for wealth or comfort, and yet he squanders those blessings because of selfishness, this person is judged differently than, say, someone born in poverty, who has no knowledge of God, but who still strives to live a decent life. The poor man may not be an important person—not a king or a lord—but in the next life it could be that he is far more blessed than many earthly kings or lords."*

*Lamanai was looking in the opposite direction, into the jungle. He wasn't even listening to me. Three and a half weeks ago he thought I was a goddess named Ix-Chel. How times had changed! I guessed he'd finally realized how human I really was. Or worse, how* female *I was. It occurred to me that my influence upon him was now less than anyone in our group. In fact, for me to have taken on the role of Miss Guru may have been more insulting than I could have comprehended.*

*Apollus took over, his voice still gentle, seeking with all his heart to enlighten the Prince's mind. "I can relate to your initial repugnance of such beliefs. Where I am from, my people are the masters of the world— the undisputed conquerors of hundreds of other races and tribes. It was not easy to submit my will to a God who I thought was only the God of the Jews—a nation despised and mocked by every other civilized people of the Roman world. But by submitting to this God, I was embraced by a Holy Spirit whose love and power is greater than any love or power of this earth. Each day I must relearn ways and ideas that I have stubbornly clung to since I was a child."*

*He glanced at me, and met my adoring eyes. I suddenly forgot all of our petty arguments and disagreements. I regretted my frequent snideness and sarcasm. Again I was reminded that I could never love a man more than this coarse, unpolished Roman centurion. There was a gem inside that roughness—a Celestial gem. I'd seen it, and I wanted to hang onto it with all that I had.*

*The look in my eyes was probably too much for Apollus. A faint tide of color came to his cheeks and he turned away self-consciously.* "Well," he concluded. "This was my experience, and I am glad that God felt I was worthy to know His true ways."

*Ryan tossed in his two bits:* "I grew up in the Church, but the journey for me was just the same. I still had to submit and be taught by the Spirit. The trick is, you have to want to learn. You have to pray and ask for answers—sometimes with all the energy inside you. But the answers do come. Soon I'm going to be a full-time missionary, spreading that message wherever God decides to send me."

*Wasn't there a quote in the Book of Mormon that said something like,* "If all men had been like unto Captain Moroni . . . ?" *Well, to paraphrase that statement, if all future missionaries were like unto Mr. Ryan Champion, I felt sure the powers of hell would quake and tremble.*

*But the prince remained silent. I couldn't tell if any of these noble statements were sinking in. But next, as Jacobah—humble Jacobah!—decided to speak, I realized that Lamanai had been listening carefully to every word.*

*Ryan's bodyguard looked pleadingly into the eyes of his future king:* "It is true, Prince Eagle-Sky—all that they have said. I have knelt and sought to understand the ways of this Messiah Jesus, and I have felt the same Holy Spirit that Apollus and Ryan have—"

*That's when Lamanai erupted. Hearing these testimonies from us was one thing, but hearing it from his own countryman was too much. He leaped to his feet and screamed at Jacobah,* "You are LAMAYA! You are a son of Tepeu and Gucamatz, the Mother and Father of life, created from the Sacred Corn to be a guardian of the earth!"

*Lamanai looked monstrous—fists clenched, body shaking, face waxyellow with rage. I felt sure he was about to strike Jacobah, but Moroni, Apollus, and Ryan intervened before he could deliver a blow. The prince stood his ground and scanned everyone in the gathering, nostrils flaring,*

*lungs pumping furiously. Finally, he walked away—just left the area
around the fire and stepped into the darkness of the woods to be alone.*

*The climate remained intense. We looked at one another, our hearts
clamoring. I heard Gilgal quietly chuckling at the edge of the encampment, where he'd been sitting all evening. There was a definite "I told you
so" in that awful, caustic laugh. Tz'ikin merely grunted and shook her
head, as if this event was more a reflection of the general idiocy of all
mankind rather than a statement about god or religion or culture.
Jacobah looked particularly distraught. He stood and watched after his
Prince, wanting to follow, but Apollus grabbed his shoulder and firmly
shook his head.*

*"Let his blood cool," Apollus advised. "You do not know what a man
will do in the darkness."*

*Our eyes turned to Moroni. The son of Mormon looked the saddest of
all, even heartbroken. I felt so stupid. What idiocy had made us think
Lamanai was on the verge of conversion? But would it have been so
earthshaking? Jacobah had witnessed all the same events and miracles as
Lamanai. What was the difference between them? How had the message
reached Jacobah and completely whooshed over the head of Eagle-Sky-
Jaguar?*

*Remarkably, almost as if he'd heard my silent question, Moroni
uttered a single word: "Pride." The Nephite prophet sat down and heaved
a miserable sigh. "It's always the same."*

*His tone carried the weight of the world. For an instant I glimpsed in
his eyes the full depth of his heartache, not just for Lamanai, but for all of his
people, the Nephites. Despite Lamanai's assurance, I think Moroni now had
serious misgivings that a treaty between his nation and the Lamaya would
ever be possible. I began praying inwardly. It tore me up seeing the faces of
Moroni and Apollus and Ryan. Was it really so hopeless? But then I shook
myself. What was I saying? Wasn't something like this inevitable? I knew the
ultimate destiny of the Nephites. I knew what awaited them. I realized we'd
all been fostering a mindless hope. Then I shook myself again. Maybe when
it came to the larger question of avoiding war, it was a mindless hope. But
what about Lamanai? What about saving the soul of this one man whom
God surely loved with all His might? Lamanai just needed time—a chance
to work it out in his mind. Tomorrow things would be better. Apologies
would be made; words would be retracted.*

*So be it, the next day, there was a modest apology. Or maybe it was more like a confession of overreaction. As we trudged up the valley on the last leg of our journey to Tz'ikin's home village, Lamanai said to Moroni, "My behavior last night was . . . not the behavior of a king. I will do better in the future to maintain the dignity of my birthright."*

*Moroni pondered his reply, then said, "I am sure you have the potential to be a great king, Lamanai, so long as you always remember where you have been, and how far you have come."*

*Lamanai stared at Moroni, expressionless. I couldn't tell if he appreciated this bit of wisdom or not. Then finally the prince nodded, and walked on ahead. Not the warmest exchange I might have hoped for, but a start.*

*Not long thereafter we began to pass the first palm-thatched huts and cooking fires of Tz'ikin's people, the Lacandones. Men were out working their small family farms, or milpas, in the midst of the eternally encroaching jungle. Many of the women assisted their husbands, carrying bales on their backs with a leather strap across their forehead, or weaving fabrics on outdoor looms. Naked and* mostly *naked children scurried about. Kids older than six worked right alongside the adults. With her good arm, Tz'ikin often sent them her traditional greeting by raising an open hand, much like the Indians of old Western movies, except that she did not hail them with the old cliché greeting "How." Many returned the gesture, but with reluctance and suspicion. Certainly our group had a strange, possibly* threatening, *appearance—not only because of our race, but because we were heavily armed. Tz'ikin's presence probably comforted them, but their faces still betrayed heavy concern. I wasn't sure how many of these folks Tz'ikin knew, but they definitely recognized her as a member of their tribe.*

*What struck me right away was the number of dogs. Each home seemed to have its own skinny-legged, big-shouldered dog, usually white, but sometimes brown or mottled, about as tall as Labradors. No need for doorbells. These canines notified the entire neighborhood of a stranger's approach long before they could have reached the entranceway. And none of them wore leashes, so the entire time as we passed by they would yip and yowl as if facing off a pride of mountain lions. Then they would nip at our heels until we were well up the trail. Several got close enough that Gilgal—and once even Apollus—managed to deliver a swift kick to a mongrel's mouth.*

*The second thing that struck me was how* beautiful *these people were—not only the women, but the men. I don't mean the men had a "handsome" or "rugged" kind of beauty. I mean they had long hair, thick eyebrows, and other facial features that made them appear distinctively effeminate. The Lacandones did not cover their bodies in tattoos or flatten their foreheads at birth like other Lamanites. (Actually, I wasn't sure if these people were Lamanites at all. Or even if they were related to Nephites.) Like Tz'ikin, they all possessed silky, shimmering black locks that flowed like hair in a Pantene commercial. And unlike the Lamaya, most of the adults wore simple white cotton tunics that hung down to their ankles, or shifts fashioned much like Hawaiian muumuus. The girls also seemed to have an affinity for colorful bead necklaces.*

*Several of the men in our group could hardly help themselves from gawking at the women, especially since so many were gawking right back, as if sizing up the quality and appearance of these strange new males who had entered their domain. However, I noticed that my man, Apollus, remained alert, keeping an eye out for danger, and seemed oblivious to all sultry and smiling females.*

*"I'm impressed," I said to him.*

*"Impressed with what?" he asked.*

*"With you," I replied.*

*He scrutinized me with drawn eyebrows. Without inquiring what I meant, he declared, "I'm glad to hear it."*

*My heart felt heavy, remembering some of the awful things I'd said to him: my accusations of narrow-mindedness and chauvinism and goodness knows what else! Tears came to my eyes and I said, "I love you, Apollus."*

*Still unsure what had brought on this gush of sentiment, he smiled and said, "I am in love with you too, Meagan." As his eyes went back to watching out for danger, he added, "But if you do not know this by now, I must have made a despicable effort at communicating it."*

*"No," I said. "I do know it. Maybe that's . . . that's why I feel so bad about the way I act sometimes, the things I say."*

*"Hm," he grunted. "Well, I am equally inclined to foolish statements. Besides, many of the words you speak regarding my shortcomings are true."*

*"I don't think so," I said. "Not from where I'm standing now. You are . . .* miraculous, *Apollus. A true miracle and hero in every way I can express."*

*"My!" said Apollus, putting his arm around me. "You really are feeling good today, aren't you?" He planted a kiss on the side of my forehead.*

*"Okay, you two break it up," said Ryan from behind. "Much more and I'm gonna be nauseous."*

*There was one habit that made the Lacandones cumulatively unattractive. Virtually every adult—male and female—had pinched in their fingers or dangling from their lips a homegrown and hand-rolled cigar. I even saw children as young as twelve or thirteen puffing on stogies. Ryan had noticed as well. At one point he turned to Tz'ikin and asked, "Does everyone around here smoke?"*

*"Of course," she said. "The Lacandones grow the best tobacco, picietl, and peyotl in all of the One World."*

*"Peyotl," Ryan repeated. Then it hit him. "Peyote?"*

*Tz'ikin nodded. "They also brew the best balché. And nowhere is there found a more ample harvest of 'flesh of the gods' mushrooms than in these mountains."*

*Ryan was appalled by the apparent rampant drug use. "Have you used all of these things?"*

*The question confused her. "Some are only for men, some only for sacred ceremonies—"*

*"What about cigars?" Ryan asked tentatively.*

*Tz'ikin shrugged. "Of course. Whenever I'm home."*

*He suddenly looked pale. "I'm beggin' ya . . . You're so pretty, Tz'ikin . . . If I were to see you with one of those . . . foot-long . . . I'm not sure I could take it."*

*Tz'ikin narrowed one eye and said thoughtfully, "You are a strange man, Ryan Champion. I have heard that some peoples do not like their women to indulge—"*

*"Or their men," Ryan added hastily. "I mean, at least, not among my 'direct' people."*

*"Is partaking of tobacco also proscribed by your curious religion?" asked Tz'ikin.*

*"Well, yes. It is. But that's only the cherry on the topping. Where I'm from it's also condemned by just about every intelligent person you can find. Our doctors have proven that it causes cancer, lung disease, and many other potentially fatal illnesses. Even breathing someone else's smoke can shorten your life."*

"*My great-grandmother lived until she was one hundred years old. I don't recall that I ever saw her without a cigar in her lips. Are you saying if she had refrained she might have lived to be a hundred and fifty?*"

"*Yeah, fine,*" said Ryan. "*Make fun if you want. Somebody can always find the rare exception. But you must have noticed how much sicker smokers are in general from non-smokers.*"

"*How would I have noticed that?*" she asked. "*I do not know any Lacandones who do not smoke.*"

*Ryan shook his head, realizing he wasn't making any headway.*

"*But,*" said Tz'ikin finally, "*if it pleases you, I will not indulge.*"

*To me it seemed a rather pointless request for Ryan to make. We only planned to remain among the Lacandones for one, perhaps two days. Then we would be off again on the final leg of our journey to the besieged lands of the Nephites. After tomorrow it was unlikely that Ryan or any of the rest of us would ever see Tz'ikin again. It occurred to me that Ryan may not have fully internalized this fact.*

*It was nearly dusk by the time we reached Tz'ikin's part of the village. It was situated on the eastern shore of a small lake tightly enclosed by mahogany and cypress. As we emerged from the jungle, the melodies of parrots and other songbirds quickly gave way to the artificial sounds of reed flutes and a few other instruments wafting from the shadow-darkened interiors of one or two huts. The fiery colors of the sunset were mirrored perfectly in the dark waters of the lake. I smelled woodfire and I heard the sizzling of tortillas on unseen clay griddles. Very few people were out and about, no doubt because of the hour. Most appeared to be inside with their families, though inquisitive eyes sometimes peered through wooden slats.*

*I finally did see one frail, gray-haired man. He was carrying a fiber sack toward a curious stone formation in the center of the village. The formation was natural, though many artificial carvings, murals, and other decorations had sprung up around it. To me it looked almost like a rocket had burst up from beneath the ground, causing the earth's crust to explode upward, piling up huge limestone boulders around the open hole. The "rocket" analogy also seemed apropos because much of the stone near the peak of this formation was blackened by ceremonial fires. The pit's interior wasn't visible, but its edge appeared to be the old man's destination. Before he climbed the final steps up a stone stairway, he paused, set down his sack, and ceremoniously washed his hands in a basin while chanting some kind of prayer in a low, guttural voice.*

*That's when I noticed that the sack was* moving. *Something was* alive *inside it! After his prayer concluded, the man glanced at us, then quickly concluded his task. He climbed to the edge, overturned the sack, and dumped in its contents. I squinted in the dimming light to confirm what it was.*

*"Did he just dump in what I* think *he just dumped in?" I asked out loud.*

*"Rats and mice," said Tz'ikin. "He is feeding the sacred serpents."*

*"You mean that thing is a* snake pit*?" asked Ryan incredulously.*

*"Yes," Tz'ikin confirmed. "Where do you think I obtained the yellow-chin viper that I'd intended to put in Fireborn's bedchamber?"*

*It had been a while since we'd heard the story of Tz'ikin's failed assassination attempt. I'd forgotten the particulars.*

*She went on: "Among the Lacandon, the 'nauyaca' serpent is worshipped as a deity of dark powers. People who are killed while capturing one alive to be placed into the pit are honored by our gods. Or, if the snake is accidentally slain, the person and their family are sorely cursed."*

*Tz'ikin stopped speaking. For the first time I realized how nervous she appeared. This wasn't the emotion I might have expected from a girl returning home after such a long separation. She led us slowly toward a wooden structure that stood near the lakeshore.*

*It was oval-shaped, about forty feet long, with rounded ends. Like the rest of the houses in this village, the doorframe, posts, and crossbeams were carved of hard, durable mahogany. The two-sided roof was thatched with the leaves of thorn palms, as were the windowless walls. Smoking braziers hung from both sides of the entrance; the smell of copal incense was heavy. There was no door in the entryway, and there was another opening on the opposite side of the house. As we peered inside we could see the silhouette of a man sitting in the opposite entrance, his back to us, staring across the lake. Tz'ikin motioned for the rest of us to wait and then approached the doorway. The man must have heard our arrival. If nothing else, he'd have heard the barking mutts as we entered the village, but he did not turn around. Tz'ikin entered the structure and paused near its center. She waited in silence.*

*"So you have arrived," said the man in the opposite doorway.*

*Tz'ikin nodded, as if the man could see her with eyes in the back of his head.*

*The man continued, "Last night I dreamed of your onen, your kindred animal spirit, the hummingbird. I reached out to touch it, just as I have on other nights when I dreamed such a dream. But instead of fluttering just out of reach, I snatched it out of the air. So I knew that you would soon be coming home."*

*The man had not yet turned to confirm that the person standing in the center of the hut was indeed Tz'ikin.*

*"Yes, I am home, Father," said Tz'ikin, her voice subdued.*

*After she'd spoken, the man finally slid around. As I saw his face, I flinched slightly. There was terrible scarring, mostly on the left side, from his nose all the way to his ear. I couldn't make out very much detail. The setting sun behind his head cast a shadow over his features. But there seemed to be a peculiar pattern about the scars, as if . . . I wasn't sure. He wore the same long white mantle as other Lacandones, so I didn't know if the scarring was anywhere besides his face. But his movements were awkward, so I knew that his feet were handicapped in some way.*

*"In my dream," her father continued, "when I opened my hand again, the hummingbird fluttered helplessly, so I knew that you had been injured."*

*"Yes," Tz'ikin admitted, glancing down at her sling.*

*"But also, I noticed that the hummingbird had no eyes. Therefore . . . I knew that you had failed." He took a puff on a fat, homegrown cigar.*

*Tz'ikin stared down at the ground, racked with shame, and peeped, "Yes."*

*My heart clenched. He was certainly referring to her mission to assassinate Fireborn. It seemed unspeakably cruel after all that Tz'ikin had endured—nearly losing her life more times than I could count—that her father's first words made sure to label her a failure. I'd always assumed that Tz'ikin had wanted to kill Fireborn out of vengeance for some great evil that Fireborn had perpetrated upon her. It was starting to appear as if the story might go somewhat deeper.*

*For the first time, her father acknowledged our presence. "You have brought strangers to our land."*

*"They are friends," said Tz'ikin. "Without their help, I would not have made it home. I would not have survived."*

*At that he looked away and said coldly, "Perhaps this would have been better."*

What? *I couldn't believe my ears! I came forward, stood in the doorway, and declared, "Tz'ikin's acts have been noble—more courageous than any woman I've ever seen. We may have saved her. But she has also saved many of us."*

*Tz'ikin glared at me. She didn't seem to appreciate my interruption. Instead she looked embarrassed and irritated. This was all very bizarre. I suddenly regretted that none of us had pushed Tz'ikin for a fuller explanation of why she'd tried to kill the commander of Teotihuacán's armies. More than ever I was eager to finish our visit to these mountains and be on our way. I even considered asking Tz'ikin to continue traveling with us. No matter where she went, it had to be better than staying here with a father who felt she should have died rather than return home a failure.*

*Tz'ikin made a clumsy introduction. "This woman—she is called Meagan." Tz'ikin turned to me. "This is my Father, Chief K'ayyum of the Wild Boar Clan of the Lacandon." Back to her father, she said, "Behind Meagan are Apollus and Ryan. They, and the woman, are Guardian-Messengers who I believe were sent here by our lord creator, Hachäkyum."*

*"Guardian-Messengers?" asked the chief.*

*"Yes," said Tz'ikin. "Guardian-Messengers of power."*

*I cringed. Why would Tz'ikin say such a thing? She knew better! By now she'd doubtlessly observed that we were about as human as humans could be.*

*She added, "Apollus and Ryan are great warriors of K'ulel Ah, the Whirlwind. I have seen them in many battles—in many circumstances where they should have perished. They cannot be defeated by the weapons of men. Apollus, of the tribe of the Romans, cannot be injured. All three of them can converse with beasts of the forest."*

*All at once it struck me that Tz'ikin's mystic religion* allowed *for supernatural 'guardians' who displayed human attributes. I wasn't sure why this hadn't occurred to me before. After all, these people worshipped* kings! *Surely they saw human failings in their kings. Yet their kings were also gods. Maybe we should have continually reminded her of our straightforward, unembellished humanity. But would this have helped?*

*We were, after all,* time travelers! *Totally dispelling our miraculous presence might have been impossible—that is, to all but Moroni. I felt sure that at least Moroni understood us. He may not have realized that we were from another century, but he recognized that we were no more than plain mortals, the same as other human beings.*

*Tz'ikin continued her introductions: "That man is Jacobah, Ryan's servant, of the people of the Water-Lilies. And those two are Moroni and Gilgal—Nephites from the regions of Cumorah of Desolation."*

*Chief K'ayyum stiffened in contempt. "You have brought* Nephites *to our land?"*

*Tz'ikin quickly explained, "Moroni is the son of the Nephites' highest-ranking war general. He was sent to Tikal as an emissary and was held as a prisoner with me in the Temple of the Morning and Evening Star. We were marked for sacrifice, but the Guardians, Apollus and Ryan, attacked with an army of Lamayans to set him free. They freed me as well, so that after I am healed I may again seek justice against the invader from Teotihuacán. And that man—" She referred to Lamanai. "—That last man is most important. His name is Eagle-Sky-Jaguar. He is the son of Great-Jaguar-Paw. He is the Prince of Tikal."*

*K'ayyum's eyes widened. Then he exploded with a cackling laugh, cigar smoke sputtering out his nose. I heard other laughter and realized more Lacandones were just outside the opposite entrance, listening.*

*"Prince of Tikal!" the chief sneered. "What nonsense is this? What Lamayan peasant have you brought to our village?"*

*"It is true, Father," Tz'ikin defended. "He is the son of Jaguar-Paw."*

*"Then I am the son of a boa constrictor," said K'ayyum.*

*"Indeed you are." Lamanai came forward until he stood just ahead of Meagan. "But we Lamayans have always believed Lacandones were the sons of boa constrictors. I am the Prince of Tikal, son of Chak Toh Ich'ak—the Great-Jaguar-Paw."*

*Some of the men outside the back door began to wander into view so they could see with their own eyes the person who dared proclaim such a title. I also noticed three women inside the house. They'd been standing in the shadows behind the glow of two hearthfires—one on either end of the building's interior.*

*Chief K'ayyum finally took the matter a bit more seriously. He studied Lamanai, and said, "Why would the son of Jaguar-Paw be traveling to my village with Nephites and holy Guardian-Messengers?"*

*"We journey to Cumorah and Tehuantepec to strike an alliance with the Nephites and all the scattered Lamaya of the One World," said Lamanai. "Fireborn is coming. He will arrive here any day. He comes with his armies—the Lightning Warriors and all the hosts of the people of the Water-Lilies."*

*K'ayyum shuddered. "Coming? Here?"*

*Lamanai nodded. "He must be defeated. Our alliance with the Nephites will drive Fireborn and his Lightning Warriors back to their northern wastelands forever."*

*I heard the men outside anxiously muttering. There was now some credibility behind the prince's words.*

*Lamanai continued, "Your people once bowed before my father and brought him tribute. Soon you will bow before* me." *He carefully scrutinized K'ayyum's scarred face. "I remember you now. You came to Tikal when I was a boy, just before the arrival of the armies of Spearthrower Owl. You met the Great-Jaguar-Paw in the Hall of Serpents with your retinue. Yes, I remember the meeting well. I was at court that day with my tutor, Hapai-Zin. But your face was not the mask of hideousness that it is now."*

*Lamanai's lack of respect was abominable, like it had never dinged in his brain that these people could wipe us out in a heartbeat, then go on about their lives as if we'd never crossed their paths. K'ayyum looked unnerved. But it wasn't anger; it wasn't Lamanai's blatant rudeness that had upset him. Something about that memory from long ago made K'ayyum squirm—so much so that he didn't react at all to the insult.*

*K'ayyum's cigar hand swept past his face as he explained, "This is Fireborn's pretty work. His minions splattered me with pine pitch and set me aflame. They made me a cripple by cutting off my toes. My first wife, Tz'ikin's mother, is dead because of Fireborn's evil. She was the most beautiful woman of these mountains—a bird of paradise in a swirl of butterflies—but the invader from Teotihuacán could not endure to think that a woman of such grace and beauty belonged to someone else."*

*So that explained it. It apparently wasn't Tz'ikin who had been the direct victim of Fireborn's insatiable cruelty. It was her parents. Tz'ikin was avenging wrongs done—not to her—but to her family. The sun continued to sink. As the orange glow of hearthfires created most of the light inside the building, I began to see K'ayyum's face better. The scars still showed residue of tar and grit beneath the skin. The pain he'd endured at Fireborn's hands must have been horrible. But did this justify his awful words to Tz'ikin, telling her it would have been better if she'd died rather than return home a failure?*

*People started coming forward out of the woodwork. They came from the backside of the building, from neighboring houses, even from the foliage to the right of K'ayyum's house. There had been far more people eavesdropping and spying on this conversation than I had suspected. Some were young warriors, carrying weapons.*

*Suddenly the Lacandon chief, so cold and mean when we first arrived, started playing the part of hospitable host. "Enter my home," he invited with a smile. "Come inside and join us, son of Jaguar-Paw! Bring your holy guardians and sit this day with the* Hack Winik—*the true people of the gods. Enjoy the bounty of our good fortune from* Akinchob, *the lord of corn."*

*But the bounds of his hospitality ended there as he added, "Only the Nephites may not enter here."*

*Moroni and Gilgal, who had started walking forward, stopped in their tracks.*

Unbelievable! *I'd had just about enough of these hillbillies. I clenched my fists and said brusquely, "If Moroni and Gilgal may not enter here, neither will I."*

*I displayed the back of my head and stomped outside. Ryan, who was momentarily taken aback by this rude exclusion, reacted next. "I agree with Meagan." He turned and followed me.*

*Next, Apollus said, "If you will forbid men as noble as these Nephites to enter these premises, no doubt you will also forbid a Roman." He joined us beyond the entranceway.*

*But as I walked up to Moroni, he stopped me with his eyes. Taking my shoulders, he whispered, "No, Meagan." He took in Ryan and Apollus as they arrived close behind me. "Do not insult them in this way. It could become highly dangerous. Go back. Gilgal and I will wait outside. There is a history here that you do not understand. The Lacandones have been the Nephites' sworn enemies for two centuries. This prejudice is now a part of their religion. These mountain tribes are among the first who began again to call themselves Lamanites. Now they have many names— Tetzali, Chamula, Zapotomak—not only Lacantūn. According to the words of Ammaron, theirs will be an existence of isolation and poverty until they begin again to repent and embrace the God of their fathers. Do not despise those who already face God's judgment. Go on. All of you, turn around. Tell them you're coming back. And if you can, convince Lamanai to hold his tongue, or we may all lose our heads."*

*I gawked at Moroni, his eyes radiating deadly seriousness. Reluctantly, I turned around. "We're coming back."*

*I reapproached the doorway along with my two time-traveling companions. To my surprise, Chief K'ayyum did not appear offended by our behavior in the least. He almost seemed amused, puffing on his wretched cigar like a smokestack. This was almost worse. I certainly did not want to be his "entertainment." I wished I could have stuffed that stogie down his throat. Twenty other villagers had also entered the rear door, all of them glaring at us with intense curiosity. Truthfully, it was only Lamanai who looked annoyed that we had almost declined the chief's invitation.*

*I glanced back one last time at Moroni, then I drew a deep breath and said, "So . . . didn't I just hear somebody mention food?"*

\* \* \*

## Apollus

Based on what Moroni had spoken to Meagan, I was beginning to believe that if we hoped to leave this village alive, we would do well to behave exactly as the chief had requested. Or, as I often said, when in Greece, do as the Greeks.

Before our meal was even served, K'ayyum's house was beset by nearly every warrior and elder of the village. They sat along the wall, filling every quatratus of space, and giving those of us who sat at the center less than two arms' length of breathing room. Dozens more were outside. I could hear grunting through the walls and see eyeballs blinking through slats in the thatching. The six of us—me, Meagan, Ryan, Lamanai, Jacobah, and Chief K'ayyum—sat upon a central square of banana leaf mats and rugs of rough fabric, our faces lit by the glowing coals of the two hearthfires. The roof was blackened with cooking and incense smoke, especially around the twin ventilation shafts. Soot also ingrained the faces of the three women who served us. I deduced quickly that they were K'ayyum's wives. Their demeanor toward the chief was comparable to that of polygamous wives whom I'd observed in wealthy Syrian homes—always deferent, but with behavior much more particular than that of servants. Despite their soot-blackened complexions, all three were beautiful, and at least two were half the age of the crippled chief. Tz'ikin herself could not have been much younger than two of her stepmothers.

Tz'ikin did not sit with us at our introductive banquet. Ryan seemed particularly concerned about her whereabouts, though he received no reply when he put the question to the eldest of K'ayyum's wives. Instead, the dignified but sorrowful-looking woman slunk away as if tribal proprieties would not have permitted her to speak to any man besides her husband.

The house itself had few impractical additions. Shelves were lined with drinking gourds and clay dishes. From the rafters hung unfinished arrow shafts, bundles of bird feathers, stacks of dried tobacco leaf, and other primitive odds and ends. The only decorative feature, other than the twelve incense burners called "god-pots," were dried stocks of corn which hung from the eaves. The cobs were red, white, and blue, much like the twenty-first-century flag of Meagan's home nation. Not dyed or painted, but natural in hue, and evenly interspersed—three reds, three blues, and three whites—all the way around the house. This was the extent of lavish furnishings for the chieftain of the Boar Clan of the Lacandon.

Prince Eagle-Sky-Jaguar was, without doubt, the object of greatest curiosity. Now and again I heard someone mutter that he did not believe Lamanai was truly a royal personage, but others seemed deeply and solemnly convinced. It was these skeptical observers who concerned me most. The feeling they exuded was not reverence, but fear and disdain. True to character, Lamanai seemed utterly oblivious to the opinions of others, iron-firm in the conviction of his immortality.

As our meal was served—white tortillas, white beans, red sweet potatoes, plum-sized red tomatoes, red chili peppers, and strips of red paca meat—the chief offered Ryan, Meagan, and myself an unusual observation:

"The great Lord Hachäkyum originally created the Lacandon tall and fair-skinned like the three of you, with hair like yours"—he indicated Ryan—"the color of golden sunlight. My ancestors also had curly bangs and thick beards of red and blue. It was Kisin, the Lord of Death, who spitefully darkened our complexions, and spoiled our hair with a little round stick while Hachäkyum's back was turned."

The details of the myth reminded me of the story of the Lamanite curse as recounted to me from the Book of Mormon, though this version must have contained many interpolations. I felt K'ayyum's eyes upon me. I tried to ignore him and eat my half-cooked beans.

He said to me directly, "You are, perhaps, the fittest-looking man I have ever laid my eyes upon. My daughter believes you cannot be defeated or injured in battle. Is this true?"

I shook my head. "No. It is *not* true, noble Chief. I can be defeated or injured the same as any man."

"So you do not concur with Tz'ikin that you are invincible through your powers as the Prince's holy guardian?"

I exchanged looks with Lamanai, who seemed curious how I would answer. Finally, I replied to my host, "I strive to defend not only Eagle-Sky-Jaguar, but *all* of the members of our party. If I have any powers, it is through the grace of my Heavenly Father and Lord Jesus Christ."

"Ah!" said K'ayyum excitedly. "Then you *do* concur that you carry within you the powers of the gods."

I raised an eyebrow. Strangely, I'd said exactly what he'd wanted to hear. "I do not carry such powers 'within.' Or what I mean is, I do not carry them 'of myself.' They are given to me, just as they are given to other men who strive—"

But K'ayyum was no longer interested in my semantics. He said, "Over the mountains, in the valley of Lake Mensäbäk, our enemies, the Chamula, have sent word that they have found a champion who can defeat our strongest warrior. It is a contest that we engage in every four cycles of the sun, in the season of rains. Two champions wearing the garb of Kisin, Lord of Destruction, and Sukunkyum, Lord of the Underworld, will fight to the death on a platform of stone. The tribal chief of the victor may choose thirty of the enemy's warriors for blood sacrifice at the ancient altar in the ruins of Desolation, the city of ancient kings. It is a sacred tradition of our peoples, and one which diverts our lusts for a more open and bloody warfare. What, my fair

Guardian, would convince you to fight for the Lacandon on the holy platform? What, besides the eternal gratitude and honor of the *Hach Winik*—the true people of the gods—could entice you undertake such a challenge?"

I finished chewing my mouthful of food, swallowed, then said to K'ayyum with great regret, "I'm afraid there is nothing that could convince me to fight in such a contest, noble Chief. Please understand; I am on an errand of peace, not a campaign of bloodshed."

There were grumbles of disappointment from the audience. The chief continued to study me, blowing great clouds of blue smoke from his cigar. Meagan looked green from the foul tobacco stench. Indeed, half of the people present held lit cigars. The clouded atmosphere had discouraged Meagan and Ryan from eating much of their food. Meagan ate only her tomatoes—a delicacy that I think she relished. Frequently she and Ryan could be seen holding their breath as the exhale of tobacco wafted from one direction or another.

At last the chief slapped the mat and said, "I would reward you with thirty of the most beautiful daughters of my people—one for each Chamulan sacrifice at the altar of Desolation. You could keep or sell them as you wish, or you could raise up an entire kingdom of your own progeny."

Some gasped at the munificence of the offer. Several men at the rear laughed, no doubt fancying themselves the master of such a harem. But I shook my head apologetically and replied to K'ayyum, "My mission is one of a most urgent and sacred character. I could not, in good conscience, divert myself from that task to which I am entrusted. I could not betray the faith of Eagle-Sky-Jaguar and the other members of my expedition."

The chief glared at me. His face reddened. It was apparent that I had insulted and embarrassed him, perhaps to the very depths. This may well have been the most liberal offer he had ever made for a task such as this. I had been afraid that something like this would occur. I searched my mind for something to say that might restore good feelings.

K'ayyum glanced at Ryan, as if he considered making him the same offer. Then he seemed to dismiss the idea. Though Ryan was strong and fit, he simply did not carry himself like a battle-seasoned warrior, and K'ayyum could sense the difference. Besides, I was the one who supposedly had never been injured—a skill not attributed to Ryan, presumably because Tz'ikin had seen the cuts he had sustained at the river.

Suddenly the chief's face brightened. He turned to Prince Lamanai. "Of course! How uncouth of me. I beg the Prince's forgiveness not to have recognized that the Guardian is a servant of the son of Jaguar-Paw. Perhaps it is not the Guardian's decision to make, and perhaps it is not to him that our gift of gratitude should be offered."

We waited for Lamanai's response. It infuriated me that he did not answer immediately. Was he flattered by the question? Did he believe he had the remotest influence upon such a decision? I knew the importance of giving Lamanai his due princely respect with this audience, yet I nearly tossed propriety to the wind and answered K'ayyum's asinine assumption myself. Finally, Lamanai spoke. But his reply angered me all the more!

"I do not have need of thirty young virgins, Chief K'ayyum," he said smugly. "Perhaps if there was something . . . more substantial that you could offer, I would do my best to persuade my Guardian otherwise. However . . ." He let the word linger in the air.

My eyes became firebrands, searing the soul of young Eagle-Sky-Jaguar. Nevertheless, I held my tongue. I did not undermine his authority in public, though by the cold snout of Cerberus, I confess it took great self-discipline. Then Lamanai, always eager to harvest the manure in his mind and spew it from his mouth, decided to dredge up further memories from his youth.

"On that day when you held audience with my father in the Hall of Serpents, I seem to recall that he asked you a question. Do you remember what it was?"

K'ayyum's expression changed markedly, darkening like a storm cloud. "I don't recall."

Meagan recognized the potential tension and tried to interrupt. "Maybe the chief would prefer it if we reminisced about such things at another time. I would like to ask the chief how it is that his people look so young, even when they are old, and how it is that they are all so beautiful."

In an act of utter contempt, Lamanai took it upon himself to answer her question. "I will tell you why. It is because the Lacandon are quick to adapt to all circumstances and eager to please all those who might otherwise disturb their pastoral existence. Their loyalties are to themselves alone. Not to lords, not to kings—certainly not to my father. And because they are so eager to avoid conflict at any cost, they face very little that might age them prematurely or spoil the beauty of their mountain paradise." He turned to K'ayyum, "Would you say that this was accurate?"

Frowning heavily, suddenly emitting more *steam* from his nostrils than tobacco smoke, the chief replied, "Your father never questioned my loyalty."

"My father never had the chance," said Lamanai coldly. "Since you pretend not to remember the question he asked you, I will repeat it now for all to hear. He asked, 'Does Lord Fireborn intend to bring his armies farther south into Tikal? Or will he remain in the north?' Do you remember your reply?"

"I told your father all that I knew," K'ayyum said in a low, simmering tone.

"You replied, 'I am convinced that Fireborn's intentions are peaceful. Much of his army has gone home to Teotihuacán. If he comes to Tikal, it will only be to expand trade and establish a deeper friendship with the Lamaya.'"

"And so that is what Fireborn told me!" snapped K'ayyum.

Lamanai was on his feet. "He told you his army had gone *home?* Fireborn showed you this *personally?* You could not climb a tree and see for yourself? You had no reports from other villages? My father *believed* you! Now he is dead! You were summoned to his palace to give him intelligence. Instead you gave him lies! What did Fireborn promise you? Riches? Power? Protection? Now you have reaped the rewards of his friendship. It's there on your face! It's there in your decrepit limp for all to see!"

He was insane—no other way to frame it. Our friend Lamanai had lost his mind. Any moment I expected weapons to be drawn. Feminine-looking or not, I did not doubt the Lacandones' ability to put arrows into our hearts. And—*curse Poseidon!*—I had only my short blade, having left our more lethal weapons outside with the rest of our provisions. We'd done this out of courtesy. *Courtesy!* It seemed now that our courtesy had made our situation twice as dire.

During Lamanai's surreal tirade, I noticed Ryan's head bobbing. He seemed to be having a difficult time staying awake. Was the drama of this scene not enough to hold his attention?

Chief K'ayyum broke down and began to weep. His fury had given way to tears. For a long moment he kept blubbering, onlookers remaining as still and silent as a winter's day.

Finally, K'ayyum confessed, "I was a fool, Lord Eagle-Sky. Fireborn blackmailed me. He held all my wives and children for ransom. My village was threatened with decimation. His army seemed as vast as the trees of the forest. I did not believe that my insignificant report could ever truly hurt your father. I did not believe it could extinguish the indomitable powers of the divine ancestors of Tikal—a dynasty that had been upheld by the gods for longer than my grandfather's memory . . ."

Now Meagan's eyelids seemed to be getting heavy. What was happening to everyone? She shook her head to try and reinvigorate her senses. Ryan looked ready to fall into his bowl of food, every scrap uneaten except . . . the tomatoes.

In my own eating bowl one plum-sized tomato remained. I snatched it up for inspection. The skin was undamaged, and yet I noticed a small puncture in the very top, at the spot where the stem had been attached. I was astonished. How could I have suspected foul play? Nature often created the very same puncture by plucking the stem. But on closer examination, this puncture went deep, piercing the fruit to the center. Plainly something had been inserted—a foreign substance injected deep inside. But would this poison induce sleep—or *death?*

I leaped to my feet in alarm. At the same instant, Ryan Champion fell forward onto the banana-leaf mat, eyes glazed and empty. Meagan looked around in a daze, her vision finally focusing on me. I drew my knife. Several warriors grabbed up clubs and spears, but no one attacked. They feared me. No one dared to be the first to confront the "Holy Guardian."

I eyed the exit—my escape. I had to leave, but not without my friends. Suddenly Jacobah, his hand still holding a half-eaten tomato, fell over onto his side, body limp. No time for protracted analysis—I could only save one. Brandishing my knife, threatening any warrior who appeared ready to rush me, I grabbed Meagan around the shoulders and hoisted her to her feet. She was teetering badly, but still conscious.

I glowered at Chief K'ayyum. Even with eyes still wet from tears over Lamanai's castigation, he watched me intensely.

I gritted my teeth. "What did you feed us? What was in those tomatoes?"

The chief didn't reply, just patiently observed, eyes glittering strangely, sending out rays of feverish light from those deep sockets. I looked at Lamanai. Why was he just sitting there? Why hadn't he risen up and drawn his blade? He just watched me. I glanced at his dish. No tomatoes. Had he already consumed them? *No.* I realized he'd taken none for his plate! As the first wave of delirium poured through my mind, I said to the prince, "You were warned, weren't you? Who warned you, Lamanai? What have you done?"

His expression was like a monument of stone, emotionless and detached. I might have struck right then—stabbed my knife into his foul, festering heart—but another wave of delirium nearly buckled my knees. I faced the entrance, still supporting Meagan while pointing the knife with my other hand. I lunged twice, lashing and causing those who blocked my way to clear a wider path. I reached the entryway. I made it outside into the torchlit night. Meagan became flaccid, eyes closed, head tilted to one side. I dragged her forward. I made it as far as the tree where we'd laid our provisions. Moroni and Gilgal were gone, as were most of the provisions. I might have expected Huracan to leap forth from the jungle, ferociously tearing apart Lacandones to the right and left. Our jaguar was not to be seen. I could only hope she even now aided in Moroni and Gilgal's escape.

I turned back to see that the villagers had followed my steps. They were surrounding me, pressing closer, keeping only enough distance to avoid the swipe of my weapon. Their faces began to blur and smear, like paintings left out in the rain. Then I saw only glowing firelights—pine-pitch torches and the bright orange tips of their cigars. These lambent flames left lightning trails in the air, like fast-moving fireflies, as my head swayed and my body staggered. I dropped Meagan. I fell to the earth, closed my eyes, and drifted into oblivion.

## NOTES TO CHAPTER 10

The Lacandon Indians are a modern-day tribe that presently congregates in only a few settlements in the highlands of Chiapas, Mexico. They have been the subject of exhaustive research by anthropologists of the twentieth century because it is believed that they, unlike other native peoples of Mesoamerica, have retained many of the traditions and lifestyles that have their roots in Pre-Columbian culture. In other words, they are seen by some as a bridge to the actual religion and culture of the ancient Mayans and Aztecs. Only a few hundred tribal Lacandones have survived into the present century, though they are commonly seen at the archeological site of Palanque, Mexico, hawking their wares of handcrafted bows and arrows and other novelties.

The origin of the tribal name "Lacandon" is likely the plural form of the Yucatec Mayan term *äh akantunoob,* which means "those who set up (build and worship) stone idols." In other words, this was not the name they gave to themselves, but a label placed upon them by their Mayan neighbors who had converted to Catholicism. Early Spaniards wrote of the *Acantunes* (the "Pagans" or "Maya Wild Indians") and referred to their jungle habitat as *El Acantún.* At one time or another some author changed the pronunciation to *El Lacantūn,* which also became the name of a local river. Finally, the word was deformed even further to Lacandón. The Lacandones refer to *themselves* as the *Hach Winik,* which means, as the novel states, the "true or real people" (Victor Perera and Robert D. Bruce, *The Last Lords of Palenque: The Lacandon Maya of the Mexican Rain Forest* [University of California Press, 1982], 8).

Some Latter-day Saints have wondered if the name Lacandon somehow relates to the Nephite leader named Lachoneus, whose domain in the land of Zarahemla may have encompassed the area where present-day Lacandones reside. After a careful study of the word's etymology, this hardly seems likely. A more fruitful study might focus upon the syllables of a name like Lachoneus and other unusual Nephite names, relating them to ancient languages in Mesoamerica and the Middle East. A number of studies have been undertaken and were discussed in the notes to Chapter 15 of *Warriors of Cumorah*. Interestingly, non-LDS anthropologists Victor Perera and Robert D. Bruce, without any acknowledgment of LDS beliefs, concluded after swapping Hebrew and Maya phrases that the two languages were "astonishingly sympathetic, both phonetically and structurally" (Perera and Bruce, *The Last Lords of Palenque,* 62).

The author chose to retain the term Lacandon as the name of the fictional tribe in this book because it seems plausible that even the ancients of Mesoamerica—perhaps even Nephites of the fourth century AD—might have referred to the inhabitants of this rugged, inhospitable region as "primitive, wild, and uncultured pagans," much like the Spaniards and their Maya converts some 1200 years later.

Though in this novel many of the terms, traits, and practices of the Lacandones are borrowed directly from books and articles on the Lacandon culture, the author has also taken considerable license for the purposes of telling his story. Most scholars describe modern Lacandones as a peace-loving, dignified, and spiritual people. However, it is the author's personal observation that this same characterization is also given by anthropologists to other primitive cultures—usually the ones they happen to be studying. In some cases such a characterization may be more a reflection of the nostalgic desire of urban societies to return to the idyllic life represented by rural peoples like the Lacandon, rather than reality.

The reality is that the Lacandon, like many other primitive societies of today's world, suffer from a wide range of social ills, including a depletion of their population to near extinction by such factors as interbreeding, loss of land and resources, and tribal infighting. Victor Perera and Robert D. Bruce in their book *The Last Lords of Palenque,* write, "There is almost a Sadie Hawkins Day casualness to the way northern Lacandones marry, unmarry, and remarry cousins, nieces, aunts and nephews." He also recounts many instances of tribal and family violence, infighting, and abuse. A report is cited wherein he recounts "forty cases of homicide . . . nearly all of which involved clan feuds or quarrels over women, and innumerable rapes, abductions and incestuous marriages." Beyond these kinds of crimes, Lacandones suffered until very recently from deplorably high infant mortality rates and lower life expectancy. They *still* suffer from a high occurrence of malaria, encephalitis, hookworm, ascaris, and other parasites and diseases, a high incidence of death by snakebite, rampant substance abuse, frequent domestic violence, illiteracy, and poverty (*The Last Lords of Palenque* 148–149). These points are not illustrated to say that the Lacandones are any worse than other cultures that suffer from poverty and encroachment, but merely to dispel the idyllic perceptions of some scholars of the last fifty years.

Many Lacandones, like other modern Maya, yearn for the opportunities and benefits of the modern world, while politics, exploitation, and prejudice often serve to keep them in squalor. Ironically, some anthropologists who study primitive cultures may perpetuate this condition by encouraging modernized society to "leave them alone" so they may continue in their traditional beliefs and practices, even though some of these beliefs and practices may interfere with efforts to incorporate the very modernizations that would improve health, education, and opportunity.

It would be interesting to discover all the reasons why certain cultures and peoples of the world have remained in utter physical and spiritual isolation into the nineteenth, twentieth, and twenty-first centuries. In LDS theology, it is logical to assume that all tribes and cultures of the world can trace back to a single ancestor (or ancestors) who rejected—for whatever reason—the fullness of the gospel. Therefore, it becomes possible that particular societies have literally been "cursed" for their apostasy. Such a statement must be viewed with caution so as to avoid unrighteous bigotry and stereotypes, though it may represent a vital fact of world history (see Gen. 4:15, 9:25, 27:29; Deut. 30:7; Zech. 8:13; 2 Ne. 5:21–24; D&C 98:29–46; Moses 5:52; Abr. 1:26).

In any case, we are comforted by the doctrine that the Lord chastens only those whom He loves, and that the ultimate solution for combating all cycles of isolation, ignorance, poverty, and squalor resides in the teachings and practices of the gospel of Jesus Christ (see Alma 23:16–18; Rev. 22:1–14).

# CHAPTER 11

## Ryan

I awoke to the feeling that my nose was on fire—blistering all the way down my throat and into my lungs. As my eyes popped open, I saw a ceramic bowl filled with a yellow mud, fizzing and smoking from some kind of chemical reaction. The effect was like smelling salts, but twice as potent. I tried to push the bowl away, but my hands wouldn't work right. They were tied together in front.

The chemical was taken away as soon as the people saw that I was awake. I raised up my eyes and tried to focus on the swarm of faces. I recognized Chief K'ayyum and many other Lacandones who'd sat in the audience the night before.

*Night before?* I could hardly believe it was daylight. We were outside. The sun was blazing straight overhead. It wasn't even morning—it was *noonday!* It seemed only *seconds* ago that I was sitting in K'ayyum's house with Meagan, Apollus, Lamanai, and Jacobah. Fourteen or fifteen hours had passed like the flash of a match. I tried to get a handle on the last things I remembered. I recalled suffocating cigar smoke. Eating a tomato. Some kind of shouting match between Lamanai and the chief. But beyond that, the details were fuzzy. At some point the video of my memory banks got stuck on fast forward, then blacked out entirely.

I searched the faces frantically for my companions. I saw only one—Jacobah. He was lying directly beside me, hands also bound, and also wheezing and spitting as the same bowl of fizzing chemicals was removed from under *his* nose.

My sense of reality whipped back. I became so awake and alert that it was hard to believe I'd ever slept. Three seconds and I put it all together. *Drugged.* I'd been drugged. It must have been slipped into my food.

The crowd comprised the same white-cloaked, bleary-eyed spectators as yesterday. I swore every one of them was high on something. But I was no longer their guest. I was their prisoner, like a captured animal. *I'm a long way from BYU,* I thought. A long way from Utah. A long way from anything I'd ever imagined in my meager life. If I ever made it home alive, a mission to the grimiest, slimiest grunge-pit on earth would seem like a walk in the botanical gardens of paradise.

I shut my eyes against the bright sunlight and demanded, "What's going on? Why are you doing this to me?"

K'ayyum announced, "You are awake, Ryan."

I said sarcastically, "Brilliant observation. Where is everyone? Where's Apollus—and Meagan? Where's Tz'ikin?"

The chief ignored my questions and said, "Your hair and flesh are as white as 'He of the Sun'—*K'in Ah.* But what are your powers? Are you the great warrior and destroyer of armies that my daughter proclaims? Can you talk to beasts and commune with deities of the Underworld? Can you see the ghosts of the dead in the darkness?"

I blustered at him, "What are you talking about? You're all crazy. Untie me! Why are you doing this?"

I heard Jacobah say, "They fear you, Ryan. They will kill us both. Call on your God. Do not wait. *Call on Him now!*"

The villagers gasped and backed up a step, as if I had the power to do exactly the thing that Jacobah was suggesting. What did my oh-so-faithful bodyguard expect me to do? Ask Heavenly Father to conjure up an earthquake? Zap all onlookers with an electric shock? Jacobah believed in Jesus Christ, but there was much he didn't understand. Or was it *me* who didn't understand? Jacobah really believed I could do this. His voice carried no doubt. What was wrong with me? I shut my eyes and prayed for help.

Chief K'ayyum continued speaking. He also sounded like he was praying, but to *whom?* It almost sounded like he was praying directly to *me!*

"Guardian of Lord Hachäkyum, if you are indeed an incarnate spirit of K'ak' Ah, the Lord of hunters and warriors, prove yourself to us! Prove your magical powers and we will worship you! We are but humble servants of the gods. It is our right to test the divine nature of Hachäkyum's messengers. You belong to *us* now, Ryan Champion. Permission is granted by your former master, the Prince of Tikal. Let us test your powers to see if you are worthy of the veneration and homage of the *Hach Winik*."

*Permission is granted?* What was *that* supposed to mean? Granted by *Lamanai?* That was impossible. Lamanai was our *friend.* I rolled onto my side and pushed up on my knees to try and see over the heads of those in front.

"Lamanai!" I called out. "*Lamanai!*"

K'ayyum kept right on babbling. "If you survive the first test— the nauyaca pit—we will begin to believe. If you survive the second test—the cauldron of fire—we will know that you are sent of the gods. And if you survive the third test—a trial of your own choosing—we will bow down to worship at your feet until the end of all things, until the *Hach Balam*—the Holy Jaguars—shall be set loose to devour all life so that everything may be reborn for the New Heaven and the New Earth."

The nauyaca pit . . . *The snake pit!* They were going to cast me into that disgusting pit where the old Lacandon had dumped the rats!

I screamed at K'ayyum. "Cut me loose, you psychopath!" I yelled at the others: "What's wrong with you people? If you throw me in there you'll kill me! You know it! *LAMANAI!*"

The Prince of Tikal didn't answer. He wasn't here. Either that or he was hiding in one of these huts like the cockroach he was. The chief also did not respond—just nodded to four of his henchmen. I was seized on all sides. They stood me on my feet, facing the weird rock formation in the center of the village—the same one with the bizarre graffiti written in blood. My body was instantly drenched in sweat. I fought like a wolverine with all my strength, kicking and punching with my bound fists. I broke free! I ran all of two steps before more Lacandon warriors pounced and wrestled me to the ground. They carried me by all four limbs, struggling and fighting. I cried out in terror, "*Stop! Please! You don't know what you're doing!*"

Yet I suspected that miserable Chief K'ayyum knew *exactly* what he was doing. That speech sounded too rehearsed. I surely wasn't the first would-be god he'd ever tossed into that infernal pit. I'd have bet anything I was only the latest in a long list of men, women, and children executed this way.

My prayers became vocal: "Heavenly Father, help me! Stop them! Give me strength, Lord!"

Behind me I could hear K'ayyum talking to Jacobah: "The Guardian-Messenger no longer requires your services. If he passes the three tests, he will have the whole Lacandon nation to see to his needs. Stand tall and your death by the blade will be swift and painless."

The next moment passed like a dream—like a nightmare—in slow motion. In my mind flashed the faces of my mother and father, my older brother, Rory, and my older sister, Kay. I saw my grandparents, my bishop, my twelfth-grade Seminary teacher, and even Valerie Vanbeekam, a girl I'd had a crush on in the second grade. The warriors climbed the stone steps to the summit of the limestone formation. The pit's fire-blackened edge loomed closer. I could smell the odor of death; I swore I could hear the sound of hissing. Still, I fought my executioners, yanking one arm free and grabbing a man's hair. After they pried it loose, my fist was full of greasy black strands of hair, pulled out at the roots. An instant later I was staring face-first into the abyss. Below I could see the bones of the dead. The bottom appeared to open up into a larger area. I couldn't see any snakes. It was the hottest part of the day; they were doubtlessly just beyond the edge of the sunlight. The blood was rushing so loud in my ears I couldn't hear the words of my continuous prayer.

"Lord, help me! Lord, save me!"

Then it was over. With a mighty heave, I was flung into the darkness, my hands still bound. That's when I experienced the day's first miracle.

It was not a straight, clean fall. There were many jutting rocks and boulders. I bounced off the first sharp ledge with the kind of impact that should have shattered my collar bone like a china dish. Yet I hardly felt anything at all.

My bishop—the same bishop whose face had just flashed through my mind—had once told me about a car accident he'd had at the Point of the Mountain. Another driver had forced him off the highway. His car, he claimed, flipped three or four times. I saw the picture they'd taken. His Nissan Altima looked like an accordion. No one would have believed anyone could survive. But Bishop Hoffman walked away with hardly a scratch. One Sunday he told me and the other priests that he firmly believed two angels had sat on either side of him. He didn't see them, just felt their presence. They buffered and buttressed him against the collapse of the chassis, the grinding of metal, and the shattering of glass. He wasn't sure why they'd aided him, or what he'd done to deserve their intervention. But they were present just the same.

So my bishop and I now shared a common miracle. I didn't see angels. I don't remember seeing anything at all. But there must have been an explanation for why my shoulder didn't shatter, or why my hip, two yards later, wasn't pulverized on the next ledge. My guardian angels somehow flipped my body upright like a house cat. I landed feet-first in the stew of rotting bones, my knees collapsing perfectly to cushion the impact.

As I came to my senses I perceived movement in the shadows all around me. But there were no snakes inside the dust-filled beam of sunlight that shined down from above. I balanced myself on my knees, using the ribs of a skeleton for leverage. That's when the first snake slithered out of the darkness.

It crawled into the light underneath a femur bone, then past the gaping jaw of a hair-covered skull. The serpent stopped, the eyes on its triangular head lasered right into mine. I didn't budge a muscle, my bound hands balanced against my belly.

We both remained in that position for several seconds as its forked tongue tasted the air. It must've been six feet long, with a bright yellow throat—hence its name, yellow-chin viper. The rest of its body was a pattern of rich copper and crimson diamonds. But those eyes—those *eyes!* If eyes are the window to the soul, it was plain to see that this creature was as soulless as a vampire. It glided toward me another six inches, and stopped again. I sucked a breath, and I swear the snake heard me. If it ever had doubts that I was there, four feet away, it doubted no longer.

I thought of Huracan. I thought of my unusual ability to talk to beasts. Would it work with a reptile like it had with a jaguar?

"H-hello," I said, my throat as dry as the encircling bones. "I mean you no harm. If you don't mess with me, I won't mess with you."

*I've lost my mind,* I thought. *I'm talkin' to a flippin' snake!* But did it understand me? It darn well hadn't lost interest. Slowly, it slithered closer—its speed now uniform and determined. If anything, its crawling speed was *increasing.* Then its neck and body rose up into the shape of an 'S.' Looking into those soulless eyes I felt sure that it *had* understood me—and it didn't give a hoot. *It was preparing to strike!*

I gasped to the depths of my lungs; my limbs chilled to ice as every drop of blood rushed to my heart. I heard commotion above, but I did not glance up. The snake owned my gaze. The strike would come any instant—so fast I'd never see it. The only evidence would be fang marks in my skin and burning venom in my flesh. It would strike *now!*

Something crashed down. A pair of sandals landed right on the snake's head! The person inside those sandals grunted sharply and rolled into the bed of skeletons, flipping bones into the air.

"Jacobah!" I shrieked.

Somehow my Lamanite bodyguard had fallen into the pit! Had K'ayyum changed his mind about executing him with a blade? I reached out with my bound hands and grabbed his cloak. The yellow-chin viper still convulsed in the throes of death, its head mushed like a fritter. Jacobah's face was a picture of pain. He reached down toward his shin.

"Jacobah, what happened?"

"I ran! I jumped!"

"You *what?*"

"I broke free and ran for the pit."

"You jumped in *deliberately?* Have you lost your mind? *Why?*"

"To save you—if I could."

Again he winced in pain, grabbing his hamstring. I was so blown away I couldn't speak. *Save me?* He might as well have committed suicide! He'd surely busted his leg. The foot appeared to be twisted almost forty-five degrees. There was already purple swelling around his ankle. The purple color was darkening right before our eyes. Yet Jacobah seemed more concerned with me than his own predicament.

His face still showing great strain, he asked, "Are you bitten?"

"No."

"Where are the snakes?"

No need to answer him as two more triangular heads entered the beam of light, tongues a'flicking. One grayish-colored specimen was only three feet above Jacobah's head. I grabbed his arm and dragged him into the center of the lighted area.

Above us I heard laughter. Lacandones were gazing down at us, reveling in Jacobah's stupidity in thinking that leaping into this pit was any kind of escape.

I said, "Gimme your hands."

With the knot on the backside, it was impossible to untie my *own* hands, but relatively easy to untie Jacobah. Afterwards he untied me, our eyes continually watching every corner of the shadows as three or four more snake heads slithered into view.

I asked Jacobah, "Did you see Apollus or Moroni?"

He shook his head. "No one but you."

"Why are they doin' this, Jacobah?"

He said through clenched teeth, "We were betrayed. By Prince Lamanai."

Bleakly, I replied, "I figured that one out already."

With our hands free I reached under Jacobah's armpits and hoisted him to his feet. He let out a yelp from the pain in his leg. I feared he might faint, but ol' tough-as-nails Jacobah balanced himself on one foot. He'd even grabbed up a skull, ready to pummel any serpent who even thought of crawlin' closer. I'd gathered up a couple of fist-sized stones with the same idea in mind.

Jacobah asked, "Why didn't you call upon your God?"

"I did. He sent *you.*"

Though I said it with irony, the emotion of it welled up in my chest. I was sure no king or president ever had a more dedicated servant—a more loyal friend—than I had in Jacobah. I never *did* understand why my welfare meant so much to the guy. I decided, in a very real way, Jacobah was a gift sent to me from heaven.

Three more flicking tongues crept into the light. The contrast of sunlight against the shadows was so stark that I couldn't exactly tell how many total slitherers we were dealing with. Nor could I guess the size of the room—and I didn't dare stick my head into the shadows so I could find out.

Jacobah hurled his skull at a pair of vipers, hitting both. One snake curled into a ball and disappeared back into the shadows, but the other one only flinched and continued creeping forward. Wouldn't such creatures have naturally feared any animals larger than themselves? They showed no such concern and continued gliding toward the vibration of movement and the smell of warm blood.

Jacobah observed, "Your God must send more than me if we are to live."

I replied, "One miracle at a time. I hope I'm not the only one praying for help."

"You wish me to pray?"

"Well, *yeah!*"

Four more heads appeared. I threw both of my rocks, nailing one. Jacobah armed himself with a leg bone. He poked it aggressively at several snakes just a yard away. The vipers struck at the bone. One imbedded its fangs into dried cartilage and hung on, releasing an ooze of poison. Jacobah flung both bone and snake into the shadows, nearly tripping from his injury. We heard the snake hit an unseen wall.

This strategy of standing here wasn't doing us much good. More and more snakes were slithering into the light. I had to see into the shadows. If I could just shade my eyes—

There was an overhanging ledge ten feet above. It caused a shadow to cut into the beam of sunlight. Unfortunately, the area with the shadow was also occupied by three advancing snakes. I reached down and picked up an entire human skeleton, much of it held together by decaying sinews and tendons. I thrust it upon the three serpents at once. Then I flung everything else at my feet, driving them back. Those things were *tenacious!* Our abuse only seemed to irritate them. Some of the vipers inside the circle of light were striking at empty air. The inches separating us continued to shrink.

At least the three snakes in front of me had been driven back. I stepped forward until my face crossed into shadow. I blinked as my eyes adjusted. The room was larger than I'd imagined. And every square yard was occupied by at least one yellow-chin viper.

Jacobah asked, "What do you see?"

"I see a tunnel."

"Truly? A tunnel?"

I feared I'd sounded too optimistic. Yes, there was a narrow shaft that seemed to go in for some distance, but I couldn't see where it led. And which of us had the nerve to venture blindly into a dark tunnel filled with venomous serpents? Besides, three steps toward that shaft and my legs would become a dart board for snake fangs.

Something else encouraged me. I sniffed the air. Above the smell of rotting flesh, snake filth, and cave dust, I caught a very encouraging whiff in the direction of that shaft—a fishy kind of scent, like the odor coming from the rear of K'ayyum's hut. Was it my imagination, or did I smell the lake? I'd lost my bearings in the fall, but perhaps that tunnel led back toward the water.

I announced to Jacobah, "We gotta go *that* way."

"How?" he inquired through gritted teeth. The agony in his voice reminded me that darkness and snakes weren't our only challenges. I'd have to practically carry Jacobah as he hopped on one leg. But we weren't going anywhere unless I somehow cleared a path.

I looked again at the skeleton I'd just tossed. The leg bones had broken off when it landed, but the rib cage, arms, and skull were intact. I had an idea. As Jacobah threw more stones at advancing reptiles, I gripped the spine and pelvic bone of the skeleton.

"Watch out!" Jacobah yelled.

Unseen, a small viper had hidden behind the pelvis bone. I tried to react, but the snake struck. It bit the sole of my boar hide sandal. The fangs did not penetrate. The viper was only two feet long. I brought down my other foot on its head, stomping several times to make sure it was history.

Again I gripped the skeleton and swung it across the floor in a wide circle. Several of the creepy-crawlies hissed furiously as I swept them out of the way. I took two steps forward and made the same sweeping motion. The skull broke off and rolled across the room, but several more snakes were moved out of striking range.

I called back to Jacobah, "Stay with me, buddy. Can you hop?"

He made the attempt, but tripped on the tangle of bones. As he fell to the side, a snake six inches above his head coiled to strike.

"Jacobah!"

To my amazement, the wily Lamanite struck first. Jacobah grabbed it just below the head, brought up his other hand, and with a swift twist, broke its neck. He flung it away and scrambled back into the cleared pathway before two more slitherers could mosey into position to take revenge.

I continued sweeping the skeleton back and forth, sending snakes scurrying out of our path. With each sweep I'd lose an arm bone here, a rib bone there. This whole effort was rather psychotic. Was any of this even worth it? Soon it would get so dark we wouldn't be able to see the ground.

I asked Jacobah, "Are you still praying?"

"I'm praying! I'm praying!"

With a final sweep I pushed aside four vipers—one of them nine feet long. The sucker attacked the skeleton with three or four strikes. A rib bone dripped with strings of sticky venom. But at last it looked like the pathway into the narrow shaft was clear. I abandoned the skeleton and lifted Jacobah back to his feet, pulling his arm around my neck for support. For the next twenty feet, as we entered the shaft, there were no serpents. Then the tunnel made a tight turn. Our last hint of light cut off abruptly. And to our further dismay, I saw a viper's orange tail slip into the same darkness. It was the only time a snake had fled from us!—and down the very path we were about to trod. For all we knew, there were hundreds more of 'em waiting for us just inside the shadow.

Jacobah's teeth remained clenched, but his lips were moving, whispering a prayer. "Give him your power, Father God of Jesus. Give Ryan your power."

I said to Jacobah in total seriousness, "Do you believe we can walk into that darkness? Do you believe God can protect us?"

He replied, "I will believe if you believe."

"I *do* believe it. I believe God can do anything. He can protect us, Jacobah, if we got enough faith."

"I will have faith if you—"

"*No,* Jacobah. I can't carry your faith—not on this one. You have to have it for yourself. And put it in the *Lord.* Not in me."

He swallowed, but stiffened his jaw and nodded. "I will have faith. My *own* faith. And in the Lord."

Jacobah's declaration filled in the gaps of my faith as well. I drew a deep breath, blew it out, and then I said, "All right. Let's go."

So there was Daniel in the lion's den. There was Moses parting the Red Sea. And there was Ryan and Jacobah walking blindly through a tunnel of yellow-chin vipers.

We forged ahead with Jacobah hopping painfully on one leg, his arm around my neck. No creepy-crawlers sank their fangs into our flesh. I heard hissing in the blackness. I accidentally kicked something that quickly slithered away. Once, as I grabbed the wall for balance, I reached into a crack and swore I felt something scaly and cold-blooded. But no reptiles attacked us.

Need a scientific explanation? Okay, here's the best I got. Even deadly snakes liked to see what they were biting, and these serpents were no less blind than ourselves. And yet *any* scientific explanation would've been utterly unsatisfying. It was a miracle. True blue. Pure and simple.

Soon we were trudging through water. A short distance farther and it was up to our waists. I carried Jacobah onward. We discovered that yellow-chin vipers can swim. I swore I felt several scaly bodies squirming past us. So apparently those serpents weren't prisoners in that pit. They could come and go as they pleased, though most of them likely stayed in place so they could benefit from the regular entrée of rodents.

About the time that the water reached our shoulders, I began to see light. But before we reached it, I was swimming breast stroke as Jacobah clung to my back. Soon we could see the wide opening where the cavern exited into the waters of the lake. And just inside that opening we saw a girl in a canoe.

Breathlessly, she cried out, "Ryan! Jacobah!"

Such a welcome voice. The voice of Tz'ikin.

\* \* \*

"Keep your hands in the boat," Tz'ikin whispered, still guiding our dugout along the lakeshore with her pole. "The sword grass below the surface can slice off your fingers."

She was talking about the water plants that clogged much of the lake and made the going slow. Though I manned the oar, it wasn't half as effective as Tz'ikin's pole. We might've tried to cross the lake through deeper water, avoiding the shoreline, but that would've put us in open view of the village, which would've unquestionably prompted dozens of dugouts to take up pursuit. I'd survived the nauyaca pit. I had no interest in testing God's patience with my second "trial" involving fiery cauldrons. We'd gone far enough around the lake that I could clearly see Tz'ikin's village. If I could see *them,* they could certainly see *us.* But perhaps we were too far away now to be distinguished from other average-Joe fishermen.

Because Tz'ikin had insisted that we remain quiet, I hadn't asked her to explain her actions of today or last night. Nor had I asked what had become of our friends. But if she was willing to talk to warn us about the sword grass, I figured it was finally time to make inquiries.

"Why, Tz'ikin?" I began. "Why did you tell your father that Apollus and I were sacred Messenger-Guardians? Why would you say this when you know it isn't true?"

She continued to kneel at the bow, working the pole. Without turning around, she replied, "I do *not* know this."

Frustrated, I asked, "You still think we're gods, eh?"

"I did not say that you were gods. I said that you were holy. I said that you could talk to beasts. I said that you could not be killed. And because I know it is true, I went to the entrance of the water cavern and waited."

I sat there aghast. I glanced at Jacobah. His eyes were closed, face still full of anguish. I pondered Tz'ikin's words. Yesterday I'd thought her introduction of us to her father had been an outright lie on her part—that she was somehow covering for her failure to kill Fireborn by claiming that she'd befriended a couple of gods. But now, after seeing us emerge from that snake pit, her theories about our supernatural abilities only seemed to be reconfirmed. I even wondered . . . was it true?

*No, no.* I tossed the idea right out. If I started to really believe I was invulnerable, the Lord would smite me for sure.

Jacobah spoke. "Where are you taking us?"

So my faithful bodyguard wasn't unconscious after all, though his eyes remained closed.

Tz'ikin replied, "To Moroni and Gilgal."

I felt a rush of exhilaration. "They escaped?"

Still facing forward, she said, "Yes. My father had food brought to them, but they did not eat it. They fled into the jungle. They were aided by the balam. Huracan killed two of my father's warriors. I found Moroni and Gilgal this morning hiding in the forest. I stole one of my uncle's dugouts for them to use and told them to meet me at the far end of the alligator swamp."

I asked, "Where's that?"

"Through here."

We'd reached a narrow channel banked on either side by tall reeds, sword grass, and impenetrable jungle. The water trail led west. I might've missed it if Tz'ikin hadn't pointed it out. It didn't even look like water. What I mean is, the channel was so thickly carpeted by green, white, and yellow lily pads that I could've easily mistaken it for earth. She continued working her pole while I used the oar to push us past roots and other shallow-water obstacles.

I asked, "What about the others? Apollus and Meagan?"

She didn't answer for a long moment, then said, "On their way to Desolation."

"Desolation? A *city?*"

She nodded. "Yes. An abandoned city. Abandoned by Nephites."

I said urgently, "What'll happen to them?"

"Apollus will fight."

I remembered now. The contest that Chief K'ayyum had mentioned—the fight to the death where thirty warriors were destined to be sacrificed by the winning tribe. "When? How soon?"

She replied, "A few days. I'm not quite certain."

A single blade of sword grass whisked my arm, nicking the skin like a razor. I looked at the tiny trickle of blood, then I said to Tz'ikin, "Apollus will not fight. I *know* it. He'll give up his own life rather than cause the deaths of thirty innocent men."

She said simply, "I would not count on it."

I raised my eyebrows. "You *wouldn't?*"

"They will use Meagan . . . as leverage."

I shook my head. "Won't matter. He still won't kill for them."

But Tz'ikin wouldn't be swayed. "They will find a way. I assure you, Apollus will fight. Even if . . ."

"If what?"

But she wouldn't reply. She still hadn't glanced back this entire time. I hadn't even seen the girl's face since we'd climbed into the dugout. I demanded, "Turn around. Talk to me, Tz'ikin. Tell me what they will do."

She shook her head. "I . . . I cannot face you."

"What? Why not?"

I leaned out over the dugout to see part of her face. Before she turned away again, I saw for the first time that she was weeping. This surprised me. I'd have never known it by the tone of her voice. But with tear-streaked cheeks, she added, "I cannot look upon you. I am . . . ashamed."

"Ashamed of what?"

"Of my people. Of myself."

Flabbergasted, I said, "Tz'ikin, you just saved our lives—*again.*"

She said nothing to that. I set down my oar and came forward. After placing my hands on her shoulders, I turned her around. Still, she kept her eyes downcast.

I implored, "Tz'ikin, it's not your fault. You didn't cause this to happen."

Her face was turned into her shoulder. "I cannot look at you, Ryan Champion. I am not worthy to see your eyes."

I almost laughed. It sounded ridiculous. Instead I only said, "Don't be silly."

"Please," she said, her voice totally serious, "don't make me."

I released her and backed away, still perplexed. It was like something religious or superstitious—as if she believed there would literally be some terrible consequence if she raised her eyes.

I said, "Tz'ikin, I am your friend. You have done nothing to betray that friendship."

She shook her head in disagreement. "I brought you to my village. I did not warn you of the danger. I knew that my father would not approve of the Nephites. I thought, perhaps, because of you and Apollus, and because of Prince Lamanai, that he might forbear any action."

I said, "You couldn't have known that he'd end up actually *conspiring* with Lamanai."

"I knew that he would try something. I knew it when he ordered me to leave the feast. But I made no effort to warn you."

I sat back. "Okay. So you were afraid. Still, I don't think your warning would've changed anything."

"It might have changed . . . something."

I pondered this, then I spoke again. "You said a moment ago that you believed I couldn't be killed. I'm sure to you that's probably how it appears, but I don't think it's entirely true. Even so, the reason for my survival would not be because of any power I possess. It's because God is protecting us. Not just me. I believe He's protecting everyone in our party."

She shook her head. "I do not believe this same protection . . . applies to everyone."

"I do," I said firmly.

She turned around again, pushing us forward with the pole. "I can never go back to my village. I can never return to my people."

I thought about this, and then I replied, "Why would you *want* to?"

She was silent. I was afraid my response was too callous. To be more compassionate, I added, "You've been in the vengeance business a very long time, Tz'ikin. But it seems like you've been doing it mostly for your father. I certainly understand your hatred. If a man like Fireborn had killed my mother, I'd hate him for the rest of my life. But our God teaches us that vengeance is His, and He will repay—"

Tz'ikin corrected me. "Fireborn did not kill my mother."

I blinked in surprise. "But last night the chief—"

"Fireborn *defiled* my mother. My *father* killed her. He . . . *saved* her . . . from Fireborn's corruption."

She continued pressing forward through the lily pads, seemingly emotionless, the pain of it pushed back so far she may have hoped it was gone forever. I sat there with my mouth dangling, wondering if I'd ever heard something more despicable and evil. What could I say in reply? My mind was blank with loathing. I hated Chief K'ayyum. I hated the entire Lacandon nation.

Under his breath, I heard Jacobah say in utter contempt, "Lacandon fungus-eaters." Apparently it was a rather harsh epithet, though to me it sounded a bit odd.

We emerged from the channel into a very shallow, swampy pond, also carpeted with lily pads. True to its name, dozens of alligators basked on the muddy bank. Most were unruffled by our presence, though some crawled into the water and sank into the slime, as if playing the odds that one of us might fall overboard. Herons and other long-legged birds walked across the lily pads, poking their beaks into the muck. The going continued to be slow. In many places my oar touched bottom, so I used it like a pole.

As we neared the far shore, I saw another dugout, pulled into the cattails. Before we'd reached the bank, Moroni and Gilgal came out of the forest. My heart soared. There was nothing like the sight of a prophet to restore confidence and security. Also accompanying them was Huracan. The jaguar's tail was diving and dancing; she was very enthused to see us.

"What happened?" Moroni inquired.

As I recounted the story of the snake pit and Tz'ikin's rescue, Moroni and Gilgal helped Jacobah from the canoe. Gilgal pulled our dugout into the cattails alongside their own boat while Moroni and I carried Jacobah into the trees where they'd set up a temporary camp. He and Gilgal had salvaged most of our supplies and weapons as they fled the warriors of Chief K'ayyum. Gilgal rejoined us as we examined Jacobah's leg. The muscle was now a rainbow of colors—dark red, purple, and black. The shin was thoroughly swollen and contorted.

Gilgal commented, "This boy's not going anywhere. That bone is probably broken. May take months to heal."

I said testily, "We don't *have* months. And we're not gonna leave him here."

Gilgal shook his head. "Got no choice. I'm not going to wait around to be tossed into a snake pit by K'ayyum and his crazies." He glared at Tz'ikin, who continued to make eye contact with no one.

Pleadingly, I said to Moroni, "We can give him a blessing. I have olive oil."

The prophet said curiously, "*Olive* oil?"

I took out my vial. "Yes. It might be a little rancid, but . . ."

I gave it to the prophet. He twisted it open, sniffed. He said with great reverence, "So this is olive oil."

"You mean you've never seen—?" I stopped myself. Stupid question. Olives were an Old World thing.

Moroni continued, "The Nephites use other oils—the cottonseed or the ramon nut—very hard to extract. But my father once told me that the oil of olives—as from the fruit of the allegory of Father Jacob—was the most appropriate. Where did you obtain it?"

I stammered, and fortunately didn't have to answer as Gilgal declared, "No balm can heal *that* wound."

Having been a party to many miracles already in one day, I said to Gilgal, "*Faith* can heal it."

I got into position to anoint Jacobah's head. There wasn't much oil left. I had to wait a long time for the tiniest drop to emerge. The honor of pronouncing the actual blessing belonged to Moroni. As I laid my hands on top of the prophet's hands, I tried as hard as I could to soak in the experience—the opportunity—of participating in a Priesthood blessing with one of the greatest men in all of human history. I feared, because of all the other pressures and stresses, that I wasn't able to fully grasp the experience. But over time I would realize that I'd rarely enjoyed a greater honor in all my life.

In the blessing, Moroni said, *"I would exhort you, Jacobah, to come fully unto Jesus Christ, who is your Lord and your God. It is by faith in Him that you will be strengthened in your hour of need. Deny not His gifts, nor His powers, and through His mercies you will be enabled to walk, though at times your pain may seem too great to bear. Remember that the Son of Man bore all pains and afflictions so that you, Jacobah, might repent and be healed by His cleansing blood. Let your pain be swallowed up by your faith in Him . . ."*

I listened in awe. For the first time I was able to place a voice—a real human voice—to the words of the Book of Mormon, and in particular the verses of Moroni, chapter 10. As he closed the blessing in the Savior's name, Gilgal was pacing contemptuously.

Afterwards, Gilgal said emphatically, "We cannot linger here, Moroni. And we cannot bear the burden of an injured man."

The prophet turned to his fellow Nephite and said simply, "He will not be a burden."

I looked again at the injury. To me it appeared just the same, but Jacobah's *face* was different. It seemed to be shining, and his eyes were moist with tears. The Lamanite pushed himself up to a sitting position, and then attempted to stand. Immediately he crumbled to the ground in intense anguish. Gilgal shook his head in frustration.

But Jacobah insisted, "I'm all right. I will try again."

As he did so, I turned again to Moroni, "We have to go to the city of Desolation. Tz'ikin says that Meagan and Apollus are being taken there."

"To Desolation?" asked Moroni.

"Yes. They'll try to force Apollus to fight to the death against a warrior from a tribe called the Chamulans."

The prophet pondered this and said, "Desolation is to the west— a journey of two to three days over these mountains and across a wide river."

Again Gilgal interjected his caustic negativity, declaring to Moroni, "Fireborn's armies are coming. They will overrun this place in a matter of days. We must reach Cumorah as soon as possible to warn Judge Zenephi and your father. The Nephites must prepare! *There is no more time to delay!*"

I faced Gilgal nose to nose. "Back off, Jack! This is Apollus and Meagan we're talking about. *Apollus*—who has saved your life more times than—!"

Moroni interrupted, "No more shouting. No more fighting. We must have no conflicts among us if we are to succeed and survive. The power of God is given to men who govern their passions. Yes, Ryan, have no fears. We will go to Desolation."

I sighed in relief. Gilgal stood there a moment, fuming. Finally he threw up his arms and walked away.

I added to Moroni, "Somehow we gotta rescue Apollus and Meagan before the fight begins. I feel certain Apollus will let them slay him before he'll participate in such a contest."

I heard a whimper from Tz'ikin. Though she'd moved apart from us, I could see her shoulders trembling from fresh tears.

I stepped closer to her. "Tz'ikin, stop blaming yourself and join us. No one holds any grudges. And we still need your help."

She said quietly, "If I had done more . . . if I had acted sooner, it might have saved . . . her life."

The words shook inside me like an earthquake. "What are you talking about? *Whose* life?"

She whispered, "Meagan's."

My heart clenched. No air could enter my lungs. "What do you mean? You told me she was with Apollus—on her way to Desolation. *Tell me what you mean!*"

Contrary to my earlier instinct, I grabbed her head and forced her to look into my face. She tried to fight me, but then at last she focused. Finally she pulled away and sank onto the ground.

Still shaking, she said, "They will kill her, Ryan. She is probably dead already. They will show her bloody garments—or even her decapitated head—to Apollus as a way to entice him to fight. It is what they *always* do. Sometimes they will murder the entire family of the Lacandon warrior who is chosen. But they will not tell him until the day of the contest. They will do it to provoke the greatest possible hatred. They will tell him that his family was butchered by his opponent. Sometimes it is true. Sometimes the warrior's loved ones are delivered to the Chamulan for him to slay. But even if the Chamulan does not do the killing, they will *say* it was him."

My energy seemed to drain out of my limbs, my mind convulsing with fury and terror. Then I let out a yell from the back of my throat, shaking off the terror like a black curtain. The sound startled Huracan, who released a growl of her own.

I said sternly, "No, Tz'ikin. Meagan is alive. I won't believe anything else."

Moroni stepped toward us, "Well spoken. Neither will I."

Even Jacobah declared, "Nor will I." He was standing on his own—no assistance—and even putting some weight on his broken leg. Did I say broken? There was no way, ten minutes ago, that *anyone* could have stood upon that leg in any fashion whatsoever. The Lamanite's teeth were still gritted and there were beads of sweat on his forehead. As Moroni had stated in the blessing, Jacobah would not be entirely relieved of pain. Gilgal watched with astonishment. Then Jacobah took several limping steps forward.

"Well?" Jacobah asked. "Is there a reason that we hesitate? Desolation is not getting any closer."

Gilgal looked nonplussed. He had no response for Jacobah or Moroni or anyone else. Yet after all that we'd experienced, the thing I found most surprising was that Gilgal should be surprised at all.

NOTES TO CHAPTER 11

Nauyaca is the Mayan name for the Fer-de-Lance, or *Bothrops Asper*, which is widely regarded as the deadliest snake in Central and South America, not only because of the size of this viper (up to ten feet in length) and its ability to inject large amounts of highly toxic venom, but because of its naturally aggressive temperament. Without treatment, a bite will generally cause death within forty-eight hours. Even for those who survive, the poison causes massive tissue damage around the wound, literally rotting the victim's flesh, and frequently leading to limb amputation. The snake commonly inhabits crop fields, especially sugarcane and corn, where it comes into contact with farm workers. Until recent years, a bite from this viper was one of the most common causes of death among adults of the Lacandon Indians of Chiapas, Mexico, and other rural-living Central American tribes (*Encyclopedia Britannica* and *The Last Lords of Palenque*). The Fer-de-Lance is also a possible candidate for the snake that caused the Jaredites so much trouble in the ninth and tenth chapters of Ether.

Priesthood holders in The Church of Jesus Christ of Latter-day Saints are counseled to only use olive oil when performing sacred ordinances. Olive oil was used to anoint in ancient Israel, and likely has served this function since the dawn of time. Of course, olive trees did not grow in the New World. Still, it can be assumed that priesthood holders among the Nephites performed ordinances and blessings in much the same manner as they are performed today. It is unknown what oil the Nephites may have used for blessing the sick. There are, of course, many possible alternatives, from corn oil to cottonseed oil. In the absence of olives the Lord would have certainly allowed His faithful followers to use a substitute. It is the author's speculation that Mormon or Moroni would have understood that olive oil was the "appropriate" or "preferred" oil for sacred ordinances. It can be assumed that Mormon and others would have known about olives and olive oil from the brass plates as well as from the allegory of Jacob, the brother of Nephi, found in chapter 5 of his book.

# CHAPTER 12

## Garth

*I had accepted it.*

*I felt I had accepted that my son was no longer a young boy. Or perhaps I was only stowing the emotional pain in the back of my mind. I did not dwell upon it. I would deal with it later. For the moment I was not nearly* as concerned about *my son's life, his age, or his physical condition, as I was about the state of his soul. I could accept any fate for a loved one—even death—but not the corruption of their spirit. Not the loss of their salvation. This was a fate that I would never accept—not while there remained the slightest breath in my loved one's body.*

*And yet for Joshua I felt, of late, a resurgence of hope. To me there were strong hints that the honor and nobility that I would have expected to see in my son were slowly reawakening. I felt certain that a burning testimony would soon reignite in his heart. He had not forgotten—only briefly lost his way.*

*As for the scripture in the Book of Mormon that spoke of . . . of fallen captains at the battle of Cumorah . . . I did not think of this. Marcos had refused to accept it—had suggested that there might be another interpretation. But I dared not even to contemplate this. I put the subject out of my mind completely. Such things were in the hands of God. For now, perhaps forever, this was where they would remain.*

*It was after dark when we reached the city of Zenephi, a short distance from the base of the Hill Cumorah. The silhouette of Cumorah's elevation loomed above us like a sleeping Goliath. I may have called Zenephi a city, but it appeared to me more as an encampment. There were but a few structures of stone, and probably none erected in the past four years. Most homes were of unstripped branches, shoddily thatched roofs, and stretched canvas. In truth, the city was little better than a shanty-town. I smelled the scents of roasting meat, rotting garbage, and the foulness of human waste. Although ditches and pits utilizing the natural flow of Cumorah's spring waters had been excavated for sewage disposal, the system was not well tended, and raw waste overflowed in many places, even over segments of the roadway. Every direction where I cast my eyes I was met by the hardened gaze of men, women, and children whose faces reflected the baser instincts of malice and fear. In none of those gazes did I see the gospel light of hope. My heart ached for them, especially the young ones—those who had no idea of the storm that was coming.*

*It was evident that most of their time and effort had been expended building massive and elaborate defense works in the tradition of Captain Moroni of old. It was no secret that Captain Moroni was a personal hero of Mormon. He'd named his own son after the great war commander. So it was understandable that his defense works were quite similar to those described in Alma, chapter 50. The barriers included deep ditches with steep earth embankments cast up against the inner wall, stands of timbers with sharpened pickets, and a multitude of towers. We passed through three layers, or checkpoints, displaying these types of earthworks as we neared Zenephi's city center. At each gate was posted a strong garrison of Nephite soldiers who demanded of us our names, ranks, and a count of the warriors in our company. Of a truth they seemed to require everything but blood samples and social security numbers.*

*At each gate we were met by military officers of increasingly higher ranks who demanded greater and greater details regarding the purpose of our visit. At the final gate—the gate that would access the offices of government* and *the headquarters of the army—our progress was halted by an officer whose rank finally exceeded that of my son. His name, according to the sentry who went to fetch him, was Lamah.*

*As he emerged from his office, his stern face and stiffly set jaw scrutinized Joshua in the torchlight.*

*"Why have you abandoned your post in the north, Captain Josh?" he inquired with harshness, knuckles balanced heavily on his hips.*

*Joshua raised his chin in defiance and said stiffly, "I have left my men of the Fox Division in the capable hands of my first officer, Kigron, whom you know well, Commander Lamah, since he served under your leadership at the battle of Jordan."*

*"As did you for a time, young Joshua," retorted the commander. But then he heaved a dismal sigh, as if the images conjured by the memory of that terrible battle were most unpleasant. Shrugging it off, he said, "Yes, I know Kigron, but that doesn't answer my question."*

*"I'm here on a matter of urgency—" My son glanced in my direction. "—the details of which I wish to discuss only with General Mormon."*

*"It's late," said Lamah. "Mormon is probably preparing to retire for the evening, if he has not retired already. We all have an early day tomorrow."*

*"What's happening tomorrow?" Joshua inquired.*

*"Council meeting. All the judges and war commanders. Bound to be some tension. If you remain in Zenephi, your presence may also be required."*

*"What will be discussed?"*

*"Money," said Lamah. "Gold. Commanders need more. Judges won't share it. People don't have it to give. What else do they ever bicker about?"*

*Joshua grunted and nodded. He said to Lamah, "I hope to return northward at dawn. I would be most grateful if you found out whether General Mormon can receive me tonight."*

*The commander furrowed his brow while considering the request. I sensed that he respected my son, though perhaps he considered him a bit of an upstart. Finally he heaved an additional sigh. "All right. Wait here. Have your men wait over by the fire."*

*Lamah departed. Ammonchi began commanding the men to form ranks close to a hearty blaze that burned a stone's throw to our right, fed with wood by the tower guards to ward off the evening chill. Myself, Marcos, Josh, and of course, Nompak—who utterly refused to leave Joshua's side for any reason—stood nearer to the gate.*

*I must confess that my heart was pounding. I mean, yes, I was just an old dullard—a devoted bookworm who thought that he'd turned his back on adventures like this long ago. Nevertheless, the prospect that I might find myself, in a matter of moments, standing face-to-face with a man who had been a hero of mine since earliest boyhood, got the ol' blood pumping a little faster. I tried to place aside all preconceived notions of what to expect, hoping merely that I would maintain my dignity and not stammer like an adolescent.*

*As we waited, an entourage of men and soldiers approached the bridge and gate which crossed into the government compound. It was an easy matter to pick out the most prestigious member of the entourage—a gentleman adorned in a bright red mantle with excessive embroidery and featherwork. He also wore fine leather sandals, a red cone-shaped hood, or helmet, with circlets of gems, and some kind of fancy breast- or neck-plate fashioned of silver or iron—it was difficult to be certain in the dim light. I assumed the neck piece and helmet were a brand of insignia designating his office, along with spindle-shaped earrings out of which hung a strip of un-spun cotton. The uniform was much reminiscent of the Huaxtec noblemen who would not occupy these coastal lands for another thousand years. But I'll not encourage narcolepsy with such scholarly comparisons.*

*Anyway, this man paused after noticing Ammonchi and the other soldiers who warmed themselves by the fire. He called over to them, "Men of the Jaguar—where are you from?"*

*Ammonchi replied, "We are of the Fox Division of the northern coasts."*

*"Captain Josh's division?"*

*"Yes," said Ammonchi.*

*Before Ammonchi could speak further, the well-dressed man broke away from his entourage and approached the soldiers of the Fox Division with urgency, saying, "It has reached my ears that a great tragedy has befallen your division. Please tell me, what is the fate of Captain Josh?"*

*Awkwardly, Ammonchi raised his hand and pointed it at us. "Perhaps you should ask Captain Josh yourself."*

*Even in the darkness I perceived that a state of surprise seized the man in the conical hat. I do not think these were the words that he expected to hear. The strangeness of his reaction was obvious, though I could not quite decide how to interpret it. But despite his temporary befuddlement, the man seemed to recover well enough. He approached those of us who stood near the gate, followed closely by his entourage.*

*"Captain Josh." His greeting had a tone of authority.*

*Joshua and Nompak both bowed respectfully. "Yes, your honor, Chief Judge Zenephi," said Josh.*

*The chief judge continued to gape at my son, mouth tightly shut, as if a cat had caught his tongue. Finally, he said, "I am relieved to see that you . . . are well. There are rumors that you may have suffered some nasty business, even an attempt on your life."*

"Yes," said Joshua slowly. "Though I can't imagine, Sir, where you would have heard this rumor . . . especially since the violence occurred only a few short hours ago."

Zenephi must have perceived the subtle accusation, yet he shrugged and said innocently, "The rumor was one of impending danger. Unfortunately, the same rumor is circulating about several of our noble captains who fight so diligently for the Nephite cause."

"I see," said Josh. "Well, as you can see, I survived any attempts of violence."

"That you did," Zenephi conceded, nodding three times. There was an awkward pause. Finally, he said, "Well, obviously I am inclined to take such dangers and threats far too seriously. I should accept that our captains are quite capable of looking out for themselves."

"Yes," said Joshua, with a peculiar curtness.

The chief judge waited another uncomfortable moment before replying, "Well, I am very pleased. Since you are here, perhaps you will join us tomorrow for the war council. Important matters are to be discussed that may determine our fate as a nation."

"If possible," Joshua replied, "I will be in attendance."

"Very good," said Zenephi. "Until tomorrow then. Good night, Captain."

"Good night, Judge Zenephi."

The chief judge took his leave and was admitted through the government gates with his entourage. I could feel the tension stirring in my son—and also stirring within Nompak and Marcos—as the judge's men passed by and disappeared inside. As soon as he felt sure that Zenephi's attendants were out of hearing, Nompak said to Joshua, "Did you see that? The reaction on his face?"

"I saw it," said Josh.

"What does it mean?" asked Marcos.

"It means," said Nompak, "that our situation is more grave than I could have ever presumed."

My son's eyes turned to Ammonchi. The Banner Chief, when he caught Joshua's stare, turned away conspicuously and faced the fire. I felt a crushing weight in the pit of my stomach. Was it really so obvious? So clear? In these past moments—in these few brief exchanges—it appeared that we had suddenly learned the identity of several of Joshua's principal enemies.

*Lamah emerged from within the compound. He approached and said to Josh, "General Mormon will see you. He said that he was expecting you."*

*For the second time in as many minutes, my son looked thoroughly astonished. "'Expecting' us?"*

*"That's what he said. He commanded that I send you to him immediately."*

*Once more, I experienced an unusually swift surge of blood through my veins. The moment was upon us. I was about to enter the presence of the Prophet Mormon.*

* * *

Joshua

My mind was reeling. I hardly remembered walking from the gate to the residence of General Mormon. Zenephi had confessed nothing. I had no hard evidence to prove my case. Yet there was not a shred of doubt in my mind—the chief judge of the Nephites was guilty of treason. This conspiracy that had nearly taken my life ran much deeper than I would have ever suspected. The question kept pulsing: Why would Zenephi—why would any Nephite—betray his people on the eve of their potential destruction? What could they possibly hope to gain? I needed time to collect my thoughts—to sort out what I was going to do, what I would say when I returned to my men.

Ammonchi. He was part of it. I was sure of it now. It suddenly seemed incredibly fortunate that I was on my way to speak with the supreme commander of the armies. Yet what would I say to him? How would he handle the news? He would dismiss me as young, brazen, and paranoid—I was sure of it. Lamah said that he was *expecting* me. How was it possible that Mormon expected my arrival considering that yesterday, at this hour, I wasn't even aware that I would be here myself?

Mormon's personal guard quickly ushered us into the building that had become the general's residence. It was a sturdy, square structure built around and on top of the ruins of an older structure. Supposedly the older ruins dated back to the days of Teancum and Captain Moroni, his son's namesake. The recent carpentry and woodwork was shoddy and hastily executed, like every other structure in

Zenephi, but the great Mormon had frequently commented that he felt very comfortable here, dwelling among the ghosts of those who had lived in the days of former heroes.

As we approached the general's office, I was reminded of the preeminence of this moment by looking in my father's eyes. Beyond the next doorway was a prophet of God. I had known Mormon for five years. I had known him as a great war commander, the most respected man in the Nephite nation, and perhaps as the most determined and energetic person I had ever met. But for some reason the significance of that other title—Prophet of God—resounded more loudly in my mind than it had ever resounded before. I wasn't quite sure why. I could only assume it was the expression on my father's face that drove it home. I had met General Mormon on several occasions. He had approved my commission as a captain. Yet strangely, because of the reverence in my father's eyes, I felt as if I was meeting him for the very first time.

As we entered his office, the general was standing at the other end. His back was to us. Mormon's office was the largest room of the residence, with a roof ten feet overhead and a wide circular opening that offered a portal view of the stars. The opening was covered at the moment because of the day's rains, but there was a space for smoke to escape. A pair of torches flickered on poles on either side of his round stone table, but most of the room's illumination seemed to come from dozens of beeswax candles situated throughout the room. General Mormon was in the process of lighting even more of these as we entered, presumably in anticipation of my arrival, almost as if he wanted as much light on this event as could be had.

As I glanced around I realized that the general was completely alone—no bodyguards or attendants, or at least none in the same room. I felt a twinge of disapproval over this. Considering who he was, I would have insisted that he remain in the perpetual shadow of a dozen men like Nompak. But there was no one else within hearing, unless he decided to yell at the top of his voice.

Finally, he turned to face us, feet bare, wearing only his well-worn cotton mantle—one that I suspect he had owned for twenty years. My father drew a breath. Marcos was also captivated and silent. The prophet's presence was no less breathtaking than it ever was, and yet to me he also looked older than I had ever seen him before. I mean, Mormon was certainly not a young man. Some speculated that he was in his mid-seventies, though no one seemed quite certain. However, tonight every muscle in his body seemed tired and drawn. The lines in his face looked as gnarled as the ancient olive trees in the Garden of Gethsemane. But as soon as he recognized me, the familiar spark of robust energy and power seemed to return. He smiled warmly and waved us deeper into the room.

"Come in, Captain Josh, Nompak. Sit upon my floor. Who are these other two men?"

There was no alarm in his voice as he asked this. Just kind curiosity. But here was the first example of my lack of preparation. I'd given no thought as to how I might introduce them or explain who they were. Caught off guard as I was, the only option seemed to be stark, simple honesty.

"This is my father, Garth," I said. "And my cousin's husband— uh—" Suddenly it seemed inconsiderate to say it that way, so I said, "I mean, *my* cousin, Marcos."

Mild amazement crossed the prophet's face. Mormon knew that I had been found wild and alone in the wilderness. I had never mentioned my parents, and whenever I had been asked about my family and kin, I had always been vague and evasive. But despite whatever he might have been thinking, the general took my father by the shoulders and drew him forward until they touched foreheads, in the customary Nephite embrace. My father remained speechless, even overcome.

Finally, in a dry-sounding voice, Dad said, "It is an honor."

Mormon looked into my father's eyes. The longer the prophet gazed, the more interested—even fascinated—he became. At last he declared, "There is . . . *light* in your eyes."

At first I wasn't exactly sure what this meant. But my father seemed to understand. However, he made no reply, just smiled broadly, his eyes moist, ready to overflow.

Mormon further added, "You *know*. You *understand*."

My dad nodded and said in a whisper, "Yes."

I began to grasp what they meant. Mormon was referring to the gospel. Or truth. Or perhaps that the prophet recognized—just by my father's eyes—that he had a testimony of Jesus Christ. As this settled over me, I started to realize how lonely it sounded. What I mean is, for Mormon to have recognized this in my father's eyes meant that he rarely saw it—rarely enough that it was surprising and unique.

He then looked at Marcos and said, "You also."

Marcos nodded.

I started to feel a little uncomfortable. Unworthy. I felt a familiar ache inside me. A longing. Something I wanted. Something I missed.

Nompak looked impatient, but he remained at attention in the presence of his supreme commander.

"I wish," said Mormon to the others, "that I could ask everyone to stay. There is much I would like to know and hear." To my father and Marcos he added, "Your presence confirms . . . many things. But first I must speak with Captain Joshua alone."

There were no objections from Dad or Marcos. Nompak faithfully followed after them to the front part of the residence where the general's guard was situated. After they were gone, the great commander just stood there looking me over, as if he wanted me to speak first.

Finally I said, "Lamah told me that you were expecting me."

"Yes," said Mormon.

"But . . . how could you know that . . . when I didn't even know it myself until—"

"I prayed that you would come," he said calmly. "And God has heard my prayers."

I just stood there, stunned, and at last said, "You *prayed*—prayed that *I*—?"

"—that *someone* would come," he clarified. "It was your face that appeared before me. Plainly the Lord has selected you, young Joshua."

I fidgeted. I had no retort. Honestly, it sounded utterly ridiculous. Not that God had answered Mormon's prayer, but the idea that God would select *me*. This seemed preposterous. But how could I doubt the word of a prophet of God?

Slowly, I said, "I . . . have also come for my own reasons."

This statement sobered his mood a bit. Mormon nodded succinctly and said, "Yes, of course. Please tell me your concerns, Captain. Then I will tell you my reasons for asking the Lord to bring you here. It may be that both matters are closely related."

I began by saying, "General, I believe . . . there is a dangerous conspiracy at work in the government of the Nephites."

"Hm," said Mormon, again nodding. I had the firm impression that I wasn't telling him anything that he didn't already know.

Yet I persisted. "I believe this conspiracy involves many of the highest-ranking members of our government." I paused again.

"Go on," said Mormon.

"Last night . . . and again *today*—during our journey to the settlement of Zenephi—there were two separate attempts on my life. One involved a calculated attack on my column by a company of Wolf Witches. I believe the attack may have been somehow supported, or instigated, by high ranking officers of the Fox Division."

"Do you know who these officers are?"

"I may know who some of them are," I replied. "But I have no proof. And also . . ."

"Yes?"

"I believe that this conspiracy may involve other captains and commanders in the field, and it is my *strong* suspicion . . . that at the root of this conspiracy . . ."

He waited.

". . . is Chief Judge Zenephi."

Mormon let this sink in, then replied simply, "I see."

"Again," I added, "I have no proof, but—"

"So you have come here to make these accusations against officers and judges without any proof? Just based on suspicions and feelings?"

"Somewhat more than that, but . . ." I looked down in shame. "Yes, mostly. Mostly suspicions and feelings." I looked up again, my face set, tone much bolder. "And *instinct*. My Snake Seeker, Nompak, if I may call him in, will support what I say by giving—"

"There is no need," said Mormon in the same calm voice. "I believe you."

My eyebrows shot up. "You do?"

He nodded. "I have known of various intrigues stirring among the Nephites for some time."

"You *have?*"

"Yes."

"And you know that such intrigues may involve the chief judge?"

He sighed darkly. "Yes, I know it. Zenephi is a vain and cruel man. It was only a matter of time before he fell in with the authors of secret combinations."

"But *why?*" I asked desperately. "I mean, what do the conspirators want? What could they possibly hope to gain?"

"Power," said Mormon. "Vengeance. They are weary of living in poverty for so long here at Cumorah, putting all of our energies into defense works and pit-digging rather than reconstructing the beautiful cities that our people have abandoned and fled during my lifetime. Satan fills their hearts with an appetite for blood and a foolish pride that deceives them into believing that because the Lamanites have not attacked in great numbers for four long years, they must be weak. They imagine that they are trembling in their strongholds, praying that the mighty men of the Nephites will not rouse like a sleeping dragon and come upon them with unspeakable fury. The adversary whispers this cunning deceit in the ears of our warriors from morn until eve, until they begin to believe it. And because these words are pleasing to the carnal mind, they can no longer hear the whisperings of the Holy Spirit, which would testify of their folly."

Breathlessly, I said, "But why kill *me*—a captain of the army that is defending them? How will this aid in their cause?"

"As you wisely supposed a moment ago, you are not the only object of their wicked designs. They have carefully identified *all* captains and officers who they feel would oppose them in a renewed campaign of aggression against the Lamanites, and against the Gadianton armies from the north."

I looked squarely at the general. "But . . . if they have targeted *me,* they will also target . . ." I stopped as I realized that there was nothing I could tell Mormon of which he was not already keenly aware.

He nodded solemnly, painfully, and said, "Yes. I have no doubt that I am also viewed as an obstruction to their plans. Once they looked upon me as their deliverer. Now that opinion has faded. For four years have I directed the attention of the Nephites to the sole cause of our defense in and around Cumorah. I have made no preparations whatsoever for a campaign of aggression to retake our lost lands and fallen cities. I had hoped—I had prayed—that during these four years perhaps the Nephites might turn their hearts . . . that they might once again become a delightsome people and come back to . . ." The voice of the Lord's servant choked and for several moments he couldn't speak.

I just stood there. I could think of nothing to say, so I waited for him to wipe away his tears and continue.

Finally he said, "I do not doubt, Captain Josh, that like you, I will soon become an object of their dark intentions."

"Then we have to do something," I said with urgency. "We have to thwart their plot. We have to expose Judge Zenephi for who he is!"

But to my bewilderment, Mormon was shaking his head. "No, young Joshua. There is no need. There is no longer any time."

"No *need?*" I retorted. "No *time?*"

"Captain Josh, you are a brave warrior," Mormon declared. "From the moment I first set eyes upon you in the land of Desolation, the Spirit has whispered to me that you are a remarkable soul. Wandering, perhaps. Full of much anger and confusion. But we both knew the reason for this, and so that reason was removed. I knew that you were a boy whose heart was good at its center. I even saw you much as I once saw myself—eager, headstrong, determined to set the world aflame, and sober enough to make a lasting difference for the sake of the Nephite nation."

Again a response escaped me. Why was he saying these things—pouring out compliments and observations—at a moment like this?

He continued, "But you are also encompassed by many mysteries, Joshua. Once I prayed to know the answers to such mysteries, but the Lord told me only that you are in His capable hands, and that I should be satisfied with this for the present. Now, after meeting your father and your cousin, and seeing the light of Christ in their eyes, I am reminded that you are without a doubt an exceptional soul. And I believe you are deeply beloved of our Father in Heaven."

My eyes watered, clouding my vision. I realized I had forgotten this, or at least I had not heard such a thing seemingly in forever. But even if I had, I wondered if there could ever be anything more powerful than hearing it from the mouth of a true prophet. I steeled my nerves, determined that I would not shed tears.

Mormon continued, "So because of this, I will tell you, Joshua, what the Spirit has whispered to me over the past few days."

I felt as if I already knew what he was about to say. My mood changed again as I braced myself, trepidation already stirring within.

"The enemy is moving," Mormon declared. "His armies are assembling from the east and from the south, from the west and from the north. The Lamanites and the Gadiantons march swiftly toward our lands. They will begin to arrive and surround the regions of Cumorah at any hour. In their hearts is only one objective: the complete and total destruction of the Nephite peoples."

I did not want to hear this. I could *not* hear it! Everything I had fought for—the whole purpose of my life until this day!—seemed to be sinking from my grasp. I shook my head, "We can fight them. We can drive them back."

Again the eyes of this spiritual giant filled with tears. "Not this time, my young captain. Yes, we will fight. We will fight with all our might and power. Even I, though I begin to bear the infirmities of age, will fight alongside the people whom I love. But . . . we will not be victorious."

"No," I said, the anguish now overflowing. "It can't be true. All our preparations. All our defenses. They will hold. *They will hold.*"

Mormon came forward as I spoke. His wrinkled hands—still as powerful at seventy-plus as a man of twenty—took hold of my shoulders as he said, "Listen to me, Captain. You must accept the truth of what I have said. I *know* you, Joshua, just as I know myself, and I know that you would fight for the Nephite people to the very death if that time came. But that time is not yet, and before it comes I have a task for you that I am confident is more important than all the lives of every man, woman, and child of the Nephites throughout our thousand-year history. On the surface it may not seem so difficult or dangerous, but you must understand that the very powers of Satan may conspire to defeat you. In performing this task you cannot return to your men at the gate. For a short time your army will not know your whereabouts. Some will fear you are dead. Others may believe you have deserted and will proclaim that you are a coward. I regret that I will not be able to come to your defense and tell them what I have asked you to do. I cannot reveal this at the risk that Judge Zenephi will assemble all the forces at his command to try and stop you. He may do this anyway, and issue a call for your imprisonment. By agreeing to this assignment, you will put at risk everything that you have attained among the Nephites. Your rank, your standing—your very life. Yet I ask you, Captain Josh, will you help me?"

My thoughts were whirling. I had absolutely no idea what was coming. Yet I stood up tall, squared my resolve, and said, "What is it that you request of me, Commander?"

His eyes turned toward the stone table behind us. This table—in fact much of the general's office—was bursting at the seams with deerskin scrolls, stone and wooden tablets, stacked copper sheets, and other articles covered in writings and hieroglyphs. And not just the writings of the Nephites. I knew that Mormon also collected the writings of the Lamanites, Jaredites, and every other people and tribe who had kept records on this continent. What I saw in this room was surely only a small sampling of the records in his possession, many of which were handed down to him by the Prophet Ammaron when Mormon was a young man. I knew that the bulk of these records were gathered into a great library, the location of which I had never been told. But because of other events that had transpired between myself and Mormon, I had reason to believe that it was some kind of secret cave vault. At the moment the prophet's eyes were not directed at any of his record-filled shelves or nooks. His gaze was aimed at something in the very center of the table, covered by a sack of rough, maguey fiber. The hidden article wasn't really all that conspicuous in the midst of the other odds and ends in the room. But it was still the most prominent thing on the table.

Mormon kept one hand on my shoulder and led me closer to the hidden thing. He looked into my face a final time, as if peering into my soul for reassurance, or perhaps for some glimpse of what the future might bring if he revealed to me the thing that was underneath the cloth. Then Mormon grabbed the edges of the sack and pulled them aside.

I recognized what it was immediately. Of course I had known of its existence, but surprisingly it had not crossed my mind in a very long time. The candlelight in the room danced excitedly upon its shimmering gold surface.

"The golden plates," I said, my breath little more than a whisper.

I was struck with the realization that few people in history had ever been allowed to see them. Of those who had viewed them in the latter-days, the number could almost be counted on two hands: Joseph Smith, of course. And then the Three Witnesses, and the Eight Witnesses—the same men whose testimonies were emblazoned upon the first few pages of every copy in print. My mother once said that Emma Smith and one or two others might have also seen or at least felt the plates, but that's where the list ended. And now there was me.

Just like the pictures I'd seen in books and paintings, the Golden Plates consisted of a stack of shining metal sheets, about eight inches long and six inches wide—bound by three rings. And like replicas I'd seen in the Church museum and elsewhere, two-thirds of those metal plates were bound up within a separate gold-colored metal binding, like the dust jacket of a dictionary, or the paper ring around a sheaf of typing paper. These two thirds looked older—more tarnished and dull—than the other plates outside the binding. The plates inside that binding, I knew, comprised the *sealed* portion of the Book of Mormon, or the portion written by the Brother of Jared. It occurred to me that Mormon had modeled those plates that he had fashioned for his abridgement after plates originally designed by Ether—or perhaps by the Brother of Jared himself—with the specific objective of combining the records into one volume.

A small number of the newer gold plates were turned aside on the metal rings. There were no etchings on these. The book wasn't finished. There was room for more. Those blank sheets, I knew, were destined to become Mormon's record of events that were yet to occur, along with a few words to be added by his son, Moroni.

"You appear to recognize what this is," Mormon marveled.

I reached out, like I was going to touch it, then reverentially withdrew my hand. "Yes," I admitted. "I recognize it. And I know what the things written on it will one day mean to the world."

Mormon was awestruck. He found it hard to believe that anyone besides himself, or his son, might know the plates' contents. I could tell he wanted to grill me for more details, but then a flash of understanding entered his eyes, and he refrained from asking for further information.

I swallowed and asked, "What do you want me to do with it?"

"The plates are in danger," said Mormon. "I should have removed them from the city long ago, as I have already done with other sacred records, but of late I have added many things that I believed to be of great worth to the children of men. Wherefore, I may have put at risk all of my painstaking years of labor. The Nephite council is presently searching out every public treasury, hunting diligently for anything of value—every remnant of jade and precious gems, but more especially *gold*. A large number of Nephite kinships south and west of Cumorah are threatening to defect from our cause. Many have mingled their seed with the children of the Gadiantons and have become divided in their loyalties."

I nodded. "I'm aware of this problem."

"Then you know that among them are thousands of able warriors. I am convinced that for some time Zenephi and others have been planning a secret attack against Lamanite strongholds. They have persuaded themselves that without the participation of these kinships, they cannot succeed."

I raised an eyebrow. "But they can't succeed anyway. You just said there won't be time for any such campaign—"

"Yes. Yes, I know. But *they* do not know. So with whatever spoils they can find, they will fatten the purses of as many kin leaders as they can to insure their loyalty—as if their loyalty can be bought with gold."

Again I looked at the plates. "I'm beginning to understand."

He continued, "These plates of gold, mingled with other ores so that I might engrave upon them and make them lighter to carry, constitute the largest amount of precious metal that is left in our treasuries. I obtained the gold when I had greater authority in public affairs, knowing only this alloy would resist the corruption of time, and be preserved until a day when the Lord will bring these sayings to light by the hand of some future prophet. Zenephi, regrettably, knows of their existence. So do many other judges and council members. Tomorrow a decree will be passed permitting Zenephi's men to ransack my residence and seize these plates. Afterwards, they will surely be destroyed. The smelters will molten the ore before the setting of the sun. So you see, time is very short."

"Yes," I said. "I agree."

Mormon smiled warmly, but then his eyes became serious and grave. "Josh, I cannot allow these plates to be destroyed. The Lord will not permit it. But it is only by our faith that the Lord strengthens men and allows them to accomplish His righteous purposes. I would attempt to carry away the plates myself—I would do so tonight—but Zenephi's spies are watching me. They have been watching my house for many days. Also, I must concede that I am not as swift and spry as I once was. So I have prayed for the Lord's guidance and wisdom. I know of no man among the Nephites, Joshua, whom I would entrust with this task—not even my closest advisors and bodyguards. I had hoped and prayed that my son, Moroni, would return from his diplomatic mission to the Lamanites in time, but . . . this was not to be. If and when he will return, I do not know. So the Lord, in His infinite wisdom, has sent you to accomplish this task."

"But," I asked, "where will I take them?"

"To a secret vault of records that I have established on the slopes of the Hill Cumorah. When the time comes, it is from these slopes that I will direct the movements of the Nephite armies in their final conflict. I do not expect that I will survive this conflict, and yet there is more that I wish to add to these plates before the hour of my death. If I can only get them to the cave, I will trust that the Lord will provide a future hour wherein I may complete the sacred record. So I must place them in your hands, young Captain Josh, to safely remove them from the city of Zenephi so that they might be hidden up in the secret vault along with the plates of Nephi, the plates of Ether, and other sacred records."

I shuddered inwardly, not in fear of the assignment, but in fear of something else entirely. "This cave . . . this vault. You told me once before about a secret vault, when I first came among your people. You told it to me in the presence of Captain Cumenihah before he took me in as his servant. Is this the same vault where . . .?"

Mormon studied me closely. "Yes, Joshua. It is the same cave where . . . *it* was hidden—the thing that was in your possession when you were first discovered by Cumenihah's soldiers."

I looked at my hands. They were trembling. My heart felt like it was being seized in an iron clamp. "But I cannot go there. You *know* I can't. I can never again be in the presence of the thing that I had in my possession. There must be another way."

He shook his head slowly. "There is not. At least not tonight. And perhaps not ever. But you need not fear, Captain Josh. No man who girds himself in the power of God need fear the power of darkness. I believe there is a reason that God has sent you above all others to accomplish this task. I am convinced of this more than ever after meeting your father and your cousin. They will help you. The cavern is only a day's journey from here, up the southern slopes of Cumorah. I will provide you with a guide map that will give exact directions. But just as the plates cannot be allowed to fall into evil hands, neither can this map. So I must ask again, Captain Josh: Will you accept this sacred assignment? Not as your chief captain do I ask it. But as your *prophet.*"

My flesh was crawling with nauseating waves of hot and cold. I feared, despite everything, that Mormon could not fully understand what he was asking me to do. Had he forgotten the state of my mind when we first met? The depths of despair and helplessness to which I had fallen? And all because of this *thing*—this weapon—this abomination in my possession.

Yes, I had lied to my father and Marcos. The silver sword of Coriantumr had not remained behind in the kingdom of Akish. After Queen Asherah had cut the rift in the fabric of time, I wrenched the sword from her hands and leapt into the void. The voice inside that sword had always hated and despised me, but never with quite the same passion and determination as now. I had always supposed that when I fell into the boar trap set by Cumenihah's soldiers that the sword had deliberately *allowed* me to fall into the pit. It had *wanted* me to lose possession of itself, perhaps hoping that it might find an owner among the Nephites with a little more power and rank. That way it could wreak its objectives of destruction more effectively. But what the sword had not counted on was the presence of General Mormon.

The chiefest of chief captains of the Nephites happened to be in the area of Jordan to help with local conscriptions. It was to

Cumenihah's credit that he brought Mormon directly to that pit in the wilderness. Cumenihah had personally observed how the sword protected me as his soldiers made sport of my life, firing arrows and tossing spears. They had discovered that, so long as I held that sword in my hands, I could not be slain. Cumenihah brought Mormon to witness the phenomenon for himself. The prophet commanded them to leave the two of us alone. He ordered me in his powerful voice to release the sword and toss it away.

To this day I'm not sure where I found the strength to heave it out of that pit. I'm convinced only a prophet of God could have issued such a command and given me the will. After Mormon took possession of it, I was rescued from the trap. They bound up the wounds that I'd received from the spikes in the pit's floor. Cumenihah took pity on me and made me his personal servant. And the sword . . . Akish's sword . . . was taken away by General Mormon. The last thing the prophet said to me was that it would be laid in a secret vault where I would never again have to listen to its corrupting voice.

That was five years ago. It seemed more like five millenniums! And now the man who'd saved me from the sword was asking me to save the gold plates of the Book of Mormon, and thereby place myself again under the sword's evil influence. The timing was uncanny—right on the very eve of a massive invasion that threatened to sweep the Nephites from the face of the earth. It was almost as if . . . as if the sword had *planned* it this way! Didn't Mormon understand? Didn't he realize the temptation that I would face? How was it possible that I had been chosen for this sacred task? Why would Mormon take such an incomprehensible risk?

Yet there sat the golden plates, shining like a beacon before me. And there was Mormon, his eyes filled with such love, such undeserved confidence, that I felt as though I was already standing on Cumorah's lofty summit. I can't say that I fully comprehended the task that I was accepting.

Nevertheless, I started to nod, and after a sharp, deep breath, I replied to the prophet, "Yes. I will do as you have asked. I will save the golden plates."

## Notes to Chapter 12

The character named Zenephi in this novel is based on the Book of Mormon figure mentioned briefly in Moroni Chapter 9. Earlier in this novel, Garth expresses reservations about this person based on his memory of what he had read of him in his studies of the Book of Mormon. The scriptural reference describes an earlier time in Zenephi's career. His tendencies toward cruelty and ruthlessness are recorded in Moroni 9:16–17.

In this novel, the use of military terms like general, commander, garrison, brigade, division, etc. are mostly for convenience. Such terms are actually European, though they have corollaries in most armies of the world.

The Book of Mormon itself only uses very generic military terms. A grouping of soldiers is simply called an "army" and is never defined by its composition of spearmen, bowmen, infantry, etc., or its number of troops. A military leader is referred to as a "captain" or "chief captain," as with Captain Moroni. However, these same two ranks—"captain" and "chief captain"—are *also* used to describe leaders who served *beneath* men like Moroni or Gidgiddoni (see Alma 49:16; 3 Ne. 3:17). The most detailed reference for how military rankings worked among the Nephites is found in 3 Nephi 3:18: *"Now the chiefest among all the chief captains and the great commander of all the armies of the Nephites was appointed, and his name was Gidgiddoni."* Mormon may have deliberately used these generic terms to make his record more universally understood by any culture, or he may have used the more specific terms from his experience as a Nephite war commander, and afterwards, Joseph Smith, in his inspired translation, chose terms with a more general and universal meaning.

We have detailed descriptions of how armies and army officers were organized among the Aztecs, Mayans, and other Mesoamerican civilizations. Many of these rankings or divisions had European or Middle Eastern equivalents, but often were quite unique. Among the Aztecs, for example, there was the *Tlotoani*, who was the commander-in-chief of the army. Then there was the *Cihuacoatl*, or "Snake Woman" (a position held by a man, despite the name) who was the head of a war council drawn from princely nobility called the *tetecuhtin*. A *xiquipilli* was a regimental division of 8000 men, while there were also 400-man units and 20-man squads. But unlike European armies, such regiments were generally comprised of men living within certain geographic boundaries or city wards. In European and modern military organizations less concern is given to the concept of having neighbors and kinsmen fighting side by side, and is often rigorously avoided to avoid cliquishness (John M. D. Poul and Angus McBride, *Aztec, Mixtec and Zapotec Armies* [Reed International Books, Ltd., 1991], 9).

Among the Mixtecs their leaders and supreme army commanders were called Oracles or "Great Seers" because of the ability that a commander was expected to have for receiving advice and counsel directly from the gods (unlike Romans or Greeks, for example, who received godly advice secondarily from priests or other religious advisors who interpreted signs and portents) (Poul and McBride, 36). This corresponds to the Nephite custom of combining captains and prophets as reported in 3 Ne. 3:19: *"Now it was the custom among all the Nephites to appoint for their chief captains, (save it were in their times of wickedness) some one that had the spirit of revelation and also prophecy; therefore, this Gidgiddoni was a great prophet among them, as also was the chief judge* (Lachoneus)."

During the time period of this novel, Mormon would have been approximately seventy-three years old. This conclusion is drawn from Morm. 1:6, where it states that Mormon was eleven years old in AD 322.

The matter of sources for the Book of Mormon, as well as the composition and nature of the Golden Plates, is more complex than it first appears. For example, Joseph Smith said of the Book of Mormon that it was *"engraven on plates which had the appearance of gold, each plate was six inches wide and eight inches long and not quite so thick as common tin . . . The volume was something near six inches in thickness . . ."* (Joseph Smith, *Times and Seasons*, Vol. 3:9, March 1, 1842, 707.) From his exact wording that the plates had the *"appearance* of gold," and also the same wording from the Testimony of the Eight Witnesses, it is assumed that the Book of Mormon plates were not *pure* gold. A pure, 24-carat gold block of 6"x 8"x 6" would have weighed approximately

200 pounds. Even allowing for unevenness in the hammering of the various plates, pure gold would have still weighed close to 100 pounds. Yet William Smith, Martin Harris, and others who hefted the plates estimated their weight at 40 to 60 pounds. (*FARMS Update,* Oct. 1984, revised Feb. 1985, quoting *Saints Herald* 31:644).

In this chapter, the Prophet Mormon is depicted as saying that the plates were a gold *alloy,* meaning that it was mixed with other metals for durability and convenience. This is consistent with suggestions made by modern LDS scholars and researchers, and also with metallurgical practices in ancient America. Pure gold may have been too brittle for engraving or long-term preservation, as well as being too heavy to heft.

The goldsmiths of various cultures in Mesoamerica often mixed gold and copper together—an alloy that the Spanish called *tumbaga.* Many examples of this alloy—including hammered sheets or plates— have been found in the New World. Consistent with the description of Joseph Smith and others, this alloy indeed would have had the "appearance of pure gold," though its actual gold content could have been anywhere from eight to fourteen carats. LDS researcher Reed H. Putnam wrote in 1969: "Tumbaga, the magic metal, can be cast, drawn, hammered, gilded, soldered, welded, plated, hardened, annealed, polished, engraved, embossed, and inlaid. Yet with all this versatility, tumbaga will destroy itself if it is improperly alloyed, improperly stored, or improperly finished" ("Were the Golden Plates Made of Tumbaga?" *Improvement Era* 69:9, September 1969, 788–89, 828–31).

It is assumed that Mormon commissioned skillful artisans of his day to fashion the gold-alloy plates (if indeed he did not fashion the plates himself under the Lord's guidance), and then mastered the skill of engraving for the purpose of abridging his collection of sacred records. It is the author's assumption that since the sealed portion of the Book of Mormon may have already existed, Mormon modeled the design of the plates upon which he would write his abridgement from those sealed plates. (However, it is also possible that the words of the Brother of Jared were translated and transcribed by Mormon onto the newer plates of his own design.) If we assume that the plates were between eight- and fourteen-carat gold, their weight would have been consistent with descriptions by William Smith, Martin Harris, and others. (See also Michael R. Ash, *Supposed Book of Mormon Anachronisms,* 1998, www.mormonfortress.com/gweight.html.)

It may be interesting that the Book of Mormon does state that the twenty-four plates of Ether (which were later abridged by Moroni and engraved upon his father's golden plates) were made of pure gold (Mosiah 8:9), though the record itself mentions no particular metal composition in connection with the final 6" x 8" x 6" plates engraved by Mormon, which included the sealed portion by the brother of Jared. (The author is not certain if this record was part of the original twenty-four plates of Ether, or a separate record.) Nor do we know the composition of the original small and large plates of Nephi that were handed down by the Nephite prophets for a thousand years. Most of the Book of Mormon is an abridgement of those large and small plates.

The Book of Mormon also mentions the plates of brass that Nephi obtained from Laban. These plates recorded the same information as found in the Old Testament until the days of Jeremiah, or the time when Lehi departed Jerusalem.

We know that Joseph Smith only retained possession of the golden plates of the Book of Mormon until he "had accomplished by them what was required . . ." (JS—H: 1:60). They were then delivered back into the charge of the "messenger," i.e., the Angel Moroni. But what about the twenty-four plates of Ether, the plates of brass, and the small and large plates of Nephi?

We do know that Mormon established a vault for record-keeping in the Hill Cumorah just prior to the Nephite destruction. Many Latter-day Saints have assumed that this repository and the stone box found in upstate New York were one and the same. However, there is much to suggest otherwise. Today this hill near Palmyra is known as Cumorah, though it is unclear what local New Yorkers may have called it in 1823, when Moroni first led Joseph Smith to it. Nor is it entirely clear that this hill was *ever* called Cumorah by Joseph Smith. By the 1840s there is evidence that some Church leaders were calling the hill in New York Cumorah, but there is no evidence that it received this name because of its correlation with the hill of the same name in the Book of Mormon. In fact, it seems possible that it was given this name only by tradition. Another possibility is that it was so named because, like the Cumorah in the Book of Mormon, it also became a repository of sacred records. Moroni himself may have called it by this name in memory or commemoration of the hill of the same name in "the land of his fathers." None of this assumes that the hill in New York is the same location as the last battle between the Nephites and Lamanites. (For a comprehensive treatment of this subject, see Matthew Roper's online article entitled "Limited Geography and the Book of Mormon: Historical Antecedents and Early Interpretations," F.A.R.M.S., 2004, http://www.farms.byu.edu/display.php?table=review&id=555.)

In Morm. 6:6 the Prophet Mormon tells us that all the sacred records were hid up in Cumorah except "these few plates which I give unto my son, Moroni." Obviously these "few plates" comprised the record that Moroni later delivered to Joseph Smith. (It also likely included the twenty-four plates of Ether since the abridgement known as the Book of Ether which was added to the gold plates of the Book of Mormon was made by Moroni, not Mormon. See Ether 1:1–2.) This assumes that somewhere inside the Hill Cumorah of Moroni's homeland there existed a secret vault for record storage. What did this vault contain? Naturally, it included the large and small plates of Nephi, possibly the brass plates of Laban, perhaps the twenty-four gold plates of Ether, and perhaps even scores of other records that Mormon deemed sacred or important. It was therefore a much more spacious repository than the stone box unearthed by Joseph Smith. Mormon's motive for hiding up all these sacred records was that, if found, "the Lamanites would destroy them." This novel suggests that this repository may have also been intended to protect them from corrupt Nephites. If this is true, very few people—even in Mormon's day—would have known the vault's location.

Many Latter-day Saints are aware of the story told by Brigham Young of an event reported by Oliver Cowdery, wherein Oliver states that when he and Joseph were returning the golden plates to Cumorah, ". . . the hill opened, and they walked into a cave, in which there was a large and spacious room. He says he did not think, at the time, whether they had the light of the sun or artificial light, but that it was just as light as day. They laid the plates on a table; it was a large table that stood in the room. Under this table there was a pile of plates as much as two feet high, and there were altogether in this room more plates than probably many wagon loads; they were piled up in corners and along the walls" (*Journal of Discourses,* 17 June, 1877, 38).

Brigham Young defines this as a secondhand account, not a personal experience. Furthermore, it was recorded almost fifty years after the event. Even when reported by a prophet of God, a clear distinction should be made between secondhand accounts and inspired revelation. However, this does not mean that the account should be dismissed. It's interesting that Brigham Young would recall Oliver's confusion about whether he was viewing this room with artificial or natural light. Such a description may place it more in the category of a vision or a manifestation, rather than an incident where a hill actually splits open, etc. An earlier account of this story from Heber C. Kimball indicates the record repository was seen in vision, and may not have referred to an actual event (Heber C. Kimball, *Journal of Discourses,* 28 Sept., 1856). Regardless of the differences in these accounts, we would do well to ponder the relevant *message* of the tale rather than get hung up on peripheral details, such as looking for treasure vaults inside the hill in New York. Since the geological processes that formed the Hill Cumorah in New York normally do not produce caves or caverns, it seems plausible that this vision may have been of the *larger* record repository described in Mormon 6:6. One day perhaps, in the due time of the Lord, the location of these records may be revealed.

Most scholars remain convinced that the hill referred to in the scriptures as Ramah/Cumorah was located in Mesoamerica, not New York. Dr. John Sorenson, PhD., first suggested in the 1950s that the hill which seems to best fit the criteria outlined in the Book of Mormon is *El Cerro Vigia* ("Lookout Hill") in Veracruz, Mexico (John L. Sorenson, *An Ancient American Setting for the Book of Mormon* [Salt Lake City: Deseret Book, 1985], 343–350. See also David Palmer, *In Search of Cumorah* [Horizon Books, 1981]). The Hill Vigia in Veracruz is rife with caves and caverns. The author was personally shown photographs of some of these secret caves, found directly beneath the hill's eastern slopes, by local residents of the village of Santiago Tuxtla in 2001.

Though some Latter-day Saints still feel strongly about the New York model, most believe that placing Ramah/Cumorah in New York is neither logical nor necessary for a fuller understanding of the Book of Mormon. (For additional reading on New York vs. Mesoamerica, refer to Matthew Roper's article cited earlier, or John E. Clark's article entitled, "The Final Battle for Cumorah, Review of *Christ in North America* by Delbert W. Curtis," *F.A.R.M.S. Reviews,* 1994, 79–113. This article is also found online at http://farms.byu.edu/display.php?table=review&id=153).

# CHAPTER 13

## Jim

After our confrontation with Bar Abba at the villa on the River Jordan, Jennifer and I were forced to spend the night in exactly the kind of accommodations I would have expected from a band of robbers—a flea-infested cave in the desert hills. Nearly all of the ruffians from the estate at Jericho had joined their leader as we departed that evening. We might have been able to reach Jerusalem shortly after dark, but it was Bar Abba's intent that we enter the capital early the next morning when, by his estimate, the market district of the Lower City would be bustling with listeners.

As we reached the cave, our ragtag army of horsemen and footmen doubled in number. I estimated there were now about three hundred Zealots in our band, half of them armed only with reshaped or modified farm tools. These men were mostly from the poorer classes of Judea, but with a few wealthier idealists sprinkled in between.

There were actually three caves set in the rocks around our encampment. Bar Abba erected a tent for himself—and another for me—just outside the largest cave. Jenny was forced to sleep inside the cave itself with Heli and several dozen other ruffians, along with the regular contingent of fleas and scorpions. She and I hadn't spoken for many hours, and Bar Abba made it a point to keep the two of us as far apart as possible.

The Zealot leader repeatedly said to me—especially when in the company of others—"Do as you like, James," or "You may go anywhere you please." Then he would post three of his most vicious henchmen around me. Like a pack of guard dogs, these men hemmed me in against the hillside where my tent had been erected. Only rarely did I catch of glimpse of Jenny.

Bar Abba greeted, with a hearty embrace, several other Zealot leaders who were trailed by their own small squadrons of lean and hungry-looking followers. To one such leader whom he called Dysmas of Cana, he said in a low conspiratorial voice, "There are surprises awaiting us in the Street of the Coppersmiths."

Those who heard this would wring their hands excitedly and declare, almost in jubilation, "The time is here! The time has finally come!"

The whole scene sickened me. They truly looked to Bar Abba as their promised "messiah"—a messiah of blood and vengeance against Rome and all other enemies. They forced me to wear an old, scratchy, camel-skin robe, rusted buckles up the front. It was frayed on the edges and still stank of the dead animal that had originally worn it. But other than this awful outfit, Bar Abba put up the pretense of treating me like a royal guest. He even fed me a portion of his honey-dripping figs, sweetbread, and pastry-wrapped meats. He spoke *of* me to everyone, but never *to* me. I was, as Bar Abba put it, "a worker of miracles who will prepare the way before me as I enter Jerusalem."

Once the leader named Dysmas started to approach, presumably to speak with me directly, but Bar Abba quickly dissuaded him, saying, "The Forerunner must not be disturbed this night. He cannot be bothered with the trivial things of the world. He must only contemplate the events of tomorrow."

Dysmas and others nodded in complete understanding.

Many times the story was recounted of how I'd raised a woman from the dead. Few made it a point to connect this miracle with my sister, possibly to avoid any requests to bring her forward for an interview. In each telling, it became further embellished in some small way, until they were saying I was "famous throughout the wilderness of Judea and Moab," and had "a wide reputation as a great prophet and healer."

I listened to it all as I sat against the hill behind my tent, the guilt festering in my stomach like an open wound. To my right I could dimly see the bluish level of the Dead Sea, sunk deep in the silver, moonlit mountains of Moab, like an open eye in a wild face. Narrow . . . watching . . . waiting to see if I would actually betray my God.

I'd realized many hours ago that I couldn't go through with this. Despite the risks, despite the awful likelihood that I would lose my life and watch my sister killed before my eyes, I could not do as Bar Abba had requested. I would not just remain quiet and stand by his side. Even letting the people *assume* that I was a supporter, or forerunner, of this vile pretender was a betrayal of all that I held dear—a betrayal of my very testimony. I believed ardently that the worst kind of betrayers were those who remained quiet and did nothing as evil increased around them. I had to expose this fraud. I had to raise the curtain and reveal this charlatan for who he was. But each time I tried to stand and express the truth—even that night as the other Zealot leaders gathered at their messiah's side—the same essential thought came to my heart: *Not now. Wait.*

I thought I understood the reason. Clearly the object was to expose the lies of Bar Abba when my words might have the maximum impact—before the largest possible crowd. I wasn't entirely certain what the Zealot messiah was planning in the morning, but I was confident that when the right moment arrived, I would recognize it. With that understanding clearly in my mind, I was finally able to relax and go inside my tent.

Sleep, however, was a different matter. This was no time for sleep. It was a time to pray. I poured out my whole soul to God for as long as I could hold my eyes open. So many thoughts tore at my consciousness. I felt as though I'd never needed God's courage as much as I did right now. I wondered if I'd ever felt such a cold, bleak, darkness as I felt tonight, as if the whole weight of the universe was pressing down, crushing, grinding, and foretelling certain doom. *What art Thou trying to tell me, Father? Is it really so hopeless? Is there really no chance that my sister and I will come out of this alive?* I found myself weeping, and I wasn't sure why. I even wondered if something had happened to my wife or my infant son, Gid. I prayed for them with *all* of my strength. I prayed for all of my children, whose circumstances in the fabric of time only God could know for certain.

I pleaded for greater insight into Jenny's unusual vision—the one where she expressed that someone in this time period would save her family—and possibly *mine*—but that we first had to save *them*. The vision had too many specifics to have been conjured in her imagination. She'd said this person was someone with great power, but not necessarily physical, spiritual, or political power. Just "great influence," whatever that meant. I certainly hadn't met anyone yet who could fit this description. She'd hinted that this person might be in Jerusalem, but without Jen at my side, how would I ever recognize them? Or could I receive my own inspiration? Despite the passion of my prayers, no insights came into my head. Nothing but empty, suffocating blackness. I knew it was a matter of faith and trust. Just as with the moment when I finally exposed Bar Abba as a fraud, the Lord possessed all power to make it known. I knew He also had the power to speak comfort to my soul this night, and yet the heavens seemed to be silent, like the terrible quiet before a devastating tsunami.

After a night of tossing and turning, I was awakened at the crack of dawn. Unlike the previous night, Bar Abba gave me nothing to eat. I might have heard him inform others that I was fasting. Actually, I decided this was an excellent idea, but not for any reasons that Bar Abba might have expressed. I decided to fast on my own and opened it by uttering a powerful prayer in the silence of my mind. The gloom that I'd felt in the night had lifted some with the advent of daylight, but not entirely. I continued to feel that today—perhaps of *all* days—I needed all the spiritual strength I could dredge up from within. The sole purpose of my fast was that the Lord would help me to find this strength. If, as I genuinely feared, today was the day I would finally die, or the day that I would witness the death of my loving sister, I knew that I needed to tap into a vein of inner courage heretofore undiscovered.

We mounted our horses and rode west. They continued to keep Jenny and me apart, though her guardian, Heli, did send me a wicked grin that was meant, I suppose, as a warning. In contrast, Jenny sent me a smile of confidence, and I loved her so much for it. No one on earth had ever had a better sister. She rode with Heli at the rear of our column while I remained at the front with Bar Abba. Our horses passed through some hill country and smaller villages. The roads were lined with pilgrim's tents and beasts of burden, all living things just awakening or eating meager breakfasts in preparation for their final push into Jerusalem.

An hour later, we reached what appeared to be the backside of the Mount of Olives. At this juncture, Dysmas and many others split off and went a different direction with instructions to meet up again later at the "Street of the Coppersmiths." Heli and Jenny went with them. I watched her go with a deeply stricken conscience, again blaming myself for getting us into this mess in the first place. Last night's cloud of doubt returned, as grim and suffocating as ever.

We continued toward Jerusalem. The faces of the Zealots were set with determination. The strong implication in their hushed, excitable tones was that some kind of armed revolt was planned—a revolt to be incited by a rousing speech from Bar Abba himself. Coupled with all of this was an incredible assumption: they truly believed the general citizenry of Jerusalem would join them in this uprising. Without them, the revolution couldn't succeed, and Bar Abba knew it. But the idea that the city would suddenly unite behind the Zealot messiah wasn't even in question. Bar Abba firmly believed it was inevitable.

Only about twenty horsemen remained in our party, including the four henchmen whose job it was to make sure I didn't misbehave. As we continued down the main road and around the southern flank of the Mount of Olives, Bar Abba spoke to me for the first time this morning.

"We will soon be in sight of the city," he said, his voice only loud enough for my ears. "At that point you will ride ahead a short distance and lead the way. Do not attempt anything, for Gestas is the finest archer in Judea. His orders are to kill you immediately should you attempt to say anything untoward or undermine our cause. And be assured, your sister will also be slain."

Gestas was one of my guard dogs—a balding, middle-aged ogre whose forehead reflected the rising sun like a shiny piece of porcelain. Though he couldn't hear us, he was smirking, as if he knew precisely what Bar Abba was telling me.

In his typical schizophrenic fashion, the Zealot suddenly slapped me on the back as if we were old army buddies. "But of course, there is no need to tell you this. For I know that these thoughts are as far from your mind as the snows of Mount Ararat. You, my noble friend, are a man of honor. And before this day is through—mark my words—you will become my most ardent proselyte."

I paid him a backward glance, then faced forward again so I could roll my eyes unseen.

"And one other thing," he added, as if it was an afterthought. "I would very much like it if you would say—on occasion, and in a moderately loud voice—*Make way! Make way! For the Kingdom of Heaven is soon at hand!*"

I turned on him like a lion. "I will say no such thing. Not now. Not ever."

He stared at me a moment, as if ready to explode in anger, then threw back his head and exploded with *laughter,* although the laughter sounded strangely forced. "I am only jesting! Do not be so dour, James! Loosen your sandal thongs! For whether you speak or remain silent, you are about to play a most vital part in our nation's history."

He rode back a short distance to his other men, still laughing, but out of the corner of my eye I saw him pay me a sneering glance. If I didn't know it before, I knew now that the instant he felt he no longer needed me, I was a dead man. Again I prayed for the Lord to reveal the right moment to expose him.

As per Bar Abba's instructions, I rode a few horse lengths ahead, all the while feeling nauseous to be participating in this charade in any capacity. Shortly, the road drew up over a rise and then . . . my nausea fled; my breath was taken away.

Spreading out before me like a shining jewel was the city of Jerusalem. This wasn't the smoldering ash heap I'd seen in the days after the Roman decimation of 73 AD. This was *Jerusalem* in all the magnificence that the word implies. Against the city's eastern extreme—reflecting back from countless golden thresholds, lintels, and gates—was the Holy Temple of God. Some phenomenon of the morning light seemed to bring the kaleidoscope of colors and shapes right up to my face. At the moment I couldn't have said if stone or wood was included in its construction, for it seemed comprised of one singular, living flow of molten gold. So massive in size, so simple and solid in design, yet because of all the fluttering curtains of purple and blue on the surrounding walls, it gave off the illusion that it was floating in midair. The sanctuary stood on foundations of blinding white marble, while guarding it tenderly on all sides were the celebrated courtyards, themselves divided by gateways, niches, rows of columns, and towers—all fantastically high by ancient standards.

I counted it miraculous—or at the very least a sweet gift from God in my hour of turmoil—that at the exact moment I recognized the Temple, a stirring peal of rams horns resounded from the balconies about the gate. Two enormous golden doors against the eastern cliff swung inward to open, allowing those crammed outside on the bridge to enter. Within seconds the courtyards, which had previously showed no signs of life beyond a few barefooted, white-robed priests, began to flood with the mass of humanity. The first day of Passover worship had begun.

I think in other circumstances—if Bar Abba and his villains hadn't been my tour guides—my heart would have leapt with the same joy and pride felt by all the Jews of Judea at this time of year. But as it was, I felt only grief that I was leading a man who would shortly claim ownership of that edifice for himself.

My eyes took in the whole of the city—walls and bridges, columns and gates, palaces and towers. On the northern side of the Temple rose the Antonia Fortress, presuming to dominate and over-shadow the House of the Lord with Roman might. It sprang from a pyramid-like base, framed on the east by the cliffs of the same rocky plateau upon which all of Jerusalem was built. From the four towers and galleries of the citadel Rome's soldiers could spy and gawk and jeer down upon the sea of faithful pilgrims preparing to make their Passover offerings. I tried to imagine how it might have felt if a foreign invader had built a similar fortress overlooking Temple Square. No doubt it caused a lot of teeth-grinding among the people of Israel and helped to inflame the violent passions of the men riding behind me.

Another gate opened on the Temple's western wall. This gate was connected to an elevated causeway that crossed the whole length of Jerusalem from east to west. Upon it were hundreds more ant-sized figures making their way toward the Temple district. My eyes followed the causeway all the way to the city's western extreme where stood another sprawling vista of stone structures, towers, marble columns, and lookout posts. This, I guessed, was Herod's palace, the largest building in Jerusalem other than the Temple, and also headquarters to the Roman procurator whenever he was in town, which was always during major feast days in case of an uprising—much like the one that Bar Abba was planning. Otherwise the procurator could be found soaking up rays in the Romanized city of Caesarea on the Mediterranean seashore. In the days of Jesus, of course, the procurator was Pontius Pilate, though I couldn't be certain who it was now. The procuratorship of Judea wasn't a popular appointment, so it changed hands often.

My eyes continued to swim over the city, even as I spurred my horse onward, knowing that my gawking might try Bar Abba's patience. The clarity of the day allowed me to distinguish all of the city's celebrated quarters. I easily identified the Upper City of Jerusalem's aristocratic nobility from the Lower City with its market district and poorer classes. I could also distinguish the newer quarter on the north established by Herod the Great for the "new rich" of Jerusalem—prosperous merchants, tax collectors, and foreigners— and the priestly district south of the Temple where resided the Levites and their servants, and where the great Sanhedrin had a palace of its own. I also picked out the Circus Maximus and the Hippodrome, constructed by Herod to entertain his Roman masters. Knowing Jewish proscriptions against theatrical amusements, these buildings must have been eyesores nearly as offensive as the Antonia.

It was a mistake to assume—as with so many modern-day models and paintings—that the city of Jerusalem was entirely contained within its fortification walls. Like modern-day Jerusalem, it spilled over into the valley below, splashed up the surrounding hillsides, and leapt from hilltop to hilltop like a jackrabbit. In fact, I swore this metropolis was *more* populous and cramped today than it was during any other period of its long history, including the twenty-first century. I recognized Mount Scopus, where BYU had built its modern extension, and of course the Mount of Olives. Cascading down the slopes of these hills were terraces of rooftops with water cisterns and garden areas with artificially planted trees and hedges. As I looked upward at the Mount of Olives I made out a few olive groves, especially two-thirds of the way toward the top, but not as many as I might have expected. It seemed the local demand for housing was such that orchards and farmland were being necessarily squeezed out.

But in contrast to these wealthier hillside estates were the swarms and tangles of mud and clay dwellings directly below us in the Kidron Vale, and also farther southward within the Vale of Hinnon or Gehenna. Little more than heaps of stones, these structures were a continuation of the general architecture of the Lower City. The abyss separating Jerusalem's different social classes was here displayed for all eyes to behold—the swollen opulence of the higher elevations, and the grinding poverty below. It seemed a mystery to me how the rich could have borne looking down from their lofty terraces to see these decrepit dwellings filled with the suffering and the starving without doing something about it. I took it as evidence of something terribly evil stirring beneath the surface.

The roadway that we took around the base of the Mount of Olives was quickly filling with pilgrims. Since I had refused to say what Bar Abba had requested, I soon began to hear his men shouting to fellow travelers, "Make way! Make way! For the Kingdom of Heaven is soon at hand! And look! Leading the pathway for Yeshua, the Great Messiah, is his Forerunner, the miracle worker of Moab—the voice of one who cries in the wilderness!"

I cringed as their bony fingers pointed at my back, while the fingers of their opposite hands pointed at Yeshua Bar Abba upon his steed. Even hearing them call him by his first name—the same name as our Savior—caused every cell in my body to wither and recoil. The reactions of the pilgrims to all this shouting were quite diverse. Some dismissed the proclamations of Bar Abba as if they'd heard similar sayings attributed to other men, only to be disappointed. But I was surprised at how many *were* affected, and how they stopped to gaze at Bar Abba or turned aside in the roadway to let him pass. I heard whispering and muttering, many wondering if it could be true—if this man might actually be the promised Messiah. Others seemed to recognize the Zealot leader from previous encounters and repeated his name to those who might not have known him. "Ben Abbas. It is Ben Abbas!"

I internalized again what I'd first felt in the presence of Baruk and Mordecai. There was a strange tension in the air, an unusual expectation in the minds of pilgrims far and wide that this Passover might be different from all others. Bar Abba had sensed it well beforehand, and was quite determined to exploit it. But not all were so eager to fall in line.

"Robbers," I heard one man declare to his companions. "Sicarii. There's going to be trouble. Let's enter by another gate." They turned off the road and quickly went another direction.

However, many other listeners said, "Let's follow him. Let's hear what he will say."

So a train began to form behind us, consisting mostly of the curious, but also of some who sincerely believed that Yeshua Bar Abba might be the bonafide Messiah. Again I prayed inwardly: *Is it time?* Was it the right moment to say something to end this charade? But again the feeling resonated: *Not yet. Patience.*

I realized I was terribly jumpy and needed to relax. Was I really so eager to bring about the moment of my death? And then I wondered—What if I *did* watch my sister die? Could I still follow through and say what needed to be said? I shook myself. Somehow I needed to stop these thoughts—just focus on each moment as it unfolded.

We arrived at a crossroads. One roadway went toward the Temple's Golden Gate, while the other led toward the Lower City. Here the people also divided. Those with no interest, or only moderate interest in Bar Abba, separated from those with genuine interest and conviction. Curiously, Bar Abba did not head toward the Golden Gate, but instead directed our train toward the Lower City, and into the slums of Kidron and Gehenna. This choice, in and of itself, offended some who might have otherwise been believers. I heard one man scoff, "Another pretender. Everyone knows that the true Messiah will go first to the Temple to proclaim himself."

Those who remained with us were mostly the poorer pilgrims— farmers and camel drivers, fishermen and sailors—men and women whose faces were beaten hard by fierce winds or hollowed and pitted by hunger. Their bodies were covered in camel skin, sheepskin, and sackcloth—not silks and golden sashes. The men's beards were combed by the wind, not curled or braided. But these people were the lifeblood of Israel, and the ones who I'd always been told would be the most receptive to the Gospel of Jesus Christ. Unfortunately, at this moment, their hopes for a Messiah had also made them the most gullible, and Bar Abba was taking full advantage.

People began to fall in behind us in frightening numbers as we continued through these scummy neighborhoods. And not all were pilgrims anymore. Many were citizens of the city—beggars, cripples, and the poorest of the poor. We passed by an establishment where the lowest classes of Levites were skinning temple sacrifices and washing the hides in bloodstained gutters. We passed mounds of refuse where women and children were scraping and culling through the filth for scraps of food. They all turned to look at us on our horses, their interest increasing with every step. Chanting broke out fore and aft— "Bar Abba!" or "Ben Abbas!"

The smell alone in this district was enough to curdle my stomach, but the primary cause of my sickness and heartache had nothing to do with the stench. It was the loathing I felt for Bar Abba—his willingness to exploit the sacred longings of these people. *Please, Lord,* I prayed again, *help me to expose him.*

At last we abandoned our horses, leaving behind some men to watch them while I continued to lead our procession toward a city gate accessed by a rocky staircase. From the piles of garbage around it, and because of the assembly line of women—mostly, I gathered, maidservants to the rich—who descended the steps to dump buckets of human waste into an adjacent stream, I felt sure this was the infamous Dung Gate. But before we reached the stairway, a disturbance began that seriously threatened to compete with Bar Abba's "triumphal" entry. All around us I began to hear a clamorous tinkling of bells, as if someone had stirred up a herd of sheep or cattle. Voices above us, inside the city, were crying, "It is agitated! The waters are smitten! It is agitated!"

I had no idea what this meant, but to scores of loiterers within and without the Dung Gate it signified something of paramount importance. I heard members of our procession start shouting, "Unclean! Unclean!"

People were reeling backwards or leaping to the sides to clear a path for a rushing torrent of human figures, all with bells or clappers attached to their bodies or hung about their necks. I quickly realized that every figure with a bell was somehow crippled or afflicted—whether halt, or lame, or blind. Some were crawling on all fours, others supporting wretchedly broken limbs. Still others were carried, or dragged along on wooden sleds. The blind tapped the ground with their sticks, screaming helplessly for someone to lead the way. The people in our train shrank back as far as possible to avoid being touched, as if merely brushing against a blind man might cause his infirmity to take root inside them.

They fled toward what appeared to be a pool to our right, surrounded by a number of covered colonnades. To the north of it was a large pen for sheep. The pool appeared to be a natural spring. Out in the middle I could see rising bubbles, which caused a ripple to travel outward across the surface. No doubt this was created by some kind of geological phenomenon inside the earth, but to the people of faith in Jerusalem's Lower City and outer vales, it was a miracle. In an instant I remembered the name—the Pool of Bethesda—and I also remembered the supernatural legend associated with it.

Many Jews believed that from time to time an angel would visit Bethesda and smite the surface. Whenever this occurred, anyone who could go down into the waters would be healed of all sickness and infirmity. It was here that the Savior told—or *would* tell—a certain man who'd been crippled for thirty-eight years to take up his bed and walk. I gathered from the uproar that this "smiting" was not such a common event. I observed Bar Abba's face as he watched people splashing about, churning up the pool to a thick, muddy soup. He was highly irritated. This mud pond had stolen his thunder. Many of our followers were turning back, discouraged by the presence of so many of the "unclean."

Bar Abba's men were shrugging, baffled as to how he might regain everyone's attention. Then one of the cleverer Zealots turned to his leader and said, "It's a miracle! And it happened because of you!"

Bar Abba's eyes lit up. "Announce it!" he commanded. "Tell them!"

I shook my head in disgust as his men began to cry, "The waters are smitten because the Messiah passes by!"

A few of those who'd been following us heard and had their interest restored. But then something happened that I felt was heaven-sent, for it threw the crowd into such a tizzy that Bar Abba's hopes of regaining the attention of those around the gate were permanently shattered. There were more screams among the populace—far more dramatic and terrified. A colony of lepers who'd made their home in Gehenna had broken through whatever barriers had cordoned them off from the rest of Jerusalem. At least forty of the most afflicted and disease-ridden people I'd ever seen were making a mad dash down toward the waters. Some had only stumps for limbs and all were covered in sores and tumors. I quickly realized that even to the city's run-of-the-mill cripples and handicapped there was a whole other class of truly "unclean" souls. As the lepers arrived at Bethesda, the previous occupants ran out from under the roofed colonnades. Those in the water scrambled for shore, as if the pool was now a wellspring of pestilence and disease.

This was the final straw. Now *everyone* was vacating the area, rushing back in the other direction—including many of the Zealots. Those closest to Bar Abba threw up their hands in frustration.

"The Temple guards will come to disperse the lepers," warned one of his men. "We must get far away."

The Zealot leader shuddered angrily, then announced, "We'll go to the Street of the Coppersmiths, see if the others are obtaining what was promised."

As we climbed the stairs to the Dung Gate, I heard a few feeble voices calling out Ben Abbas's name, but the Zealots ignored them and continued into the city. After passing by another natural spring called Siloam, we entered a district where sheep were being sheared and pyramids of wool sat inside covered warehouses. Bar Abba directed us into a narrow alleyway. We soon emerged into the first official street of Jerusalem's vast marketplace.

My senses were assailed by a new convergence of sights and sounds. The place was already stirring with early-morning shoppers, moving through the assemblage of stalls and tables. The hawkers and hucksters seemed well prepared for this Passover season; inventories of exotic goods were stacked from floor to ceiling, even spilling out into the street. Passover week in Jerusalem seemed much like Christmastime in the modern world, where commercialism sometimes overwhelmed spiritual significance.

Moreover, I noticed that in every free space—in alleys, under archways, arcades, and viaducts, between pillars and market stalls, and in the shadow of public buildings—campsites had been claimed. These spaces inside the city must have been the *best* campsites, snatched up by the earliest arrivals. In this regard, Jerusalem's citizens seemed incredibly hospitable. Everywhere were families—husbands, wives, grandparents, and children—eating meager breakfasts and holding in their laps snow-white lambs, bundles of grain, cruses of oil, and other articles intended as Temple offerings. Children as young as five and six were responsible for sacks of food and supplies. Men displayed little leather boxes on their arms and foreheads, each one enclosing the sacred writings from the Torah, or books of Moses.

All at once the Zealots came to a halt. Near a table stacked with exotic fabrics and textiles, three Roman legionnaires in full regalia were fingering the merchandise and conversing with the shopkeeper. Bar Abba's eyes narrowed. One of his men grabbed his shoulder, turning his face away. We walked on quickly, avoiding the possibility that Bar Abba might be recognized. However, I happened to see a *fourth* soldier just down from his comrades, standing between two racks of brightly colored silks. The merchant held a purple bolt under his nose, trying to close a sale, but this Roman's gaze was squarely set on us. I seemed to be the only one who noticed how his eyes followed Bar Abba all the way up the street. His lips might have even mouthed Bar Abba's name, but then our party passed into the next avenue.

My nervousness was mounting as we moved quickly along the thoroughfare, past streets representing every possible trade, from tailors to saddle makers to perfume sellers, until we reached an area of side streets a bit more murky and soot stained than the others. I heard hammering, smelled greasy smoke, and felt the heat of the bellows even before we'd entered. This was the market quarter devoted to metalwork—gold, silver, iron, and copper.

I recognized more and more faces from Bar Abba's band of robbers. They were milling about, tense, impatient. Upon seeing their leader, many approached him with mischievous grins and pulled back a segment of their coats or cloaks to reveal items hidden underneath. As I might have guessed, the hidden articles were weapons—usually swords. With a jerk of their chins, some followers indicated toward the rear of a certain alleyway that revealed several cavernous shops. This, I gathered, was where weapons for the upcoming revolt were being distributed. My eyes searched anxiously up and down the avenues for Jennifer and her "keeper," Heli, but to my distress I couldn't seem to spot them.

The Zealot named Dysmas approached Bar Abba and leaned closely to say, "The inspectors of Edom came through the day before yesterday to find only pots and pans. Since then our allies among the copper and ironsmiths have been hammering out nothing but blades. Every man of us carries two to three hidden weapons."

"Very good," said Bar Abba. "Spread the word. Have the men wander slowly to the open square by the shops of the wine and oil sellers—but not all at once, and do not congregate. Not yet. I will mount one of the old millstones with my prophet in a quarter of an hour."

He gave me a narrow glance to confirm that the "prophet" he was referring to was me. As Dysmas nodded and withdrew, Bar Abba leaned toward me and said with a threatening hiss, "So far you are a grave disappointment to me, James. You will mount one of the millstones beside me and make a proper introduction. Otherwise, I will have no further use for you. Do I speak plainly?"

I stared back at him, my mouth shut, my heart calm.

Suddenly the Zealot messiah grabbed me around the throat with a single monstrous hand. *"Do I speak plainly?"*

I seized his arms to try and thrust him back, but instead he thrust *me* back. I was caught by Gestas, the henchman with the shiny forehead. Bar Abba turned away and started off furiously toward his destination, as if uninterested in my reply, confident that I had understood his message. Gestas pushed the back of my head to follow.

I wasn't sure if I wanted this walk to the wine and oil district to take forever or happen quickly. My heart was racing. I was praying desperately under my breath. Whatever happened, I wasn't about to stand on some millstone like a circus ringmaster and announce, "It's now my pleasure to introduce to you your *Promised Messiah!*"

And so I would die. Jenny would die as well. This seemed the only way that these next few minutes could play out unless, of course, God intervened. But maybe the episodes where I was spared by God's intervention were over. Joseph Smith had been snatched from the clutches of his enemies a thousand times, but then, finally, his time had come. Would it shortly come for me? It crossed my mind that I could make a break for it. I could easily slip into any one of these narrow alleys and quickly find myself in a labyrinth where no one could follow. But not this time—and not without my sister. But even if Jenny had been at my side, I would not have tried to escape. Not yet. I felt strongly that God still had something for me to say, and no matter what happened after I said it, I wasn't about to flee before that moment arrived. *Please Father,* I prayed, *even if I have to die today, just save my sister. Save Jenny.* I took several deep breaths to try and settle my nerves.

Soon every stall and arcade around us displayed all varieties of cruses and vases and vials. We'd entered the wine and oil district. Right away I saw the millstones that Bar Abba intended to use as his pulpit. There were three of them, old and abandoned, one cracked in half. I guessed they'd been left in place for occasions much like this when a rabbi or some other speaker wished to address an audience. Despite the early hour, the district was already quite active. Precious oils and exotic wines from across the globe were clearly a featured commodity of the Jerusalem market. Bar Abba must have known this and had selected this area on purpose.

Soon the other Zealots began filtering into the crowd, clutching their cloaks, ready to draw hidden weapons at a moment's notice and quickly distribute the excess to all citizens willing to join in their cause. Again my eyes searched for Jenny, but to no avail. I started to recognize a few of the pilgrims and citizens who'd followed us to the Dung Gate. As they spotted Bar Abba, they pointed toward him enthusiastically.

"Ben Abbas!" several shouted at once.

The Zealot messiah turned to me, accepting these shouts of his name as a final cue. "The time has come," he snarled. "Climb this millstone. Tell the people who I am. You *will* be my forerunner and prophet, James. It is the role for which you were born. Now climb!"

I glared at him, unmoving. The Spirit had not confirmed that this was the moment. I needed to wait a little longer. After swallowing the football in my throat, I shook my head in firm resolve and said, "I will not."

Bar Abba's face turned three different colors, from red to crimson to purple. His teeth were gnashing hard enough to crush a box of nails. Gestas raised his fist to strike me, but Bar Abba caught his arm.

"Do not strike him here," he told Gestas angrily. "You will not make a further scene. Put a knife to his spine and keep him close." He turned back and raised his dirt-crusted fingernail to my nose. "You have sealed your fate, miracle worker."

He turned away again. The air eased slowly from my lungs. I was still alive. His fear of inciting the crowd too soon had saved me.

A chant broke out, probably initiated by Bar Abba's men, but infectiously spread by others. "Ben Abbas! Bar Abba! Ben Abbas!"

As the Zealot messiah took in the gathering and their growing enthusiasm, I sensed that he began to wonder why he'd been so worried about my inaction. Perhaps, as originally hoped, my mere presence was enough, dressed as I was in a smelly camel-hair coat with rusted buckles. I marveled as the chant rose in volume.

The entire wine and oil district was focused on us now—every shopper, shopkeeper, servant, and beggar. From a corner building that might have been a synagogue, an old, wizened rabbi and his young students emerged. Like everyone else they stared at the object of attention. Much of the audience had become enraptured, fully anticipating that something extraordinary was about to take place—much more extraordinary than the smiting of the waters at Bethesda.

Bar Abba drank in the spontaneous show of adulation. I watched the lines of his jaw grow firm with self-assurance. Of *course* they were reacting this way. After all, it was what he'd anticipated all along. It was *destiny*.

In a single bound Bar Abba mounted the highest millstone. The crowd erupted with applause. The steady chant of his name shattered into a hundred frenzied exclamations of *"Ben Abbas!"*

He raised his hands, but this hardly silenced them. Instead, the persistent chant became louder than ever. *"Ben Abbas! Bar Abba! Bar Abba!"*

And that's when it hit me. My heart froze. That name. It was suddenly, unmistakably familiar. In fact, this whole scene resembled something right off the pages of the New Testament.

"*Hear O Israel!*" Bar Abba bellowed at the top of his lungs. "The day of your deliverance is at hand!"

Despite the volume of his voice, none but those closest heard the cry. He repeated it again, and then a third time: "*Hear O Israel!* The day of your deliverance is at hand!"

A few shouts arose. "Silence! He's speaking! I want to hear! I want to hear!"

At last a sense of order was restored, the roaring was hushed, and a semblance of reverence took hold of the marketplace.

"*Hear O Israel!*" he repeated a fourth time. "The day of your deliverance is at hand! The time for the fulfilling of God's holy covenant is upon us! The bond between Abraham and Adonai begins to be established this very day in the city of the Lord! Awake, O children of the Covenant! No longer shall you remain the slaves of a cruel and merciless taskmaster! No longer shall you endure the shame visited upon you by the unpurified, by the unbelieving, and by scavengers and thieves! The time has come to rise up! The sword of the Torah must now be sheathed until the sword of steel has conquered! So hear me, O Israel! Take up your sword! Join with me and *fight!*"

He paused to let this sink in. I might have expected some fearful gasps to accompany this proclamation, but except for murmuring—mostly among the students of the rabbi—there was relative silence. I'm not sure the people knew yet what to think. Perhaps many had been under the impression that the Messiah would do their fighting for them. They weren't rejecting the idea of swords and violence out of hand, but they needed reassurance.

At last someone in the crowd was brave enough to ask, "Are you the One then? Tell us plainly! Are you the long-awaited Messiah?"

Bar Abba's face fell into smiling repose. His arms dropped slowly to his side, and his body straightened to its fullest height.

"What is your answer, Yeshua Bar Abba?" cried another. "Let us hear it from your own lips!"

As if chastising them for doubting, Bar Abba said boldly, "What will it take, O Israel? What will it take for you to recognize your deliverer when he appears? Will your messiah be a man of words or of actions? Will he be a preacher on a hilltop or a mover of mountains? Will the only wind he produces issue from his mouth, or will it be stirred up by his hands as his storm of vengeance is unleashed upon the enemies of God? Will he be a man who says 'Go thither!' or one who cries in a voice of thunder, 'Follow me'? You should not *need* to hear an answer from my own lips. If Israel has not the courage to recognize the Messiah when He appears, perhaps it does not *deserve* a messiah! Perhaps it should remain in misery and suffering forever, feeling the hobnails of the Roman boot eternally grinding upon its neck, kissing evermore the jeweled rings of Herod's blood-stained fingers, or licking the crumbs from the floor in the House of Hanan!"

At last there were gasps from one end of the avenue to the other; I guessed this was because Bar Abba had mentioned *names*. No more metaphors. The oppressors were defined. Every soul in that market-place was now a potential witness against him. Moreover, by continuing to listen, every person made *himself* a traitor, and therefore vulnerable to brutal repercussions. Someone near the front grabbed his friend and said, "Let's go. His words are full of scorpions."

But the vast majority remained where they stood, feet planted, minds rapt. Besides, if Bar Abba was the Messiah, shouldn't they *expect* him to speak with such boldness? If he was truly the One, it would not matter what he said, or who he accused. His cause, his mission, his revolution would be unstoppable.

My own mind was still reeling. I gaped in shock at the Zealot leader with heightened, invigorated understanding. Why hadn't I recognized it before? Why hadn't I realized who this person was?

Bar Abba continued speaking, his charges now much more specific. "The Romans have stripped us of our lives and our dignity. They try to set up their images inside our holiest precincts, slay our countrymen in the Temple courtyards, corrupt our citizens and make them publicans and thieves; they bring their vices, their diseases, and their heathen gods to our streets and synagogues, turning the very air we breath into a noxious poison. They set up for our kings the sons of the Edomites—illegitimate children of the Covenant—bringing famine and pestilence to our lands while their own bodies crawl with maggots and reek of death even before their hearts have stopped beating!

"But for all this evil, no crimes are greater than those of the High Priesthood and the House of Hanan! Their iron weapons hold the

House of God as if in a vise! They raise the price of doves for the purification sacrifices and cheat us at the tables of the money-changers! They hold for ransom our very souls! This Passover they will sacrifice a Red Heifer—Israel's first in more than a generation! Do any of you think you shall be so privileged as to have its ashes sprinkled upon you? I tell you that none but the very *richest* shall ever receive its sanctification! So, because of the House of Hanan, we are *all* unclean! *Unclean!* We have been pushed away, thrust out of the sight of God, where His eye can no longer reach us! We are locked out of all right-eousness, and the key is in the hands of Caiaphas and his wicked father-in-law, Annas. It is a golden key, and only gold may buy it! Is it not enough that we hunger in the streets, and cover our bodies in the rags of slaves? Must we also live in filthiness of soul? The High Priests of Hanan have made us *all* into stinking corpses, into decomposing beasts, into lepers! But no longer, O Children! Take up your swords and join us! Today we march on the Temple and the palace of the Edomites! Today Jerusalem! And tomorrow the whole world!"

Deliberately timed with these words the Zealots of Bar Abba withdrew from their cloaks the weapons they had concealed. Many weapons were offered to other men in the crowd. Suddenly a hundred swords pointed at the sky, surrounded by a forest of angry fists. The people were in a frenzy, cheering madly, wildly, as if their hatred was a drug, and their minds were all heavily intoxicated.

In the midst of all this noise I found myself pronouncing his name aloud—only now with the traditional "s" and without the slightest breath between the syllables. "Barabbas. Barabbas."

I don't know why it had taken me so long, or why I had to hear the name over a hundred times before it sank in, but finally I realized that I was in the company of one of the most famous—or *infamous*—characters in all the Four Gospels of Jesus Christ. I had to wonder why my gift of tongues hadn't cut through the confusion of Aramaic and Hebrew and made it immediately clear in my mind. I think I missed it because I was not *looking* for it. Now it all made sense—so much more sense than I would have ever imagined.

Yet even as I pronounced his name, I heard another voice in the crowd—high pitched and persistent. This voice kept repeating the same question over and over. It was repeated until at last those around him stopped shouting to listen. This reaction had a domino effect until more and more people understood and became intrigued. I saw now that the questioner was the old rabbi—frail, gaunt, a knobby cane in his trembling grip.

At last I heard his words: "Who else will speak for you? Who else will speak for you? You speak well for yourself, but who will speak for you?"

Initially the point of the question escaped me, though many Jews in the crowd comprehended. As the rabbi realized he had listening ears, he clarified his question further, and finally I grasped its purpose.

"Who is your forerunner?" asked the rabbi. "The Messiah cannot declare himself. Where is the voice of him that crieth in the wilderness, according to the prophecy of Esaias, saying 'Prepare ye the way of the Lord'?"

It was Barabbas's men who answered, particularly those who had not yet caught on that I was only a decoy, a fraud, and a play actor cast only in case some annoying old rabbi posed exactly this question.

"Do you not see him?" said one of the Zealots. "He is there, before the millstones! James, the miracle worker, from the deserts of Edom. He has already spoken for Bar Abba!"

"Then let us hear him!" another voice yelled. "Let us hear the words of the forerunner!"

Some people in the crowd objected. "No! We will hear the Messiah!" But the general clamor was that they wanted to hear at least some statement from me.

Barabbas tried to prevent it. "He has already spoken more than is required! The forerunner has nothing more to add! Nothing more than what he has already testified!"

This was the moment. I sensed it with every fiber of my being. The power of it percolated inside me like a geyser ready to blow.

"I will speak!" I declared.

Barabbas glowered at me, fists clenched, jaw set in antipathy. But there was nothing he could do. The crowd was already chanting, "Let him speak! Let him speak!"

I did not wait for an invitation from Barabbas. Instead I stepped forward, toward a neighboring millstone, a mere six feet away from Barabbas's strangling grip. Gestas grabbed my shoulder and made a feeble attempt to stop me, but the will of the crowd was too strong. As I stepped away, he clumsily hid the knife that he'd been poking into my back.

I mounted the millstone and looked at Barabbas. His expression was now stoic, as if convinced God would not *allow* me to say anything that might undermine his objectives. I turned my eyes toward the multitude, and then I saw Jen. She stood near the back, by the corner of the synagogue. Heli and several other Zealots were right beside her.

The crowd hushed, waiting. Prayers continued to resound in my heart, pleading for the Lord to fill my mouth with the right words. I knew I wouldn't be allowed to talk long. I had to deliver my message quickly, before Bar Abba and the others had a chance to react. I was fully aware that this was a suicide speech. In sixty seconds I expected to be dead, lying in the street. Not only me, but my sister as well. And yet, to my inexpressible gratitude, I caught a smile on Jenny's face—warm, loving, persuasive. She nodded to me, as if fully comprehending what I had to do, and completely accepting any and all consequences. My heart overflowed. I'm sure my tears would have done the same, but suddenly the words came into my mind.

I drew a deep breath and declared, "People of Jerusalem and Judea! Listen closely to what I have to say. You have heard much this morning. Much talk of vengeance and swords and fighting. Listen to your minds! Listen with your whole hearts! Are you seeking a messiah who promises worldly triumph and the destruction of your enemies? Or do you seek a Messiah who can save your souls—one who will promise you eternal life in the world to come? I tell you that there is a Messiah whose power is greater than all earthly kings, priests, and empires. He is the Bread of Life, the Good Shepherd, and the King of Kings. He will bring salvation to all who come to Him with broken hearts and contrite spirits, repenting of evil, and embracing His holy righteousness. By His blood will all men be cleansed from their sins, never again having to fear the darkness. He will enter Jerusalem as a mortal man and depart as a resurrected God."

No one spoke. There was perfect silence, so quiet I could hear the whisper of the wind. Until now most people seemed to think I was just using poetry or devices of language to describe the man beside me—Jesus Barabbas. Some appeared confused. The Zealots looked ready to pounce. But it hadn't yet sunk into everyone's minds that I was speaking of someone else. All doubt ended, however, with my next sentences.

"I say to you the Messiah is not in this square. I do not know when He will arrive in Jerusalem. But He *is coming!* And His name is not Barabbas! It is Jesus of Nazareth! He is the true Messiah! *Jesus Barabbas is a fraud and a deceiver!*"

Mouths dropped so far and so fast that I thought I might hear a clunking sound as chins hit the street. For a moment—a precious, sacred moment—I would have sworn that my testimony had entered the hearts of every soul in my hearing. The Zealots hadn't yet pounced. They just gaped in shock. I wasn't sure why they hesitated. Had God's power stayed their vengeful hands? But with my next words I seemed to unleash a firestorm.

"Depart from here all those who love righteousness and despise wickedness!" I cried. "Leave this square! Flee from the presence of these villains as fast as you can and seek the true Messiah of Israel!"

These words transformed the square so quickly, so furiously, that I could hardly comprehend it. A primal, gut-twisting yell was wrenched from the lungs of Barabbas. He screamed, "*Liar! Liar!* Child of Hell! You are an imposter! This man is not my forerunner! *He is a spy of Pontius Pilate!*"

I blinked, nonplussed.

"It's true!" cried another voice. "I saw him conferring with the Hegemon of the Antonia! He is employed by the Roman Legate! *Spy! Traitor! He will see that we are all scourged and slain!*"

I honestly wasn't sure if these shouts were from one voice or many. Certainly it first erupted from Barabbas's men, but in a matter of seconds *everyone* seemed to be yelling, shaking fists, or throwing punches at each other. Some were departing just as I'd advised, but in the midst of a growing melee. My eyes searched for Jennifer, but I could no longer see her.

Objects were flung—at me *and* Barabbas! I dodged a clay pot. Then something was launched at me that I could not dodge. Gestas had flung his knife at my heart. There wasn't even time to register that it was a knife before I felt the metal hit my chest. I fell backwards, partly from the force of impact and partly from losing my balance. I remember falling, but the next thing I realized I was laying flat on my back on the cobbled street. The sound in my head was literally like a tuning fork, but a tuning fork the size of a gong. For several seconds I heard nothing beyond a twanging, deafening echo. If these were the choirs of heaven they were terribly off-key.

Then, steadily, my normal hearing returned. I raised my hands to feel my chest. To my astonishment, no knife was imbedded in my ribs. Instead, I felt one of the rusty iron buckles of my camel hair coat. Beneath this buckle was a tender bruise, but no puncture, no blood. I saw the knife on the ground. I couldn't say whether the tip was deflected by that buckle, or whether I was struck by the butt-end of the knife's hilt.

As I got up on my knees, a tumult began beyond anything I'd yet witnessed today. It began with a blast of ram horns from several directions at once!

"The Temple guards!" I heard people shrieking.

Within seconds, squadrons of soldiers began to descend upon the wine and oil district, lances and shields in hand. They sallied forth from three side-streets at once—east, west, and south—in lethal battle formation. I might have expected them to be Romans, but the uniforms of the vanguard were altogether different. By their long beards, leather helmets, and darker complexions, I discerned that they were *Jews*. But then came the Romans from the north, indomitable in their steel helmets, bronze corselets, and leather skirts, swinging broadswords left and right. Behind the Temple guards were Roman horsemen wielding lashes interwoven with bits of lead.

Many of the Zealots raised their swords and refurbished farm tools to fight back, but they were no match for the discipline of the Temple guards and Roman auxiliaries. I saw men cut down where they stood, hardly even slowing the soldiers' advance. Several in the crowd who'd accepted swords from the Zealots dropped their weapons in the street, but this hardly mattered to the soldiers. Terror erupted in my breast as I realized that the armed men were cutting down every living thing in their path. Where was Jenny? What had happened to her? The screaming multitude rushed one direction, then the other, breaking against walls, canopies, and tables like ocean waves in a typhoon. Someone tripped over the top of me, accidentally kicking me in the stomach. After he'd scrambled away, I managed to get to my feet, gripping the edge of the millstone to keep from being crushed back to the ground.

The marketplace was in chaos. The screams were deafening. I climbed onto the stone to find some bearings, search for Jenny, and discover any routes of escape. Bodies were piling up around the soldiers. My eyes caught sight of Barabbas and Gestas and several more Zealots. They vanished into one of the wine shops, presumably in search of a rear exit. I suspected Bar Abba had been in tight spots before, and that his men had calculated all escape routes beforehand.

Then I saw her.

"Jenny!" I yelled.

She was fighting her way toward me through the crowd. There was no sign of Heli. Somehow in the confusion she'd freed herself from his clutches. I leaped from the millstone and struggled to reach her. I realized immediately that I should have remained on the millstone and allowed her to come to me. I'd lost sight of her in the rush of bodies left and right.

But then I turned around and my heart soared to the height of an eagle. She was right beside me! My sister threw her arms around me in a bear hug.

"Are you all right?" I asked.

"Yes! You?"

I nodded, but that ended our conversation. I'd have to hear later how she'd escaped from the Zealots. I took her hand and we fought to reach the same shop that Barabbas had entered. Others had also spotted this escape, creating a terrible bottleneck, overturning every vat and vase of wine near the entryway. The crack of whips, the clatter of hooves, and the piercing cries of the dying were drawing closer. Finally, we squeezed inside. Much of the rear wall had been broken down. We charged through and soon arrived at the narrow alleyway beyond only to see that this escape route had been anticipated by the soldiers. Roman auxiliaries were rushing from the west, forcing people to flee in the other direction. I was about to turn the same way, but Jenny stopped me.

"No! Follow me!"

She climbed onto a wooden barrel and hoisted herself onto the roof of what appeared to be a storage facility. I followed her with all due speed. As she helped to pull me up onto the roof, the soldiers barreled past us down the alleyway, broadswords swinging, too busy with other fleeing citizens to worry about the two of us. I wondered if I'd ever witnessed anything so ruthless. There were *women* in that multitude!—and *children!* I was sickened to think of it. Obviously that Roman in the fabric shop had reported seeing Barabbas—a report eagerly received by Roman and Temple guards. The authorities weren't taking any chances that the Zealot messiah might slip away, so they'd quickly assembled all available forces.

I looked across the housetops and the maze of narrow streets and alleyways.

"What do you suggest now?" I asked my sister.

"We leap from roof to roof," she replied.

I groaned and said, "We're getting way too old for this."

"Says who? Come on!"

We continued westward, leaping from building to building. The distance was normally only two or three feet, but then we reached an edge where the gap was at least nine feet. When I was twenty I might have tried, but not at fifty.

Regretfully, I led the way as we prepared to climb back down to street level. But as soon as my feet hit the ground, I was struck from behind. Jenny let out a scream. I staggered forward and tripped onto my face. Rolling over again, I saw the flaming eyes of Barabbas. Only one of his men had remained with him—Gestas, the knife thrower. Barabbas had another blade inside his cloak, but he did not arm himself. Instead he marched forward to throttle me with his bare hands.

There was no doubt his powerful limbs could have done the job, but my fingers searched for a weapon. I found a wooden crate and threw it at Barabbas's head. He easily deflected it with his arm. I found something more substantial—a broken piece of lumber. As he reached for my throat, I swung it with all my might, landing it solidly against his right temple. Then I raised it back, ready to deliver another blow.

A second blow wasn't necessary. Barabbas went down, dazed and disoriented, crawling on his face while holding his ear. I looked up at

Gestas. Barabbas' faithful thug would have gladly taken up where his master had left off, but suddenly his eyes turned west. Hooves were galloping toward us—two Romans on horseback. Gestas sent me a scowl, then bolted in the other direction.

"Jump!" I cried to Jenny.

She leaped. Miraculously, she cushioned her landing by bending her knees, keeping herself from falling. Quickly, she grabbed the sleeve of my cloak. "This way!"

Apparently she'd spotted something while on the roof—a possible escape route. She led the way into a shadowed nook between two buildings. Twenty feet later we found an open hole, like a storm drain. Hastily, I climbed inside, helping Jenny down after me. She started crawling into the darkness. I couldn't resist looking back toward the alley. The Roman soldiers had dismounted.

"It's him!" one of them announced. "It's Barabbas!"

The second soldier let out a hoot of triumph, but his celebration was premature. Barabbas recovered enough to draw his knife. He sprang at the Roman, his blade aimed directly at the soldier's unprotected neck. As his comrade was struck and fell, the first legionnaire managed to wallop Barabbas in the back of the head with the hilt of his broadsword. This time he was knocked completely unconscious. But it also appeared that at least one soldier had fallen victim to Barabbas's violence.

Additional auxiliaries arrived on the scene. It appeared as if the soldier who'd walloped the Zealot might finish the job with a plunge of his blade. Then I heard someone say to him sternly, "Our orders were to take him alive."

The soldier lowered his weapon. "He's alive," he assured his comrade regretfully. Obviously he would have wished otherwise.

They surrounded their unconscious quarry and began binding him with cords. Yeshua Bar Abba, the Zealot messiah, was now in the custody of the Roman Empire.

I'd seen enough. I pulled my head inside the hole and followed Jenny, crawling through a narrow passage on my hands and knees. The tunnel went for some distance. I was still convinced it was some kind of drain pipe. The sleeves and hem of my camel-hair cloak were soon caked in muddy silt. My heart continued pounding like a jackhammer. I could hear several squeaking vermin running ahead of us.

"I see an opening!" Jenny whispered excitedly.

A short distance later our heads were poking out of the exit. We were in the middle of the cliff face on Jerusalem's eastern wall. The height wasn't excessive—a drop of nine or ten feet to a rocky ledge. From there it was a relatively easy climb to the bottom of the Kidron Vale. But we couldn't climb down now. It was too risky. I could see Roman troops wandering just below us among the huts and hovels. It seemed as though every soldier in Jerusalem was on the lookout for Zealots and disturbers of the peace. Climbing down now would make me very conspicuous.

I sat back against the wall of the tunnel, closed my eyes, and tried to calm down, relax my breathing. "So how'd you do it?" I finally asked Jen. "How'd you get away from Heli?"

"I didn't," she replied. "I mean, it wasn't me. Not exactly. It was the students of the rabbi—one in particular. Right after your speech, they started arguing with Heli and the other Zealots—got right in their faces. Several had accepted swords from the Zealots and one of them used theirs to threaten Heli. The timing was perfect. Heli was about to kill me. That student saved my life. I can still see his face. Young and full of energy. I pulled away, and then the soldiers rushed in and . . . then I found you."

I smiled, though my eyes remained closed. It was clear that God still had a few miracles left for us. Still, this did little to explain the suffocating cloud of darkness that I'd felt earlier. It was still morning. The day had only just begun. What events might still transpire before this day was through? I couldn't think about that. For the first time I realized the back of my head was throbbing, probably from when I'd fallen off the millstone. Or maybe from when Barabbas had struck me. It was likely a double bruise. I wasn't sure.

I think I fainted momentarily. The next thing I knew, Jenny was slapping muddy water on my face.

"Jim," said Jenny. "You have to stay awake. The soldiers have moved on. This is our chance."

I forced my eyes open. If she'd have let me, I think I would have allowed the entire day to pass as I slept in that tunnel. I looked out across the valley that lay between the city wall and the slopes of

Olivet. The roads around the southern extremity of the Mount of Olives were still packed with pilgrims. Villagers in the slums of Kidron and Gehenna were tending to their animals and other chores. The legionnaires of Rome and the soldiers of the Temple had indeed moved on in the direction of the Dung Gate.

"Are you strong enough?" Jenny asked me.

"Of course," I said.

"How's your head?"

"Hurts," I replied. "But I'll make it."

I swung my legs out over the lip and lowered myself down toward the rocky ledge. I dangled for a few seconds and finally dropped, slipping a bit in some mud. Somehow I managed to stay on my feet and helped Jenny down after me. We looked about to see if anyone was observing us. I presumed it wasn't exactly a normal thing to see two persons climbing out of a sewer drain. We spotted some women near a stream to the south. They'd stopped gossiping and washing clothes to glare. No doubt others had noticed us as well.

"We should get out of here," I said.

"Leave Jerusalem?" asked Jenny.

"Yes."

"What about my dream?" she inquired. "The person who'll help us is inside the city. I know it."

"We'll find them later," I said, "in a day or two, after things cool down. A lot of people saw me on that millstone. By now there's probably an all-points bulletin."

Jenny scoffed. "It's not like they can broadcast your picture or put up 'wanted' posters. There are a million strangers in this city."

"Just the same, I'll feel better when we're out of town—and after I've shed these stinking camel hides."

We found a trail that curved past several huts and tanner's shops with the pungent odor of rotting meat. A moment later we reached the road—the same road I'd trod earlier with Barabbas around the southern shoulder of Olivet. The day was still relatively young; we were still very much traveling against the tide of cheerful pilgrims headed toward the city gates.

My head throbbed badly. I could feel a tacky scab on the back of my scalp. After wandering for a short distance along the road, Jenny noticed that I was tottering in my steps.

"Let's take a rest," she suggested. "We'll find some shade."

We turned off the main highway and walked a short distance uphill toward a modest hamlet with a single street. The street passed beside a grove of fig trees and gardens clothed in spring verdure.

"There's a well up ahead," said Jenny. "A drink should refresh you. Just a little farther."

I shook my head. I was just too dizzy. Involuntarily, I sat in the shade of a fig tree that stood closest to the road. Jenny sighed and decided not to push me anymore.

"Wait here," she said. "I'll get you some water."

I grabbed her wrist. "No. Stay with me."

"Jim, I'll be right up the street. I'll never be out of your sight. Don't try to tell me you're not thirsty." She set my hand back on my knee and started off toward the well.

I sat there for a moment, then I called out, "No wait! I'm . . . fasting."

She didn't hear me and continued on. The chatter of pilgrims on the main road below us was loud enough to drown me out. I leaned back against the fig bark and closed my eyes. *Oh, well. She can relieve her own thirst. Should have told her about my fast earlier.*

Once again I shut my eyes, and for an undetermined amount of time, the lights in my head blinked out completely.


## Notes to Chapter 13

The New Testament figure called Barabbas is mentioned by name in each of the Four Gospels, yet the significance of the role he played in contrast to the Savior's Atonement is sometimes overlooked. Firstly, his name—Bar'Abba or Ben'Abbas (depending upon whether it is spoken in Aramaic or Hebrew)—means "son of the father." Yet the term *Abba* in Hebrew means more than just "father." The best translation into vernacular English might be "Daddy." It was a very familiar and personal title of honor, and was used in the most intimate associations. The Savior used this term right before His arrest in the Garden of Gethsemane when He prayed, "*. . . Abba, Father, all things are possible unto thee; take away this cup from me; nevertheless not what I will, but what thou wilt*" (Mark 16:32).

Several ancient New Testament manuscripts proclaim that Barabbas's first name was Yeshua, or Jesus. Some scholars are convinced that the double name was used in the original rendering of the gospel texts, but that the name "Jesus" was eventually removed because of the repugnance Christians felt to think that such a reprehensible person had the same name as the Savior. (Ancient New Testament manuscripts that retain the name Yeshua as the first name of Barabbas include the Theta, Sinaitic, and Palestinian Syriac versions. Many apocryphal manuscripts also refer to him as Jesus Barabbas.)

If the parallels ended here it would be fascinating enough, but add to this the likelihood that Barabbas was from Galilee. During this time period Galilee was the principal hotbed of Zealot activity and most Zealot leaders, including the movement's founder, Judah, and also Menahem who led the revolt at Masada in AD 73, and so many other notable Zealots were also from Galilee (as was Simon the Zealot, one of the Savior's apostles). It would seem in keeping with the Adversary's character to raise up in the Savior's own neighborhood a man who would become a rival for Jesus Christ in every way, diverting the people's attention, and twisting the definition of "Messiah" to suit his own ends.

Then of course there is the ultimate parallel wherein the people of Jerusalem were given a literal choice of who they would like to see released according to the tradition of the Roman procurator. Would they prefer to save the life of Jesus Barabbas ("Yeshua, the son of the father) or Jesus the Messiah ("Yeshua, the son of *Heavenly* Father")? Or in other words, would they prefer a messiah who promises triumph over earthly kingdoms, revenge against all enemies, and the glory of the world, or would they prefer a Messiah whose kingdom was *not* of this world, but whose promise was one of eternal life, and glory in the world to come?

Reflecting upon this parallel should embolden our comprehension of the fact that this same choice—Jesus Christ or Jesus Barabbas—is made in the lives of all men and women virtually every day. We each make this choice for ourselves, and on many occasions in our mortal lives.

The location of the Pool of Bethesda is still a point of some controversy among Bible scholars and archeologists. The only mention of such a pool is in John 5: 2–4: *"Now there is at Jerusalem by the sheep market a pool, which is called in the Hebrew tongue Bethesda, having five porches. In these lay a great multitude of impotent folk, of blind, halt, withered, waiting for the moving of the water. For an angel went down at a certain season into the pool, and troubled the water: whosoever then first after the troubling of the water stepped in was made whole of whatsoever disease he had."*

The most popular site for these events is an ancient artificial pool found close to the Church of St. Anne, a little north of the Temple area and the Antonia fortress. Excavated just in the last quarter century, this site reveals a rock-cut, rain-filled cistern, fifty-five feet long and twelve feet wide, approached by a steep and winding stairway. Though no evidence of five "porches" (covered colonnades?) is mentioned, a fourth-century Christian church was built over the top of the site supported upon five commemorative arches. There is also a medieval fresco, now defaced and fading, representing the angel troubling the waters.

However, John's description sounds more like a natural, intermittent spring. Even today, springs are frequently reputed to have miraculous, curative powers. Therefore, a man-made cistern like the one near the Church of St. Anne would not have qualified. Some scholars have also suggested that the story of a man being forbidden to carry his bed on the Sabbath implies that the incident occurred outside the city walls. Others have said that the "five porches" describes Roman-era architecture around the Pool of Siloam in the lower city.

There is, in fact, another spring a short distance below the Pool of Siloam called the Virgin's Fount or Spring of Gihon. This spring is still visited by Jews today for its curative powers. However, its terrain doesn't seem to allow for multitudes of the sick, blind, halt, and withered to be lying about.

In light of these uncertainties, the author created a site just outside the city, nearby where waters from the Pool of Siloam flow out of Hezekiah's tunnel. This is at least in the area where natural springs are to be found in Jerusalem, and also the likely spot where large flocks of sheep would have been kept in connection with Temple rituals. Until more is known, such a location seems to suffice (E. W. G. Masterman, *International Standard Bible Encyclopedia–Bethesda,* 2003; www.reference-guides.com/isbe/B/BETHESDA).

In his speech to the crowd, Barabbas makes several references which ought to be further explained. He mentions, for instance, the sons of the Edomites who bring evil to their lands while "their own bodies crawl with maggots and reek of death even before their hearts have stopped beating." This is a direct allusion to descriptions of the death of Herod the Great—the first Edomite ruler—as given by Flavius Josephus in the first century AD. This Herod, of course, is the same King Herod mentioned in the Bible as being responsible for the murder of the infants in Bethlehem. He is also known for many other reprehensible acts, including the murder of many of his own wives and children. Right before his death he even ordered all the important personages of Jerusalem to be shut up in the Hippodrome and executed at the very moment of his demise so that the whole country would be unified in mourning. Fortunately, this order was not carried out.

Josephus tells us that Herod's physical condition before death included fever, intolerable itching that caused him to scratch himself to bleeding, terrible ulcers, tumors of the feet, inflammation of the abdomen and "gangrene of the privy parts that produced worms" (*Wars,* I:33:5). Modern physicians have made an effort to diagnose his condition as chronic kidney failure mingled with cancer and even venereal disease ("Mysteries of Herod's Death," CNN.com/Health, Jan. 25, 2002).

In this novel, Barabbas also makes mention of an incident where the Romans killed his countrymen (Galileans) inside the courts of the Temple. This is a direct reference to Luke 13:1, where it is reported to Jesus that certain Galileans were killed inside the Temple precincts by Pilate, thus "mingling" their blood "with their (Temple) sacrifices."

# CHAPTER 14

## Apollus

My mind was vexed to the boiling point. My heart was crushed by a battering ram of grief and pain. They kept me caged like an animal, like Spartacus the gladiator, and not unlike a captured chieftain of the Britons I'd once seen displayed along the Appian Way when I was a child. To my shame, I was no better than other children that day. I'd taken my turn at tormenting the poor man, tossing rotten garbage upon him and abusing him with a stick. Now I was suffering for my sins. The Lacandon children treated me no differently, spitting in my face, shouting abuses, and assailing me with stones and refuse.

For three days the Lacandon warriors carried my cage along the forest pathways toward the ruins of a city called Desolation. Despite the sturdy bars that surrounded me on six sides, they also bound my hands for fear that I might reach out and injure any one of the four porters who supported my cage on their backs.

My suffering might have been bearable if I had only known what they were doing to Meagan. If I could have just seen her, spoken to her, touched her hand . . . But I only saw her once, right as we were departing the village of the Boar Clan of Chief K'ayyum. She was imprisoned in a cage smaller than mine. Meagan called out to me. She reached toward me through her bars. I called back, shouting words of courage, of hope. But then they carried her out of my sight.

The anger boiled inside me like molten metal. I wanted to tear Prince Lamanai limb from limb—slowly, savoring the moment. Never in my life had I been the victim of such betrayal, such outright malevolence and inhumanity. If my enemies wished to treat me as an animal, I was determined—if I ever got out of this cage, if my wrists were ever unbound and I was handed a weapon—that I would also *act* like an animal. Like a monster. I would become a cyclone of violence to all who stood in my way.

I did not see Meagan again, though I suspected that the Lacandones in charge of her were traveling several hours ahead of us. The agony of not knowing her whereabouts, her condition, was the worst pain that I bore. I could endure any torture, but not the torture of being kept in ignorance about Meagan's well-being, the torment of not knowing if she was even alive. None of my prayers were for my own relief, but for hers. I also prayed for Ryan, Moroni, Jacobah, and the others. As to their fate, I knew nothing. I hadn't seen any of them since the terrible night that we were drugged in the house of K'ayyum. Nor had I seen Chief K'ayyum himself or Prince Eagle-Sky-Jaguar. The two cowards did not have the backbone to face me— at least not before our arrival at Desolation.

For three days they fed me only greasy meats, according to the regulations of some myth of theirs that a fighter would be more fit if he was denied grains and vegetables. The only drink I was given was some concoction of herbs mixed with additional drugs that heightened my senses, caused my nerves to stand on end, and made me feel as if I ought to be able to snap my bonds and tear my cage apart like a lion in a paper box. But it was merely an illusion, for my strength was not altered. After they gave me one draught of this formula I spat the next mouthful back into their faces, utterly refusing to drink more, notwithstanding that they offered me no other liquid to quench my thirst. After nearly two days of dehydration they relented and gave me water, fearing that I might become so weak that it would threaten my chances of victory.

Apparently my upcoming opponent was significant—the champion fighter of a tribe that had been a long-time enemy of the Lacandon. The tribe was called Chamula. But significant contender or not, I did not want to fight this champion. I would not become an object of amusement to these swine. I did, however, fantasize that if I was handed a weapon, I would immediately abandon the contest and attack my true enemies—Lamanai and K'ayyum. It was this fantasy that kept me going, and gave me the strength to endure all my suffering.

After three days of baking in the sun, suffering thirst and abuse, my cage was finally transported across another wide river and carried into the ruined city of Desolation. Much of the destruction here looked relatively recent—within the last decade. Though squatters and other human vermin had settled the outlying lands, the city center with its impressive stone buildings and monuments had been entirely abandoned. It was after dark when our dugouts arrived at the river's opposite shore and entered Desolation from the east, so I depended mostly upon the moonlight to tell the sad story of this city's fate. I perceived evidence of terrible fires and carnage; a more detailed observation would have to wait until daylight. I knew only that it had formerly been a Nephite community and stronghold. Some warriors in my company also remarked that it was once occupied by the people of Zarahemla, and prior to that by a people called Jaredites, who had called it by a different name. It was plainly a metropolis with a long and remarkable history, but all that had come to a violent end only a few years earlier. I could not help but observe that its present condition was much more representative of its Nephite name.

Exactly thirty Lacandon warriors had accompanied my litter to Desolation. There were other packs of Lacandon mongrels in the vicinity when we arrived, but though I searched frantically with my eyes, I could not find Meagan. My cage was carried into a stone corridor with an arched roof, and there it was dropped with a thud. I heard someone mutter that we were inside the ruins of a "holy temple," but whether this meant a Christian temple or that of a pagan cult I could not have said. On the wall in front of me was a mural, and near the ceiling I swore that the image had once represented the Savior coming down from the clouds, but the faces of the Savior and those who greeted His arrival had all been smashed and chipped away. Much of the remaining image was either scraped off or covered with black paint. Still, I did my best to draw comfort from it, and to imagine the glory of what this place once had been.

My hands remained bound behind my back. The muscles ached, and my wrists were swollen. If I had hoped that Meagan and I might at least be kept in the same room upon our arrival in Desolation, such hopes were dashed. My only companions were the same thirty idiots who'd brought me, but even if I'd wanted to carry on a conversation with them, they acted wholly uninterested. Or perhaps they were incapable. I had to wonder if these mindless sycophants had any capacity for intelligent thought. It was my conclusion that these thirty warriors were the same thirty whose lives would end if I failed to win tomorrow's duel. If I fell, they would each have their throats cut by the Chamulan chieftain. No loss, I decided, to humanity at large.

I called out to the stone-faced drone who'd led our party, "Where is the girl?"

He approached and said simply, "She is here."

"Where?" I demanded again.

"Near," he replied.

The only name that I could discern for this dolt was Chan. That's all I had ever heard him called. And yet "Chan" also seemed to be the name of about a quarter of all Lacandon males. The only male names I'd yet heard were Chan, K'in, Bol, and K'ayyum. Just more evidence of their stunted imaginations.

"Tell me, Chan," I said. "Where is your pigeon-hearted chief, K'ayyum? And that traitorous pig, Lamanai?"

"They are also here," he said.

"I want to speak to them."

"That is their decision."

"Then you give them a message," I snarled. "You tell them that this was all a waste of their time. I have no intention of fighting tomorrow. You and these other twenty-nine warriors are going to die—and you will die for *nothing!* Deliver this message to K'ayyum and Lamanai."

"This message has already been delivered," said Chan. "It is the same message that you have been repeating morning and night for the last three days."

"Then why have you gone through with all this?" I asked in exhaustion. "Why bring me all this way when you know I have no intention of fighting the Chamulan champion?"

"Because it was the will of Chief K'ayyum."

"So you really are just an incognizant animal," I said. "You do the will of your chief even when it means certain death? The Lacandones are nothing but slaves. Slaves and cowards!"

His expression didn't even flinch at my insults. I realized an insult is only useful when those being insulted feel the sting of it. I wasn't sure if this salamander of a man had enough pride to be insulted. I wasn't sure if *any* of them had any pride. They were gawking at me from their places along the wall where they intended to bed down with the same blank curiosity as slaves in the Roman markets—particularly those from the remotest corners of the known world. But with the slaves it was because they didn't speak or understand Latin! What was the excuse of these pluckless bovines?

I sat back in disgust. As on every night, there was excessive cigar smoking in our poorly ventilated corridor. While living in Albuquerque and Mexico I'd grown accustomed to the stench of tobacco, and this did not smell exactly like tobacco. There was something else in those cigars—marijuana or the drug they called peyotl or some other substance. Whatever the extra narcotic was, it did not deaden or slow their physical reactions. It only seemed to deaden their powers of rational thought—their consciences.

I sat upon the floor of my cage and had started to doze off when suddenly my hands were cut free. Like a leopard, I sprang to my feet and faced the man with the knife. To my surprise—and disgust—it was the Prince of Tikal, Lamanai.

He was alone. It was very late. Most of my Lacandon escorts were asleep. Lamanai gaped at me, his expression blank and emotionless, much like my thirty companions. I stared back, the fire in my gaze scorchingly hot. Still, my enmity seemed to have no effect upon the son of Great-Jaguar-Paw.

He said calmly, "Your hands have been bound for days. The limbs should be given a chance to recover for tomorrow's . . . events."

"It's more than my arm muscles that are stiff," I seethed, massaging the rope burns on my wrists. "For three days I've been kept in a cage unfit for a dog."

He grunted without sympathy. "I do not think your muscles will suffer a permanent disability. You are Hunaphu, the Evening Star of War."

"I am the Evening Star of *nothing!*" I spat back. "You know this."

He raised his eyebrows. "On the contrary, I am more convinced now than ever. More convinced even than I was the first moment I saw you emerge from that cenote in the forest. It was only during our journeys that I began to doubt. But in the Lacandon Mountains, on the evening before our arrival in Tz'ikin's village, I was visited by the spirit of my father. He reminded me that I must trust my first instincts, and trust in my own unalterable destiny."

"You are *drunk* with visions of your unalterable destiny, Lamanai. I tell you that you are deceived. When a man betrays his friends, he is in the clutches of the devil, not the power of God." I gritted my teeth and said, "I saved your life."

His eyes went wide. "Saved my life? You never saved my life, Apollus Hunaphu. You merely fulfilled your purpose—your reason for coming to this world. I *risked* my life to save the son of Mormon."

I shook my head in consternation. "You are crazy, Lamanai—driven insane by your vanity. If you believe all things exist to fulfill your 'purposes,' then why *did* you risk your life to save the son of your enemy?"

"Because it fulfilled my purposes," he said evenly. "By freeing the son of Mormon, it stirred up the anger of Fireborn and Lord Crocodile. The long-anticipated battle to annihilate the Nephite nation will soon commence. And when the conquering armies of the dispersed Lamaya are all gathered at Cumorah, I will at last unite them under the banner of the gods of my fathers."

The depths of his self-delusions staggered me. "What about the healings in your village? What about all the testimonies borne of Jesus Christ and His Priesthood?"

He hesitated to answer, his tongue working the inside of his cheek as he contemplated his response. Finally, he threw the question back. "What about them?"

"You witnessed for yourself the great power of this Priesthood!"

"I witnessed *your* power—the power of Apollus Hunaphu and Ryan Xbalanque."

"Then are we liars? We testified that this power is not ours—but a power conferred on us by the One God and Savior of the world!"

"I am convinced," said Lamanai, "that Kukalcan—or as you say, Jesus Christ—has great powers. But His powers are not greater than the gods of my fathers. Your present predicament confirms this."

I leaned back against the far side of my cage. This conversation was futile. There was no arguing with the devil. I finally asked, "Where is Meagan? Where are Moroni, Ryan, and the others?"

"By now they are dead," he said, a mystifying absence of emotion in his voice. "That is, except for Meagan. And of course, Tz'ikin, who no doubt aided her father in his desires. They are all slain by the hand of Chief K'ayyum and the people of the Lacandon."

My mind echoed with the words. I gripped onto the cage for support. Grief resonated in every sinew of my body. My soul felt the pangs of a hatred that I'd never before experienced. Even if he was lying, even if *some* of my beloved companions had survived, certainly not *all* could have survived. Like the strike of a cobra, I reached through the bars, attempting to seize him by the throat, but Lamanai anticipated my strike and moved just out of reach, mild amusement at the corners of his mouth.

"*Why?*" I shrieked. "Why have you left the two of us alive? Why not kill me too?"

"Because it is Chief K'ayyum's will that you fight."

"But I will *not* fight! What is K'ayyum to you? What are the Lacandones to the Lamaya but a tribe of insignificant, drug-addicted savages? Why do you care about K'ayyum's will?"

"Because he owes my father a debt of honor, and he will repay me with his undying loyalty, or he knows that the gods will smite him, and his people will be destroyed. You, Hunaphu, are simply a token of my gratitude for that loyalty. And as to whether you will fight, Chief K'ayyum is confident that you can be persuaded."

I gaped at him, terrified to think about what leverage they might apply to force me to do their bidding. At last, fury pulsing through every vein, I declared to the prince in a voice of low thunder, "I will kill you, Lamanai. I swear it by the blood of those you have caused to be slain, and also by the blood of my father, mother, and sister—that you will pay for your crimes. You'd better pray that I die tomorrow, because if I don't, it is my oath that I will smash you with all the powers of justice that my God will grant me. I will become His destroying angel. This is my promise to you, *Prince* Eagle-Sky-Jaguar."

Lamanai's eyes narrowed with a hatred of his own. "I do not fear you, Apollus Hunaphu. You are but a god in human form, and your powers are fading. Soon they will be extinguished entirely. It is the nature of your spirit to attempt to rise above your allotted purpose. And it is a testament to the far greater power of the gods of my fathers that I recognized your treacherous ambitions in time. So here you are, like a caged panther, your claws clipped and your fangs ground down to the gums. Take my advice and fight tomorrow with all that remains of your waning powers. Let it be your final act of glory. Afterwards your spine will be broken and your spirit delivered back to the Underworld from whence it sprang, never again to return to the world of light. For you are cursed, Hunaphu. I curse you. And unless I lift this curse at some future day, yours will be an existence of eternal torment in the fires of Yum Cimil, Lord of Death of the Lamaya, and Kisin, Lord of Death of the Lacandon."

I stared at him a moment, then uttered, "We shall see who is cursed."

With this, Lamanai faded back down the corridor and disappeared into the darkness. Many of the Chans and K'ins and Bols of the warriors who guarded me were muttering and chuckling among themselves, thoroughly entertained by the drama they'd just witnessed. Little did they know I hoped that they, too, would become the inheritors of this curse.

The air was dank and full of stertorous breathing. My grief was so overwhelming that I trembled in the muggy heat. Sleep, no longer the gentle brother of death, had become an evil, mocking spirit, staring back at me from red-rimmed eyes. I thought on Ryan and Moroni, Jacobah and the rest. But I was beyond weeping. The anger fully consumed me and no tears came to my eyes. I saw only my own frenetic hands snuffing out the life of Eagle-Sky-Jaguar. I knew full well that such hatred carried its own curse but—God forgive me—my lust for vengeance was unparalleled. I yearned to become an instrument of God's wrath, and determined that before I died I would find myself alone in the presence of the Lamayan prince. Such thoughts laid siege to my mind like Titus's legions burning and pillaging, until the daylight began to disperse the gloom of night.

But if I did not think my enmity could grow more intense, I was about to discover a heretofore unfathomable level of hatred. I was not asleep, but in the midst of some kind of vengeful trance when I heard the voice of Chief K'ayyum.

"Guardian Apollus!" he called.

I did not move. I remained as still as a sleeping statue, head bowed, eyes closed, secretly hoping that K'ayyum might draw near enough that I would succeed where I had failed last night, and seize the Lacandon chieftain by the throat.

"Apollus, awake!" he said again.

Still, I did not move.

I heard K'ayyum say to someone—probably Chan—"I thought you told me he refused our nectars?"

"He did," Chan assured him. "But even so, the only nectar he was offered would have produced alertness, not sleep."

"Then that explains his weariness. He must be roused."

For several seconds I heard only a soft shuffle upon the stone floor as someone drew near. A hand touched my shoulder to shake it. Like the strike of an Egyptian adder, I seized the hand and yanked it into the cage. Then I turned and grabbed the back of the head of the person who'd roused me and smashed it *two!—three!—four!* times against the bars of the cage. Several other men sprang forward, grabbed my wrist, and pried open my fist to set him free. I had attacked Chan, the leader of the thirty warriors. He was not dead, though his nose and face were appropriately smashed; I predicted his consciousness would not recover fully this day.

I looked up into the scarred but delighted face of Chief K'ayyum. "Ah! Your reflexes have not atrophied in the least as some had feared. Truly you are a Guardian of the Gods, Lord Apollus."

"I only regret," I said, "that it was not *you* who tried to rouse me. But I should have expected no less from a writhing maggot like yourself."

"And your fiery temper burns no less hot!" he raved. "I think the unsuspecting Chamulan champion doesn't stand a chance."

"He stands *more* than a chance," I responded. "For days I have tried to inform you that I will not become a pit bull for your spectacle entertainment."

K'ayyum became thoughtful. He stuck out his lower lip—the half not scarred by fire—and studied me carefully. "I am aware of your reluctance. But I believe I can make you feel differently."

I shook my head, but he continued:

"There is a tradition associated with this annual contest. It is an essential part of the ritual, for it heightens the passions of both our tribes—and helps to purge our mutual enmity, if only for another season. Unbeknownst to your opponent, the Chamulan chieftain, Mensäbäk, has brought the wives and children of his champion to Desolation. They are imprisoned at this moment in a cell overlooking the sacred altar in the courtyard. In a few moments you will be taken to their cell with a weapon of your choice. There it will be your privilege and honor to slay them as they are bound and lying with their faces to the floor. News of your actions, along with their bloodied garments, will then be delivered to the Chamulan champion."

My body began to shake with anger. "You hideous, faceless wretch!" I spat. "I will do no such thing. I would slice my own throat before I would harm innocent women and children!"

"Perhaps you will change your mind," he continued, eyes sparkling like gems, "after I show you this."

My lungs became as cold as an Alpine lake and my heart withered in its chamber as he took several awkward steps to the left on his toeless feet and reached into a basket held by one of his attendants. With his eyes set on mine to relish the reaction, he pulled out a blue and white woman's cotton pullover, covered in blood. He held it toward my face, grinning widely to show the gaps between his rotting teeth. From the pit of my stomach I wrenched a cry of agony.

The pullover was Meagan's.

The strength was sapped from my limbs. I crumbled to my knees on the bottom of the cage, my mind cast into a cyclone of grief.

Chief K'ayyum continued to speak. "The Champion of the Chamula performed a similar execution of your companion, Guardian Mee-gan, only moments ago—and with considerable relish and pleasure. You do yourself a great disservice, Guardian Apollus, not to repay this gesture by shedding the blood of his loved ones to your own satisfaction. It is what Kisin, the Lord of Death, and Sukunkyum, the Lord of the Underworld, would have you do. Just as these gods are the eternal enemies of one another, so you should feel the same eternal hatred toward the Chamulan champion. Only in this manner may the enmity between our two tribes be satisfied. And of course, if you are victorious, it will be my honor to cut short the lives of thirty Chamulan warriors. In this way, warfare is averted for another year, and a far greater number of the warriors of *both* tribes are spared. So that you know, even if you refuse this honor, his family will still be slain and the Chamulan will still be told that it was you who carried it out. Therefore, you are invited to slake your thirst for vengeance to the fullest. What say you, Guardian Apollus? Will you slay the wives, daughters, and sons of your adversary?"

My mind still reeling in the abyss, I raised my eyes, teeth clenched so hard the blood vessels in my temples should have ruptured. "No," I replied. "But I will fight *him.*"

A smile climbed the chieftain's cheeks, visible at least on the side where scarring had not destroyed his face muscles. This is what K'ayyum had wanted to hear, what he knew that he *would* hear as a result of this report.

Meagan was dead. My flower, my life, my only joy—murdered by the Chamulan filth that I would soon meet in combat. Murdered with "relish and pleasure." I did not doubt it. I did not doubt that this same pleasure in bloodshed was felt by all these beasts—these creatures of hell. I would kill this champion. This had now become the prime focus of my being. But though I would kill the Chamulan, it could never be as satisfying as the moment when I finally sent K'ayyum and Lamanai to their Maker. I was determined to carry it out this day. Perhaps the warriors of the two tribes would try to kill me first, but by all the power in my burning heart I would not let this happen. I would survive long enough to carry out what needed to be done. Sheer will would sustain me.

"Hands behind your back, Guardian," demanded K'ayyum. "Your arms will be rebound until you are inside the fighting arena, ready to mount the altar stone upon which you and the Chamulan will grapple to the death."

Men were already standing by with ropes. They acted far more leery than they would have otherwise been after seeing what I'd done to their commander, Chan. But my wrath was channeled now. The only men in danger were those who stood between me and my prey.

I positioned my hands as requested and backed up against the wall of the cage. I clenched my fists as they tied their knots around my wrists. After rechecking their bonds, the door of my cage was thrown open. My eyes burned with blistering heat as I walked out into the corridor. Awaiting me were a half-dozen nervous warriors aiming spearpoints at my chest.

I turned and saw another attendant holding up my "costume" for the arena. Judging by the hideous dark leather mask with boar teeth and black feathers, and the thick wooden headplate carved in the shape of a ghoulish monster with Dionysian horns, I presumed that I was to play the role of Kisin, Lord of Death. As he held up the mask and the shoulder plates with dangling straps, I walked toward him with a seemingly stoic resignation in my posture.

Abruptly I turned to the side. My initial kick knocked aside one of my escort's spears. With my next kick I planted the heel of my sandal between his eyes. The warrior's head snapped back; his spear dropped. Twisting around, I caught his spear behind my back in the palms of my bound hands. The men hesitated in confusion as I worked the weapon into the best possible grip. A second brave escort unwisely lunged to disarm me. I leaped and twisted the spearpoint, slicing the flesh of his arm and knocking him back. Immediately, I set my sights upon the Lacandon chieftain. He gaped at me, mouth open, eyes wide, blood draining from his face as I rushed at him with lethal speed. I had the entire motion worked out in my mind—leaping like a gazelle, twisting, and decapitating him where he stood. But then I was tackled from behind. Not one, not three, but five men smashed me to the earth, pried the spear from my grip, and knocked me several times in the head for good measure.

"Enough!" cried K'ayyum. "Raise him up. Hold him steady."

Two of the men held my shoulders, two others hugged my legs, another seized me around the waist, and all of them hoisted me upright in obedience to their master's command. Three other men pressed their spearpoints into my sides as K'ayyum stepped close, his face ebullient.

"Incredible!" he gushed delightedly. "Amazing! Truly invincible! This shall be the most satisfying duel ever witnessed by the *Hach Winik!*"

I responded by spitting in his face.

K'ayyum's expression hardly changed as he wiped the spittle from his scarred cheek and continued staring at me with wild, glittering eyes. "Take him to the altar stone. Let him meet Lord Sukunkyum!"

Their ridiculous costume was applied to my body. The visage of Kisin, Lord of Death, was terrible and violent, reflecting well how I felt inside. The Chamulan deserved to die. They *all* deserved the shortest span of time possible between this moment and God's judgment. I was led through the corridor and out into the sunlight. I realized the area had once been a civic and religious center. I saw just ahead, through the eyelets of my leather mask, a pyramid-like structure, not as tall or prestigious as Tikal's Temple of Venus, but much wider in girth. The steps were whitewashed and the stone and wooden walls were colored yellow and brown. Much of the paint had faded, and many of the intricate designs and facades were shattered and defaced. At the uppermost level of the building were shadowed galleries with narrow windows. Below these stretched another level with larger arcades. These compartments were presently occupied with onlookers, much like the Imperial boxes of the Emperor and high-ranking nobles at the Coliscum. Though it was too far away for me to be certain, I thought I saw a man in the center arcade with a profile like Lamanai. The prince of pigs stood with several other white-cloaked men who might have been kin leaders of the Lacandones.

To the right and left stretched additional buildings with platforms, archways, and pillars, every facing brightly painted in earth tones—red, yellow, black, and brown. Below, in the central courtyard, was laid out a sort of improvised stadium amphitheatre, benches and other seats made from wood and available rubble. One side of this amphitheatre was occupied with Lacandones while the opposite side was presumably reserved for citizens of the Chamula. There were also a good number of local squatters and riff-raff, either sitting on stairways or loitering in the shadows of buildings, eager to be entertained by the day's festivities.

In the very center of the courtyard lay the platform upon which I would fight. It was an interesting stage for a gladiatorial contest—a flat, circular stone block, roughly fifteen paces wide and as high as my chest. I assumed at first it was constructed of black cement, but looking more closely, I perceived that it was several triangular blocks of basalt set in place so skillfully that I suspected not even a weed could grow between the gaps. At one time this may have been an altar of sorts, like the one at the Jewish Temple in Jerusalem. Or if not the altar itself, perhaps a platform upon which the *actual* altar had sat and whereupon animals were sacrificed. But at present it had been transformed into an arena for combat. Set out about two paces from the edges of this raised basaltic stage was a wide barrier of hundreds of sharpened spears or pickets. Each spear was aimed back toward the rounded platform at an angle, manifesting that if a man were thrown off the stone, he would most likely be impaled upon these pickets.

Presently, I was forced to wait upon a portico looming fifteen stairs above the level of the courtyard. My hands remained bound, but to my left a Lacandon warrior held a six-foot battle lance. The stone tip was the length of my forearm, but the lancehead was more than just a point. It was intricately carved with many points and edges, like the jagged spine of a fish. It was also curved like a Spartan scythe. There was another spear in his opposite hand, longer, though less ornate, so I assumed that this shorter, fiercer weapon was meant for me. At my right shoulder stood a man with a second weapon—an obsidian sword. I did a double-take. It was *my* sword!—the one that I had so carefully crafted after commencing our journey from Seibalche—its edges augmented by lancetips and a three-inch point for stabbing, like a legionnaire's broadsword. I stared at the man who held it, but there was nothing in his eyes that indicated he knew that the weapon had originally belonged to me. I could only assume that K'ayyum had preserved it for just this purpose.

Would they give me a choice of one weapon or the other? If so, the obsidian sword would be my obvious selection. Or perhaps, if I had any good fortune on this blackest of days, they would place *both* weapons in my hands. I felt if I had any particular combat expertise, it was my ability to fight using both arms with equal focus and agility. I did not want this to be a long contest. My objective was to make very short work of the scrawny Chamulan, leap over the fence of spears, and pursue with all ferocity Chief K'ayyum and Eagle-Sky-Jaguar. If I died in the attempt, so be it. I would again be in the presence of Meagan, my eternal love, in the Elysian fields of Paradise.

Then I caught first sight of my competitor.

He emerged from the shadows of an opposite corridor across the courtyard and stood upon a similar portico to mine. He was arrayed in the blood-colored garb of the Lord of the Underworld, not unlike the vicious Salii of the traditional Roman war dance. Almost the instant that he came to a halt at the edge of the steps, his gaze found me. Immediately I saw in his eyes a hatred that seemed no less visceral than my own—but he was about to learn differently. My enmity could not have been matched. Nevertheless, even from across the courtyard I could hear his breath crashing against the inside of his clenched teeth, like a bull making ready to charge.

He was not the scrawny opponent I might have hoped, but more the size of a Chamulan Hercules. Still, this hardly mattered. Even if he'd been one of the Titans, my wrath would have remained unquenchable, like the fury of Vesuvius. The only mercy I would show him was a quick death.

And then the real storm would begin.

## Notes to Chapter 14

The city of Desolation, where this chapter takes place, was the scene of much bloodshed during the Book of Mormon, and particularly during the later years. The name was presumably given it by the Nephites, and derives not from its topography, but from its history as the region where the terrible civil wars took place that destroyed the Jaredite nation. It was upon this land that the Nephites discovered the bones and cankered weapons of the Jaredites (see Alma 22:30; Ether 7:6).

The city itself, we are told, was located very close to the narrow pass which led to Zarahemla in the land southward (see Morm. 3:5). It was therefore a critical defensive position for the Nephites after the treaty of AD 350 because it kept the Lamanites from completely over-running what was left of the Nephite nation. It appears to have become the central headquarters of the Nephites by about AD 360, and was the launching pad for the ill-fated Nephite invasion of the land of Zarahemla in AD 363, which ended with the city falling into

Lamanite hands. The Nephites took the city back in about AD 365, but lost it again a year later. The Nephites retook Desolation in AD 367, but then lost it permanently about AD 375. This continuous warfare was the basis for the author's presumption that the city was a shambles by the mid-380s, and attracted very few permanent occupants.

It may be interesting to note that several LDS scholars seem to agree on its basic location. Both Joseph Allen, PhD, and John Sorenson, PhD, place it in the state of Veracruz, Mexico, near the Gulf Coast, and in the northern part of the Isthmus of Tehuantepec (commonly proposed as the Book of Mormon's "narrow neck"). Although John Sorenson proposes the modern city of Minatitlán, Joseph Allen's site is less than 30 miles away, near the modern city of Acayucan and the ancient Olmec (Jaredite) ruins of San Lorenzo. Both of these locations are only about a hundred miles from the Hill Vigia (Cumorah) in the Tuxtla Mountains.

# CHAPTER 15

## Steffanie

We'd found them.

After nearly a week of tracking them across the woodlands and hill country of the land of Desolation, it appeared that tonight we'd finally caught up to the Nephite marauders who'd kidnapped Harry, Gid, Becky, Mary, Micah, and Jesse. The villains were camped in the forested ravine about three hundred yards away. We'd taken up our position along a ridge overlooking the serried woods. Though I hadn't yet seen our loved ones, I felt certain that they were close.

It seemed doubtful that we'd have found them at all if it hadn't been for Rafa. Just a few hours ago our loyal falcon had landed beside me with the jubilant news that we were getting very close. The bird's report was confirmed by several Lamanite scouts who'd been sent ahead to investigate.

For the past five days Pagag and I had been traveling with about eight hundred of the warriors of King Sa'abkan. The Lamanites were no less eager than we were to bring about the end of this band of Nephite savages. These Nephites with their painted faces and checkerboard-colored teeth had murdered countless Lamanite villagers and sacrificed their children to heathen gods. My only worry was that in their desperation for vengeance, the Lamanites would kill Becky, Mary, and perhaps the rest of our loved ones— either deliberately or accidentally. But despite my fears, there was no doubt that in the next few moments Pagag and the Lamanites would launch their assault.

Because of the thickness of the trees and the lateness of the hour we could only see a few shadows moving about, and the glow of

CHRIS HEIMERDINGER

several campfires. There was no way to tell exactly how many men we were facing or where their prisoners were being kept.

I had crept to the edge of the hill on my hands and knees along with Pagag and First Deer. First Deer was the name of the Hummingbird Captain in charge of the Lamanite battalion. He wasn't much older than Pagag or myself, and like other Lamanites, he was decorated from top to bottom with tattoos. But uniquely he'd also tattooed the skin of his nose. I assumed this had to do with his name, and as a result his nose was black, much like the snout of a deer. First Deer seemed to me a very fidgety, nervous man. But like every other Lamanite warrior, his prime objective in life was to kill as many Nephites as humanly possible.

The rest of the Lamanites were crouching just behind us in the brush, waiting anxiously for the order to swoop down upon the patch of woods where our enemy was encamped. The only thing that prevented us from attacking was Rafa. We were waiting for him to fly back and give us one final reconnaissance report. I was hoping to learn the exact location of Gidgiddonihah and the others and somehow stage a rescue in the midst of the assault. First Deer, however, was chomping at the bit. I was deathly concerned that he was about to shout the attack command before we received our report. First Deer acted far less interested in saving our family and friends than in slaying each and every human being in those woods. I was particularly worried about Gid. Though we'd done our best to describe the features of every prisoner, for obvious reasons I'd omitted the fact that Gid was a Nephite. Even if they recognized him by our description, I worried that Gid might get hold of a weapon in the confusion. If he did, I feared that he'd start killing Lamanites right and left. If that occurred, I doubted I would have had much influence in preventing them from slaying him. This whole thing was such an awful risk, and I could only pray that God would help it to come out all right.

Finally, I saw the falcon's sleek body zip out from the trees, flap its wings, and fly toward us. He perched on a stone just behind the lip of the hill, just a few feet from where we were crouched. Immediately he began squawking up a storm.

First Deer watched in astonishment as Rafa communicated his message. It was this miracle alone that I think had kept First Deer loyal to King Sa'abkan's command to help us. If he hadn't respected me as one who could "speak the tongue of birds," I was sure he would have kept me at the rear of the battalion and probably treated Pagag like any other warrior under his command.

Lamanite officers and soldiers were highly obsessed with rank and authority. They wanted to know who was in charge of whom in any given situation. Unfortunately, Sa'abkan had not personally explained our plight to First Deer. He'd delegated the task to one of his senior officers. The only thing First Deer understood was that he was to accompany us in pursuit of a band of Nephites and, if possible, help us free some prisoners. Because no one had specifically spelled out who was in charge, there was a little bit of a power struggle between First Deer, Pagag, and myself. First Deer felt that the priority was to destroy the Nephites while, of course, *our* priority was to save our loved ones. It was a difference in understanding that could easily spell disaster for my brother and the others. Because of the power struggle, I was very grateful for my ability to comprehend Rafa's chattering. First Deer recognized the importance of Rafa's information, and he couldn't get that information without me. This provided much-needed leverage, and forced him to keep us in the loop as to all of his plans and schemes.

"What does it say?" First Deer asked me, whispering.

But Rafa wasn't quite finished. I listened to a few more chirps, then replied uneasily, "He's . . . not very happy."

"Not very happy?" Pagag asked.

"How many Nephites are hiding in the trees?" First Deer impatiently demanded.

"All of them," I replied.

First Deer looked confused. "What does that mean?"

"A falcon doesn't think in exact numbers. He just said that all of the men who kidnapped Harry, Gid, and the rest are here."

"But I must know how many!" First Deer gruffed.

I asked Rafa the question a second time, but again the bird replied something to the effect of, "I already told you! Everyone is here that we were expecting!" Just once I wished First Deer could have had a conversation with our feathered friend. I was sure the two of them would have driven each other loopy with their mutual impatience.

Pagag spoke up. "Earlier I estimated the number to be about a hundred based on tracks that I saw when our companions were first kidnapped."

First Deer made a nervous sound in his throat. "I hope you are right."

Pagag turned back to me, "So what's wrong? Why isn't it 'happy'?"

"He couldn't find Harry."

Pagag raised an eyebrow. "What does *that* imply?"

"I'm not sure. He said that others from our group are here, but not Harry."

"Those woods are thick," Pagag noted. "Is it possible that the bird simply did not see him?"

"I don't know," I said, feeling insecure. I wasn't about to ask Rafa again. It just made no sense to ask a falcon to repeat itself. It wasn't in their natures to say any more or less than precisely what they knew. Because of this, I started feeling more and more apprehensive. If Harry wasn't among them, what had become of him? Was he dead? Had he escaped? I couldn't imagine Harry escaping and leaving the others to their fates. He would have kept following them, desperately trying to devise a way to stage a rescue. But the alternatives were too terrifying to consider. What if my brother had been injured and left behind to die?

"But the bird has confirmed that the *others* are here?" asked Pagag.

Rafa wasn't quite clear on this either. I decided this was a question I could ask. "Rafa," I began. "The others besides Harry—are they still being kept as prisoners?"

But at that Rafa almost went into a tizzy fit. He kept repeating, "Others are here! Harry is *not* here! Harry is *not* here!" He'd grown quite attached to my brother and could not seem to focus on any other angle of the question.

After I communicated this to Pagag and First Deer, First Deer said, "We have learned all that we can from the bird. It is time to strike."

Another rush of tension went through my veins. The moment was upon us. I asked First Deer again, "And you're sure your men understand that we must not harm the prisoners?"

"They understand," he snarled.

Pagag tilted his head at me questioningly. "What do you mean 'we'? *You're* not going down there."

"Oh, yes I am," I stated. "I can take care of myself. I'm going to sneak down on the right—see if I can at least spot Becky and Mary."

Pagag shook his head. "No. You will stay right here. You are not a warrior."

"Tell that to Prince Mardon and other men that I've bested."

Pagag turned to First Deer, "Can you spare two of your men to keep her on this ridge?"

First Deer nodded.

I turned on Pagag with all my feminine fury and growled, "If you prevent me from helping save my family and friends, I'll never forgive you."

Pagag widened his eyes at the forcefulness of my statement. Then he stiffened his resolve and said, "Better I am not forgiven than you are dead."

First Deer waved for two of his warriors. They weren't pleased at all to be called out of the battle to act as my babysitter. I gave Pagag the crustiest look I could manage as he and First Deer got back into position to prepare for the attack.

Pagag was by far the most aggravating human being I had ever encountered. For the past five days I'd continued to play my role as the alluring female—or at least I *tried* to play it—but Pagag had become so overprotective! I'd hardly been allowed to leave his sight for more than thirty seconds at a time. He was concerned that there was too much ogling going on from all these lonely Lamanite warriors. I will admit that the Jaredite took very good care of me. He carved a beautiful new splint for my injured arm—two pieces of hard wood and soft cloth that fit my wrist, forearm, and thumb so snugly—so perfectly—that I couldn't imagine how a plaster cast could have functioned any more effectively. With this kind of attention there was no doubt that if I had liked him, I'd have been swept right off my feet. That is, if I had *liked* him.

If I'd been the least bit attracted to him my heart would have melted whenever I was in his presence, or at least it would have melted far worse than what was to be naturally expected. I mean, let's face it, Pagag was a good-looking guy! Honestly, he was one of the most breathtakingly beautiful men I'd ever encountered. Any normal girl who allowed her defenses to slip would have experienced *some* shortness of breath, *some* mild dizziness, and *some* obsessive daydreaming. But whenever I'd found myself falling into this trap, I was very quick to nip it in the bud by focusing on something else, like the plight of Harry and Mary, or the blueness of the sky. *Mind over matter*—that's what I kept repeating to myself, though it was annoying that I had to repeat it so often.

It was as if Pagag and I were engaged in a strange, contorted kind of dance. It was so hard to act casual. Nothing came naturally. I wasn't in control, and I hated it, *hated* it! But Pagag acted no less conflicted—no less schizoid. We seemed drawn together like magnets, but as soon as we got too close, the magnets flipped, and the energy switched to repel. We argued every hour on the hour about something. We were driving each other crazy! But this didn't stop us from coming back for more.

I simply couldn't shut off that moment—those few seconds when we'd been in each other's arms—just before we'd discovered the Lamanite children. That moment flashed in my brain like a broken traffic signal. I was convinced that it had done something to *both* of us. Yet neither of us wanted to admit it, or face it, or acknowledge anything about it. Part of me wished it had never happened, but another part wanted to relive it over and over—if only to prove that it meant *nothing*. Oh, if only something would happen to make my feelings clear!

Maybe that moment was now, because all I could think about was how much I *loathed* him for forcing me to stay on this ridge while Becky, Mary, Jesse, Micah, and Gid were facing possible death below. One of the Lamanite bullies placed in charge of me—a man with tattoos on his face that reminded me of a circus clown—reached out as if to ask that I hand over Jesse's swordblade.

I thinned my eyes. "Try to take it from me, Bozo. I *dare* you."

He tried to narrow his eyes right back at me, not about to back down to a woman. The second Lamanite made a crooked grin, also intrigued by the challenge. He stepped nonchalantly to his right to get on the side with my injured arm. *Pul-lease*, I thought to myself. *What a pair of rookies!*

As the clown-faced Lamanite asked me again for the swordblade, the second one tried to move in behind to seize me around the neck. For his efforts he got a stiff blow to the forehead with my wooden cast, dropping him flat on his rear. I didn't quite play fair with the first one. Before Bozo could even move in, I raised up my knee and snapped a roundhouse to his left ear. Like his companion, he too said hello to Mother Earth. I stepped ahead of them to take my place with the others for the impending attack.

Pagag did a double-take as he saw my two babysitters on the ground, dizzily shaking their jowls. First Deer had noticed as well. He looked at Pagag, as if to say, "What are you going to do about this now?"

I swear I saw a flicker of admiration in Pagag's eyes. He wanted to laugh. But the Jaredite quickly suppressed this reaction and heaved a petulant sigh at me.

"Why can't you ever be sensible?" he scolded. "A battle is about to commence. It's no place for a woman."

"No place for *other* women," I replied. "But fine for me."

That crossed the line for Pagag. He stepped toward me, blocking my path. "You will not go."

"Oh, I'm afraid I will, unless you can come up with a better way to stop me."

He shook his head in disbelief, then reached out his hand. "Give me the sword."

"I don't think so."

The next moment was a blur. Pagag started with a move that was wholly predictable—a simple feint to the left, and a lunge to the right, to take advantage of my injured arm. I wasn't sure if he pulled a double feint or if it was his intention to attack the side where I carried my sword all along. I still don't know exactly how he did it, but the next thing I knew he had me in a half nelson, one of his hands gripping my wrist until I dropped Jesse's sword onto the ground. One of my Lamanite babysitters was quick to snatch it up. I let out a howl of humiliation, yanked away from Pagag, and faced him with a look of rabid contempt.

He had the gall to say to me, "I care about you, Steffanie, and I will not see you die today."

I was still so furious that I didn't know what to reply, which is probably good because I don't think my word choice would have been very ladylike. I just stood there, shaking with rage. The two Lamanites were chuckling contemptuously. Pagag said nothing further, just turned away and rejoined First Deer.

At last, the Hummingbird Captain sent a signal to his second-in-command, who in turn sent signals to the men. In unison, all eight hundred of the Lamanite warriors rose to their feet—not noisily, not obviously, but with deadly determination. As a single body, the battalion, including Pagag and First Deer, walked down the hillside toward the forest. Still nursing my ego, I watched without trying to follow, anxious for the next time I could face off with the son of Mahonri Moriancumr. Next time I wouldn't be so gullible. That is, if I could just figure out what he'd done.

Rafa was still perched at the edge of the ridge. He fluttered his wings excitedly. The falcon knew precisely what was about to take place. In fact, I swear he was looking around for his old master, the one-eyed falconer of Shinar, waiting to be commanded to fly back and forth with reports of troop movements or escaping soldiers. Or perhaps he was just eager to go back and look for Harry. I decided it would be best to accommodate his wishes before he self-combusted.

"Fly, Rafa!" I said, "Find Harry! Find the others! Protect them if you can—especially little Rebecca. Go!"

He'd launched back into the air even before I'd said, "Go!"

I watched Pagag and First Deer continue steadily toward the woods. As of yet there was no indication that the Nephite marauders had spotted them. But you couldn't keep eight hundred approaching men a secret for long. Approximately a hundred yards before they reached the first line of trees, I heard the blast of a conch shell. This sound inspired First Deer to sound the charge. The Lamanite battalion erupted into a full run, aiming their swords and spearheads into the forest. My heart started pounding wildly, like an oversized fish in a plastic bucket. First Deer's archers fired a volley into the trees, but I couldn't imagine that their arrows penetrated very deeply. Bowmen seemed useless in this kind of terrain.

As I heard the first clashes of combat, I caught my breath and started forward. The second of my Lamanite babysitters stiffly raised his spear before my face to discourage the very thought. I gave him a dirty look, then I pointed at the swelling bruise on his forehead. "Nice goose egg. A horn becomes you."

He eyed me malevolently, but made no reply. Soon I heard screaming—dying men on both sides. The woods suddenly seemed very misty; I wasn't sure if this was a natural phenomenon for this hour of the day or if someone had set fire to the trees. I couldn't take this. *I was going insane!* I had to get down there. I had to *help!* But how could I shake off my obnoxious babysitters?

Then I heard something intolerable. It was a scream—not a male scream, not a woman's scream. But a *child's* scream. It was *Becky!*

Again I started forward. Again the spear shaft was thrust in my face.

"Please," I begged them. "I have to get down there."

The Lamanite shook his head, sending me a tight-lipped smile.

I looked at the other Lamanite with the clown tattoos—the one holding Jesse's sword. I moved closer to him. He backed up a step, wary. But then I played the oldest trick in the book. I looked down the ridge, where there was another stand of trees, and gasped loudly, widening my eyes in fear. Like clockwork, Clown-face turned his head to see what I had found so frightening. That's all the opportunity I needed. This time I brought up my foot and nailed him right under the chin. Bozo managed to hang on to the sword, as well as his spear, but not after I stomped down on his hand. I reached down and grabbed the hilt. Next, the second Lamanite was lunging at me. I think his intention was to strike me with the shaft of his spear—maybe put a goose egg on my forehead to match his own. But some people never learn. I raised up my wooden cast and let him run right into it—putting a second knot right on top of the first one. He was out like a light.

I barreled down the hill, but soon I felt the grimy fingers of the clown-faced Lamanite as he tried to grasp my shoulders. I'd been half expecting this, so when I felt his hands, I ducked into a ball. This caused me to roll once end over end, but Bozo flipped right over the top of me, landing far more clumsily and painfully. It was an added tribute to Pagag's skillful cast-making that my wrist had thus far sustained no additional injury. In the blink of an eye I was up and running again—sword firm in my grip. The Lamanite with the double goose egg wasn't far behind his companion, but instead of continuing the chase, he paused to help his comrade to his feet. I got the impression they'd both thrown up their hands at me. If I wanted to get myself killed, they were more than happy to oblige. I continued forward and shortly entered the misty woods at a full run.

The fog seemed thicker than ever; I nearly collided directly into the trunk of a tree. The sounds of battle were raging all around me. I could see dueling shadows and silhouettes in the waning light. In a few minutes I was certain it would be impossible to tell ally from foe. I continued forward through the mist, listening desperately for another scream from Rebecca. I paused, and then I heard it—a second scream. Though it wasn't as loud as the first, I was still sure it was Becky.

Swiftly, I altered my direction, but two seconds later I tripped on the body of a fallen soldier. After I landed on the ground, I turned to look back at the dead man's face. His mouth and eyes were circled in gold and black paint, just like each of the five Nephite goons we'd faced in the land southward. There was another dead body to my left—this time a Lamanite. And behind him was another Nephite.

I rose to my feet, but I saw no more silhouettes in the mist. The fighting seemed to have moved farther west. I suspected the Nephites were fleeing for their lives and First Deer's regiment was in hot pursuit. At that instant one of the Nephites at my feet sprang to life. He'd been playing possum! Now he came at me with his hatchet. He must have thought that killing me would take no effort, because it was a klutzy swing, and I quickly avoided it by leaping back. I noticed a nasty slice to his abdomen. He'd been wounded. I confess I took full advantage of his weakness. As he swung his hatchet again, I raised Jesse's sword and caught the hilt of his weapon, digging my blade into the wood. After that it was almost poetry. Just like in the movies, I made a circular motion with my arm and disarmed him entirely. The hatchet was thrown into the air, landing somewhere off in the mist.

The Nephite gaped at me in astonishment. Still, he refused to believe that a woman could be any real threat. If I wasn't so pumped with adrenaline, I might have shaken my head at him and rolled my eyes. Were all men this stupid? He didn't even seem to care that I was armed with a sword. He ran at me with his arms fully outstretched. It was almost embarrassing. I could have killed him on the spot. Instead I threw another blow with my wooden cast, clobbering him on the crown. The Nephite beat a crazy pattern in the dirt with his feet for several seconds, then crumpled, dropping face first, unconscious.

At that instant someone grabbed my hair from behind. I gasped and swung my blade. But this attacker was not as clumsy as the others. He'd anticipated this move and seized my arm in a powerful grip. The next thing I knew, there was a knife blade at my throat and desperate eyes boring into mine.

The eyes softened. "Steffanie?" said the voice.

I let the face fall into focus. "Micah!"

He embraced me in glorious relief. "Steffanie! Thank heavens you are alive!"

I threw my arms around him in return. It was unbelievable! It was *Micah!* But then I pulled back. "Micah, where are the others? I heard Rebecca scream."

"Come!"

He took my hand and led me through the mist, toward the north. Or perhaps it was toward the east. I couldn't tell anymore.

"Jesse!" Micah yelled. "Rebecca!"

An instant later two shadows slipped out from behind some trees. The two figures came forward; their features coalesced from the mist.

"Steffanie!" Becky cried out.

My heart sprang to life. *It was them!* Rebecca's voice sounded as sweet as music, as soothing as chocolate. Jesse had a grin as big as Mount McKinley. I realized their hands were still bound in front. Another rope attached them together at the waist. Micah had remnants of a similar rope around his waist and one wrist. Somehow the Essene had managed to find a blade and cut himself loose, but he hadn't yet had a chance to free the others—a fact of which Jesse quickly reminded him.

"Cut us loose!" Jesse demanded. "Hurry! The Wolf Witches might return!"

*Wolf Witches.* That was a term I hadn't heard before.

After Micah severed their bonds, I embraced everyone in a flurry of relief and joy. But then I asked in desperation, "Where's my brother? Where's Mary and Gidgiddonihah?"

All smiles ran away.

I heard footsteps in the underbrush and whirled around. Five Lamanites stepped out of the mist, coming toward us, weapons ready.

"Stop!" I shouted. "These are my family and friends! They are not Nephites!"

They slowed their approach, but still looked skeptical. Several were covered in blood—not their own, but the blood of the slain. Before this day ended I didn't think too many "Wolf Witch" Nephites would still be breathing. But these Lamanites didn't seem to find it easy to switch off the killing mechanism in their brains. Two of them didn't care what I said. They kept coming forward. Instinctively, I raised my sword to meet the attack.

But then, with the timing of a comic book superhero, Pagag leaped out of the fog. He came between us and the Lamanites.

"Back away!" he snapped. "These are the prisoners—the people you were told about. If any man comes closer, he will contend with me."

The men stopped. More Lamanites started emerging from the misty forest, but like the others, they kept their distance and allowed our reunion. Rebecca was overjoyed to see Pagag. She threw her arms about his waist and squealed like a puppy.

Pagag looked at me and groaned. "I just can't seem to get you to obey, can I?"

"I guess not."

"It's a problem."

"I'll work on it," I promised—not.

Just as I had done, Pagag asked Jesse and Micah, "Where are the others?"

Heavily, Jesse replied, "Gone. We haven't seen them in three days."

"Three days!" I repeated in shock.

"The Wolf Witches sold them," said Micah. "They were planning to sell us as well."

"Sold them where?" asked Pagag. "To *whom?*"

"To some villagers in the mountains," answered Jesse. "There was a fight."

"They tried to hurt me," Becky added. "But Gid wouldn't let them."

Micah nodded. "Gidgiddonihah killed three of the Wolf Witches and two of the villagers in a scuffle."

"We were certain they'd kill us all after that," said Jesse. "But they didn't. These villagers were looking for a gladiator of some type—someone to fight for them in a contest with another tribe."

"So they bought him," added Micah. "They bought Harry and Mary as well. But not us. The Wolf Witches had other plans for us."

"Plans that I don't like to think about," added Jesse.

"Where is this village where Harry, Mary, and Gid were sold?" I demanded. "What was the name of the tribe?"

"Chamula," Micah replied. "The people were called Chamulans."

# CHAPTER 16

## Harry

*I held Mary tightly by my side as we sat in the darkness of our prison cell. The place smelled stale and humid. The ceiling was crisscrossed with a thousand spider webs, while the floor had a thick carpet of bird droppings. The birds got in and out through a narrow window about six feet off the floor on the outer wall. Five inches high and five feet wide, this window was also our only source of sunlight.*

*We'd been in this room inside the temple ruins of Desolation for about three hours. I'd already gripped the rim of the window and hoisted myself up several times to see outside. Our cell was overlooking the central square. People had been gathering practically from the moment we'd been dumped inside here. Just looking at the stone platform surrounded by a circular band of inward-pointing spears, it was obvious that this was where the fight would take place between Gidgiddonihah and the Lacandon champion.*

*"How are you feeling?" I asked Mary.*

*She'd been quite nauseous since yesterday, undoubtedly on account of the scant amount of food and water they'd given us over the past few days.*

*"Better," she replied. "I'm feeling much better."*

*I wasn't sure I believed her. It was rare that I ever heard Mary complain. She always seemed to feel there was no point in whining or groaning about things that couldn't be changed. This was especially true in circumstances like this.*

*"Are you sure?" I pressed.*

*She looked into my eyes and smiled. "Yes. I'm with you now. I told you once before, if I'm with you, nothing else matters. They can do whatever they want, as long as they keep us together."*

*A stab of pain pierced my heart. I felt the emotions well up inside me. How I loved this girl! What an idiot I'd been. Was I really so foolish at one time as to question my feelings? Did all males go through such moments of utter stupidity? Mary Symeon was the best thing in my life— the best that had ever happened to me. I didn't deserve her—no sense denying it. But here she was, more in love with me than I'd ever thought a girl could be.*

*Despite what she said, I had serious doubts that they would allow us to stay together much longer. We'd been captives for many days now. I'd almost lost count. For almost a week we'd been in the hands of Chief Mensäbäk of the Chamulans, a miserable imp of a man with a sagging face and the intelligence of a prairie dog. I could hear his whiny voice occasionally from one of the viewing boxes directly underneath our cell. Mensäbäk had purchased us, along with Gidgiddonihah, from a group of degenerate Nephites who called themselves "Wolf Witches."*

*The Wolf Witches had been more than happy to get rid of Gid. Shortly after discovering that our captors were Nephites, Gid had told them to their faces how disgusted he was that he and they belonged to the same race—the noble blood of Lehi, Nephi, King Benjamin, and his namesake, Captain Gidgiddoni. The Wolf Witches didn't take the insult well. They untied Gid. I think their original plan was to humiliate and slay him, but the end result was the death of several of their best warriors.*

*They wanted so badly to take out their vengeance upon him—flay him alive and feed his entrails to the vultures—but at the last second the Wolf Witch leader decided that Gid's fighting skills might prove to be a highly profitable commodity. Apparently it was widely known that a mountain tribe called the Chamulans would pay a high price for a cham- pion fighter during this season of the year. As for why the Chamulans had wanted to purchase me or Mary . . . this was still a bit of a mystery. Chief Mensäbäk had been just as anxious to purchase Becky, Jesse, and Micah as well, but the Wolf Witches refused, explaining that they were "too valu- able to trade." This seemed particularly true of ten-year-old Becky and fifteen-year-old Jesse. In actuality, I was more terrified for their lives than I was for my own. I'd observed and listened to the twisted habits of the Wolf Witches enough to realize that blood sacrifice was vital to "feed" their corrupted religion. My heart ached with desperation. Yet I knew that the Lord had not forgotten us. I felt certain that somehow this whole mess was going to work out. But if we didn't get out of here soon, I feared my precious cousin and friends would become the latest victims of the Wolf Witches' satanic appetites.*

Mary felt the reason they'd purchased us had something to do with the contest that would be underway in the courtyard in the next few minutes, but I couldn't quite grasp how the two concepts related. Earlier that morning my heart quaked as it appeared that they were going to kill us just before they threw us into this cell, but for now it seemed they were determined to let us live—at least long enough to witness the outside events about to unfold.

There seemed to be considerably more noise and activity in the square than before. I arose and grabbed the ledge again, pulling myself higher to see through the window. I caught my breath as I recognized Gidgiddonihah standing on the platform directly below us. His hands were bound. He was arrayed in some sort of fighting costume—a red helmet with odd symbols and shapes, a mask over his face like some kind of demonic monster, and a short cape that came off the shoulders with plenty of streamers and red feathers.

I raised my eyes and looked across the square, and for the first time I saw Gid's opponent. My blood pressure rose as I studied him. His helmet was black. His mask had horns and some sort of tusks. These two costumes must have represented some kind of Chamulan and Lacandon deities. A battle of the gods was about to begin.

"I see them," I announced to Mary. "Both Gid and the man he's going to fight."

"What does the other fighter look like?" Mary inquired.

I studied Gid's opponent a moment longer, then replied, "Don't worry. I've never met the man who could best Gidgiddonihah—not in a one-on-one duel."

"But Gid told Mensäbäk that he would rather die than fight for anyone's entertainment."

"That may be what he said, but . . . something must have changed. I think—or at least it appears—that Gid is going through with it."

I must confess, even as I tried to reassure Mary, there was something about the Lacandon warrior that I found terribly unsettling. Even from this distance I could see that his eyes scintillated with flames of hatred.

*But what bothered me—what genuinely disturbed me—was his overall demeanor. The man was not cocky or overexuberant. His hatred was not reckless, but seemed menacingly concentrated and calculating. The Lacandon warrior was much larger than most Chamulans, and his skin was considerably paler. Not blindingly white like my own flesh, but . . . I had to wonder if this man, like Gidgiddonihah, had been recruited for this fight from another tribe. I also noted that the Lacadon's hands were bound, much like Gidgiddonihah's. I found this curious. Was it part of the ritual to bind the fighters' limbs? Or were such warriors simply considered so dangerous and unruly that their actions couldn't be trusted? And if indeed they were both fighting against their will, then I had to wonder why the two men didn't just lay down their weapons, shake hands, and defy the will of the Chamulan and Lacandon chieftains. Again, I felt certain that something was going on here that I didn't fully understand.*

*My wrists began to ache from holding myself up, but I couldn't let go of the ledge now. Like tigers stalking prey, the two fighters were on the move . . .*

* * *

### Apollus

The drums started booming. In addition, there was a shrieking volley of other queer-sounding instruments, primitive and brutish. I watched as my adversary, the Chamulan champion, began descending the stairs, followed by his entourage, including those who carried his weapons. The spectators in the galleries, as well as those seated around the courtyard, began singing and chanting, the volume increasing and the tone growing ever more boisterous.

I descended the stairs as well, followed by my flock of attendants. My eyes were fixed upon the Chamulan the entire distance as we reached the ground level and crossed the courtyard, approaching the round block of dark stone. Because his hands were also bound, I concluded that he was most likely a slave. Since he owned nothing else, his family had been his most prized possession. This explained the fierce enmity in his eyes. How would he react, I wondered, if he knew that it was not me who had slain his family—but the

Chamulan and Lacandon chieftains? Not that it made things any different. It would not change the fact that he'd murdered Meagan with "relish and pleasure." There was a certain look in the eyes of a man who knew how to kill and kill *well*. This man's eyes radiated that look.

We reached the circle of pickets surrounding the fighting block. There were two places—one exactly in front me and the other in front of the Chamulan—where a "gate" was established. At this narrow entryway the spears were in a single line—not spread out in a wide band or "nest" as they were the rest of the way around the platform. Men on either side yanked three spears out of the earth, much like pulling up tent stakes. This opened the entrances. My arms came loose; my bonds were cut. The Chamulan was freed as well.

The fighting lance was placed in my hands. They also handed me my obsidian sword. *So,* I thought, *I'll fight with both.* My teeth set tightly in satisfaction. A stone dagger was also tied to my waist. In all, I would carry three implements of death—no less than the number of weapons in the hands of my adversary. He received a lance like mine. A bulky stone hatchet was tied around his waist. But his *final* weapon actually raised my eyebrows.

It was a sword. A *metal* sword. If I hadn't known any better, I might have thought it was a *Roman* sword. But that was ludicrous. Until this moment I'd seen no evidence that Lamanites or Teotihuacános or even Nephites could smelt metals with the same skill as Europeans. Apparently I was wrong. Whatever improvements I'd made to obsidian sword-making, it was still a weapon of stone, while his was of steel. Who was the idiot in charge of providing an equivalent arsenal? My measly dagger was no match for that hatchet either. So be it. No matter. The hatchet did appear somewhat cumbersome. Maybe in that I would find some advantage.

We were also given shields decorated with the same symbolism as our costumes. They were strapped to our left forearms, freeing up our left hands for the lances. No less than twenty warriors surrounded each of us as we accepted our weapons, each bearing spears with an arm's length advantage over our lances. The Chamulans and the Lacandones weren't taking any risks that we might try to use our weapons for purposes other than killing each other.

Again the shrieking horns resounded—our cue to enter the arena. As I stepped into the narrow pathway, the sharpened pickets comprising the "gate" were hastily replaced into their three empty sockets in the ground. Once again, my eyes fixed upon my adversary. The more I studied him, the less I liked what I saw. I had expected the Chamulan champion to be as bumbling and ill-trained as the rest of the warriors I'd encountered in this land. As a boy, and before my father had accepted his commission in Syria and Palestine, I'd whiled away far too many afternoons at the *Ludus Gladitorius,* watching some of Rome's most famous gladiators in action and in training. Despite being a Roman soldier, my father (like most parents) considered it a disreputable waste of time, and he was right. But what those afternoons taught me was that all gladiators who survived the games year after year carried themselves the same—as if eyes were permanently affixed to the backs of their heads. Even at leisure their feet never stood in a position of imbalance. Their hands always floated a short distance out from the body. And above all, there was just . . . an *air* about them—a general manner of heightened awareness, of lethal dexterity. Only someone who possessed similar skills could recognize it. Fortunately, I had these skills, and I perceived each of these deadly attributes in the red-masked Chamulan on the opposite side of the stone.

I was glad to have recognized it. Otherwise I might have lowered my guard—I might have allowed even the narrowest thread of overconfidence to enter my mind. This may have been fatal. I could not afford to be cocky. Hatred could make a man sloppy, careless, and overexuberant. *Harness your hatred,* I told myself. If I wished to pursue my ultimate object of scaling those walls behind my opponent to spill the blood of Lamanai and Chief K'ayyum, I had to be prepared to utilize every expertise in my arsenal. I wasn't taking any chances. The Chamulan champion—though still a vile murderer—was but a pawn of far more insidious villains. It was *these* men whose lives I sought to destroy. This cockroach was only in my way.

Added to my advantage, I felt—or *hoped*—that I had noticed several "chinks" in my adversary's armor. He was older. Although our heights were nearly equivalent, he was stouter in build, not quite as lean in musculature. I presumed these factors would give me greater quickness and agility. Though this gorilla might have bested me in the shot put, I could assuredly best him in any contest of speed. Such knowledge would affect my strategy on every level. Also, though he tried hard to disguise it, I perceived a stiffness in the Chamulan's left shoulder, most likely from an old injury. *Very good,* I thought. All these weaknesses would allow me to slit this dog's throat in short order, thus permitting me to pursue my true quarry with all passion and vengeance.

The Chamulan and I came to a halt at the foot of the platform, the curved basaltic edge only inches away from my abdomen. I knew why *I* had hesitated to climb the stone, but I was not certain why my opponent had done the same. His manner of climbing would tell me volumes about his conditioning—endurance, flexibility, stamina, and perhaps a betrayal of further weaknesses in joints or knees. Did he hesitate for the same reason—to observe my flexibility and conditioning? Those phantom Chamulan eyes remained locked into mine, burning with a cold, consuming flame. Fortunately, I did not believe that I had any particular weaknesses to expose. Or so I hoped. In case he *was* sizing up my physical prowess, I decided when mounting the stone that I would *feign* a weakness—on my right side, exactly facing his ailing left shoulder.

There was a sudden cessation of the drums, followed by a singular flurry of blasts from shell trumpets, and shrieks from those other wooden instruments—the ones that created a sound strangely akin to the death knell of a cow. Afterwards came the black-robed priests, toting urns of smoking incense. They marched in a circular fashion around the outside of the fence of sharpened pickets, leaving a trail of smoke, as if purifying or preparing the space inside for the advent of certain death. I thought to myself how this spectacle was really not so different from those of the Coliseum with its costumed attendants representing Pluto, Hermes, Charon, and other funereal deities. The march of the priests was followed by a strange, dissonant chanting-singing from brightly dressed figures who stood at the head of either side of the makeshift bleachers—one side representing the Chumula, and the other representing the Lacandon. Following this, the thirty warriors from the ranks of both tribes filed out of the darkened corridors like rodents from a cave. They took their places at the head of their respective audiences, seating themselves on the ground facing *away* from the fighting platform, as if to signify that whatever the outcome, they were utterly resigned to their fate, and thus could pretend indifference to the unfolding action of the contest.

I took in all of these rituals with a quick sweep of my eyes, but when I returned my stare to my adversary, his granite gaze had not budged. Those fire-filled eyes had remained fixed, either because he was already intimately familiar with the pageantry of this event, and therefore had no interest, or because he was inordinately focused on perpetuating my untimely death, and would therefore let nothing else distract him. *Not a concern. Just keep watching me you vermin, you jackal. In five minutes my weapons will be stained with your putrefied blood.* This would complete the first phase of seeking retribution for the lives of Moroni, Ryan, Jacobah . . . and Meagan.

Sorties of taunts and jibes emanated from the audience, demanding that we climb onto the platform. The Chamulan didn't move, still watching me the way a crocodile watches an animal that comes to the river to drink. *Very well,* I thought. *I will mount first, you cretin, just to satisfy your fecund curiosity and toy with your villainous mind.*

In a single leap I mounted the stone, sword and lance firmly in my grasp and control. Ah, but my landing was not so perfect. I allowed my right leg to buckle a little and clenched my teeth ever so fleetingly in pain. Very subtle. Nothing obvious. I doubted that the audience had even noticed, but I was sure that the *Chamulan* had noticed. Even now those scorching eyes danced with a new awareness, a valuable secret that he hoped to exploit. Oh, how I *yearned* for the moment when he attempted to exploit it! It could not come soon enough. The Lacandon spectators were already cheering and banging stones together. This was either their manner of applause, or they were arming themselves to kill the victor when the fight had concluded.

I waited patiently on my side of the platform as the Chamulan set down his sword and lance. Slowly, awkwardly, he lay flat against the platform, shield still strapped to his arm, and drew up one leg, then the other. For the first time, he took his eyes off me entirely, as if necessity demanded that he devote all of his energies to pulling his body up onto the stone. His clumsiness produced laughter and booing from the audience. I shook my head minutely. The display was somewhat disconcerting. Did he think I was an outright fool? That I was so naïve as to launch across this platform and attempt to skewer him with my lance while he *appeared* to be vulnerable? Some of the Lacandones were offering just this advice.

"Kill him!" they shouted. "Hurry! Kill him now!"

But my father did not raise such a slow-witted son. Rather, I waited indulgently for him to finish his game, his ruse. At one juncture he became still, eyes cast down, as if he were stuck or winded or broken in some way. Again, I made no move to strike. Finally, deliberately, he raised his eyes and gave me a fresh look of icy contempt. I replied with a sagacious smile. So disappointing. I had not taken the bait. He'd certainly hoped that I might rush him, or better yet, cast my lance. Had I done so, I would have discovered that he was far more prepared than it seemed. His weapons were not so sloppily placed. He'd carefully kept them within inches of his fingers. Had I lunged, he would have rolled and most likely flung his lance. Had I cast my *own* lance, he would have quickly hoisted his shield and I would have found myself shy one essential weapon. He looked irritated. I winked in response, then sent him my most wrathful scowl. This got his goat. He jumped to his feet, jaw again firmly set.

The two of us were now upright, poised, our weapons bristling and ready. The drums, which had thumped a consistent rhythm for the past several minutes, suddenly ceased. Clamor from the audience had stopped as well. But this silence was short-lived. A single raucous blast erupted from every wind instrument in the courtyard. I had not been informed as to the official signal that would start the contest, but it wasn't necessary. I recognized it anyway.

Noise from the spectators was renewed with greater intensity, each side cheering, hailing, lambasting, taunting, and cursing the champion of choice. I took the initiative of moving several steps toward my adversary. He matched my steps, and within seconds we were less than ten feet apart, circling in the center of the platform like male lions competing for domination of the pride. Blood coursed through my veins, awakening my instincts, alerting every particle of my flesh. *"For Meagan,"* I whispered under my breath. *"For Meagan."*

The impulse to initiate attack came to us both at the same instant. In unison we raised our swords and flew toward one another. I knew better than to meet his strike with my obsidian-edged weapon. Instead I raised my forearm shield to take the blow. Alternately, I felt my obsidian dig into his own shield. We spun around and faced one another again, only now on opposite sides. The dance of death had begun.

I glanced at my shield. It had held up rather well, though I could clearly see where his sword had cut into the wood. No matter how well this shield may have been made, without the steel crossbands and plating of its Roman counterpart, it would not withstand too many blows like that one. My adversary continued to circle, hissing at me through his clenched teeth. I mocked him by making a similar sound, though mine might have compared more accurately to the huffing of a winded mule.

This provoked an expected second lunge. As our spears and swords clashed, he released a furious howl from his gut. He certainly was a noisy beggar. Again, my shield took the impact, but this time I heard the splintering of wood. There was a smirk on the Chamulan's face. He'd heard it too. Though on each pass I'd wisely turned my sword to the side to avoid breaking the obsidian blades, several of the volcanic glass points had shattered anyway. Blast these inferior weapons! I needed to employ a different tactic.

Before our next go at it, I switched the lance into my right hand, letting the sword dangle awkwardly from my wrist. The Chamulan frowned, trying to ascertain my thoughts. This time I took the initiative and sprang forward. My adversary raised his shield and swung his blade. At the last second I swerved straight into him. This caused my shield to receive a harder blow, but as we passed I stuck out my lance tip, and as I turned to face him, I reveled to see a trickle of blood across his chest, parallel to his lowest rib. The cut wasn't particularly deep, but drawing first blood in a contest like this was critical. Its effect was always debilitating, often making an adversary overly cautious or reckless, dulling perceptions and muddling instincts. To a seasoned gladiator it often meant that a duel was as good as won. It was now only a matter of time.

To my disappointment, the Chamulan did not touch or even glance down at his injury. Surely he'd felt it, but apparently it hadn't affected his range of motion. The next lunge belonged to the Chamulan. I thrust out my lance, but he easily parried the tip and battered my shield with several vicious strikes. To my shock and alarm, I lost my balance. My knee met the stone surface of the platform, causing it to vibrate with pain. I threw myself to the right, rolling once and then finding my stance again. My adversary had continued to pursue me with his blade, but the deftness I'd displayed in coming back to my feet took him by surprise. Instead of pummeling me with further blows, he found my lancetip aimed directly at his navel. His forward charge was stopped, and once again we were circling.

My shield was quickly turning into a shambles. The frame was split in several places and a portion was hanging down, as if held together by hinge joints. It was now but half a shield. Of greater concern was my throbbing knee. My limp was impossible to hide. The flaw that I'd so cunningly tried to fabricate as I'd leapt upon the platform was now painfully real. The honor or advantage of having drawn first blood had dissipated. I was starting to acknowledge the reality of my situation. This was no less than a fight for my life. Accepting this fact might prove my best hope of surviving long enough to pursue my true objective.

My adversary was radiating confidence and power—but not in any kind of gloating manner. No, he was too astute for that. But he knew full well that he had the upper hand, and his tactics seemed more focused than ever—as if religiously determined that from here on he would make no further errors—not even the slightest miscalculation. I swallowed my rage. I swallowed my pain. And I prayed. Never before had I prayed for strength in the midst of combat, relying far too heavily on what had ever been my far superior skills as a fighter. All such pride suddenly fled. I prayed instead for the power of God.

Curiously, my adversary's lips were *also* moving, as if he, too, was silently engaged in some kind of prayerful chant. This thought emboldened me. Whatever demonic deities this filth was addressing, they could only be dismally inferior to the Father of Heaven who received my supplications.

I renewed the attack, but again switched my lance to the left hand and gripped my sword in the right. Considering the shabby state of my shield, I knew I might need the lance to ward off further blows from his blade. I walked around him swiftly on his left side—the side wherein I'd perceived the existence of an old battle wound. He turned with me, as if privy to my motives. At the last instant I twisted to the right and raised my shield straight up. His sword chopped right through the top of my shield—nearly biting into my wrist. This maneuver was precisely what I'd hoped for. For an instant his sword was stuck—imbedded in the tangle of wood and hide. I swung both of my obsidian blades—not toward his face, but toward his *arm.*

The prize of entirely severing off his limb was before my eyes, but at the last second he pulled himself unexpectedly downward. Instead of cutting off his forearm, the stone edge of my sword struck his sword's metal hilt just above his fingertips. In a flash I realized I'd been duped. This was *not* his weak side. He'd played exactly the same game with me that I had played with *him!*

In spite of this, my strategy was not without its rewards. Even as two of my obsidian points shattered, the Chamulan's steel sword was completely knocked from his grip. His knuckle was bleeding, likely from the shrapnel of shattered obsidian. His sword clattered onto the stone, spinning to a stop at the opposite side of the platform. Now was my chance to move in—to *kill!* But instead . . . I *paused.*

In my entire fighting career I'd never behaved quite so foolishly, but I literally hesitated to seize the advantage that I had earned. Like a novice I squandered my moment of superiority! My forward attack froze—almost in mid-motion—allowing my adversary several precious seconds to regain his footing and reappraise his predicament. And the reason for my hesitation? It was because my eye was fixed on his steel sword. I could hardly comprehend what I was seeing!

The Chamulan's blade did not just *look* like a Roman broadsword. It was a Roman broadsword! The spiral grip, the engraving of the Roman eagle upon the pommel—it was *unmistakable.* Where in the name of all the Olympian gods would a Chumulan warrior half a world away from the Seven Hills have found an authentic Imperial cavalry gladius? The sight of it nearly staggered me.

I turned back to the Chamulan in astonishment, my mouth gaping open as if I were about to pose to him this very question. I'd turned back none too soon, because he was coming at me again, this time with his lance swiping directly at my throat. I parried it just in time, the black lance tip brushing my whiskers and very nearly granting me a fatally close shave. One of the boar's teeth on my helmet was severed clean. To my dismay, I realized that my feet had found themselves precipitously close to the platform's edge.

Though the Chamulan's strike had only caught a piece of my helmet, it was enough that I lost my balance. To prevent myself from toppling over backwards like a felled oak and impaling myself on the pickets, I *leaped* backwards in an attempt to land flat-footed. Upon hitting the ground, I curled forward into a ball—again to avoid tripping onto the pickets. I finally rolled onto my hip, but I lost my grip on the obsidian blade! Furthermore, my mask was now *askew!* For a terrible instant my eyes saw nothing but the sweaty interior of the hood. Quickly, I readjusted the eye-slits—and to my horror I found myself looking up into the flaming eyes of the Chamulan. He stood above me on the platform. He'd drawn back his lance to hurl it straight down at my chest. I pulled my tattered shield tight against my body and jerked to the right. By God's grace the lance tip clipped the edge of my shield and imbedded in the soil between my left arm and torso.

Now unarmed except for the hatchet strapped to his belt, the Chamulan had no alternative but to dive on top of me. Before I could bring up the scythe-shaped head of my lance, his knee crunched into my stomach. Fists arrived an instant later, punching me twice in the face before I'd pummeled him in the ribs with the butt of my lance. Using sheer body strength, I threw him off to the right. His back crashed against several in-leaning pickets, but at an angle that unfortunately did not impale him. Rather, he used his impact against the pickets almost like a springboard to propel himself back at me.

I don't know how he did it, but somehow in all of that desperate crashing and propelling—never once taking his eyes off mine—his fingers managed to find the hilt of my obsidian sword. He was now armed with my own weapon!

I was on my feet again, using the shaft of the lance to parry multiple blows as he skillfully wielded my own expertly crafted stone blade. Most of the jagged points had broken down to much shorter points, but as is often the nature of obsidian glass, the broken points were ofttimes sharper than the originals. My lance suddenly broke. The top of it flipped out over the pickets. Spectators among the

Lacandones threw up their arms for protection as the lance head found a target, slicing a nasty cut in the backside of the naked shoulder of one of the warriors who'd escorted me to Desolation.

The Chamulan was still coming at me. I'd turned sideways and was practically fleeing at a full run around the perimeter of the platform. All at once my eyes caught hold of a glorious sight. My hand grasped out at an article more precious than diamonds—the Roman broadsword. I snatched it up and turned to face my adversary.

He skidded to a halt—his relentless assault at an end. We were now wielding each other's swords. Oh, how appropriate it was! Each of us now possessed the primary weapons of our native cultures. Truly poetic—no less than divine! A wicked smile climbed my cheeks. My opponent's face may have blanched slightly under that crimson helmet. Or was this only my wishful thinking?

I shook off the useless, broken shield from my left arm, and postured myself in the aggressive stance of a Roman swordsman—right leg forward, left arm and leg back, horns of my death-god mask aimed right between his eyes.

The Chamulan's chest was streaked with blood from the wound I'd inflicted with my lance. The gruesome appearance highly entertained the audience, and many were pointing and making remarks. Still, he did not seem to notice the injury or care. Nor did I. I still believed the cut was only superficial, but the pounding of his heart, so close to the laceration, made its appearance seem worse.

As we stood facing one another for several precious seconds, catching our breaths, steeling our nerves, before the next, and possibly final, clash of violence, I considered my adversary with renewed interest. I will not say that I respected or admired this swine who'd slain the woman I loved, but I felt a certain degree of . . . recognition. I could acknowledge his skills. It seemed such a shame that the devil could recruit warriors with such deadly talent. And yet I was more confident than ever that I would prevail and kill him in the next moment. That obsidian sword—though perhaps the finest specimen ever fashioned—was nonetheless no match for Roman steel.

The audience was clamoring for us to resume the battle. Instead, I surprised myself and spoke to the villain, caring not whether he believed my words, but feeling compelled that I must say what I had to say.

"I did not kill your wife and children," I sneered.

He looked confused for a moment, then those glistening white teeth clenched anew. "You might as well have. You killed my friends. They were family in every way but blood."

I furrowed my brow. It was an odd reply. So odd I cocked my head in dismay. Exactly which of his friends did I kill? Someone in Tikal or Seibalche? Was he a friend to one of the Lightning Warriors I'd slain at Korihab? How strange that a Chamulan tribesman would have friends in such remote and obscure locations.

He continued his vituperation. "And for their lives, God grant that I may be an instrument of His wrath. May He grant me the power to slay you."

Sounded familiar—a prayer to God for a just execution. So be it. I thinned my eyes and raised my sword.

"Yes," I echoed. "May my God grant me the power as *well*."

\* \* \*

*Harry*

*"What do you see?" asked Mary from the shadowed space below me.*
*"He has Gid's blade!" I declared.*
*"What?" cried Mary.*

*I looked down upon the battle between Gidgiddonihah and the Lacandon champion, my nerves frayed from anxiety. The man in the black, horned helmet and mask was far more formidable than I would have believed.*

*Frankly, I found Gid's behavior a little confusing. He'd vehemently stated to Chief Mensäbäk that he'd rather let himself be slain than commit murder for the entertainment of others. Yet here he was, fighting with more savagery and fury than I'd ever seen him exhibit. Was it that fighting was so ingrained in Gid's psyche that he couldn't resist? The look in Gid's eyes was so vicious it was downright disturbing. What was it about this Lacandon that had brought out such hatred in him?*

*My arms ached as I gripped the stone ledge of the narrow window, my feet dangling above the floor of our prison cell. The window space was so frustratingly narrow! Finally, I couldn't take it anymore. I dropped down and began frantically shaking the blood back into both limbs.*

I repeated to Mary, "The Lacandon now has Gid's Roman sword."

Mary eyes widened in alarm. "Does Gid still have the Lacandon's obsidian club?"

"Yes."

She gave it a positive spin. "That's Gid's weapon of choice—the one he's trained with all of his life."

"Actually," I corrected, "his weapon of choice is the one still on his belt—the battle hatchet."

"Then why hasn't he used it?"

"Not sure. Hasn't had much of a chance. I've never seen Gid in a fight like this. I would never have thought he had an equal. My arms are killing me!"

It was killing me even more that I wasn't up there watching. Mary also wanted desperately to see what was happening. Unable to wait for me, she leaped up and grabbed the ledge. I heard her gasp.

"What is it?" I asked, still earnestly massaging my fingers and forearm.

"They're fighting again! They're not on the platform!"

"I already told you that."

"They're exchanging blows! The Lacandon champion is driving him back! Oh, Harry!"

That was it. Forget the pain. I leaped up and again grabbed onto the ledge beside her, determined that I would hang on even if it meant my arms would fall off.

She was right. Gid's opponent was driving him back—back around the narrow perimeter between the fighting platform and the circle of spears. Just as Gid's sword had destroyed his opponent's wooden shield, now his shield was being destroyed. Each blow left it further splintered and battered. The Lacandon seemed to relish that metal blade. Somehow this Mesoamerican warrior understood exactly how to use it. Any second Gid's Roman weapon would cut right through his shield and amputate his arm at the shoulder.

What was Gid doing? It didn't even look like he was fighting back! He was allowing that Lacandon slimeball to wail on him with blow after blow. But then I saw the strategy—or thought I saw it. Gid was driven back far enough around the perimeter that he reached the place where he'd flung his spear downward, sticking it in the earth.

In a surprise move, Gid thrust out his obsidian blade and caught the Roman sword. I watched one of the stone points on Gid's weapon shatter like glass. Gid used the opportunity to toss his battered shield away and pluck the lance out of the earth. The Nephite was again armed with three weapons!

The Lacandon's onslaught was halted. Gid had changed the dynamics—coming right back at him with both weapons—crossing them and twirling them like a Samurai. It was a beautiful sight! Then Gid brought his lance smack down on the Lacandon's black shoulder armor. My heart soared! The Lacandon fell to one knee—his bad knee. I'm not sure how deep the wound was, considering the thickness of that shoulder armor, but Gid wasn't resting on his laurels. He twisted up the butt end of his lance and landed a savage chop to his enemy's jaw, sprawling him back in the dirt—nearly impaling the jerk on a spear.

It looked like it was all over. Gid brought up his obsidian sword and plunged it downward for a death blow. Incredibly, the Lacandon brought up his own weapon, caught the sword, and deflected the tip, causing the sword point to strike the earth. The slippery worm rolled out of harm's way, leaping to his feet with such agility I might have thought an angel had grabbed him under the arms and hoisted him upright.

Gid recovered quickly, bringing his other weapon into play, forcing the Lacandon to spin outward. I realized that Gid's opponent had slipped into the narrow, two-foot gap that approached the platform's exit. Gid had the maggot trapped. There were deadly spikes on three sides of him. All the Nephite had to do was keep driving his opponent backward and the man would inevitably impale himself against the outermost circle of spikes.

Then—once again—the Lacandon did something completely unexpected—something I wouldn't have thought possible from that angle. With a single mighty swipe of his Roman sword he chopped off two of the wooden spikes that had acted as a gate to prevent him from exiting the arena. He'd actually cut himself an escape route! As Gid rushed at him—weapons a-twirling—the Lacandon leaped out into the courtyard. Gid pursued him through the same gap. Holy cow! They were both on the outside. They were free!

Mary had to let go of the ledge. Her arms gave out, but not mine. My arms were numb with pain, but I wasn't going to miss a single moment of this. Despite my terror for Gid's life, there was no denying—this was the fight of the century. Prayers for Gidgiddonihah repeated furiously in my brain.

*Audience members were coming to their feet—many screaming and scrambling to get out of the way as the two warriors took their death duel right into the bleachers.*

*"Harry," said Mary, sounding thoughtful.*

*I barely heard her—my focus riveted.*

*"Harry," she repeated.*

*"Yeah?"*

*The Lacandon swung his metal blade and nearly split open Gid's abdomen. My hero jumped out of the way in the nick of time.*

*Quietly, Mary said, "I think I know."*

*"Know what?"*

*Gid raised up his lance, but the Lacandon champion clobbered down right on top of it. Gid's lance finally snapped in two!*

*"I think I know why the Chamulans purchased you and me along with Gid," said Mary.*

*I finally gave her my attention.*

\* \* \*

Apollus

He was tireless! Brilliant! Did age and youth offer me no advantage whatsoever? The Chamulan had the stamina of a yearling bull! My own lungs were on fire, yet I fought on. He couldn't keep this up forever. The fight had to end. Someone had to die.

He parried my every blow, dodged every strike of my steel blade—attacks that would have split in half nine-out-of-ten of the best Roman legionnaires—but not the Chamulan. Then, to add to the insult, he would round back on me in a manner always deadly and unexpected.

I could feel sweat pouring into the wound on my shoulder. I did not know how deep the injury was. I hadn't had a second to examine it! But—*oh!*—I felt the sting. Yet it did not hinder my aggressiveness. Empowered wholly by rage, my limbs seemed unaffected as I pursued him across the wooden benches that—until seconds ago—had been occupied by Lacandon spectators. The rabble had tripped over one another like peasants at a grain riot, desperate to get out of our path. Some shouted, calling for our deaths, claiming that because we'd escaped the fighting arena, we ought to both be slain. But few listened to these outcries. Neither did I. Free or not, my objective had not changed. Before I could pursue Lamanai and K'ayyum, I had to kill the Chamulan.

He now wielded only my obsidian sword, the blades now so blunt it was little more than a club. That is, except for that three-inch tip—a personal innovation that now concerned me. For that tip I'd employed a particularly thick and sturdy stone. My ingenuity had now become his best hope of killing me. Frequently he tried to seize the hatchet at his waist, but drawing it from his belt wasn't so easy. The weapon had to be untied, and I kept him far too occupied for that.

I drove him back against the stairway that led up toward the corridor where I'd spent the previous night. The prestigious spectators in the upper galleries were on their feet, leaning out to watch as our duel further intensified. I had to wonder if the Chamulan was climbing the stairway deliberately. These stairs gave him the advantage of height, but his weapon was still no match for my sword. One or two more blows and I would certainly smash the obsidian club completely, giving me the opening I finally needed to finish him for good. But then—once again—he did something that left me stymied. Tossing his club to the opposite hand, he began parrying my blows from a new angle. I had to take a moment to adjust tactics—and in that instant I made a foolish error. I swung and missed. My steel struck the stone steps. For this error I was well punished as the Chamulan thrust the bottom of his sandal right into my forehead.

I fell backwards, tumbling to the bottom of the stairs. I heard the dagger on my belt clatter on the stone floor, but miraculously, I maintained my grip on the sword. I was momentarily disoriented; my sense of direction had fled. And before I could regain full focus, I saw a massive red blur leaping toward my face—

\* \* \*

*Harry*

"*They told him that we're dead, Harry,*" Mary announced. "*I know it.*"

*I watched the Lacandon tumble to the bottom of the stairs. Gid swooped down the stairway right behind him—his obsidian sword now drawn back like a spear, prepared to plunge it straight into the Lacandon's heart. It seemed unbelievable that Gid's opponent had managed to keep his fingers clasped around the hilt of that sword after such a painful landing. But his grip was like iron, and as Gid arrived to deliver the fatal blow, the Lacandon did something spectacular.*

*Even in his dazed condition, he brought that sword in front of his chest, turned the blade to the side, and—I couldn't believe it—as Gid tried again to thrust that black stone tip into his heart, the obsidian collided directly with the two-inch-wide blade. I could hear the tip shatter even from up here. How did he do it? Two inches wide! Luck! It was the vilest stroke of luck I'd ever witnessed! That was Gid's moment—he'd earned it! The Lacandon champion should have given up the ghost right there. Instead, Gid's weapon was now lying on the ground, a useless chunk of wood.*

*Gidgiddonihah backed away from his opponent, fully cognizant of his grim situation. He was now unarmed—except for that crucial hatchet! Why wouldn't he use it? What was preventing him from removing it from his belt?*

"Gid's in trouble!" I said breathlessly.

"Harry, did you hear me?" Mary snapped. "He doesn't know we're alive!"

"Why would they tell him we were dead? What difference would it make?"

"Motivation," she answered. "They know how much we mean to Gid. So they lied to him to make him fight harder."

"Saying we're dead would make him fight harder?"

"Yes! Think about it! What if they told Gid that the Lacandon champion had executed us? Would that explain the hatred in Gid's eyes?"

I nodded. "Yeah. I guess it would."

"He needs to know, Harry," she said. "He needs to know that we're alive."

"How? You want me to cry out to him? Do you hear the audience? Gid would never hear us over this clamor."

"You have to try," said Mary.

"But what does it matter now?" I asked.

*"Gid might murder an innocent man."*

*"Murder? You call this murder? The man has nearly killed Gid a dozen times! A hundred ways!"*

*"What if the other fighter was told the same lies? You said yourself that he doesn't look Lacandon. What if they've manipulated some outsider—just like Gid? What if they kidnapped his family? Don't you see? It explains why they purchased us. It's all part of the same, rehearsed deception!"*

*"Even if you're right, it's too late!" I retorted. "Mary, if he thinks we're alive, he might lose his edge—his will to fight. Even an instant of distraction might be fatal!"*

*Mary went quiet, her mind toiling. The Lacandon champion was coming back to his feet . . .*

\* \* \*

Apollus

Now I had him. His weapons spent, I watched his hand go again to the hatchet on his belt. The leather knot that bound it there was meant to slip easily loose, but either his "handlers" had not tied it correctly, or they'd deliberately sabotaged his cause. Either way, I wasn't going to let him solve the problem.

I moved in relentlessly. He again began backing up the staircase, and his effort to arm himself with the hatchet was temporarily abandoned. I was not overly eager anymore. What could he do? Run into the dead-end corridor? All the better. With his masked eyes glued into mine, he walked backwards up the stairs with virtually the same ease as someone walking forward. My patience was exhausted. I'd had enough. I rushed him, sword outstretched for the kill.

Hastily, he turned around. To my befuddlement, he stepped onto the short containment wall at the edge of the stairway—and sprang into the air! The infernal Chamulan leaped onto the elevated rampart of the neighboring structure—a distance of nearly three Roman yards! The rampart was slightly more elevated than the wall—tilting at the same angle as the stairway. I felt certain that he couldn't possibly hang on. He'd crash onto the stones below. But again, I was wrong. He barely caught the edge, and then, with incredible strength, hoisted himself upright. A moment later he was standing upon that tilting rampart, knees bent like a wrestler. I gaped at him furiously across the chasm, my fists clenched with excruciating frustration, causing the sword to vibrate in my grip.

At last the Chamulan had found an opportunity to examine that troublesome knot on his belt. Seconds later, he'd loosed it. At last he had his blessed hatchet. I glanced down at the courtyard and saw many of the spectators gathering below us, still cheering or shouting abuse at one or the other of their tribes' champions.

I wasn't particularly concerned with the Chamulan's new toy. Once again, it was stone versus steel. I'd disarm him of the hatchet much as I'd done with his other weapons. Seconds later he ran up the tilting rampart and again leaped across the chasm. If I'd thought the old codger might take the opportunity to rest, I was sorely mistaken. He landed upon the stairway just above where I was positioned. I lurched forward to take advantage of a bad landing, but no such luck. He was already poised to fight and coming straight at me.

I jabbed with my sword, each jab deflected by his axehead—not obsidian this time, but some harder white stone—flint or marble. One deflection caught me hard and threw my sword arm back. He used the opening to come at me fast, swinging his weapon past my face. I backed away farther down the stairs, but then I saw my own opening and drew a slice through the air.

*Got him!* My sword caught his red leather mask and sliced high across the bridge of his nose and into his cheek. Perhaps not a fatal blow, but the bleeding from his nose flowed directly into his left eye. I, at last, had the satisfaction of watching him touch one of the wounds I had inflicted as he attempted to clear away the blood around the eye-hole of his mask. I moved in mercilessly, swinging and stabbing. Again, he parried each blow. Was there a third eye in this man's head that I hadn't noticed? Somehow he again maneuvered us back down to the base of the stairs. I confess I'd never seen a man fight with a stone axe against a sword. I wouldn't have thought that it could be effectively done! Again this warrior's skills left me awestruck. After a few more deflections I began to conclude that this was the weapon he'd been born for, like a natural appendage of his right arm—of *either* arm! The hatchet switched to either hand as nimbly as a baton. My frustration was inexpressible. Each instance when I'd thought to have gained an advantage over this gorilla, it evaporated like a wisp of smoke.

Then I saw it—another opening, wide as a canyon. He raised up the hatchet with his left arm and tried to come straight at my face. This left his torso exposed. I ducked down and moved in for the kill. But even before I'd completed my forward motion I realized my mistake—my fatal error. The villain had *drawn me into it!* And at last, like a fly to a spider's web, I'd been caught in what should have been an obvious trap. In horror I watched as he spun around, letting the hatchet drop—almost casually—into his opposite hand, and then making a backward swipe as he passed. My only hope of recovery was to throw myself more off balance than I already was. In spite of this, the hatchet still bit the nape of my sword hand, cutting practically to the bone just below my thumb.

I dropped the sword and tripped, rolling until I crashed against the base of the stairway. I was a dead man, and I knew it. When I looked back at the Chamulan, he'd already retrieved my sword from where it lay on the steps. Though his chest, face, and knuckles still oozed from injuries I'd inflicted, though one eye was completely blinded by blood, he stood erect with both weapons firmly in his grasp, looking exactly like a champion gladiator filled with the knowledge that his contest was won.

He started toward me. There was no such thing as repentance for a warrior's pride. My life was over. The murderer of my beloved Meagan would also slay me. Thus it was. God was in control of all. He must have had His reasons for allowing me to die. I was at peace. Had this been the great Coliseum, I would have latched onto the victor's feet so he might place the tip of his broadsword at the back of my neck and drive its point mercifully downward in one practiced thrust. But this was not Rome. I doubted if my death would be so painless.

The crowd had gone remarkably silent, as if to reverence the victory of their new champion. He stood over me, one eye shut, the other examining me pitilessly as I lay on my back, looking up through my mask of the god of death. He began to draw back his hatchet for the fatal blow. I was not afraid.

"*Kill me quickly,*" I started to say, but as the words began to fall from my mouth, I heard a strange voice.

It resonated from somewhere above me—crying out at the peak of its volume, *"Gidgiddonihah!"*

The hand of my executioner paused. An extraordinary look flashed across his face. Was it relief? Adulation? Or gut-wrenching terror? I honestly could not discern.

My own mind had dropped into a kind of time warp. For an instant I couldn't decide if I had heard an angel's voice or that of a man. So familiar. How could it be a man? It must have been a heavenly being—my guardian angel.

The name was shouted again, only this time it was echoed by *two* voices—a male and a female. Again I was thunderstruck with the impression that I'd heard both of these voices before.

"Gidgiddonihah! We're alive!"

The Chamulan looked up at the galleries above—the ones occupied by the dignitaries and chieftains of the Chamulans and Lacandones. I recognized the box containing Lamanai and several elders from K'ayyum's village. But these people were *also* peering upward. They leaned out beyond the balustrades, looking up toward a series of narrow window slits over their heads. *Cells,* I thought immediately. The voices that had cried out were those of prisoners from within one of those windows. At no other moment would we have heard them. The crowd had simply been too boisterous.

The Chamulan turned back to me, eyes strangely wide. "You didn't kill them."

Was it a question or a statement? I put it together in a heartbeat. *His family.* Those voices—they were his family members. And they were alive and well! And yet . . . I *knew* them! I knew who they were! Where had I heard—?

It came to me—entering my mind with the impact of a charging Spanish bull. "Harry," I said, softer than an exclamation, but louder than a whisper. "Mary."

Now the Chamulan's eyes were as wide as wagon wheels—even the one blinded by blood.

"Who are you?" he demanded, voice grinding with intensity.

I didn't answer. I was steeped in amazement. Who was *he?* Even that name—Gidgiddonihah—seemed familiar, but in a very inordinate way, like a name from some faraway memory, some storybook fantasy. Had I ever met a man of that name? For a foggy moment I honestly . . .

"Take off your helmet and mask," the Chamulan commanded me.

My right hand was injured, but my left hand reached behind my head and pulled at the leather straps. It was very awkward to loose them with one hand. I slid it off enough that I could no longer see through the eye-slits. I'd forgotten about the straps which bound it in place around my shoulders. I felt the Chamulan grab hold of the horns on my right side. The remaining straps were cut with a blade. The whole contraption with its shoulder adornments and padding was abruptly yanked off my head and tossed aside.

Blinking, I looked back at the Chamulan, his own face still hidden beneath the trappings of the pagan god of the underworld. As he gazed upon me, took in every feature of my face, he staggered backward several steps.

Voices rang out from the gallery of the Chamulan and Lacandon chieftains. "Slay them! Slay them *both!*"

I'd have sworn that the Chamulan recognized me. But that was impossible. However, it took only a word—or actually *three* words—to disperse all doubt.

"Apollus Brutus Severillus!" he exclaimed.

From a window above the gallery I thought I might have heard my name spoken again above the renewed and rising furor of the crowd, but more as a breathless gasp—*"My gosh! It's Apollus!"*

An instant later, the Chamulan had severed the bindings on his own helmet. After he stripped it off and stood before me, I experienced the most astonishing rush of memories that I'd ever experienced, like someone pouring hot liquid into an empty vacuum of space. Had I met this man? Yes, I *had* met him. In a place called Ephesus, on a ship bound for home, and in a cave where we had bid one another a fond farewell. So peculiar, as if for a moment *another* memory had filled that void—the memory of a man I'd never actually met—a man who'd died defending those very voices that I had heard shouting from the cells above.

But those memories would have been wrong. I knew this man *very* well, and I almost choked with horror as I realized what had nearly occurred—what we'd almost done to each other in these forsaken ruins of the city of Desolation—all because of unbridled, all-consuming hatred. That choking sound in my throat must have been apparent as I finally uttered his name—the name of my friend and fellow warrior. The name of—

"Gidgiddonihah!"

## NOTES TO CHAPTER 16

Just as with the Romans, ritual combat among the ancients of Mesoamerica was also very popular and usually steeped in religious mysticism, colorful pageantry, and elaborate costumes. For the Romans, gladiatorial combat originated with funeral rites and was sponsored in honor of an important personage who had died. The Romans believed that their ancestors, the Etruscans, held gladiatorial contests among the servants of a dead lord or chieftain so that this leader might be accompanied during his journey to the realms of immortality in the life beyond.

In the beginning, gladiatorial contests in Rome were limited to specific days, namely the winter and spring equinoxes. But because of their popularity, and because they became sources of substantial profit for the *lanistae* (owner-managers of gladiator troops), they were later sponsored year-round and held all across the Empire. A gladiator in Rome might fight another gladiator, teams of gladiators, or he might fight wild animals, including lions, tigers, leopards, and elephants. The Emperor Trajan once sponsored games where over nine thousand animals were slaughtered. During other years, massive land and even *sea* battles were staged involving real ships in water-filled stadiums. Such spectacles were often re-creations of famous battles in Roman history, and might involve hundreds, or even thousands, of gladiatorial combatants.

Among the Aztecs, such ritual contests between warriors were also popular. Through these kinds of displays the emperor hoped to bring home to the common people the reality of combat and help Aztec citizens to understand the purposes behind investing so much of their food and substance—not to mention their *sons*—for the support of the Imperial army.

For both societies, the competitors in such contests were almost always "socially dead" or (Latin) *infamis*. In other words, they were prisoners of war, slaves, or convicted criminals. By performing well, or surviving a large number of contests, a Roman gladiator could often earn his/her freedom and citizenship. (It should be noted that *female* gladiators were also quite popular in Rome.) Among the Aztecs, a captive who performed well might also gain his freedom. It is said that when the Aztecs captured Tlahuicol, a war captain of their sworn enemies, the Tlaxcalans, he was forced to fight upon a large circular stone like the one described in this chapter. (Several such stones, though smaller than the one described herein, are on display in Mexico's National Museum of Anthropology and the Museum of the Great Temple.) After Tlahuicol had killed no less than eight Jaguar and Eagle knights, he was offered not only his freedom, but a command position in the Imperial army. Tlahuicol, however, considered this an insult and asked instead to be ritually sacrificed to the war god, Huitzilopochtli (John Pohl, PhD, and Adam Hook, *Aztec Warror: Weapons, Armor, Tactics* [United Kingdom: Osprey Publishing Limited, 2001], 61).

These kind of aggressive, militaristic cultures, lacking gospel values or enlightenment, were obsessed with the idea of killing and dying well. They valued the "art" of killing in ways that modern or enlightened societies often cannot comprehend. As with most ancient civilizations, mortality rates within the general populace were high and most people did not anticipate that they would reach an old age. Men did not expect to live much beyond thirty, so at the age of twenty or so they began to think about how they might die with honor and dignity, or in other words, die in a way that would give their lives meaning. Sadly, gladiatorial combat was one way for them to do so (*Roman Civilization: The Gladiator,* 2004, AbleMedia, http://ablemedia.com/ctcweb/consortium/gladiator3.html).

A bitter rivalry between the highland Maya tribes of the Lacandon and Chamula exists even to this day. They have been traditional enemies from ancient times and their ancestors may have fought many wars (Perera and Bruce, 312). Although the author named the actual Lacandon gods of the underworld and the dead in this chapter, the idea that such deities were represented in an annual gladiatorial contest in the manner described is purely fictional speculation.

# CHAPTER 17

## Pagag

We hunkered down in the brush just beyond the boundary of the ruined city called Desolation. The air was muggy with the smell of rain, the heavy scents of the swollen river to the east, and the unmistakable putrescence of death—*old* death from battles once waged, but perhaps in the air I could also sense the scent of the battle about to commence.

It had been two days since we had rescued the child, Rebecca, and the young men, Jesse and Micah. Our travels with the army of First Deer—now seven-hundred and fifty strong—had taken us northeast. We'd followed a pathway suggested by those we had rescued, but also directed by the aerial reconnaissance of the falcon bird, Rafa. Now we awaited First Deer's command to move in—to attack.

Unexpectedly, the falcon bird, Rafa, flew toward us from the ruins, chirping and squawking profoundly.

"Look! He's coming back!" Steffanie announced.

She held out her arm, allowing the bird to light upon the wooden cast I'd carved for her injured wrist and finger.

After a dramatic display of wing flapping and a few more ear-piercing chirps, Steffanie interpreted the falcon: "He keeps repeating, *"I see the big man. The big man is here."*

"He means Gidgiddonihah," offered the child, Rebecca.

Rebecca, Micah, and Jesse also comprehended these unintelligible chatterings. I was the only one who lacked this ability. And of course, First Deer, who acted very jealous of it.

Jesse added, "Rafa also says that he heard Harry's voice. And Mary's voice also!"

I looked off toward the ruins and nodded. "So they're all in there. Good."

The ruins juxtaposed a wide river, and were surrounded by deep ditches and a high wall on three sides. Or rather, there *had* been a wall. Most of the city's defense fortifications had been razed or buried. But in spite of the destruction, the city was not uninhabited. From our place of concealment a stone's cast outside the wall and a short run from city's central precincts, we could hear the distinct sound of cheering and applause. Or rather, we heard it until a moment ago. Upon Rafa's return, the noise had ceased.

"What is happening?" asked First Deer. "Why were they cheering?"

"A contest," said Micah. "Rafa says Gid is—or *was*—fighting 'a man who is also a raven and a bull.'"

I furrowed my forehead in confusion. "Raven and bull?"

"Probably a costume," Steffanie interpreted. "It may not be a bird or an animal, but that's what Rafa knows best."

"Is the fight over?" asked First Deer.

Steffanie was unsure, so she posed the query back to the falcon. It responded with additional chittering.

This time Jesse interpreted. "Yes. He says the fighting stopped. Both fighters are bleeding, but they are alive."

Steffanie became earnest. "We have to get in there."

I feared she might run into the ruins alone, even if no one else followed her. All of my efforts to cool the fire in her blood had thus far been unsuccessful. Despite her beauty, she was a warrioress, and I could not alter that.

"How many enemies?" asked First Deer, still failing to grasp the concept that Rafa did not exactly communicate in numbers.

"A lot," said Jesse.

"A flock," interpreted Rebecca.

First Deer looked back at his men—seven hundred and fifty strong—who waited behind us in the tall marsh grasses and brush. Since our battle with the Wolf Witches, First Deer had grown most impatient with any campaign to recover our remaining companions. I reminded him—gently—that this was King Sa'abkan's direct order to him. But First Deer had always felt the object was foremost to wipe out the Nephite marauders. He wanted now to rejoin his fellow soldiers at Jordan who were preparing for battle. This business of helping us to rescue Gidgiddonihah, Harrison, and Mary was for him an aggravating waste of time.

He spoke tartly to Steffanie. "How do I know that you speak truthfully about what this falcon is saying? How do I know that your people are really in there?"

"Are you calling Rafa a liar?" challenged Rebecca.

First Deer reddened with rage. He was not accustomed to the sharp tongue of children. For now he ignored her and said to me, "Why should my men go to battle against Chamulans and Lacandones? True, they are the accursed offspring of the Lamaya. But my men have marched from their lands to die with honor. They have come to slay the children of Nephi. There is no honor in killing Chamulan dogs."

"First Deer," I said calmly, "we are most grateful to you and your men for the help you have provided us. After this woman's brother and our other companions are freed, your obligation to us will be complete. You may then march to Jordan with your army."

First Deer made a growl in the back of his throat, and then finally agreed.

"Let's go," said Steffanie with greater urgency.

I shook my head. "Not you."

She turned to me with a look of utter exhaustion. "Oh, brother. Not again. Are you going to try to force me to stay?"

"Someone must remain behind to look after Rebecca."

Rebecca shook her head vigorously. "No one has to babysit me. I'll hide right here in the grass."

Steffanie did not approve of this idea. She turned to Jesse. "You will stay behind with her."

"*Me?*" Jesse protested.

"Please, Jesse, do this for me."

"But why me? You're a g—" An icy stare from Steffanie cut off the word before it could be uttered. Jesse's shoulders sank. "I'll remain behind with her."

I might have warned him that such an argument would be fruitless. Steffanie was certainly not a girl. She was most definitely a *woman*—without question the most intriguing woman I had ever met. She provoked feelings inside me that . . . How can I express it? I found her baffling, vexatious, and utterly unpredictable. One moment she was as hard as granite, as cunning as a tigress, while in the next she was as pliable as papyrus and as soft as lamb skin. She was truly as beautiful as any woman of the clan of Moriancumr. Indeed, as beautiful as any woman of Shinar or Salem. I found her deliriously attractive and invariably repulsive simultaneously. Whenever I did not wish to ring her neck I was memorizing the curves of her face. She dominated my waking thoughts and hovered over my sleep like an illuminant angel. It was intolerably exasperating! Every time I passed a tree I considered knocking my head against its bark to jar loose some common sense. Until a week ago I'd been indestructibly certain of my love for another woman. Was I really so inconstant and fickle?—so possessed of the double-minded contortions of an irresolute baboon? Perhaps I was unworthy of *all* women and would best serve every one of them if I remained an eternal bachelor.

It was Steffanie's fault. She was to blame for this. She'd put an enchantment upon me somehow, though I could not determine how. It was that instant—that moment—when I had held her in the forest, looked into her eyes, as she lingered in my arms. The feeling. I'd never experienced such an emotion—not with any other woman—of my own clan or elsewhere. Such a cascade of feeling. Almost spiritual. Revelatory. Like being . . . home.

I had to know if it was real or a conjuring of my daydreams. But how? I'd already twice been on the receiving end of her fist—not a particularly happy place to be. But how else could I know unless . . . unless I held her again. Unless I . . .

Soon I would have to take the risk—no matter the consequences or the disfiguring bruise that might result. I simply had to know. I could not endure life without having the answer. Thus was the state of my mind as I crouched beside my enchantress awaiting the signal from First Deer to take to the field.

The signal finally came. The falcon launched back into the skies, while I, Steffanie, Micah, and seven hundred and fifty Lamanite soldiers started forward from the brush and stealthily approached the city wall.

As we passed through a breach in the fortifications, Rafa returned, circling furiously over our heads and squawking a message that Steffanie interpreted as *"Hurry!"*

I remained as close to Steffanie's side as I could, concerned for her well being and safety. She finally sent me an irritated glance.

"Could you back off just a bit?" she whispered. "You're gonna run right over the top of me."

"Sorry," I said. Again I wished there had been a convenient tree trunk nearby. It was impossible to be an effective soldier and simultaneously an effective bodyguard. My behavior risked *both* of our lives. But as I contemplated the opposition that we might shortly come up against, I couldn't bear the idea of seeing her become hurt.

As we neared the complex of structures in the center of the city, First Deer raised his arm as a sign for us to seek concealment. Steffanie and I took shelter behind a dilapidated stone wall. Micah was a short distance away, pressing against the blind side of an empty building with a dozen Lamanites around him as we waited for the remaining soldiers of First Deer's battalion to get into position. Our hearts beat with anticipation as we watched First Deer for an announcement of the final charge.

I suppose it was the anxiety of the moment and the looming possibility of death that provoked my upcoming statements.

"Steffanie," I whispered.

"Yes?" she replied.

Fumbling my words like a child, I said, "There's something . . . something I . . . I've been desiring to tell you."

She raised her eyebrow, communicating plainly that I should either cough it out or shut up.

I hesitated somewhat longer, then said, "There is no telling what is about to happen. I . . . I just wanted you to know that . . . my feelings have changed."

"About what?"

"About . . . Mary."

Both of her eyebrows lifted now. "Oh?"

I pressed on. "It is no longer my desire to . . . interfere with your brother's engagement."

She faced forward, hiding what appeared to be a gloating smile, then said casually, "I'm glad to hear it. Why not? What's changed?"

"Well, nothing in particular. I mean, as far as my feelings for her."

She scowled at me. I sensed that I was—What was Steffanie's phrase?—"digging another hole for myself."

Hastily, I added, "What I mean to say is . . . I still believe Mary is a superior person—a wonderful woman. I was not wrong in my judgment of her qualities. But I suppose . . . I did not realize how strongly my emotions could be drawn . . . toward another."

She tried to wait for further words but then challenged me with, "What are you trying to say, Pagag?"

Just then First Deer rose up and sounded the war cry—three shouts in the air. How terrible was it that I should feel such relief to hear a cry to battle? Steffanie gritted her teeth, I think wishing she could cram a cactus in First Deer's mouth. She looked back at me, still hoping for a hasty answer.

Rather, I stood up, firmly gripped my sword, and announced, "I will tell you later."

Micah and the Lamanite warriors were already rushing forth from their places of hiding, charging toward the central buildings. I shouted the war cry along with Steffanie and joined in the charge. The battle for Mary, Harry, and Gidgiddonihah's freedom would soon be underway.

\* \* \*

Apollus

Gidgiddonihah reached for my left hand—my *uninjured* hand—and helped me to my feet. I continued to gape at him. So many questions and mysteries. How in the name of Jupiter had he *gotten* here? I would have to ask such questions at another time. The Chamulan and Lacandon warriors were shaking off their befuddlement. They'd heard the shouts from the gallery—the outcry to kill us both. Many were drawing closer, preparing to carry out their orders.

Gid whispered to me, "Can you still fight?"

I put forth my left hand. "Yes." As he passed me the Roman sword, I asked, "What about you? You need a weapon."

A spear was hurled toward us, launched straight at Gid's torso. The Nephite warrior turned sideways, threw out his palm and caught it in flight. His body spun around, but as he faced me again, the spear was tightly in his grasp.

"Thanks," he replied to me, "but I have one."

More warriors were raising weapons, drawing back spears. Gid and I threw ourselves in separate directions. He went to the left while I dashed right, toward the stairs. I became vaguely aware of other distractions in the courtyard, people reacting to some kind of disturbance—something that had nothing to do with Gid or myself. But with lances hurtling toward me I couldn't concentrate on this. I vaulted up the steps three at a time while spears clattered against the stones on all sides of me. The Chamulans and Lacandones were terrible aims. Tz'ikin was more skilled than ten of her male tribesmen combined. A single Roman battalion could have wiped out multiple legions of these louts. It was no wonder that they recruited or kidnapped fighting champions from other tribes.

As I reached the upper platform, I realized that no further arrows or spears were being fired or thrown. I gazed across the courtyard.

Then I saw the Lamanites.

Hundreds of Lamayan warriors were pouring into the square from the south, cutting down Chamulans, Lacandones, and every other squatter and beggar unlucky enough to have sought admission to the gladiatorial contest. My eyes searched for Gidgiddonihah. It appeared that he had attempted to follow me, but a rush of Chamulan guards had foiled his efforts. Attackers had forced him to move past the circular platform, killing several Chamulan warriors en route. He made eye contact with me and shouted above the chaos: *"Find them!"*

In the next moment, his direct opposition from Chamulans or Lacandones seemed to evaporate. Everyone's focus shifted to the rush of invaders. A mass panic ensued. Every Chamulan and Lacandon spectator began fleeing desperately toward the north end of the courtyard, many exiting into the general ruins of the city. Few stood their ground to face the Lamanite army.

I tore a strip of cloth from the hem of my mantle and wrapped it around my injured hand as I peered up toward the cells where I'd heard the voices of Harry and Mary. I felt a tightening of my heart. If the "family" of Gidgiddonihah had not been slain, was it possible that Meagan might also be alive? It was almost too painful to contemplate. Still, I embraced that hope. I had to reach those upper cells.

The galleries, situated directly above me and exactly beneath the cells, had emptied of all spectators. I could no longer see Lamanai or any of the tribal chieftains. I recalled my earlier oath to become Prince Eagle-Sky-Jaguar's destroying angel. That oath would have to wait. I had to find Meagan, free Harry and Mary.

From the dark tunnel ahead—the same corridor where Gidgiddonihah had earlier emerged—burst forth four Lacandon warriors. I recognized them right away as henchmen of Chief K'ayyum. They faced me with obsidian blades, trembling like leaves and sweating nervously. If the goal of these men was to slow me down, they would fail.

My right hand still bled, as did the other wound on my shoulder, yet my mind felt as alert and lethal as ever. I charged directly at them, swinging the Roman blade with my left arm. The first warrior fell easily, attempting to stop me with an awkward swipe that opened him up for a counter swipe. The second man managed to get in two worthwhile strikes, but a sudden thrust from my swordpoint ended his rampage. The third and fourth warriors tried to attack at once. I ducked, causing their stone blades to clash together. Obsidian shattered. One attacker wobbled off balance while the other apparently got a rock chip in his eye and staggered forward. I stabbed the off-balance warrior, didn't even bother with the other unworthy opponent, and rushed into the darkened corridor.

No further adversaries awaited me inside. The tunnel appeared nearly vacant. Obviously there was another exit—a way out the back side. I saw multiple stairways leading up to various galleries that overlooked the courtyard. Farther on down the tunnel I spotted a dozen trailing Chamulan and Lacandon elders. They were rushing away from me. Beyond them I saw a beam of daylight—the second exit. K'ayyum and Lamanai had undoubtedly used this route of escape.

I scanned the stairways and settled upon one that was narrower, climbing between two of the viewing galleries until it arrived at an arched entryway. I hastily ascended.

* * *

*Harry*

For a third time I rammed my shoulder against the wooden door. It was old and stirred up a dust cloud with every collision but showed no signs of busting open.

Mary and I had witnessed the commotion outside—the sudden invasion of a new tribe of warriors. We'd seen Apollus climb the stairway and fight the Lacandones, but then he rushed inside and we lost sight of him. Mary arose and I went to her.

"Apollus or Gidgiddonihah will find us," I told her. "I'm certain they heard our voices."

She smiled. "I was about to reassure you of the same thing."

Again I smashed against the door. Either this beast was gonna break down or the racket I created would attract help. Mary broke away a chunk of stone from the window ledge and started scraping out the mortar which held the stone blocks in place around the doorway. This confounded door was gonna come down like the walls of Jericho sooner or later. Something seemed to be blocking it from the other side. Not just a latch. I'd seen no latch when they'd tossed us in here. More like a wedge.

Suddenly I heard something. I stopped slamming to listen. Faintly, I heard Apollus's voice in the outside hallway.

"Meagan!" the Roman cried. "Harry!"

He was checking other rooms down the hall. As far as I could tell, the whole upper story had been converted into prison cells.

"Apollus!" I yelled.

Mary cried his name as well, then she said to me, "Harry, he's looking for Meagan. Do you think she might be imprisoned in one of these other rooms?"

"If Apollus is here," I replied, "Meagan can't be too far away."

I heard Apollus shout directly outside our door, "Harry! Mary!"

"We're in here!" I shouted back.

After listening to some fumbling and shuffling, the door crashed inward, barely giving me time to leap out of the way. Standing in the dust cloud was Apollus Brutus Severillus. Mary rushed forward to embrace him, causing Apollus to wince because of the wound to his shoulder. His injured hand was wrapped in a strip torn from the hem of his mantle.

"*Careful,*" *he told Mary.* "*Gidgiddonihah gave me a few souvenirs.*"

"*I saw that you gave him a few of your own,*" *I responded.*

"*How did you get here?*" *asked Mary.*

"*I've been in this land since the moment we separated in Frost Cave,*" *Apollus replied.* "*I should ask you the same.*"

"*Where's Meagan?*" *I inquired.*

*Apollus stepped back into the hallway, eager to search the rooms beyond.* "*That's what I'd like to know,*" *he replied.* "*They told me she was dead.*"

*Mary turned white.* "*What?*"

"*I don't believe them,*" *said Apollus firmly. He kicked open the next door down the hall. It was empty.*

"*When did you last see her?*" *asked Mary.*

"*Three days ago,*" *said Apollus. He shoved open the next door in line. Also empty.*

"*Where's Ryan Champion?*" *I asked.*

*This caused Apollus to falter. He turned to look at me.* "*They said . . . they said he was dead as well.*"

"*Do you believe them?*" *asked Mary, her face pale.*

*He turned away to search the next room, shaking his head.* "*I don't know. They said Moroni was dead too.*"

*That widened my eyes.* "*Moroni! The Moroni?*"

"*The same from the Book of Mormon,*" *Apollus confirmed as he kicked open the next door with considerable violence. This room was also empty.*

"*Moroni, the son of Mormon?*" *I asked in astonishment.* "*You met him?*"

"*Yes,*" *said Apollus, eyes focused on the final doorway.*

"*Moroni can't be dead,*" *I insisted.* "*If they told you Moroni was dead, it must be a lie. Ryan must be alive as well.*"

*Again he looked at us, frowning, unsure, not yet daring to believe it. But there seemed to be an added spring to his step as he approached the final room. He tried to kick it open, but the door wouldn't budge. It was wedged, like ours.*

"*Meagan!*" *Mary called through the door.*

*No reply.*

*Apollus stripped away the wedges at the base, also calling out,* "*Meagan! Are in you in there? Answer!*"

*I used my shoulder against the door, but it hardly budged.*

*"Something is jamming it from the inside," Apollus surmised.*

*I got into position to ram it again. Apollus stood beside me.*

*"Ready?" I said to him. "On three."*

*I counted. On three we slammed against it with all our weight. The door flew open. We fell inside in another dust cloud. But when it cleared, there was no Meagan. I could feel Apollus's awful frustration. Here he wasn't even sure if she was alive, and now this. It was tearing him up. It was tearing me up.*

*"She's alive, Apollus," I assured him. "Where else can we look?"*

*"Across the courtyard," he said. "There are other buildings. Maybe more prison cells."*

*Mary had remained outside the room. As we reentered the hall, I saw her kneeling down near what appeared to be a stairway exit at the far end. After picking something up from the dusty floor, she dangled it toward us.*

*"A necklace?" I asked.*

*Apollus practically fell over himself to reach Mary. He took the chain from her for a better look. It was a Young Women's Medallion with an engraving of a girl standing before the Salt Lake Temple.*

*"Meagan's!" said Apollus excitedly. "She gave it to me once to barter for food. The merchant refused, so I gave it back. She was here."*

*"Meagan dropped it deliberately," Mary concluded. "She wanted us to know that they took her."*

*Apollus led the way out onto the narrow staircase and out the backside of the building. The stone stairs descended to another landing where there was another entrance leading into the lower story. We looked west and south across the forests and brushlands, but I couldn't spot Meagan or her abductors. Then, as I looked north, I saw a cluster of people. There was some kind of fracas. A large knot of the invading warriors had cornered some of the Lacandon and Chamulan elders. I scanned the cluster and saw Gidgiddonihah! He was among the invaders! I also saw—I caught my breath. Could it be true? There was a woman standing in the center of it all—a girl with long, blonde hair.*

*My heart blasted off like a rocket. It was her! My sister, Steffanie! She'd made it to Desolation!*

*Out of nowhere a bird swooped down and flew at my face.*

*"Rafa!" I cried.*

*I stuck out my arm and welcomed my faithful falcon onto my shoulder. He flapped his wings and squalled in a frenzy of excitement.*

*"Watch the claws!" I exclaimed. "No padding! No padding!"*

*I thought a friendly falcon might draw some curiosity from Apollus, but he hardly paid Rafa more than a glance. Something else had caught his eye—another figure in the middle of the cluster of people.*

*He clenched his teeth and hissed the man's name with ultimate loathing:*

*"Lamanai."*

\* \* \*

Steffanie

I'd nearly fainted dead away in shock and delight. We'd found Gidgiddonihah! He was alive—though bleeding from several gashes. With cuts on his chest and the bridge of his nose it looked like he'd been through a firestorm. All my questions of what had occurred would have to come later.

For now Gid, Pagag, First Deer, and I had cornered a group of ten Chamulans and Lacandones who'd been trying to escape. Two hundred Lamanites were also with us. Most of the fighting was over now. Micah and the rest of the Earth-Stone warriors were busily dealing with any stragglers. These ten men clung together against the vine-covered wall of a building at the northwest edge of the city center. By all appearances they were chiefs and elders—older dudes with lots of jewels, necklaces, nose rings, and feathers.

One of them, however, was not old at all. He couldn't have been more than eighteen or twenty, and he was dressed much more plainly than his compadres—just a simple tunic, although his arms and chest were still covered in myriad tattoos. Despite his youth, everybody seemed to be looking to this guy for help or advice, as if he somehow had the power to prevent them all from being cut to ribbons.

Gid wasn't as concerned about the young guy as he was about an older gentleman wearing more feather bands and jewelry than many of the others put together. His earrings looked like human fingerbones cast in gold. There were so many rings on his fingers that it was a wonder that he could use them to eat or perform any practical function. The tattoos around his eyes were like starbursts, and I'm sure when he was younger the lines were straight, but seven or eight decades of wrinkles had distorted them quite a bit.

Gid strutted right up to his face, a newly acquired spear and obsidian sword firmly set in his grip.

The man fell to his knees, groveling and begging. "Do not slay me! Do not slay me!"

"Chief Mensäbäk," Gid seethed. "You lied to me. You said they were murdered."

"Only to provoke you! Please do not slay me!" The chief pointed a shaky finger toward the back of the gathering. "Look! They have come! They are here—alive and well, as you can see!"

My eyes widened. I let out a squeal. *It was my brother and Mary!* I met them as they pushed through the crowd, throwing my arms around Harry and Mary's neck. Pagag also greeted them heartily. Apollus looked pretty beaten up, much like Gid. If I didn't know any better, I'd have thought they'd been fighting each other. I embraced Apollus too, but his mind was elsewhere. His eyes were like a hawk's—focused with deadly precision upon . . . the young man?

Apollus stopped just short, his Roman blade pointed right at the young man's chest. "Hello again, Lamanai," said Apollus, his voice so virulent that a chill ran up my spine.

For his part, the young man named Lamanai looked defiant and unafraid.

"Where's Meagan?" the centurion demanded, his sword ready to plunge into Lamanai's heart.

"Gone," he replied. "Soon dead."

Instead of further inflaming his anger, this news seemed to give Apollus great relief, as it confirmed that she was at least alive as of a short time ago. He dismissed the threat with, "Soon dead? So I was told once before. I do not think so. Make your peace with God, Lamanai. Tell me where she is before I put a blade in your stomach."

"I don't know," Lamanai said with a shrug, his demeanor very unlike a man about to be executed.

Chief Mensäbäk, however, wasn't quite so cool a customer. He said to Apollus, "She was taken by the Lacandones—by Chief K'ayyum and his escorts."

Mensäbäk was only too happy to betray the chieftain of his life-long enemies, but I noticed that Lamanai was grinding his teeth. He sent Mensäbäk a vicious scowl, as if offended that Mensäbäk would stab a fellow Lamanite—*any* fellow Lamanite—in the back.

Apollus asked Mensäbäk, "Where is he taking her? Which direction did they go?"

"Do not answer him!" Lamanai barked at the Chamulan chief.

But in defiance, Mensäbäk said, "To the river crossing." He turned back to Lamanai. "He is Lacandon. They are not worthy of our silence."

Lamanai hissed, "Speak again, Chief Mensäbäk, and they will be your last words."

Mensäbäk shut his mouth tightly. This was a surprising development, especially since this person named Lamanai carried no weapon. Just who in blazes was this flat-foreheaded upstart who could bark commands at tribal chieftains?

The centurion drew back his sword to stab Lamanai. "You have voiced your last empty threat. Your usefulness is at an end."

"WAIT!" cried Mensäbäk. As if repenting of his previous offense, he lunged forward and got between Lamanai and Apollus. I couldn't believe what I was seeing. The old Chamulan chief was now willing to die for this whelp?

"Out of my way!" growled Apollus. "Or you will die with him!"

Gid said to Apollus, "He will die anyway."

"You cannot kill this man!" Mensäbäk said to Apollus, but loud enough for the entire gathering, and directed especially to First Deer. "He is the true king of all peoples of the Lamaya—of the Water-Lilies and the Earth-Stone, of the Cloud Mountains and the Weeping Forests. He is Eagle-Sky-Jaguar, the son of the Great-Jaguar-Paw!"

You could have heard a pin drop for the reaction of the Lamanite warriors—like they were staring at a ghost. Or at a *god!* I looked at Pagag. He nodded, confirming to me his vivid recollection—no less vivid than my own—of King Sa'abkan's interrogation of us where he had mentioned a charlatan who claimed to be a direct descendant of some dethroned king of the Lamanites. He'd labeled this man to be a pretender who traveled with two supernatural companions—*May-geen* and *Aryin.* Meagan and Ryan. This was all starting to make bizarre, twisted sense. But if Meagan was in the hands of this Lacandon chieftain, where was Ryan?

First Deer stepped toward Lamanai, his eyes fierce and challenging. "We have heard rumors of a deceiver from the east who claims to be a descendant of the great king. Are you this deceiver?"

"I am no deceiver," replied Lamanai sternly. "I *am* the son of Great-Jaguar-Paw. In my veins runs the blood of the sacred dynasty of Lamayan kings from Yax-Chaac-Xoc and from the beginning of time."

"What proof have you?" demanded First Deer. "Why should you not be slain with the rest of these Chamulan and Lacandon mongrels?"

Lamanai thought a moment, then he looked at Apollus and smiled wickedly. "Ask the white warrior—Guardian Apollus Hunaphu. He cannot lie. If he is made to swear in the name of his God, he will speak nothing but truth."

With that Apollus lunged. Despite his injured hand, he used it to shove Mensäbäk aside. Again he drew back his sword for the kill, but this time several Lamanite warriors grabbed his shoulders to stop him.

"He betrayed us!" Apollus ranted. "He tried to kill us all! He must pay for his crimes!"

Gid grabbed Apollus's shoulder and pulled him away from the Lamanites. He whispered to the centurion in desperation, "*But not today.* Look at their faces, Apollus. *Think!* If he is who he claims, these Lamanites will eat our gizzards for breakfast."

Lamanai wore such an evil smirk of satisfaction that I wanted to knock out a few teeth myself, the slimy little weevil.

First Deer demanded of Apollus, "Is it so? Is it true what he says? In the name of your God will you swear that he is not the son of Jaguar-Paw?"

"He is a jackal!" seethed Apollus. "He is not worthy to be king of a dung heap. Make him king and he will lead your people straight to the fires of hell!"

*"CAN YOU SWEAR IT?"* First Deer repeated his question with such intensity that I think if Apollus had refused again to answer, the Hummingbird Captain would have ordered his men to seize the centurion and beat it out of him.

Apollus hesitated, eyes still blazing, lungs heaving in and out with fury. Finally, he shut his eyes and nodded. "He is who he says. He is the Prince of Tikal."

There were gasps and murmurs from the Lamanite warriors. Lamanai stood as tall as he could, elevating his nostril that had been pierced with a black bead. He took in the audience, whose numbers had doubled in the short time since we'd cornered these men at the vine-covered wall. The effect of that gaze upon the congregation was mesmerizing. All murmuring stopped. I'm not sure who was the first to kneel. I think it may have actually been Chief Mensäbäk. But in a matter of seconds Apollus, Gid, Pagag, myself, and a handful of the Lacandon and Chamulan elders were the only people still on our feet. Even First Deer had prostrated himself upon his face to reverence this newfound king.

Apollus continued to glower at Lamanai, who now gloated with malevolence. He'd won, and he knew it. Gid and Pagag continued to watch the centurion, afraid he might hurl his Roman blade into Lamanai's chest like a spear. But Apollus remained still.

"Lord Eagle-Sky-Jaguar," said First Deer, still unwilling to lift his gaze. "I am First Deer, Hummingbird Captain of the armies of the people of the Earth-Stone, and I serve the dynasty of Yax-Chaac-Xoc and Great-Jaguar-Paw. What is your command?"

A shiver of fear started inching its way up my spine. I realized this Lamayan Prince could order our deaths with a sweep of his hand. What would prevent him from doing just that?

Lamanai glanced over me, Pagag, and Harry, and asked First Deer, "Who are these fair-skinned people that you risked the lives of your noble warriors to help?"

First Deer was at last brave enough to raise his eyes. "They saved the lives of many of our children in the wilderness of Zarahemla. We were commanded by our king, Lord Sa'abkan, son of Aaron, to help them find their companions, who were kidnapped by a band of Nephites. We were also commanded to slay those who had kidnapped them."

"Son of Aaron," Lamanai repeated, as if he was at least familiar with this name. "I see. And have you fulfilled your command? Are they all reunited?"

First Deer looked at Pagag, who nodded in the affirmative.

"Yes, my Lord," said First Deer. "The command is fulfilled. We will now return to the city of Jordan and rejoin King Sa'abkan. Our armies are marching to Cumorah for a great war against the Nephite nation. It is said that the armies of Lord Fireborn are also marching to Cumorah."

"The rumor is true," Lamanai confirmed. "He marches with your brothers, the people of the Water-Lilies, as well as many of the usurpers from Teotihuacán—all with the same objective of driving the people of Nephi into oblivion."

First Deer looked distressed. "But if you are the son of Great-Jaguar-Paw then . . . Lord Fireborn is your enemy."

"Indeed," said Lamanai, nodding. "He is your enemy as well." He said more loudly to all warriors, who began to raise their heads, "He is the enemy to all Lamaya from where the sun rises to the place it sleeps—east, west, north, and south!" Then he looked at Apollus. "And yet it seems that for a time the alliance of Teotihuacán and Tikal may serve a useful purpose—to rid these lands once and for all of an ancient pestilence."

"So it was always a lie," Apollus snarled to Lamanai. "You never intended to forge a treaty between the Nephites and Lamanites against Fireborn and Lord Crocodile."

He narrowed his eyes at Apollus. "A king does not lie. A king always does what he must. What is expedient for his people."

With those words, Lamanai reached into his tunic and produced an obsidian knife. I caught my breath. So he wasn't completely unarmed after all. Apollus and Gidgiddonihah went into a defensive stance. But to our complete bewilderment, Lamanai turned abruptly and plunged the knife into the aged leader of the Chamulans. Eyes bulging, Chief Mensäbäk gaped at Lamanai in mortification, even as he sank to his knees and keeled over, dead. It was a sickening sight. Gid appeared no less shocked than the rest of us, despite the fact that he'd just threatened to kill Mensäbäk himself. *Evil punishes evil*, I thought to myself. Several of the elders who'd been Mensäbäk's attendants rushed forward to embrace or help their chieftain, but a word from the assassin prince halted them in their tracks.

"*Stop!* Do not touch him or you will *join* him! Any man of the Lamaya who will betray his brother—no matter his clan or tribe, no matter how longstanding their feud—is not worthy to have portion in my kingdom. From this day forward, all Lamayans must unite—or they must die!"

The elders of the Lacandon and the Chamula were visibly trembling. Those who had not prostrated themselves a moment ago, did so now.

Again Lamanai smirked in satisfaction, then he turned to First Deer. "My first order is for you to take me to the city of Jordan and King Sa'abkan."

First Deer asked, "What of the strangers? What would you have us do with the white-skinned guardian and his companions?"

I could hear my heart thumping. This was the moment. As Lamanai gazed upon us I knew that life or death was staring us in the face. Retaining that same glutinous grin, he stared at Apollus. I knew what the centurion was thinking. His fingers were still tightly gripped on that sword. This really was a face-off. If Lamanai issued a command for our deaths, the Lamayan Prince would never live to see it carried out. I don't think I'd ever seen an expression quite like the one I saw on the son of Jaguar-Paw. He may have known perfectly well what Apollus would do if he said the wrong thing, yet there was absolutely no fear in him. Did this guy have a few burned-out circuits, or did he really believe he was invincible? But that was a stupid way to put it. If he thought he was invincible, he was insane.

I couldn't say for certain if it was an act of benevolence or self-preservation, but the prince finally responded to First Deer's question, and his answer was, "Let them go. Their purposes have been served. They have brought me here to this place and time. Now let them return to the Underworld and to the gods that sent them. I spit upon them. I reject them and their gods. If they ever again fall into our hands, the vengeance of the Lamaya will know no limits." He lowered his voice and said directly to Apollus, "Good-bye Apollus. Go back to the cenote from whence you sprang. If I ever again see your face, Apollus Hunaphu, rest assured, I will not be so magnanimous as I have been today."

Apollus leaned forward. Gritting his teeth, eyes as thin as dagger blades, he replied in a voice like low thunder, "If I ever see you again, Eagle-Sky-Jaguar, rest assured . . . *neither will I.*"

\* \* \*

*Meagan*

*I'd heard their voices—friendly voices, familiar voices. It was less than a half hour ago that I was lying on the floor of a darkened room, listening to all the commotion and shouting outside my prison cell. In an instant, as everything went quiet, I swore that I'd heard Harry and Mary calling out the name of Gidgiddonihah. Gidgiddonihah! If this name had been spoken by anyone else—by any other voice—I'd have dismissed it as referring to someone with the same name, but coming from Harry and Mary . . . I just wasn't sure of anything anymore. Something spectacular was happening. I could see a window six feet above me with a piercing ray of sunlight, but a gag prevented me from yelling, and a rawhide strap around my wrists kept me from raising myself up high enough to see outside.*

*Just a few moments later K'ayyum's attendants arrived and forced me to go with them. I'd dropped my necklace in the hallway, but who could be certain if the right people would find it? They took me to K'ayyum, who waited behind the ruins of the temple. I could hear the fighting in the courtyard on the opposite side of the building. Desolation was under attack. K'ayyum's litter was carried on the shoulders of his attendants. They moved rapidly through the woods and back around to the river with me and the rest of his attendants in tow.*

*Only as we boarded canoes and set forth toward the opposite shore did Chief K'ayyum's body begin to relax. He sat facing me while two servants behind him rowed with all their strength. The relief on his face only increased the anxiety inside of me. With every stroke of the oars I was being taken farther away from Apollus. There were two other canoes on either side of us, and six additional Lacandon warriors steering them. If I could have just gotten my hands loose I was certain I could have leapt overboard and swum to safety and freedom, but the rawhide was so tight on my wrists that the straps were cutting my skin. I wanted so badly to plead with K'ayyum to let me go. What was the point of taking me with him? But the stupid gag prevented that.*

*Then a moment later ol' scarface started to explain his reasoning. "It won't be much longer, Guardian Meagan. Soon you will be honored with the same test as Ryan Champion and his servant. To earn the veneration and worship of the Hach Winik, you must prove your divine nature as a messenger of Lord Hachäkyum. We will toss you into the Nauyaca pit and witness your power for ourselves. If you survive, the gods will preserve my people from the wrath of Fireborn and anyone else who dares to work evil against us."*

*Tears popped out of my eyes. Until this moment I hadn't known the fate of Ryan or Jacobah. I prayed in my heart that it wasn't true. That's all I'd been doing for the past four days—praying for Apollus, Ryan, Moroni, and the rest.*

*A moment later the strangest thing happened. We were almost two-thirds of the way across to the eastern shore when I heard a scream from the canoe on our right. I turned my head, but only in time to see the splash. There were suddenly only two people in the boat. The one who'd been rowing at the rear was gone—as if a crocodile had sprung up out of the murky depths, caught him in its jaws, and instantly pulled him under. The other two men stopped rowing and grabbed up spears, thrusting them frantically into the surface of the river, like hunters trying to snag a turtle or a manatee. Each thrust came up empty.*

*"What happened?" yelled Chief K'ayyum.*

*They pointed into the river. "Balam! Balam!"*

*Balam—a jaguar. My heart skipped a beat. Was it possible? Could it be—?*

*There was another shriek from the canoe at our left. This time I saw it—or at least a flash of it. A black shape came up out of the water, clamped its jaws around one of the warriors' throats, dug its claws into his shoulder and arm, and pulled him over the side. In their panic to grab up weapons, the remaining warriors caused the canoe to overturn. All of them were now flailing in the current.*

*Huracan! Now I was sure of it! What other balam would have a jet-black face and coat?*

*An arrow bit into the water near the canoe on our right. I saw the source as I looked toward the eastern shore. Another canoe was rowing furiously toward us. Two of its passengers stood in the boat, firing more arrows. But they did not fire toward our dugout. They fired only at the* canoe on our right. My heart sprouted wings as I recognized the archers: *Moroni and Tz'ikin!* The other three passengers were *Ryan, Jacobah, and Gilgal!* Immediately I looked at K'ayyum's stricken face. He'd recognized them too and seemed utterly dumfounded. Oh, how I wished I didn't have this infernal gag in my mouth—just to relish his expression as I said, "I guess they passed your idiotic test. Looks like you have a few more gods to worship."

One of the Lacandones in the other boat was hit by an atlatl dart fired by Tz'ikin. Despite her wounded shoulder, she seemed as adept as ever with her weapon. As the warrior fell into the river, this canoe also became unstable and tipped, spilling the third warrior overboard.

The canoe was coming toward us swiftly. But at the moment I heard a voice calling out behind us.

"Meagan!"

I turned. It was Apollus! My Roman had set forth from the western side of the river with another canoe and six companions. It was like I was in a dream. What I was seeing couldn't be real. Seated behind Apollus, rowing like a madman, was my heroic stepbrother, Harry, and behind him was my magnificent stepsister, Steffanie. In the other canoe was Micah—sweet Micah from 73 AD! The young man sitting behind Micah was hardly recognizable, but I felt sure he was Jesse! The next man in the dugout was unfamiliar to me. But I definitely recognized the final man in the canoe. It was true! The name that Harry had yelled a short time ago was not some stranger. It was Gidgiddonihah! He was alive!

Apollus stood at the front of his canoe, a Roman broadsword in his hand, offering the same pose as General Washington crossing the Delaware. His right hand was wrapped in a cloth bandage. He was coming for me! The love of my life was coming!

K'ayyum was hyperventilating. He looked like a man who did not expect to live more than another few minutes.

I was sure that Moroni and Tz'ikin would reach us before Apollus. But as the surface of the river sprang alive once more, I realized one ally was closer than them all. Huracan climbed right into the rear of our canoe, dripping wet and revealing her fangs. Both of K'ayyum's terrified attendants abandoned ship. Our canoe rocked perilously as they leaped into the river, but miraculously it stayed upright. Huracan snarled ferociously and took several steps toward K'ayyum.

*In response, the chieftain grabbed the first thing he could find to defend himself—namely, me! Next, he snatched up a weapon from the bottom of the boat. It was a sort of hatchet, or circular knife, with a short wooden handle, like the stem of a lollypop. The blade was a massive chunk of black obsidian shaped like a half moon. Any normal person would have held it out to threaten the attacking animal, but not K'ayyum. He seemed to know instinctively that this jaguar was special. He knew it was here to rescue me. Instead of threatening the predator, K'ayyum threatened me, setting the weapon's razor edge against my throat.*

*"Huracan, no!"*

*The shout had come from Ryan. Huracan stopped, her piercing yellow eyes intently watching K'ayyum. Ten seconds later Ryan's canoe got within range. Moroni and Tz'ikin had bow and atlatl loaded, aiming their missiles directly at us. The chief twisted me around to put me between himself and his attackers, always keeping one of his mangled eyes on Huracan. His cause was hopeless. What did he hope to profit? Why couldn't K'ayyum just let me go?*

*"Do not come any closer!" K'ayyum shouted at them.*

*Ryan, Gilgal, and Jacobah stopped rowing. Their dugout turned to the side to line up Moroni and Tz'ikin for a clearer shot.*

*"Release her," commanded Moroni. "Release her and you will be set free. We will allow you to go back to your village."*

*"My attendants are gone!" he whined. "There is no one to carry me. You think I can walk all the way to my village on these crippled feet?"*

*"Do as he says, Father!" Tz'ikin barked. "At least you will be alive— which is more than you deserve."*

*I felt the circular blade bite harder into my neck. His daughter's words had infuriated him. "You are my flesh and blood!" he snarled at her. "You threaten to kill me, your father whose seed gave you life?"*

*Moroni and Tz'ikin were aiming with great concentration, as if they might fire despite the fact that K'ayyum was holding me directly in front of him. I'd certainly witnessed the incredible skill that both of them had with their weapons. But I also knew that Tz'ikin, with her tender shoulder, couldn't be operating at her top level. Add to that some very tender emotions. The girl's hand was trembling like a bowl of Jell-O. Her father still had tremendous power over her, whether she wanted to admit it or not. In Tz'ikin's case, I was terrified that she might actually fire.*

*I glanced westward. Apollus and the others were coming on strong. In less than a minute they'd be as close as the others.*

*Tz'ikin replied to her father, her voice cracking, "You are the man whose seed gave me life. But you are not my father. No father would do what you have done. You killed my mother—and since I was a girl you made me blame someone else. But it was not Fireborn who murdered her. It was you. You murdered her for a sin she did not commit—a crime in which she took no part."*

*Raving like a lunatic, K'ayyum snapped back, "You are the daughter of the tribal chief of the Boar Clan of the Lacandon! And you call me a murderer? Curse you to Metlán! You are 'lo'kin'—a cannibal of the Hach Winik, a daughter of Kisin, dead to the true gods and the true people of god!"*

*"So be it," said Tz'ikin. She glanced at Ryan. "I believe there are more powerful gods than Hachäkyum. Jesus Christ is more powerful than all the gods of the Lacandon and the Lamaya."*

*The next moment played out in my mind one frame at a time. K'ayyum removed the blade from my throat, drew it back behind his head, and threw it at Tz'ikin with all his might. At the same instant Moroni let his bowstring snap and Tz'ikin flung her atlatl dart. Three picture frames later, the hatchet hit Tz'ikin's chest while both the arrow and dart struck K'ayyum. Moroni's missile imbedded in his neck, just inches away from my right ear. The long dart of Tz'ikin struck K'ayyum's shoulder, but it also skimmed the top of my shoulder. I couldn't tell at first if it cut my flesh, but the tip pierced right through the cloth of my shabby mantle. My first impulse was to drop down into the bottom of the dugout to try and keep it upright, but because the dart had connected me to K'ayyum, I was pulled in behind him as he fell into the river.*

*I'd tried to take in a breath through my nose as I hit the water, but panic caused it to fly out in a stream of bubbles. With my hands bound and my clothes attached to a fast-sinking body, there was no way to get myself out of the situation. I was kicking like crazy. It was almost as if the chieftain was weighted down with cinderblocks! Was I caught in some kind of undercurrent or whirlpool? Why were we sinking so fast? I literally watched the circle of the sun darken to black as I drifted into the murky* depths. My circumstance seemed doomed. My confidence faded with the light. Even if every able-bodied person in those canoes dove in after me, how could they ever find me in all of this impenetrable blackness?

Just as I thought this, I felt a strong hand grab my wrist. But immediately it let go. Why did it let go? Suddenly I felt it again, this time grasping the arrow that was embedded in K'ayyum's shoulder and tangled in my mantle. I heard a crack—or thought I heard it. The arm of my rescuer hooked itself inside my bound hands. I felt myself being pulled upward. With my last pulse of strength, I started kicking again. The circle of the sun reappeared above me.

At last my head broke the surface. The gag was yanked off my face. I swallowed a life-giving breath. My head felt faint, and I might have lost consciousness, but I remained alert by sheer will. I had to see the face of my rescuer. When I did, a surge of warmth surrounded my heart like an electric blanket. The face was no surprise. It was the face I should have expected. The face I hoped to see for all eternity—the deep blue eyes of my Roman centurion.

In spite of his battle wounds, Apollus swam me the last twenty yards to the eastern shore. After we arrived, I lay there beside him on the soft bank, catching my breath. He cut the strap that bound my hands.

"I thought I'd drown," I said breathlessly. "I thought you'd never find me."

"Never doubt that I will come," he replied, "so long as there is breath in my body. I love you, Meagan."

I wrapped my arms around him, crying a little as I kissed his neck, chin, and mouth.

"I love you too, Apollus. With all my heart!"

But then Apollus glanced to our left. He sat up suddenly. I rose up as well and turned my head to see. The warmth immediately drained out of me, seeping into the mud. My heart felt the weight of a thousand pounds. Tears again flowed from my eyes, but not in relief. In genuine, heart-wrenching grief.

Two more people were lying in the mud fifty yards up the shore—another rescuer and the person he'd rescued. Only in this case, the person pulled from the river wasn't moving. The rescuer sat in the mud with her head in his lap, holding her tightly in his arms, and pleading with her softly, gently, unyieldingly, not to die.

\* \* \*

Ryan

*"Tz'ikin!"* My voice was choked with emotion. Again I said, *"Tz'ikin, hold on! Please hold on!"*

She was breathing, but it was very faint. I looked up and saw the other canoes arriving at the river's edge. Harry, Steffanie, and two men I didn't recognize were swimming to shore, having leaped into the water to try and rescue Meagan and Tz'ikin. Apollus had reached Meagan. But Tz'ikin, though I'd pulled her from the water, had been seriously injured by K'ayyum's weapon. She'd lost so much blood. She was barely clinging to life.

Huracan had also swum to shore. The jaguar was behind me now, dripping with water, and watching the silent form of the warrioress.

Tz'ikin's eyes came open halfway. She looked up at me and smiled warmly, peacefully. She said in a weak voice, "Ryan. You can't seem to stop . . . to stop pulling me from rivers."

"You can't seem to stop falling in them. Moroni will be here in less than a minute. We can bless you, Tz'ikin. You can be healed."

She shook her head minutely. "No, Ryan. I am blessed already. I am . . . healed already."

I held her more tightly. "Don't talk anymore. Save your energy. You're going to make it. Don't give up. I'm not going to give up on you."

"Ryan," she said, releasing a tear, "you must let me go."

"No! I saved your life once. The Lord gave me the strength to do it, and it was for a reason. You can't die now!"

"Yes. The reason . . . is finished . . . is fulfilled."

"Nothing was fulfilled. Not yet."

"You said once maybe . . . maybe I'd be . . . your first convert."

"And so you will be. But you have to hang on. Hang on so I can teach you more. I'll teach you everything."

"You've taught me . . . so much."

I wiped the tears from my eyes. "There's so much more to learn. More than you can imagine."

She closed her eyes, tears trickling down her cheeks. "I can imagine. Oh . . . I can imagine. I can see!"

More to myself now, more in prayer to God, I said, "Please no. Don't let this happen. *Don't let it happen . . .*"

Moroni, Apollus, and Meagan had finally reached me. They stood back a pace, watching solemnly and listening.

Tz'ikin whispered, "Thank you, Ryan. Thank you . . . for giving me . . . for showing me . . . life."

I struggled for something to say—to reply—but nothing came. For a moment, she went still, like she'd fallen asleep. Then she released a long, soft sigh. Her chest sank and her body became limp.

I looked up at Moroni. I fumbled in my pocket and found my vial of oil. There was hardly anything left—if anything at all. But I'd find enough. I said to Moroni, "We have to bless her. You have to help me bless her."

The prophet knelt down and touched her forehead, brushing a strand of hair away from her face. Then he looked back at me. "She's already gone, Ryan."

I insisted again, "Help me, Moroni. Please."

He looked at me for a long moment, then looked at her and nodded silently. I unscrewed the cap. I went to anoint her head, but before I did, I found myself gazing at her beautiful, solemn expression.

My hand was trembling. I was hesitating. *What was wrong with me?* I closed my fist around the vial and squeezed it tightly. *I couldn't do it!* Why couldn't I do it? *Heavenly Father, please!* But again the feeling echoed in my heart: It wasn't right. I heard a voice in my mind—*her* voice—a memory of her words from a moment before. But was it a memory, or something more?

"Let me go, Ryan. Let me go."

I broke down. The tension, the fear, seemed to just melt out of me, and for a moment my body felt as weak as a newborn. Meagan was weeping too, and she put her arms around me. Everyone was here now. They stood around us, gazing down at the girl who'd said she was my first convert. If this is what it felt like to have a convert . . . then I didn't want . . .

But before I could even verbalize the thought, it was struck down in my heart. I felt something calming. So calming. The Spirit blessed me, and I, too, felt peace. And such . . . gratitude! For everything. Just to have known her. To have been a part of her life.

I took her hand and squeezed it. Then I leaned close to her ear and whispered softly, "Thank you, Tz'ikin. I'll never forget you."

# CHAPTER 18

## Rebecca

Mary and I waited alone on the other side of the river for a long time. She'd accepted the duty of watching over me while Jesse and everybody else went on a desperate mission to save Meagan. The waiting was awful, but finally, everyone came back to us. We were all together again. There were a lot of tears and hugs and happiness, but there was also great sadness. They said someone very special had died. Someone they had loved very much. I never met the girl named Tz'ikin, but after what so many had said about her, and after hearing how she had done so much to save Meagan and Apollus and the others, I wished that I had. The way they talked about her—especially Ryan Champion—it made me cry, and I didn't even know her.

The Lamanites had all gone. First Deer and the rest of them had all marched toward the west and disappeared before Harry and the others had even returned. It was just us now in the wilderness of Desolation. We were on our own.

I was so overjoyed to give everyone hugs and kisses, to see all those that I loved, and to meet Jacobah and Gilgal. Well, maybe it was a little more enjoyable meeting Jacobah than Gilgal. Jacobah said he was Ryan's bodyguard. He also said to me, "I will be honored to be your protector as well, little one." Wow! What a nice thing to say to someone. What a cool guy!

But by far the biggest thrill of all was to be introduced to the Prophet Moroni. I was like, "Duh, duh, duh." I couldn't believe it! I didn't even know what to say. He was the Prophet Moroni for goodness sake! What do you say to a person like that? I think I really stuck my foot in my mouth, 'cause I told him, "I feel like I sorta know you already 'cause I see you outside my window everyday."

Harry and Meagan laughed uncomfortably, I think to make him believe I was making a weird joke. I was talking about the statue on top of the Provo Temple, of course, and after I thought about it, I felt like a real ditz. But Moroni was very friendly and he told me that he had a little boy about my age. I couldn't wait to meet him.

There were so many stories to tell and so much to catch up on. We told Apollus, Ryan, and Meagan all about what had happened after we were separated in the cave with Akish and rescuing Gidgiddonihah, and the Tower of Babel, and meeting Noah, and Pagag's father and uncle, Jared, and Mahonri Moriancumr. After that everybody was very impressed to meet Pagag and learn all about him. Pagag was also thrilled to meet everyone else. He was particularly impressed when he met Huracan, the beautiful black jaguar that had been traveling with Apollus and Meagan. Huracan growled a few times and rolled onto her back. Pagag was like, "I understood that! She wants her stomach scratched! I can't believe it! Finally, an animal that I can understand!"

We also talked a lot about my brother. We told everybody how Joshua had disappeared that night in the hills above Salem. I explained that we'd come here looking for him, and how Harry and I—because of what we'd learned from the seerstone—felt very strongly that he was here somewhere in this land. I said how I also felt that my father and Marcos were somewhere around here too. Everyone seemed very hopeful and positive when we told them these things, and I had a strong impression that all of us would be reunited again soon.

As Moroni listened to us talk about Joshua, he got kind of a strange look. He told us about another young man named Joshua who had lived among the Nephites for about five years, and whose "origins" were sort of a mystery. Supposedly this guy had a "complexion" a lot like ours. Yeah, but it was obvious he wasn't our Joshua. This guy was a captain in the Nephite army and he was almost twenty years old. We told him that our Joshua was only twelve, and had only been missing for a couple weeks, so it had to be somebody different. Moroni nodded and seemed to forget about it. But I remember that Harry, Meagan, and Steffanie got a real worried look afterwards—even a frightened look. Gid, Micah, and Jesse looked concerned as well. I really didn't understand what was bothering them. What did they think?—that in two weeks my brother could actually become a nineteen-year-old Nephite army captain? I mean, come on! What planet did they think we were on?

When Apollus, Meagan, and Ryan explained that they were on their way to the Hill Cumorah, I got such a good feeling inside. You see, Steffanie had found the seerstone that we had lost, and she'd given it back to me. I'd already used it to ask Heavenly Father about Joshua and I felt sure that by going to Cumorah, we'd be going in the right direction. The only question left was where we would find him. I wondered if it was possible that my father and Joshua were already together. I was determined to ask the Lord through the stone the first chance I got.

I loved my dad and my brother so much and I missed them terribly. I got nervous whenever I thought about what kind of trouble Joshua was in, or how he might be lonely or scared or lost. But then I felt comforted, and I knew that he would be fine. But boy! was I going to give him the lecture of his life when I saw him again. I could hardly wait. I could just hardly wait . . .

* * *

*Meagan*

*Apollus approached me that evening as I was sitting alone on a crumbling stone wall overlooking the moonlit ruins of Desolation in the far distance. All his wounds—along with Gid's—were now freshly stitched and bandaged; that is, after Moroni's special recipe of herbal antibiotic paste had been applied. Each had given a beautiful priesthood blessing to the other, pleading for forgiveness for fighting with such hatred and fury, and praying for the healing power of God.*

*The moon was as bright and round as a searchlight, and there wasn't a single cloud to hide the shimmering stars. Yet I certainly wasn't thinking about the loveliness of the night. I was thinking of Tz'ikin. I was thinking of the grief that all of us were going through, but most especially Ryan.*

*I hugged Apollus for a long time when he arrived, being careful of his injured hand and shoulder, and I wondered to myself why it was that such wonderful events were so often surrounded by such terrible things? I knew what Apollus would have said if I had asked him. He would have said that without the bitter, the sweet isn't nearly so sweet, and he would have been right. But by far the sweetest lesson I'd learned was that as long as I had my Roman, and my Roman stayed close to God, there was nothing that I couldn't endure.*

*As Apollus sat down beside me, the biggest worry of all was stirred up again in my mind. I asked him tentatively, "What did you think about what Moroni said . . . I mean, when he told us about a Nephite captain at Cumorah with strange origins whose name was also Joshua?"*

*Apollus sighed heavily. "I was thinking . . . it was an odd coincidence."*

*"That's all?"*

*"Yes. For now. Until we find Joshua, or until we meet this Nephite captain, is there any cause to worry ourselves? There are many things that would point away from the notion that this captain is your young cousin. His age, rank, time among the Nephites . . . It simply seems unthinkable."*

*I balanced my elbows on my knees and set my face in my hands. "I suppose you're right."*

*He put his arm around my shoulders. "Tomorrow we will continue on to Cumorah. You must rest; let your body regain its strength. Has the Lord not shown us enough miracles today to convince us that He is present and watching over us always?"*

*I nodded and sighed. "Yes. Yes, He has."*

*He held me tighter. "Relax, my love. Clear your mind of all tension. I did not come here to ponder stressful things. I came here to speak to you. I came to talk about something far more immediate in importance."*

*"More immediate? Like what?"*

*"Like . . . us?"*

*"Like us like what?"*

*Apollus wore an expression that I'd never seen before. I might have thought it was fear, but how was that possible? I'd seen Apollus face down enemies from Jerusalem to Desolation, from multiple lands and centuries. But this was the first time I'd ever seen him with a look that I'd describe as acute nervousness.*

I noticed that he was carrying a fiber sack. He brought it forward and said, "I have some things to give you. It is fortunate that I still have them. Moroni and Gilgal saved most of our supplies."

"Oh, cool! Prizes!" I said, being silly. "What do you have?"

"Things. They are important. Please forgive a poor plebian. I am not of Roman nobility, so it may be that I am butchering the proper customs, but first—" He reached into the bag with his left hand. "—I have this."

He brought out something wrapped in cloth and placed it in my palm. I widened my eyes at him like a little girl and began unfolding the contents. Soon they were revealed. I scrunched my forehead. It looked like a cold corn tortilla. A very old cold corn tortilla. "You're giving me . . . a tortilla?"

Apollus cleared his throat bashfully. "It should have been wheat, but . . . wheat is rather . . . rather scarce around here. I also give you this."

He brought forth something else in a cloth wrapping. He started unwrapping it awkwardly with his bandaged hand. But whatever had been inside must have spilled out, because the cloth was quite sticky and unfolded with great difficulty. Finally, a cracked clay vial was displayed. I could see Apollus's perturbation mounting. I was finding it very hard to maintain a straight face. "And what was that?"

"A vial of . . . bee's honey. It, uh, must have broken. I'm so, so sorry. Confound! *This isn't going very well.*" He looked back at the sack. "I have more. Hold on."

The determination on his face was so cute it melted my heart and stirred my curiosity. His fingers dove in several more times. In each instance he pulled out a handful of small brown and green nuts. I remembered harvesting them on our journey. Jacobah had called them breadnuts. Apollus sprinkled them on the ground around us.

Again I gave him a queer look, wondering if I should check him for a fever. "Are you all right, Apollus?"

"I'm fine," he said, a little testily. "Sorry. Please. I know that I'm not doing this right. It is more proper if they are strewn along a path, but . . ." He sighed deeply. ". . . bear with me. I want to tell you what these are. The nuts surrounding us represent bounty and industry. The honey is so that our lives may ever be richly sweetened. And the bread—I mean, the tortilla, well . . . it means that I will forever take care of you, Meagan, and that you shall never want for comfort, or happiness, or the necessities of life, or anything else so long as I am yours and you are mine."

*I looked into Apollus's eyes. They were sparkling. Dreamlike. My heart started pounding like it was part of a drum parade. Was he doing what I thought he was doing?*

*"And finally this—" The bag appeared empty, but once more his hand dove inside to find one last item. Emerging, his fist was closed. He stood up, turned over his wrist, and opened his palm. My heart stopped. I looked up at him again, then looked back down. I could hardly see it now for the sudden flood of tears.*

*It was a ring. A gold ring.*

*"I fashioned it myself," said Apollus, "with the aid of Moroni, from a somewhat larger golden trinket—a piece of an idol I think—that we found at one of the ruins. Thankfully, Moroni is quite adept with such metals. I know that in your day a ring is set with valuable jewels. But in mine such a band is a simple circle—a symbol of something that will endure forever."*

*Apollus got down on one knee, then he looked up at me, his eyes as warm and luminous as I had ever seen them. "Meagan," he began, "I love you. I realize that you and I come from two different worlds. But the only world where I am interested in living is the one where you also reside. Whatever differences there are between us, I will do all that is in my power to make it work—to make us one. God will help us. All I know is, I love you, and I will continue to love you until the end of time, and well beyond." He paused, gazing into my eyes, and said, "Will you, Meagan Sorenson, be my wife?"*

*I gulped with emotion. My cheeks were now streaked with tears. I started blubbering like an idiot. "Yes," I replied, and threw my arms around his neck. "Yes, I will be your wife, Apollus Brutus Severillus."*

*"Good," he said, a little stunned, as if he was still half inside a dream. But then reality set in. "Good! Yes, very good!"*

*He kissed me there among the stars and under the moon, inside a land bathed in the lights of heaven and eternity.*

\* \* \*

Steffanie

Harry held Mary very close the entire evening as we sat around the fire in the midst of the forest. They talked, they cried, they spoke of the future, and they appeared without a doubt to be very much in love. I caught myself glancing over at Pagag quite often, watching to see if he was noticing them, waiting to see if he would go out of his way to say something stupid or make a complete fool out himself like before. It gave me great pleasure to see that he hardly paid them any attention whatsoever. As a matter of fact, most of the times when I glanced over at the tall, blond-haired, turquoise-eyed Jaredite, I was pleased to discover that he was actually looking at *me*.

A girl knows when she's won. She just knows it. And, *oh!* this particular victory tasted especially sweet. I'd saved my brother. I'd saved his relationship with Mary. No, I never expected to be thanked for what I'd done. Honestly, I never expected to even tell Harry about it. But I would know it in my heart, and that was satisfying enough.

What wasn't so clear to me was exactly *how* I'd won. In fact, my mind was in a bit of a dither about it. What was the benefit of victory if you had no idea what you'd done to achieve it?

I scolded myself. What did it matter? I'd won! I'd *won, won, won!* Wasn't that enough? It had always been enough before. So why did I feel so . . . discontented?

It was after dark. Everybody had settled into their own groups. Huracan had returned to the forest, just as Ryan had assured us that she would. Rafa, the falcon, had buried his head inside his wing, fast asleep. Apollus and Meagan had wandered off somewhere to talk. Most of the others were gathered around the fire.

It wasn't long before Pagag finally got up the nerve to approach me. He stood over me and asked, "Would you like to go on a short walk?"

I looked around. "In the woods?"

"Yes," he replied.

"Are you sure it's safe?"

He showed me that he was still wearing his sword. "I think that we will be fine."

"Okay," I said. "But not for long. I'm very tired."

He thought about this and doubt seemed to settle in. "Perhaps you're right. Perhaps another time." He started to turn away, seemingly relieved.

*Wait a second,* I thought. This wasn't how it was supposed to work. I called him back and came to my feet. "No, it's fine. I think I'd actually enjoy a walk."

We didn't walk far. Just thirty or forty yards away from the fire, into the darkness of the jungle. The forest was alive with night birds, cicadas, and other happy, harmless creatures. It seemed like a very cheerful place, and yet I was as tense and jittery as a deer in hunting season.

"I wanted," Pagag began, "to finish our conversation from earlier today."

"Which conversation was that?"

He pursed his lips, looking mildly irritated. "The one I started just before we went into battle."

"Oh, that's right," I said, leaning on a tree. "The conversation where you graciously conceded that you would no longer interfere with the relationship between Harry and Mary."

"Yes," said Pagag slowly, "*that* conversation." He perked up. "But I didn't finish saying what I wanted to say. I didn't really tell you *why* I was no longer going to interfere."

I looked at him and waited. So fun to torment a male. Finally I said, "So . . . why?"

He became flustered and started pacing. "This is very hard for me, Steffanie, and you're not making it any easier."

"How am I making it harder?"

He stopped and pointed at me. "Because you are being impertinent—and don't try to deny it."

I feigned total innocence. "Excuse me? I am simply being who I am, Pagag. If that bothers you, perhaps I should go back over by the fire."

He shook his head in seeming disbelief over my attitude and behavior. "Incorrigible female! Why are you playing this game with me?"

I turned up my palms. "What *game*, Pagag? If you brought me out here to insult me, I'd rather not stay. But if you brought me out here tell me something, why don't you just tell me?"

He went back to pacing. "Because it is . . . *very difficult for me!* And yet I know that if I do not get it out I will most certainly explode and burst into flame!"

I widened my eyes. "Oh, by all means, don't do that. You might start a forest fire."

He went on speaking, ignoring my sarcasm. "Here is what I have to say. And what I have to say is this. I may have been . . . I mean . . . I *was,* I believe, too hasty in deciding that Mary may have been the right one for me. I have discovered—to my growth and betterment, I might add—that there are others with the same qualities of strength . . . confidence . . . compassion . . . love of God . . . that I was searching for in a woman."

He stopped to see my reaction. I gave none, so he went on.

"What I mean is, over the short space of days that we have been together, I have discovered that I enjoy being in your company. I enjoy . . . *seeing* you. Hearing you. Finding you there when I awaken, and knowing that you are safe when I sleep. Do you understand what I'm trying to say?"

I cocked one eyebrow, still giving no reaction. He gaped at me dumbly. He waited. He waited a long time. I knew he was determined not to say anything more until I'd responded in some way. I made him wait as long as I thought he could stand it, and then I asked, "Why?"

He tilted his head in consternation. *"What?"*

"Why do you enjoy hearing me or seeing me or knowing that I'm safe? Why are you telling me any of this at *all?* What difference does it make now?"

He opened and closed his mouth several times like a fish, then said, "I-I don't think I follow what you're trying—*Didn't you hear what I just said?*"

I took a couple steps toward him. "Oh, I heard it all right. And I think I heard a lot of the same sort of gibberish about ten days ago when you were describing *another* woman. Shall I quote you? Here, let me try." I lowered my voice and attempted my best Pagag impression. *"'I do not doubt what any man would go through to be with Mary. She is unique! Gentle, yet as strong as iron. Fragile, but with more resolute conviction than any girl I have ever met. No woman would make a better mother for my children. Or a better wife for me.'"* I opened my eyes widely at him. "Did I misquote you?"

His face darkened. He just stared at me with those baby blues, saying nothing in his defense, and yet refusing to break his gaze. Unexpectedly, I felt a flutter of butterflies in my stomach, and maybe even a slight twinge of fear, though I wasn't sure why. I straightened myself. Intense moments had never intimidated me before—whether rushing into battle or defending my life. Frankly, the intensity here felt almost the same. Make no mistake, this was warfare.

I put my hand on his shoulder and spoke to him like a kindly therapist. "Apparently, there are far more women than you could have possibly imagined who fit the parameters of your checklist, Pagag. You should be very happy about that. You know what I suggest, Mr. Moriancumr, as a possible cure for your . . . malady? I suggest that you get out more. You definitely need to—" I patted his chest as I said the next three words. "—meet more women. Yes, if you could do that I think then you'd feel much better about your life. I certainly hope that you find her, Pagag. Your perfect, ultimate, unsurpassable female. She's out there. I just know it."

That steely Caribbean gaze of his had not flinched in the slightest.

I took a quick breath. "Okay, well, I think we've made good progress for today, don't you? Shall we rejoin the others?"

I started to turn, but before I'd gotten all the way around, a large, strong hand gripped my arm and spun me back. I found myself facing the Jaredite once more. My eyes widened as I saw his look. Pagag had never sent me a look quite like it—not in all our numerous conflicts of the past. At first I might have described it as anger. But maybe anger wasn't the right word. Would it be more accurate to call it fury? Passion? Whatever it was, it caused my heart to flutter in my chest like the wings of a bird hit by buckshot.

"You are a woman of fire, Steffanie," he declared. "Your heart blazes with it. *Consumes* in it. Uncontrollable. Dangerous. But what I must know is . . . can it also be tamed?"

Before I could react or respond or even get out a single sound, his mouth swooped down and met mine. His arms encircled me tightly, and as we kissed, I swear my body and mind disappeared. I vanished completely. Vanished from the face of the earth. Again I was gripped by that same feeling—that same overwhelming, all-encompassing sensation of warmth and wonder, peace and joy, comfort and belonging—the feeling of *home*.

At last, the Jaredite warrior drew his head back and gazed into my eyes. I saw myself swimming in there—swimming inside those beautiful, turquoise pools. And then I saw something new. His eyes seemed to light up—to illuminate. But not with love. More like . . . conviction. He nodded a subtle nod, as if he'd finally found the answer to some unsolvable riddle—one of life's perplexing mysteries.

"Well," he said softly, "now I know."

My eyebrows raised high. What kind of an asinine statement was that? Reality rushed back over me like a torrent, like a dam break. I wrenched myself from his arms, drew back the palm of my good hand and slapped him hard across the face—the same face I'd already punched twice before. The sound of it seemed to echo, and I swore that for an instant all the birds and insects of the night went silent, gulping in shock.

And what did Pagag do in response? He smiled. That's all. Just grinned like the Cheshire cat. He might have even winked. Or maybe I only imagined that part. I was seeing so much red it might have blinded me, and I couldn't say for sure. And then that beast, that ogre, that creature from the Black Lagoon actually had the nerve to turn and walk away. He sauntered back toward the campfire, leaving me there alone in the jungle, infuriated, half-delirious, and confused.

My eyes remained glued to his back the whole time as he walked away. My heart continued thumping relentlessly. I opened my mouth to speak—to scream at him—but nothing came out. There was no air in my lungs to make a noise. *Turn around, Pagag,* I thought, gritting my teeth. *Just turn around and I'll show you . . . I'll . . . I'll . . .*

But Pagag did not turn around. He did not glance back. The Jaredite passed through the trees and soon his silhouette became indistinguishable from all the other silhouettes around the fire.

I leaned back against the bark of the tree. I slid down until I was sitting at the base of the trunk and whispered in quiet, fevered anguish, "What just happened? What have I done? What . . . have I done?"

A moment later I noticed that Meagan and Apollus had returned to camp. They'd made some sort of announcement. There was a shriek of happy voices and afterwards people were giving them hugs and offering congratulations.

Moroni spoke loud enough for me to hear, saying, "On this day of strife and sadness, let us be grateful that it can also be a day of celebration!"

Oh, my! I knew exactly what had happened. He'd just asked her to marry him. Yes, it *was* glorious news! I was so happy for them. So happy. So happy I actually managed to unclench my teeth. And so I focused on this happy thought. I focused hard and let everything else dissipate. Momentarily, my heart felt lighter.

I smiled to myself. *This isn't over,* I said under my breath as I started back to camp. *No, not by a long shot.* Pagag, the son of Mahonri Moriancumr, may have thought he'd won this first puny skirmish. But I was determined that it would only be the first of many. In the end, we'd see who grinned the last grin.

We'd just see.

# EPILOGUE 1

## Joshua

Flickers of firelight from a hundred candles danced magically upon the stucco walls and richly colored curtains of Mormon's office. The prophet stood before me, prepared to lay his hands upon my head and offer me a sacred blessing. Marcos, my father, and I bowed our heads with reverence. As I felt Mormon's palms upon my head, I was certain I could also feel his power, or in other words, the power given him by God. The feeling penetrated to every corner of the room, surrounding us with an unconquerable, overflowing strength.

He began to speak: *"By the power of the Holy Priesthood of Jesus Christ, I lay my hands upon you, young Captain Joshua, and give unto you the word of God in all purity and holiness, that you may receive wisdom and power from your Father in Heaven, that you may prevail in your quest to carry this holy Record out of the hands of wicked and conspiring men, and that you may deliver it into the safekeeping of the earth until such time as I may complete the history and prophecies with which I have been entrusted."*

He paused, and suddenly I began to feel within me something unlike anything I'd ever felt before—something beyond my ability to describe—so profound that all flowery words I might have used escaped me. I say only that my mind became more attentive, more alert, than I would have ever guessed that it could. I knew even as Mormon was speaking that every sentence and phrase he uttered would be burned into my memory for all time.

*"Listen closely, young Joshua, that you may not fail. The most cunning allies of the evil one have been dispatched to foil your mission and to destroy your very soul. There is one who will most assuredly cross your*

*path—one whose evil obsessions would thwart the very work of God, if it were possible. You know this man well. He is an intimate servant of the enemy of all light and truth. He has sought to destroy you before in many realms and in many . . . times . . . and he will do so again in new and unthinkable ways, and with greater furor than you ever thought possible. But though it may seem for a time that all is lost, and that the very powers of the adversary might overcome all righteousness, do not despair. The Lord God will preserve you, and those who accompany you, and He will give you the power to utterly defeat your enemies. He will provide it insomuch as you maintain humility and meekness before Him, having an eye single to His glory and ultimate triumph. If you fall into snares, repent. If you are overcome by the follies of your nature, repent straightway or Satan will have immediate control over you, and you will find yourself at the mercy of a being who has no mercy. The shield and protection of heaven are yours, Joshua. Call upon God night and day, with all the energy of your soul, until the end of your quest. Indeed, until the very end of your life. Heed this warning, Captain Josh, and make a full repentance now before God and those who love you and have risked so much to aid you. In this way you may have His matchless power ever after to lift and sustain you in all things. Now go with God."*

The prophet closed his blessing—his revelation—in the name of Jesus Christ, the Redeemer of the world. As he raised his hands from my head, it felt as though a great weight still remained. I admit I was a little taken aback by the deadly seriousness of what the prophet had said. I looked up at Mormon and asked, "Didn't you say that this secret vault was less than a day's journey up the slopes of Cumorah?"

The seriousness did not depart from his face. He replied, "The location or proximity of the vault does not lessen the dangers you may face."

I let this sink in. Mormon, Marcos, and my father continued to study me. I shuddered visibly. A terrible dread welled up inside me as I contemplated the identity of the villain that I might face. *Akish?* I could think of no other person whom Mormon could be describing, no other soul I knew who was such an intimate servant of the enemy of truth and light. For five years I'd convinced myself that I was finally free of him—this man who had stolen my youth, my family, my peace of mind and soul.

Mormon gripped my shoulder with his powerful hand. "Do not fear, Joshua. Be serious. Be sober. And be faithful. Remember the words that I have uttered. So long as you strive to follow the Lord, the forces of darkness will be powerless against you."

I nodded, uncertainly at first, then with greater resolution. Just the sound of this man's voice stirred up incredible courage inside me.

Mormon stepped back and took in the three of us. To my father and Marcos he declared, "You are his companions. He will need your faith as much as his own, and your support . . . to the very end."

I saw my father swallow, but he nodded nonetheless.

Marcos stood a little straighter. "He will have it."

Mormon next placed a hand upon the shoulder of Marcos, and simultaneously upon the shoulder of my father. "I know that he will."

Leaning back, he added, "Now I must leave my residence. There is not an hour of the day wherein the spies of Judge Zenephi are not watching my every move. I will leave in hopes that these spies will follow after me."

"Wouldn't such men have seen us arrive?" asked Marcos.

"Yes," said Mormon. "But it is my hope that they will assume that I have brought you in as guests for the night and that you have fallen into slumber. I will approach the main gate to make a surprise inspection of the municipal guards. You will wait a quarter of an hour after my departure, and then slip out of the rear entrance." He turned back to me and asked, "Do you know the location of the water gate where our women exit to take garments to the place of springs?"

I nodded. "Yes, I know it."

"Three days ago I ordered a reorganization of our municipal forces. The detail at this gate is minimal, and the soldiers are very young and green. It is my prayer that you will be able to slip past them without the shedding of blood."

Marcos nodded. "We will do all in our power to make it so."

The prophet's gaze moved across us once more. I sensed that his eyes were filled with incredible love, but also concern—even apprehension. I clenched my fists, my heart pounding with a fortitude and confidence beyond myself. *Remember the blessing,* I told myself. *There is no reason to fear.*

"God be with you, my friends," said Mormon. "God be with you."

The chief captain of the Nephites departed his office and headed toward the front entrance of his house. Words were exchanged between Mormon and his bodyguards. A moment later I felt a mild gust of fresh air. Mormon and his men had left the residence.

"The distance," my father said to me, "from the Hill Cumorah in New York to Joseph Smith's family farm in Palmyra will one day be considerably less than the distance that we'll travel tonight. And yet Joseph will have to expend nearly every ounce of energy and faith to get the plates safely from one place to the other."

I sent my father a nod of reassurance. I looked at the deer-vellum parchment in my hands—the guide map to the secret vault hidden near the summit. Next, I glanced at the Golden Plates, still sitting on the table inside the maguey sack. My father sensed my distress. I should have known I couldn't hide such things from my dad.

"We'll be all right, Joshua," he told me. "Everything will be all right."

A portion of Mormon's blessing sprang back to my mind: ". . . make a full repentance now before God and those who love you and have risked so much to aid you, that you may have His matchless power ever after to lift and sustain you in all things."

As I stared at my father, I felt an increased burden of guilt on my heart for the weight of grief that he was enduring, and for what I'd put him through because of the awful choices I'd made. For so long I had tried to place the blame for my situation on every possible culprit—the sword of Coriantumr, Akish the sorcerer, Lamanites, Gadiantons, bad luck, the weather, the sun, moon, and stars—*every possible thing* . . . except myself. I doubted very much if passing the buck was going to work anymore. Frankly, I doubted if it would ever work again.

"Father," I said, my voice cracking. "I'm . . . sorry. So sorry for what I've done to you . . . to Mom. To everyone."

He studied me, his own eyes growing moist, and then he reached forward and embraced me with the fullness of his strength. "I love you, Joshua. I love you so much. That will never change. No matter what you do. No matter what happens."

A tear escaped my eye. "I have something to say. Something about . . ."

The name was on my tongue—that of my sister, Rebecca. I swear I tried to say it. I tried to tell him all about what had happened that night in the hills above Salem. My tongue seemed to swell inside my mouth. For the life of me, I could not speak her name. Despite all the solemnity and humility I felt, I could not give my father the report that his only daughter might have died in 3000 BC. But perhaps it wasn't so selfish. Maybe something else had stopped my tongue—that vague glimmer of hope. That persistent shred of faith in the possibility of miracles.

Instead, I told him, "I just wanted to say, I can't do this without you, Dad. I missed you so much. I need you. I need you so badly."

"You have me," he assured. "I'll never leave your side. Count on it."

I didn't know what to say. My emotions were overwhelming. All I could do was whisper, "Thank you."

I looked over his shoulder at Marcos. He was smiling solemnly until he saw my face, then he looked down.

My father realized that I was looking at Marcos and moved out of the way. I stiffened my jaw. I tried to speak to him more formally, in the proper manner of a Nephite officer, though I think my voice still creaked several times. "I've been very harsh . . . in my judgment of you, Marcos . . . for a long time. So many stupid things I've said. So much I wish I could take back. You've risked your life for me. I don't deserve your loyalty. Can you forgive me?"

He came forward. "I can."

We gripped each other's wrists in the handclasp of brotherhood, and then I pulled him toward me to embrace him as my true brother—my brother for the eternities.

A scripture passed through my mind—one of the only scriptures I still remembered word for word. My father had once told me that this scripture came to him while he was giving me a blessing as an infant. I knew that it was from the book of Ether, but I couldn't remember the verse: *"And if men come unto me I will show them their weakness. I give unto men weakness that they may be humble; and my grace is sufficient for all men that humble themselves before me; for if they humble themselves before me, and have faith in me, then will I make weak things become strong unto them."*

Weak things. That certainly described me. I wondered if anything weaker had ever been assigned such a sacred task. Yes, I needed my dad. I needed Marcos. But more than that, I needed God, and I was determined that never again would I try to do anything without Him.

"I think Mormon has been gone long enough," said Dad. "It's time."

Marcos nodded in agreement.

Dad looked at me, "Are you ready, Son?"

"Ready as ever," I replied humbly. "As I see it, if God believes we can succeed, there's no need of a second opinion."

My father and Marcos smiled broadly. I hefted the sixty-pound sack with the sacred records and laid it behind my shoulder. We walked to the rear door of Mormon's residence. Afterwards, the three of us slipped quietly into the night, into the darkness of uncertainty, and into the arms of God.

# EPILOGUE 2

## Jim

I breathed deeply, taking in the delicate fragrance of the fig tree blossoms overhead, my eyes still happily closed in a state of semi-consciousness. I'd successfully blocked out all of the terrible memories of the day—riding to Jerusalem with Barabbas, the riot in the market-place, the attack of the Roman auxiliaries and the Temple guards. For a moment, at least, I'd found an interstice of relative tranquility.

Then all at once, my eyes popped open. A strange feeling stirred within me. I glanced back up the street. Jenny was still standing at the well in the center of the village, trying to bring up the bucket to fill some gourds that might satisfy our thirst. I saw several people in the street, and a couple of donkeys tied near the door of one residence. The villagers were leaning on walls, carrying on idle conversation. The setting looked serene enough. Perfectly harmless. Still, something seemed profoundly peculiar.

I looked back toward the bottom of the hill. Two persons had broken away from a large gathering of pilgrims on the main road. They were headed in my direction. Both men wore traveling cloaks and sported Jewish-style beards, although one was quite young and didn't have much facial hair to boast of. The other man was tall and sturdy looking, with long, sinewy arms, bronze and muscular shoulders, and a resolute, serious expression. They seemed determined in their pace and even jogged a few steps to give themselves momentum up the grade. Both pairs of eyes were keenly focused on something toward the end of the street. I looked back at Jenny to make sure it wasn't her. But the object of their attention seemed closer than the well.

I wouldn't have expected these men to pay me any mind, loitering as I was in the shade of the fig grove, but the younger one—the man with a sparse beard and round, ruddy cheeks—glanced toward me. Sunlight bounced off his shoulders, illuminating the features of his face with a kind of subtle, vibrant glow. He sent me a nod and a smile.

I blinked my eyes. My heart started to swell. Abruptly, I leaned forward. *I know that man!* I cried inwardly. I'd seen his face! But where? It wasn't in Jerusalem. *Where was it?* Unfortunately the two men had kept going. They continued past me; I could no longer see their faces. Whoever this man was, he obviously hadn't recognized *me.* This was going to drive me nuts. I came to my feet, held on a second until the blood stopped rushing between my ears, then stepped out into the street to follow them, all the while straining and sifting through a lifetime of memories.

I realized their target now. It was the doorway where the donkeys were tied. The two creatures stood calmly, basking in the warmth of the morning light as the two men arrived. One of the donkeys—a young colt—appeared to raise his head in greeting, as if it had anticipated the men's arrival. I continued to watch. The sunshine and shade framed the scene before me with a sort of gentle halo as the two individuals began untying the donkeys' tethers.

Farther up the street, one of the villagers leaning against the wall became alert. He noticed what the two men were doing and stepped toward them.

"What do you think you're doing?" he snapped. "Those animals belong to me."

The men smiled unflinchingly and waited until the owner could reach them. Then the older man, his eyes glistening, replied in a placid voice, "The Lord hath need of them."

I froze. My heart took off like an orchestra. I *knew* that sentence. I knew those words.

The donkeys' owner looked into the faces of the two men for a long moment. A cascade of understanding seemed to settle over his features. He nodded his consent.

Air refused to go into my lungs. I knew who these men were! Or at least I knew who *one* of them was. In my mind appeared the face of an old beggar on the banks of the Cayster River in Ephesus.

"He was older," I heard myself whisper. "He was wearing rags."

It was *John!* That man was *John the Beloved!* My thoughts were whirling. Two Apostles sent to fetch an ass and its colt. All at once I knew the identity of the second man. He was *Peter!* The scriptures hadn't mentioned the names of the two Apostles who'd been sent on this errand. Yet my heart told me undeniably that this second man was Simon Peter.

Peter and John began leading the animals back in my direction. I adjusted my gaze and spotted Jenny. She was on the other side of the street, a gourd of water in her hands. She'd noticed me and hurried over to where I stood, passing the Apostles. She'd passed them without even noticing who they were or what was happening.

When she reached me she asked, "Jim, what's wrong? Why are you up?"

I raised my finger and pointed at Peter, John, and the donkeys, unable to speak.

She turned to see. "Do you know them?" she inquired.

"It's *John!*" I replied in an exhaling whisper. "John and . . . and Peter."

The Apostles heard me. They were passing us now. John sent me another smile—more warm than the first—and swung his chin in invitation. He wanted us to follow them!

I looked at Jenny. Things had clicked in her brain. Her mouth was open. The men and donkeys continued toward the main road and the waiting multitude.

"Jim," Jenny whispered, eyes already full of tears. "What's going on?"

I looked at her and nodded. The lump in my own throat was still too big. But that's all I had to do—just nod—and Jenny understood my meaning perfectly: *If you're asking, sweet sister, you already know the answer.*

Jenny and I followed after them, our hearts glowing like torchlight, our minds racing. Others ran past us, too impatient to wait. Enthusiasm and wonder seemed to radiate all around us—in every living creature, every inanimate object, man and beast, tree and stone. It was infectious. Intoxicating. My gaze was sweeping back and forth, searching the multitude at the bottom of the hill. I wiped frantically at my tears. I could hardly see anything at all!

But for an instant my vision cleared. The crowd parted. A figure stood out like a beacon, like a searchlight, in the midst of the multitude. My emotions overflowed—I felt as if I might drown in them. He stood there, unmoving, patiently waiting, a loving smile upon His face, the impassioned crowd pressing Him on all sides.

As we drew near, I swore there was an instant when He took us in with His perfect, loving smile. He acknowledged us. He *knew* me!— just as He knew every living soul gathered about Him.

He was here. The King had come in peace.

My Savior, our Redeemer.

The Son of God.


*To be continued . . .*

# ABOUT THE AUTHOR

Chris Heimerdinger currently resides in Riverton, Utah, with his wife, Catherine Elizabeth, and their five children, Steven Teancum, Christopher Ammon, Alyssa Sariah, Elizabeth Liahona Cecelia, and Angelina Cumorah.

*Kingdoms and Conquerors* is the most ambitious and complex of his Tennis Shoes Adventure Series, bringing together a vast collection of beloved (and infamous) characters from other novels in the series, developing multiple storylines, and steadily converging his fictional vision toward an ultimate climax. Chris says, "*With* Kingdoms and Conquerors *I was able to explore the setting of ancient America during the final days of the Nephites, as well as events at the meridian of time, in ways that no other author has ever attempted or conceived. The result has been extremely rewarding.*"

Readers can expect an eleventh volume in the Tennis Shoes series in the future. Chris is also pursuing a feature-length motion picture based on his novel, *Passage to Zarahemla*, a CD of original songs, and a host of other projects, all with the object of celebrating the rich heritage of the Book of the Mormon, the gospel of Jesus Christ, and the glories of God's eternal kingdom.

For further information about *Kingdoms and Conquerors* and other works by Chris Heimerdinger, please become a registered guest at www.cheimerdingcr.com.

# TENNIS SHOES
## A D V E N T U R E   S E R I E S

## by CHRIS HEIMERDINGER

## 1. TENNIS SHOES AMONG THE NEPHITES

Chris Heimerdinger holds you spellbound as he introduces you to teenagers Jim Hawkins and Garth Plimpton, as well as Jim's pesky little sister, Jennifer. They accidentally stumble upon a mysterious passageway that hurls them into a Book of Mormon world where danger and suspense are a way of life.

Suddenly the names Helaman, Teancum, and Captain Moroni are more than just words on a page as Book of Mormon characters come to life. Carefully researched, entertaining, and exciting, this story will motivate young people to read the Book of Mormon and will add a whole new dimension to the understanding of those who already know and love Book of Mormon stories. *Tennis Shoes Among the Nephites* is a great educational tool that will provide fun and delight for the whole family to share!

## 2. GADIANTONS AND THE SILVER SWORD

Jim and Garth are now in college at BYU, and their earlier adventures in Book of Mormon lands are revisited in a most unusual way when evil men from the past (Gadianton robbers from Nephite times) pursue them and disrupt their lives with danger and violence. This is a spine-tingling, explosive saga that transports the reader from the familiar settings of Utah and the American West to the exotic and unfamiliar settings of southern Mexico and its deep, shadowy jungles, where Jim must find a mystical sword once wielded by the Jaredite king, Coriantumr.

## 3. THE FEATHERED SERPENT, PART ONE

Jim Hawkins is now the widowed father of two teenage daughters, Melody and Steffanie, and a ten-year-old son, Harry. Jim finds himself embarking on his most difficult and perilous adventure—a quest for survival against unseen enemies and an evil adversary from the distant past. He must also solve the deepening mystery of the disappearance of his sister, Jennifer, and his old friend Garth Plimpton. Once again he returns—this time with his family—to ancient Book of Mormon times; but now the civilization is teetering on the brink of destruction. It's the time just prior to the Savior's appearance in the New World . . . a time of danger and uncertainty.

## 4. THE FEATHERED SERPENT, PART TWO

Jim and his family continue their perilous adventures in Book of Mormon times, using all of their instincts and resources to find Garth and his family and deliver themselves from the clutches of one of the most treacherous men of ancient America—King Jacob of the Moon. They encounter murderous and conspiring men, plagues, a herd of "cureloms," hostile armies, and finally earthquakes and suffocating blackness as the Savior of the world is crucified. Along the way, members of Jim's family discover their loyalty and love for one another, and the importance of the gospel in their lives, culminating in the glorious visitation of our Lord Jesus Christ to the city of Bountiful.

## 5. THE SACRED QUEST

Jim has just learned that his daughter, Melody, now age 20, has a very serious illness. During their last adventure in Book of Mormon times, Melody fell in love with Marcos, son of King Jacob of the Moon, who had been converted to Christianity. Now Jim's son Harry, age 15, is determined to go back in time, find Marcos, and bring him back to be with Melody. He and his stepsister-to-be, Meagan, embark on this journey, but are sidetracked and end up in New Testament times, about 70 A.D. They encounter both believers and antichrists who are consumed with finding a mysterious manuscript called the Scroll of Knowledge. The epic climaxes with a breathtaking confrontation between Harry, Nephites, and gladiators; but Harry's adventure of a lifetime has only begun.

## 6. THE LOST SCROLLS

Harry and Meagan continue their heart-stopping adventure as they face the awesome challenges of courage and survival in the hostile world of Jerusalem in 70 A.D. While Meagan and Jesse, a young Jewish orphan, are held hostage by the evil Simon Magus and the Sons of the Elect, Harry and his friend Gidgiddonihah must make an impossible journey to Jerusalem to find the Scroll of Knowledge, which may contain the ultimate power and mysteries of the universe. They have only a few days to find the scroll and deliver it to Simon Magus, or Meagan and Jesse will be killed. Our young heroes face breathtaking danger and high adventure as they encounter flames, swords, desperate villains, and perhaps the greatest loves of their lives in this sixth volume of the award-winning Tennis Shoes Adventure Series.

## 7. THE GOLDEN CROWN

Hang on to your seats as the heart-pounding adventure of Harry Hawkins and Meagan Sorenson in the land of Jerusalem and the world of the Romans races toward its thrilling conclusion.

In a nightmarish twist of events, Harry finds himself in the midst of unforeseen enemies who seek to separate him from all that he holds dear. To make matters worse, Garth Plimpton and Meagan are forced to make choices that threaten to leave Harry permanently lost in time.

Harry's father, Jim, and Meagan's mother, Sabrina, enter the fray to save their families, while Harry knows that to survive he must somehow reach a faraway land where resides a true apostle of the Lord Jesus Christ. "We're all on a golden journey," Harry is told by a very special person from biblical history. "A journey inspired by golden dreams, and at the end awaits a golden crown of righteousness."

Reenter the reeling world of the first century A.D. in this, the seventh book in the celebrated Tennis Shoes Adventure Series. This is also the final volume in Harry and Meagan's breathtaking New Testament trilogy that began with *The Sacred Quest*.

## 8. WARRIORS OF CUMORAH

Leave all your expectations behind as your favorite characters from the Tennis Shoes Adventure Series are reunited in a miraculous journey into worlds never before imagined, where villains old and new must be stopped to keep the landscape of history from becoming permanently altered.

Just when the children of Jim Hawkins and Garth Plimpton thought they understood the powers of the Rainbow and Galaxy Rooms, a transformation of staggering dimensions takes place. It's a mystery whose secrets can only be unraveled by a pair of small white stones—stones in a gleaming silver frame whose powers can only be harnessed by the mightiest of prophets or by one pure-hearted little girl.

Embark on the millennium's greatest adventure, an epic that one day soon will culminate in one of the most tremendous battles ever fought—a battle of tragedy, heroism, and the rebirth of dreams on the slopes of a hill called Cumorah.

# 9. TOWER OF THUNDER

The Tennis Shoes saga reaches new heights in a world where the great patriarchs of the Bible still reign, and the memory of a terrible flood remains fresh in the minds of men. While a magnificent tower is being constructed to reach heaven, the Jewish Mary Symeon, along with young Rebecca and Joshua Plimpton, face a terrible struggle to save not only themselves, but a small baby from a power-hungry king, a mighty hunter of the souls of men, named Nimrod.

Meanwhile, Harry and Steffanie Hawkins are hurled into the same turbulent world to face the warriors of Shinar and another villain, whose objectives are the most chilling of all.

Come ride the whirlwind of adventure as the next generation of Tennis Shoes heroes tests the limits of courage and endurance against tyrants and conquerors across the spectrum of time.

# DANIEL AND NEPHI

*A Tale of Eternal Friendship in a Land Ripening for Destruction*

Welcome to 609 B.C.! In a world of infinite mystery, when caravans rule the sun-swept deserts and mighty empires grapple for ultimate power, the lives of a young prince named Daniel and a trader's son named Nephi become entwined in an adventure that takes them along the razor's edge of danger and suspense as they struggle to save the life of a king—and the fate of a nation.

Join Daniel and Nephi as they learn the lessons of friendship, fortitude, and faith that shape two young boys into great prophets of God.

Carefully researched and scrutinized by scholars, *Daniel and Nephi* offers a breathtaking opportunity to explore the world of Jeremiah and Lehi.

*"In* Daniel and Nephi, *Chris Heimerdinger has once again breathed life into significant characters in biblical and Book of Mormon history."*

—BRENT HALL, FOUNDATION FOR ANCIENT RESEARCH
AND MORMON STUDIES